Coldwater

Coldwater

Mardi McConnochie

Ballantine Books • New York

A Ballantine Book
Published by The Ballantine Publishing Group

www.ballantinebooks.com/BRC

Library of Congress Control Number: 2002090594

ISBN 0-345-44812-X

This edition published by arrangement with Doubleday, a division of Random House, Inc.

Cover illustration by Debra Lill

Manufactured in the United States of America

First Ballantine Books Edition: August 2002

10 9 8 7 6 5 4 3 2 1

For James,
who gave me a mango and pushed me in the water

However much it may have been written with a bitter ambition for fame foremost in the author's mind, the novel remains firmly rooted in the furious dreams of a passionate young woman whose life never quite matched up to her own capacity for experience.

Coldwater

One

A savage place! as holy and enchanted

As e'er beneath a waning moon was haunted

By woman wailing for her demon lover!

COLERIDGE, "KUBLA KHAN"

One

Father is shot

Charlotte

The first time Father was shot there was no warning.

I was in the kitchen peeling potatoes with Emily. The warm scent of baking bread filled the kitchen and I do not remember what we were talking about. I heard a gunshot somewhere outside. The troopers liked to take potshots at the seagulls for target practice, and so I thought nothing of it. It was not until a second volley of shots rang out that I had the first inkling something might be wrong. I went to the window and looked out.

"What is it?" asked Emily diffidently. She had a bad head coming on and was out of sorts.

"I don't know," I replied, but as I watched, I saw a detachment of troopers come hurrying up the rise towards the house. They supported a drooping figure between them—someone in an officer's uniform—and as they hurried towards me I recognised the shape of a head, a familiar form, the uniform. An officer wounded. Shot. Father.

I threw the kitchen door open and ran to meet them, with Emily a moment or two after me. Panic lanced through me. Was he hurt? Dead? I slipped and slithered down the hill.

"Father?"

He lifted his head and squinted at me, then gave me a ghastly sort of grin to show me he was still alive. His face was grey and there was dark, sticky blood oozing through the heavy fabric of his jacket. I thought I was going to collapse with terror. It looked like he'd been shot through the heart. My brain boiled. What should I do in this situation? What could I do to help? I had no idea. I had never been faced with a gunshot wound before. I tried to lend my arm, to assist Father into the house—to do something—but the soldiers shoved me out of the way. They swept into the kitchen and our dinner went flying as they stretched Father out on the kitchen table—to die, I thought.

"Send for the surgeon," Father gasped.

The officer barked over his shoulder at one of the men. "Go and get Fitzwilliam." Then he turned to snap at me. "Get something to stop the bleeding."

Emily was already in motion, bringing clean dishcloths. I could not tear my face away from Father. His eyes had closed. Was it already too late? I saw his chest rise and fall. Not too late—not yet.

The officer opened Father's coat to inspect the damage. His white shirt was torn and horribly stained with blood, and beneath the shirt it seemed at first as if his chest had been torn open, it was so slick with blood. For a moment I fancied I could see through the sundered flesh to Father's heart. I could see it beating quite clearly, exposed to the air, so vulnerable, this organ of time, ticking his life away. But then I realised that the wound was not as large as I'd feared, and that, ragged though it was, bleeding profusely though it was, the bullet had probably missed his heart. (Father kept in his study a fascinating chart showing a man without his skin, flayed for the purposes of science. It detailed the position of the organs, and the paths of the major veins and arteries. We had studied it in the schoolroom with a thrilled and uneasy awareness that we were looking at something forbidden, although we were not exactly sure why.)

The trooper came running back in. "The surgeon's on his way, sir."

The officer acknowledged this with a curt nod, then turned to me. "You can manage here until he comes, miss?" I nodded dumbly. "Then we'll get out of your way."

I felt another surge of panic as the troopers began to withdraw from the kitchen. What kind of men were these to desert us, to desert their commanding officer in his time of need? What about loyalty? Didn't they care that he could be dying? Weren't they going to stay and help?

"He's going to be alright," the officer said, and then he was gone. The sun shone coldly through the open door. There was a faint wintry smell of crushed grass and mud. The floor was littered with potato peel. And Father lay on the kitchen table, breathing harshly. I gazed down at him, transfixed by tiny details—a smudge of green on his cheekbone where he must have fallen; the tiny black dots of stubble on his jaw, etched sharply against the pallor of his skin; the change of colour and texture between his weather-beaten face and neck, and the exposed skin of his chest; blood; hair; a nipple, that odd, tender brown button. It had never occurred to me that my father would be equipped with one. I reflected that I had never seen my father undressed like this before, and my heart thumped, just once. I dragged my eyes back to his face, and in that moment, his eyes opened and looked straight up into mine. He smiled.

"Don't worry, Charlotte. There's life in the old dog yet."

A shadow fell across us, and Fitzwilliam came rolling in, bringing with him the heady savour of rum.

"What's happened?" he asked.

"Father's been shot," I said shortly, not considering until the words were out of my mouth that perhaps I should refer to Father as *Captain Wolf* in this company.

"Let's have a look then."

I stepped aside and allowed him to move to Father's side. "The bullet shouldn't be too difficult to remove," he said. He turned to Emily. "We'll need some more of those dressings."

Emily nodded, and left the room. Fitzwilliam turned to me. "I'll need your assistance to wipe away the blood. There may be rather a lot of it. Do you think you can do that?"

"Of course," I said, watching as he rummaged in his bag of instruments and produced a scalpel and a pair of nasty-looking pincers. His hands looked none too steady, but I told myself I was imagining it. My disquiet only increased as I watched him drop the scalpel on the floor, almost impaling his own toe. He shot me a furtive glance, then turned his attention to Father.

"Let's see about getting that bullet out, sir," he said loudly. Father just nodded. Fitzwilliam brandished his pincers. "This may hurt a bit," he added.

Father's jaw clenched, and he fixed his gaze on a spot above the doorway as the surgeon began to probe the wound in his shoulder. Fresh blood streamed out and went coursing down Father's chest to seep onto the table. There was a faint click of metal on metal.

"Almost had it," muttered Fitzwilliam. Father's eyes were still fixed rigidly on that point above the doorway. I felt sympathetically faint at the thought of that metal point probing cruelly-opened flesh. I reached behind me for a chair.

"Got it," said the surgeon at last, as he held up the gory black pellet he'd extracted from Father's shoulder.

"It seems such a small thing to make such a mess," Father observed, trying to sound robust.

"Indeed," said the surgeon, "but if it had been just a whisker to the left you would have been with us no longer, sir." To the left and down a bit, I thought, visualising the position of Father's heart as shown on the chart of the skinned man.

"You did a fine job, sir," said Father. "I congratulate you."

I heard breathy singing coming from outside, and then Anne was there in the doorway, back from her walk, her bonnet dangling from one hand. When she saw the awful tableau she froze, her mouth falling open in dismay.

"Father?"

"It's nothing," he said. "Someone took a potshot at me. But they'll have to do better than that if they want to see the end of me."

Emily came dashing in with an overflowing armful of bandages. I thought I recognised one of my better petticoats, ripped to shreds, and gave Emily a hard look which she affected to ignore. "Will this be enough?" she asked, a little breathlessly. "I wasn't sure how much you'd need."

"That should do nicely," Fitzwilliam said, choosing not to point out that Emily had, as usual, gone completely overboard. She moved forward to hand the bandages to the surgeon, and suddenly caught a glimpse of Father, his shirt open, smeared with clotting blood. Her eyes widened, there was a quick intake of breath, and then Emily's eyes rolled up and she fell to the floor in a dead faint.

Anne and the surgeon rushed forward to assist her.

"I think she hit her head!" said Anne.

"Quick, do you have any smelling salts?" asked Fitzwilliam.

I watched in disbelief as the surgeon whipped his coat off, rolled it up, and placed it under Emily's insensible head while Anne went running for the smelling salts. Had they forgotten Father was bleeding to death?

"Would you like me to start on the bandaging?" I asked pointedly.

"Yes, thank you. If you feel you're up to it."

Up to it? Of course I was up to it. I scooped up a handful of bandage and wadded it into a bundle. I pressed it tenderly against the wound.

"Could you hold that there for me?" I murmured. Father held it with his good arm, and watched, stoically, as I bound it in place.

"Is that too tight?" I asked.

"Perfect," he replied. I met his eye and a look of complicity passed between us, a look that said *how foolish women are*, for I knew Father did not count me among their number.

Fitzwilliam revived Emily with smelling salts and helped her into a sitting position. "Do you feel any better?" he asked solicitously.

"A little," Emily said. "I don't know what came over me."

I know it is a commonplace that ladies of delicacy cannot stand the sight of blood. I have always held this view to be misguided—or, indeed, fraudulent, since most women, in the course of their adult lives, have ample opportunity to become accustomed to the sight of blood. It seemed perfectly clear to me that the only thing that had come over Emily today was the desire to be fussed over.

"Perhaps you should go and lie down," Anne suggested.

"I think it was the sudden shock," Emily murmured. "I'm fine now, really."

"You should go to bed," Father said. "Your health is so precarious."

"But Father," Emily said, an anxious note creeping into her voice, "I haven't finished making the dinner."

"Charlotte can do that," said Father firmly. "Bed. I'm not taking any chances."

Thus ordered, Emily had no choice but to go to bed for a good lie-down, but she went with an ill grace.

Fitzwilliam supervised as I finished bandaging Father's wound, prescribing beef tea to build up the blood, and plenty of rest. I promised to see to it, knowing full well that Father would not consent to spend any more time in bed than was absolutely necessary. Once Fitzwilliam had rolled off, Anne and I helped a fainting Father off to bed. Then Anne went to sit with Emily—although she scarcely needed any assistance, as far as I could see—and I returned to the kitchen, to salvage what I could of our dinner, and scrub the blood off the kitchen table.

Perhaps I should explain.

I live on an island called Coldwater, and it's a prison (I mean that in the literal sense). My father, Captain Wolf, is the prison governor, and it's a source of great pride to him that he's never had a single prisoner escape in all the time he's been in charge. We do not have many visitors here, but every so often the garrison changes, or a ship arrives with supplies from the south. Very occasionally an eminent personage will arrive from Sydney to inspect the prison. We are not entirely cut off from human society, but sometimes it feels that way. We arrived here in 1839, when I was twenty-three, Emily was twenty-two, and Anne twenty. That was eight years ago, and it's difficult to remember, now, what my impressions of the island were like upon seeing it for the first time, but I will try.

Coldwater lies off the coast of New South Wales, and the trip from Sydney takes three days by ship with a favourable wind. The island is a long way off the coast but a determined swimmer might make it to shore. Its inaccessibility, and the presence of fresh water, make it an ideal location for a prison. Approaching it by boat it seems to loom out of the water at you like a kraken petrified into stone. Black cliffs of volcanic rock with edges as sharp and brittle as glass rear straight up out of the water, and you can't imagine how humans could find anywhere to live in such a sharply inimical landscape. There's no real place to land—one tiny little beach that's underwater at high tide—and the island is completely surrounded by rocks and reefs which will rip the bottom out of a boat if you approach it carelessly. Once you've taken your life in your hands and crossed the boiling surf to make it ashore, there's a long, hard climb up the cliff to the top, where you emerge onto a rolling plain, dotted with tree stumps and tussocks of spiky, salt-resistant grass. The island was once heavily forested, but more than half of the trees were cut down to construct the settlement, a straggling collection of low wooden buildings which my father has gradually been replacing with buildings made of stone. It is said that the island was once raucous with bird life, but the first poorly provisioned settlers, faced with the prospect of starvation, slaughtered every last one of them. Now, only seagulls circle overhead, and every winter we hack into the remaining trees on the rockier slopes of the island, so that soon there will be no trees left at all. Nonetheless, it is possible to see that this bleak, windswept island was once very beautiful.

But this physical beauty is in stark contrast with the island's reputation, for around the colony, Coldwater is known as the Gates of Hell.

Incident Report

On the attempted shooting of Captain Wolf on the 3rd day
of April, 1847

At approximately three-thirty in the afternoon on the above-
mentioned date, I made an inspection of the new barracks, which is
currently being built by a convict work gang. As I entered the half-
completed building, the prisoner Thomas *Rhodes* darted at me from
among a group of his fellows shouting "Death to the tyrant!" I observed
that he was armed with a musket of standard military issue, which he
pointed at me. He then fired upon me from a distance of some five feet.
I was struck in the chest, and knocked to the ground, but the wound was
not mortal. *Rhodes* made no attempt to escape, and was swiftly appre-
hended by Corporal *Jones* and Private *Bexley*. *Rhodes* was then placed in
custody until he could go on trial for his actions. His companions on the
work gang were also placed in custody until the extent of their complicity could be determined. After a thorough investigation, several facts
came to light:

Rhodes, in company with another prisoner, William *O'Connor*, did on
the night of April 2nd break into the quartermaster's store and steal one
musket, along with a small quantity of ammunition, with the express
purpose of killing me.

They concealed this weapon in their barracks overnight.

On the morning of April 3rd, *Rhodes* concealed the musket beneath
his clothes, and took it with him to his work assignment.

It seems likely that the other prisoners on the work gang knew of
the presence of the musket and assisted *Rhodes* in concealing same.

Prisoners *Rhodes* and *O'Connor* have each been given sentences of 300
lashes—200 for stealing the musket, and a further 100 for keeping a
concealed weapon. This sentence was carried out on the 6th of April in
front of all the prisoners, as an example. Prisoner Rhodes has also re-

ceived an additional sentence of 100 lashes for insolence. Prisoners *Rhodes* and *O'Connor* have been returned to custody to await trial for the more serious offence of Attempted Murder. They will be tried when a representative of the Supreme Court next attends Coldwater. The other prisoners on the work gang have been put into double-irons for a month.

I am conducting a separate investigation into the vigilance of my officers, who appear to have been guilty of several lapses: firstly, in allowing the theft to take place, and secondly, in failing to detect the presence of a firearm, either in the barracks or on the work gang. A report on that investigation will be sent separately.

Captain Wolf's Journal.
4th April 1847

A sleepless night. The pain of my wound was considerable—any movement caused me discomfort. But once the morning came I rose from my bed as usual. I was determined to show no sign of weakness, so I ignored F's advice and resumed my duties as if nothing had happened. The one clear thought to emerge during that long, uncomfortable night was that I must turn this near disaster to my own advantage, or risk becoming a target. Once the men hear that an attempt has been made on my life, they will surely begin to dwell on the idea that I can be removed; that I am vulnerable. I must nip this in the bud; I cannot let them think that I am mortal, that I can be struck down like any other man. No: let them think that I am superhuman, made of inflexible steel; let them think it will take more than bullets to destroy me.

In the morning, while Fry was out conducting his investigation into the incident, I took the opportunity to interview my assailant, Thomas Rhodes. His frame is small and wiry; his hair is thick and curly, bleached almost white by the sun. He looks like he should have been a farmer, growing up amid fields of grain; but instead, he is a twice-convicted felon, and he spent the night in triple-irons. When he was brought in to my study his face was blackened with bruises; but I had no difficulty seeing his look of disappointment and dismay when he saw me sitting there alive and well. I informed him that his mission had been unsuccessful, and asked him what he had to say for himself.

"What is there to say?" he replied. "You're still alive, and I will soon be dead."

I asked him what he hoped to accomplish by shooting me.

"I hoped to see the end of you, for you are the greatest tyrant that ever lived; but now I see the men are right, and you are not a man, but a Demon from the bowels of Hell who cannot be killed in the normal manner."

I told him he should have another fifty lashes for his insolence, but he seemed careless of his own fate.

"Give me fifty. Give me a hundred. Maybe you'll carry me off sooner."

Upon consultation of his record I discovered that he was three years into a seven-year sentence on Coldwater; his original sentence was fourteen years, for cattle-duffing. He was three and twenty years old.

A desperate sadness came over me. This young man did not strike me as unusually vicious. He was not deranged, like some of the men who had made attempts on my life. He was simply young, and proud, and desperate for liberty, and I wondered if he'd really understood, when he raised that musket and aimed it at me, that from that very moment, his life was over. We are all crawling towards death, every one of us, every moment of the day, but we do not know how long the journey will take us, or how far; at the fateful moment when he picked up that musket, all other paths, all his possible futures vanished. He started on the shortest, cruelest journey of all, the short walk to the gallows.

"So it was your intention to seek death?" I asked.

"I prayed he'd come knocking at your door before he came to mine. But it's all one to me. Soon I'll be at peace, and you'll never be able to touch me again."

"Do you expect to find peace in Hell?"

"I don't know, sir. Maybe we can compare notes when you join me there."

While I bore him no personal animosity, I could not, of course, allow him to speak to me like that. So I added another fifty lashes to his sentence, to be administered one week after the first fifty.

At that he fell silent, and I felt the hairs prickle on the back of my neck.

There is a strange lightness, a sense of unreality, that comes over one in a situation like this. The outcome is already assured; it cannot be changed; he will be found guilty, and he will be hanged. And sometimes, something quite unexpected can emerge at these moments, some truth which can only be uttered when everything else drops away, when two men sit together in the presence of death. These are the moments I long for, those few transcendent moments when it seems that a gap has appeared in the sky, and I can catch a glimpse of the great underlying order that rules the universe.

I waited for the moment to come, but there was nothing. He stared at me dully, pugilistic but hopeless, defeated, and I realised that Rhodes had nothing to say, nothing I had not heard a thousand times before. All he could offer me was a stale mouthful of insults. Suddenly I wished very much to be rid of him.

"How does it feel to know that your life has been pointless, and your death will be utterly meaningless?" I asked him.

With this thought, I had him returned to his cell.

Two

Fifty lashes

Charlotte

As Emily slapped butter onto slice after slice of bread, her mouth pressed into a thin line, Father explained his decision.

"An attack on me," he explained, "is not just an attack on my person. It is an attack on the authority I represent, the authority invested in me by the governor, whose authority comes directly from the Crown. An attack on me in my official capacity is an attack on our system of law and order; without it, this country would descend into chaos. I cannot say we have yet succeeded in dragging this primitive place into a civilised state, but we must try. So you see, I cannot allow this to go unpunished. There is too much at stake."

Anne stirred her tea and breathed out noisily to indicate her displeasure, not daring to say anything more forthright. She had argued before that the punishments handed out to convicts were degrading to all parties involved—both to the convicts and those who administered them—and that they would ultimately cause more problems than they purported to solve.

Emily, wielding the teapot, looked decidedly queasy. We were headed

for some ghastly public spectacle of punishment, and these performances always seemed to bring on one of Emily's bad turns. Not that we
were present for them—Father thought that such brutality should be
kept from young ladies. Just the idea of it was enough to give Emily the
vapours.

"I would be obliged if you would all stay indoors for the rest of the
day," Father said. "I know"—to Anne—"you are in the habit of taking
a walk, but today you must forgo that pleasure."

"Yes, Father," Anne murmured.

"And, Emily, you must try to bear up as best you can." Father looked
at her with a soft regretful look in his eyes. "This is not a pleasant business, but it must be done."

Emily said nothing, but opened the lid of the teapot and looked
into it.

"I'm sure you will do what is right," I said, and did my best to ignore the evil looks my sisters shot me. I understood, as they apparently
did not, that Father was acting out of the highest possible motives, and
would never do anything out of simple cruelty.

Anne, Emily, and I sat in silence in the kitchen, plying our needles
as the men were mustered outside. Emily's face was pinched; Anne
scowled. What a pretty pair they made, I thought ironically, watching
them. Emily had Father's long face, Roman nose, and rather grim colouring, with dark, strongly marked brows and lashes and dark brown eyes.
Illness had carved her cheekbones into sharp lines, and her hooded eyes
were permanently in shadow. Anne was the pretty one—she had inherited our mother's heart-shaped face, pert nose, and fair colouring. Next
to Emily she looked like a changeling. Anne's features were soft and dim-
pled, where Emily and I were both inclined to the hawkish; but there was
a certain blandness to her features that reminded me of a china doll. The
only thing that marked us all out as sisters was a certain similarity
around the chin and mouth, and in the shape of the eyes.

Outside we could hear bugle calls, the shouts of the troopers, the distant murmur of the men being mustered to the triangle, which stood at the southern end of the valley. Our cottage, at the northern end, faced it across a great, grassy open expanse. The brutal end of the prison business was thus kept as far away from us as possible. Inside the house, the silence was oppressive. Anne, I could tell, was dying to get outside; her foot tapped incessantly against the kitchen floor.

"I could read something," I suggested.

Anne shook her head. She glanced at Emily; Emily looked away.

"Perhaps we should put the kettle on for tea?"

"Oh for God's sake, Charlotte!" snapped Emily.

Annoyed, I fell silent. The awful tension seeped and slithered through the room. I wished I could go away and work on something, or read, or do almost anything, but I knew that trying to concentrate on something else was impossible. My ears strained for the sound of the lash, the creaking of the rope, the crack of the whip, the cries, the groans, then the terrible silence.

"I'm going to lie down," said Emily abruptly. She got up, huddled over like an old woman, and disappeared off to her bedroom.

I found myself gazing at Anne. She had a combative look in her eye. "I don't care what Father said, I'm going for a walk."

"But what if something goes wrong," I said, "it's not safe."

"I can't stay here," she said. "I'm going."

She plucked her bonnet and shawl from the door, and headed out into the bleak afternoon light. The door banged behind her.

Left alone, I found my ears sharpening, as my stomach twisted with nerves. The kitchen fire crackled, and the clock on the mantelpiece kept its steady time. I heard the low, ever-present whistle of wind through the cracks in the walls and the ceiling. Emily had once called our house the palace of the winds; how romantic it sounded, but the reality was very chilly. But apart from the wind, all was quiet. I could not tell if the action had commenced, whether it was begun or in progress, or whether it was all over.

Then, as I sat there alone, I heard the faint but unmistakable groan of the loose board in the hall. Someone was walking, ever so quietly, down the hallway. My heart jumped. Was someone in the house? I heard a key turn—the key to Father's study door—and I realised who it was.

Anne

Feeling like she was choking, Anne burst out the back door. On a day like today, only the wind off the Pacific could blow the sticky smell of confinement from her hands and clothes. Some days it was possible to forget that she lived in a prison; but not today. She was filled to bursting with anger and disgust at the life she lived—the sober respectable façade of domesticity which masked the reality of life on Coldwater. The fact that Father chose to keep the more hideous sights away from their eyes did not cancel out their existence. The horror went on at her doorstep. The fact that she was not permitted to see it only made it worse.

Anne headed for the cliffs behind the house, moving as far away from the flogging ground as possible. Her path took her through stunted, wind-blasted trees, their roots clinging tenaciously to the ground despite the best efforts of the ocean winds to knock them over. Nothing here, she thought, remained straight and true; in time, everything started to warp and deform. She had watched Emily's increasing mental torment over the years, as the atmosphere of fear and uncertainty crept into her psyche, populating her world with phantasms, night terrors, and nervous ailments. Then there was Charlotte, with her bombastic sense of her own importance, growing into a strange, blue-stockinged monster in the perfect isolation of the island.

And then there was Father. With his ramrod spine and his sweetly reasonable voice, his quiet manners, his reserve, his enormous library of books and his interest in the human condition, he seemed like the epitome of the civilised man. Yet here he was, presiding over a regime which the *Sydney Monitor* had described as one of the most brutal in the colony

(Father had cancelled his subscription after reading that). At home, Father was the same man he had always been: conscientious in his work, polite and charming to his daughters, although always distant. But there was a subtle change in him, barely detectable, which she could only describe as a warping of the soul. There was in Father, Anne suspected, a certain relish for his work that had not been there before he came to Coldwater. The evil magic of the place had begun to work on him too.

She reached the edge of the trees. The cliff fell away below her, a tumble of great rocks and boulders. She sat down on a large flat rock, alone at last with the sea, and let the cool salty air stream over her.

And what is this place doing to me? she wondered.

Emily

Why can't I stop doing this??

My mind is gripped by a kind of dull Stupor—I watch myself as from a great distance—my feet move, my hands turn the key—and once again I am here, in Father's study, where I *should not be*—

It is a Compulsion beyond my power to control, although it sickens and disgusts me—Although my Heart fills with revulsion I *must* reach for the telescope, I *must* place my eye to the eyepiece, I must seek out the Ghastly Sight which my vile heart longs to see—

I chance to see Anne, dear Anne, hurrying away—little knowing I am Spying on her—I wonder what she thinks about? Her face is so intent, so earnest—but perhaps it's the vigorous climb that makes her look that way—

I cannot bear to watch her more, knowing her Good, Innocent Heart, and comparing it with my own—I swing the telescope—

At first all I can see is grass—then suddenly I catch a glimpse of a foot—a back—a whole army of backs—The Convicts are assembled in a great circle around the triangle to watch the flogging—They stand amid a great Swarm of Flies—there was a flogging only two days before and the ground is Soaked with Blood—

I see Father—rigid and unmoving as a statue, his eyes fixed straight ahead—he could be on a parade ground—no suggestion in his bearing that the Flogging will have the slightest effect on him—although his face is pale—

I wonder how it must feel to know that all these men assembled here are Entirely and Completely in his Power—He can do with them what he will and there is no one to stop him—Out here, some days' journey from Town, on the far side of a Dangerous stretch of water, Father is the Law—in a world that cannot be ordered or controlled in a rational way but can only be dealt with brutally, by force—

Then I see the triangle itself—and the frail body of the man who tried to kill my father—his hands tied above his head with rope, he stands, naked to the waist, awaiting the assault—soon he will be Dangling—

It begins—and a rush of excitement surges through me, electric—

The officer swings back his arm—raises the cat—brings the many tails swinging and biting into the skin—the convict shudders but does not cry out—

The arm rises again—swings—strikes—rises again—swings—strikes—

The first Cuts appear as welts on the skin—the lines redden—the skin begins to part—then splits—At first the blood merely seeps—but as the cat swings again, and again, the blood starts to stream, to pour—the Flesh itself starts to come off in pieces, so that the convicts standing nearest are spattered with tiny gobbets of meat—

Don't spare your arm, sir! cries Mr. Fry—exhorting the lash-man to greater efforts—

Father's face still quite unmoved—he watches the spectacle dispassionately—I wonder how my own face would appear to someone watching me—Would they have any idea of the revulsion mingling with excitement—and desire—and pity—and fear—and a nameless, burning, roiling something deep within my foul stinking belly—the longing to be free from this need, the inability to prevent myself surrendering to it—

As I watch I am simultaneously the man on the triangle and the man in the hood—I am the hand that strikes and the naked flesh on which it falls—

The emotions that rise up in me—choking me, overpowering me, so that I can scarcely focus, scarcely think—are quite beyond my powers of description or explanation—

The man on the triangle slumps—he is Unconscious—he has uttered not a word although he has received fifty lashes—it is over—

I turn away as they cut him down—

Already my hands are starting to shake—the black bile is creeping through my system and black specks dance before my eyes—

I am falling—

I must reach my bed—

Charlotte

It has long been accepted in our household that Emily is *the sensitive one.* She is frequently made ill by her nerves, and as a consequence we are all under standing instructions to shield her from all sources of fear or alarm. Her illnesses are many and varied, and include headaches, fainting fits, mysterious attacks of nausea, and, on one memorable occasion, temporary blindness. But her speciality is disordered sleep: she suffers from extraordinarily vivid dreams and nightmares, and goes through bouts where she sleeps too much (twelve, fourteen hours a day, staggering through the few hours when she is awake) or too little. Often after one of her attacks (usually consisting of headaches; sensitivity to light, noise, and odours; and copious vomiting) she will go into periods of frenzied activity where she won't sleep for days, or she'll stay awake all night and sleep all day, talking maniacally and attacking the housework with a burning intensity that is most disconcerting to behold. She is also prone to fits of sleepwalking, a very dangerous activity when you live on an island ringed with cliffs and populated with hardened criminals.

I am of the opinion that most of it is done for effect. It annoys me that I am the only one who appears to have noticed this.

Anne

She hurried towards the back door, worried that Father might have come back and discovered her absence. From the prickling of her scalp she sensed trouble ahead. The house had an atmosphere, like an electrical storm. But when she stepped cautiously through the back door into the kitchen, she found Charlotte alone in the kitchen, looking exceedingly sour.

"Emily's not well," Charlotte said flatly. And at once, Anne understood what she'd been sensing as she approached the back door: Emily was ill. Emily needed her.

The rhythm of Emily's illness ruled all their lives, but it was Anne who bore the brunt of it. For as long as she could remember she had been the barometer to the fluctuating fortunes of Emily's illnesses. She felt what Emily felt; she suffered what Emily suffered; and she always knew when an attack was coming on. Sometimes, the connection between them was so intense that she could almost hear Emily's thoughts.

Anne smoothed her wind-tangled hair back and began automatically to gather the things she would need. Cool water; clean cloths; laudanum. Resentment nibbled at her. Why was this always her job? Why was she tied to Emily's moods and miseries in this way? Why did she seem to live as her sister's mirror, reflecting everything back at her? Would there ever be an end to this?

She slipped into the bedroom. Emily was lying on the bed, her face turned to the wall, stripped down to her chemise. In the dimness, her waxy skin had the unhealthy pallor of a sea creature, and her dark hair, spilling loose on the pillow, gave her the look of a drowned woman. Anne felt her heart judder sympathetically at the sight of her sister, so quiet, so wretched; the beloved face pale; the vulnerability of her white hand, like an orchid curled beside her face. And as she gazed down at Emily, something stole over her, some invisible force that mazed her brain, silencing all opposition. She could not refuse her.

Anne went quietly to the window and adjusted the curtains, blocking out the last tiny sliver of light. Then she sat on the bed, very gently so as not to rock or bump Emily, and took her hand.

"Your skin is so cool," Emily murmured. Emily's hand was moist and uncomfortably warm. Anne began to bathe her face and hands with cool water. She knew it gave only slight relief, but in the quiet and calm of the familiar ritual she could feel the two of them drawing together, silently renewing the old bonds, burning away their small resentments, returning them both to the simple fact of their unbreakable connection. They were, on some deep and unfathomable level, connected, in a way that Charlotte was not, never had been; as if a single heart beat in their two bodies. They were tied to each other, for better or worse. And try as she might to tear herself away, Anne knew that she would never, never be able to leave Emily while that heart kept on beating.

Three

The Wolf sisters
consider their position

Charlotte

That night, alone in the kitchen, I found myself brooding over the events of the last few days as I washed the supper dishes. As the surgeon had observed, Father had come perilously close to death. If things had gone only slightly differently, the three of us could well have found ourselves orphaned, and that was a frightening thought indeed, for without Father, we would be completely alone. We had no family in the colony, and only a maiden aunt—Father's sister—at home in England. Should anything happen to Father we would be alone on Coldwater, unprotected, with nowhere to go, no family to receive us, no friends to call upon, for my father had none that I knew of, and any childhood friendships my sisters and I had formed had gradually lapsed during the long years of isolation. I tried to imagine what would have happened to us if Father had indeed been killed. A new governor would have been appointed, I presumed, and once he arrived we would have been evicted from the cottage which had been our home for eight years.

I was not particularly attached to Coldwater, but it was so long since I had lived anywhere else that I found the prospect of leaving it utterly terrifying. My childhood had been spent at Haworth, a generous tract of land (bought at scandalously low cost) hacked from the bush by assigned men. After some experimentation with other crops, Father ran sheep on it with great success. It was very hot out there, and very remote. I hated it. In its own way it was as isolated as Coldwater, and the thought of returning there was quite insupportable. I would be quite happy never to see that place again. But I did not know my way around Sydney, and the thought of finding lodgings in that nasty, bustling, brutish, crowded place filled me with dread.

But perhaps the army would take care of us? That thought brought some comfort. Perhaps some kindly senior officer would take pity on us, take us into his house, and introduce us to what passed for Sydney society. Maybe the tragic circumstances of our father's death would lend us a certain cachet. Maybe the more sophisticated and intelligent members of polite society (particularly the tall and dark ones with a brooding disposition but hidden reserves of tenderness and passion) would be able to look beyond our somewhat rough manners (I had no illusions about that) and see the free-spirited, unaffected, good-hearted women we really were.

But that seemed unlikely.

It seemed more probable that once Father died, we would find ourselves with nowhere to live and no way of supporting ourselves and we would soon find ourselves in a desperate plight. It would no doubt be possible to marry our way out of trouble, given that the colony was drastically undersupplied with women, but I would prefer not to have to try it.

No: something would have to be done. And I was the only one capable of doing it.

Emily was felled for two days. On the morning of the third day she rose, looking thin, drawn, and sallow, but filled with that unnatural energy which so often accompanied the cessation of one of her attacks (yet another reason for doubting her: did anyone ever jump out of bed after an attack of influenza, full of energy and raring to go? I do not think so).

Father, although still convalescent himself, was most solicitous, and encouraged her not to get up and about before she was ready, but Emily would not hear of it. She was entirely well, she insisted, and keen to resume her duties. (Emily liked to think she was the only one capable of running the household, and was always most slighting of my efforts.)

Once Father had finished his breakfast and gone off to work, and the kitchen had been set once more to rights, I sought my sisters' opinions on the matter of our future.

"Have you ever thought about what would happen to us if something happened to Father?" I asked.

Anne and Emily looked at each other. The question had not, apparently, occurred to them.

"Wouldn't we go back to Haworth?" Anne said.

"How could we live out there without Father?" I said scornfully. "It would be impossible for the three of us to live there unprotected. What about the natives? What about bushrangers?"

Anne's bottom lip was starting to protrude obstinately. "But it's our land. Why shouldn't we go back there if we wanted to?" Of all of us, I think Anne had been the most attached to Haworth, and the most reluctant to leave.

"Charlotte's probably right," Emily said, in a conciliatory tone. "We couldn't live at Haworth by ourselves. We should have to move to town."

"And what should we do there?" I asked. "How would we live, the three of us, without Father to provide for us?"

Emily, who had not the faintest idea about such things, exchanged a glance with Anne. "We could live off the proceeds from Haworth," Emily suggested, a little uncertainly. "Father has an overseer running it for him at present. Couldn't the fellow continue to do so?"

"Do you know anything about running a property?" I asked. "Would you know what decisions to make, or whether the overseer was cheating us?"

Anne was looking waspish. "You're supposed to be the clever one, Charlotte. I'm sure you could learn."

I gave her a withering stare.

"Well, supposing Father has not made any provision for us in his will—which I very much doubt—and we were suddenly left unprotected, the answer to me seems simple," Emily said. "We sell Haworth, invest the money in a decent sort of house in the town, and open up a school."

I gazed at her, astonished. "A school?"

"Yes," said Emily, as if she was quite unaware of the extraordinary incongruity of what she had just suggested. "I'm sure we could run a very good sort of school."

I thought about pointing out how utterly unsuited the three of us were to the business of setting up a school—attracting students, extracting fees, running a large establishment—given that Emily was pathologically shy, Anne was bad-tempered and lazy, and the only one of us who was capable of the task, namely me, was passionately opposed to the idea.

"Leaving aside the question of whether this is even possible," I began, "think for a moment about what we've actually got to offer. None of us have any teaching experience whatsoever. Anne's never even set foot inside a school. No one knows us. We have no connections."

"Father has," interrupted Anne. "He knows all sorts of important people."

"Who are they?" I demanded. "What are their names? How do you propose to contact them?"

Anne was silent.

"And what would we teach them? If we want to attract the better class of girl we have to provide them with accomplishments. But we don't speak any foreign languages, apart from French." And in fact I was the only one who had applied myself to the study of French, but it seemed unnecessary to point that out here. "Nor could we teach them to dance or sing or play a musical instrument."

"Anne can play," argued Emily, "and we can all draw."

"Anne hasn't played since the salt water got into the pianoforte," I reminded her. "And as for drawing—"

Anne interrupted, suddenly bored. "If you're not interested in our suggestions you may as well tell us what you have in mind, Charlotte."

"I've started writing a novel," I said. "I think we should try and make a living as writers."

Suddenly the room went very quiet.

We had always been a literary family. My father had attempted to combat the terrible isolation of this country by reading. Great boxes of books were shipped to us regularly from London, making their laborious way from Portsmouth, south via the Canary Islands to Rio de Janeiro, south again to Van Diemen's Land, then north to Sydney, and up the coast to us. Everything we received was months old; the events we read about in the English newspapers were ancient history by the time we heard of them. My father read voraciously—novels, poetry, science, politics, philosophy—and everything he read he passed on to us, his daughters. He never troubled himself about whether it was suitable for us or not—if we could understand it, it must be suitable.

I don't remember exactly when it was that our activities expanded to include writing. I remember complaining to Father once when I was quite young—eight, perhaps, or ten, although I feel as if I was even younger—that I had nothing left to read and was tired of all my old books. With the next shipment of books some months off I'm not quite sure what I expected him to do about it. Father suggested that in that case I should go and write my own book. Was he joking? I don't know; but the suggestion made a deep impression on me. As I remember, I did not follow his advice—*what's the point of writing yourself a book?* I thought. *You already know how it's going to end.* But I think that even then I must already have been writing, or he would not have made the suggestion.

"We've always written to amuse ourselves," I continued, "why shouldn't we write to amuse others?"

"Try and get our work published, you mean?" Anne said, puzzled. "In one of the newspapers?"

"Certainly not," I said. "I meant we should be writing books."

Anne raised her eyebrows. Emily snorted.

"Well?" I said.

"It's not very ladylike, is it?" Anne said.

This from Anne, who ran around with her skirts hitched up and her hair falling down, never caring if she ruined her complexion by exposing it to the sun. "When have you ever cared about being ladylike?"

"But what you're talking about—the publicity—it's not right, it's not—*decent*—" Anne stammered.

I knew what she was trying to say. The world, had you asked it, would no doubt have said that there was something distinctly indelicate about the idea of young ladies like ourselves making such a bid for fame and notoriety. For after all, a woman's place was in the home, and her one true purpose in life was to run a household quietly and competently, putting her own needs aside so that her children might thrive and her husband prosper. A woman's way lay in silence and self-sacrifice, tenderness and humility, never asking anything for herself. While a gentlewoman in distressed circumstances might sometimes be forced to seek a living, she should do so quietly and privately, without self-aggrandisement, and certainly without intruding into the public world of men—by becoming, say, a writer—for a woman's knowledge of world affairs was imperfect, her education inadequate, and her intellect more feeble than a man's. How could she possibly have anything of value to say in print?

Yet despite all this, I wanted to write. I had always wanted to write. I knew what the world's views were on the matter. I didn't care.

And I knew that my sisters must feel the same way—did they not spend as much time as I did consumed by their private world? Our lives were hard, and isolated, and disappointing. The possible futures which lay before us—bush wife, town wife, military wife—were all equally dismal and uninviting. Only on the page could I say what I needed to say, think what I needed to think. Only on the page could I really, truly exist.

"We needn't publish under our own names," I said. "We could use pseudonyms."

"But they'd never publish us," Anne objected.

"Why wouldn't they?"

"They just wouldn't."

I looked at Emily, hoping she would enter the discussion, but she was silent, staring into the middle distance, her heavy brows drawn together. It was a bad sign. Without Emily's assistance and consent, I was not sure how to proceed.

"Tell me what your objections are," I said. "If it's publicity you object to, we can find ways to avoid it. We can write under assumed names, and keep our sex a secret."

Still Emily said nothing.

I looked at Anne. She was listening, uncertain, lips pursed.

"It's surely not a question of technique," I continued. "After all these years of writing stories and sagas I'm sure we should have no difficulty writing a novel. So the problem must be something else."

I paused. "Perhaps you're wondering whether anyone cares about what you've got to say. Whether your opinions are utterly worthless or not. Well, all I can say to you is, you must decide that for yourself. I cannot be certain of it myself. But I am determined to try."

"Supposing we *were* to write novels," Anne said cautiously, "how would we go about seeking a publisher?"

"We look in our favourite books for the name and address of the publisher, and we send our manuscripts to them," I explained crisply. "It's really quite simple."

"It's really quite impossible," Emily said flatly, startling me.

"Why, pray?"

"Because we're here and all the publishers are in England," said Emily. "Suppose we did try to get a book published. Aside from the prohibitive cost of sending them a manuscript, it would take four months to get there, and then it would take another four months for them to reply. Even if they say yes straightaway, that's nearly a year of waiting. And what if they say no, and we have to begin the process all over again? We would have starved to death long since if we were relying on this as our only source of income. I think we'd be much better off opening a school."

This was disappointing, but I was not really surprised. "Well, if you're afraid to try . . ." I sighed. This was guaranteed to prod Emily into action.

"I'm not afraid," Emily snapped back. "I just think the whole idea is impossible."

She was right, of course: there was no hope of putting my plan into action while we stayed out here on the rim of the world. If we were to succeed, we would have to leave Coldwater and the colony and return home to England.

But that was a battle I was not yet ready to fight. So I said nothing more.

Anne

Retreating from the forbidding wall of Emily's silence, Anne fled the house. The place had an atmosphere sometimes—close, warm, vegetable, rotten—like a hothouse; a crazed, accelerated, confined, unnatural kind of energy that burned and surged and produced nothing—nothing but words. Whether it was Charlotte's efforts to become a great novelist or Emily's endless story-spinning or the reams of reports and journals that spilled from Father's pen, the result was nothing but more chatter, more ink spilt. So much effort, and for what? What did all those words accomplish? Men would still be flogged and dinner would still be cooked, whether the books got written or not. Sometimes—sometimes—she failed to see the point of it all. If it were not for her walks, she was sure she would go mad.

Marching briskly over the rocks, her skirts snapping like sails, Anne thought about Charlotte's suggestion. She knew why Emily was so obstinately against the idea of publishing her work: it would be a betrayal of Gondal.

Gondal was their private world. It began when they were little girls, and Emily invented an imaginary country which lay in the unexplored centre of the Australian continent. She named it Gondal, and the stories they made up were little more than a flexible framework for play as they ran around the property at Haworth, laughing, shouting, dressing up. Now there was no running, no laughing. There was a history of Gondal; it had been written down, and the new incidents they wrote had to accord with what had gone before. The story unfurled like a great banner, spinning out day after day, with no sign of an end, for this story had no conceivable endpoint. Heroes and heroines died, but new ones were born to carry on the story—and sometimes the dead came back if they found it was impossible to do without them.

Such had been the fate of Augusta, who died of love; her death scene had been terribly affecting, the funeral—a spectacle of imperial grandeur—astonishingly moving, and the grief of her husband—who had arrived at her deathbed moments too late—was the source of hitherto undreamt-of storms of passion. However, as the weeks passed, they discovered that they missed her too much. The new heroine they had devised to take Augusta's place did not have quite the same grip on their hearts (for after all, they had grown up with Augusta, whom Emily had invented at the age of nine) and so the death scene was revised. Augusta no longer sat bolt upright, with the name of her absent beloved on her lips, as the fever spiked, before collapsing back onto the pillows and expiring. Instead, her beloved reached the sick bed in the very nick of time, so that when she called out for him he could cry, "Darling, I'm here!" (having crossed the kingdom at a dead gallop, riding four horses to death in order to reach her) and take her in his arms, whereupon the fever broke, and she was returned to him from the very edge of the grave. The funeral was later recycled, to almost as good an effect, for the death of the dowager duchess.

Gondal had begun as a game, but over time it had become the stuff of life, an active mythological world which accompanied them through the days. The geography of Gondal overlaid the landscape she was walking through now, like a veil. The rocks and trees of their island home were imprinted with the tales that had been conjured here in the early days, when Emily would still come for walks: *this is the throne room, this is the secret passage, this is where Alexandrina was imprisoned, this is where Mary died in Percy's arms.* The crenellated landscape of rock which rose up behind the house had long ago been transformed into the semi-ruined castle where Augusta, Araminta, and a phalanx of dukes, heroes, and villains lived their tumultuous and eventful lives, lives that were interwoven with their own, continuing and developing on a daily basis. *The Gondals are besieged,* Emily would begin, as Anne was dusting the mantelpiece in the sitting room. *Augusta has had a letter from the front,* Anne would say, as Emily kneaded the bread.

Anne stopped in front of a tall rocky outcrop, one of the most significant Gondal sites on the island, the place where the wicked Lord Jasper was hanged. When first they climbed the rock they had not realised that from the top they could see a real gallows, not far away. When prisoners were hanged, it was from a picturesque spot overlooking the great empty ocean. The prisoners' graves, mostly unmarked, lay at the foot of the gallows, also overlooking the sea.

On a whim, she decided to climb the rock. She gathered up her skirts, tucked them out of the way, and began to haul herself up. Her body could remember the climb, although she had not done it in several years: a handhold here, a foothold here, a big stretch here. When she reached the top she swung her legs over and sat with her face to the wind, listening to it ruffling past her ears, tangling her hair into silvery strings, gazing out at the great expanse of the Pacific Ocean, ribbed with a swell that was dreamily steady, rhythmic, like breathing. The blue water looked up at the blue sky with an ancient, ageless gaze, and the place where they met, far off in the distance, was a colourless, cloudless silver. There was something mesmerising about that view. The inhuman scale of the world's largest ocean stunned her into a kind of numb, meditative trance. Here at the edge of things, all activity seemed to recede in the face of the vast indifference of the landscape. Forests could be cut down, mountains scaled, marshes drained, rivers forded, bridged, or dammed, but here, human ingenuity came to nothing. A boat was making its way north, its sails shining white in the blistering sun, distance rendering it frail and tiny. Lolloping over these vast distances in such a tiny craft seemed like an act of wanton bravado.

And looking out at the immensity, she was struck, forcefully and with a weary distaste, but not for the first time, by how utterly absurd their lives had become, locked in a draughty cottage on the perilous edge of a vast ocean, scribbling romances which no one but themselves would ever read; romances which described the passionate emotions, the love between man and woman, which they could only imagine, shaping their conjectures from descriptions in books and poetry. It was no way to live. It was a shadow existence. It was a kind of emotional cannibalism. It was time to stop.

Shocked by the thought, Anne turned and began to scramble down. Her skirt caught and she yanked at it impatiently, ripping a three-cornered hole in it. She would have some mending to do tonight.

Stop playing Gondals? The thought was sacrilege. Gondal was Emily's world. It was, Anne suspected, more real to her than their daily existence—and why not, after all? Their daily life was dreary enough. If they didn't have Gondal to entertain them, what would they have? Cooking. Cleaning. Waiting for Father to be recalled to Sydney. Dining with the officers, hoping to be chosen, trying not to be too particular. But Anne could not help feeling that Gondal was, in some subtle way, bad for them. It was another kind of poison, part of the bad magic of the island, leaching its way into their expectations, building up a dream world that could never be realised. Perhaps it would be better to give it up, to try and live in the real world, to be content. That was sensible. That was *real*.

Emily

I cannot Bear the thought of someone I don't know, but who I might some day be Obliged to meet, reading my stories—letting a Stranger into Gondal to trample on our invention, to ridicule and belittle the passions of the people who inhabit it—I can see him with his thick tobacco-stained fingers and his pasty skin, leafing through my Manuscript with his big brown shoes up on his desk, wearing a faint moue of derision as his moustached lip curls—It's like offering to let someone Tear my Skin off—

Anne latched onto the idea and was not going to be put off—very persistent—*Don't you think that perhaps we could do some good, if we tried?*

I find books that try to do good very tiresome.

Hurt feelings all round, Anne huffing: *I do not propose to write some moralising sermon disguised as fiction. That would certainly be tiresome but I think a novel can instruct as well as entertain!*

I remonstrating: *If we publish all our secrets what will be left for us?*

She: *I'm not talking about Gondal. That's ours. It's private. I wouldn't want anyone else to see it. No, I meant we could start something new, written with publication in mind. I think it would be splendid to write the kind of book I like to read myself, and to know that there were people out there like ourselves who would seize upon it and read it and be uplifted by it, and then give it to all their friends and say,* Here, you must read this. *Imagine it.*

And I do entertain a vision of myself—Emily Wolf, the Lady of the Hour—Eminent Lady Novelist—the Toast of every gathering—in silks, holding court—Emily Wolf, the most Fascinating lady in town—how delightful!

But quite impossible—I remember myself as a girl in Sydney—a small and backward place, provincial, crass, rough—but even there, I failed to make any sort of impression—conversation was almost impossible, I never knew what to do with my hands, never understood people's jokes, never looked well in clothes—women frightened me, while men left me Paralysed with Terror—No book is ever going to change that—

And yet I found myself agreeing that yes, *I would start a new book*—through a singing in my ears like the shrill of cicadas—*Yes, I already have an idea!*—no, not cicadas—the sound a crystal wineglass makes when you rub a moistened finger around its rim, a resonant, mineral song rising in my ears to drown out Anne's voice—

And then it came to me—and the sound in my ears ceased its buzzing—In the plays of Shakespeare it is very common for the hero or heroine to put on a *Mask* in order to accomplish a difficult task which they could not achieve as themselves—Not just the castaway heroines—*Viola*—*Rosalind*—but the great heroes—*Hamlet* himself—

To put on a mask is to become something greater than oneself, to become both yourself *and* the mask—Emily Wolf is a poor creature indeed, riven with all kinds of fears and doubts—But Who might not I Become if I spoke from behind the mask?

I have observed that a woman who puts her Words before the Public is rarely judged on her Merits—The most simpering, idiotic kind of Nonsense is Praised—or rather Flattered—for its *ladylike qualities*—Critics care not one jot whether it is Truthful or Honest—they would rather we parroted back conventional ideas, conventional characters—But if that is all I am permitted to do, I would rather not write at all—

So then—I cannot write as a Woman—yet I cannot write as a Man either—to do so would be a betrayal of all that I am—all that I feel and know to be true—

So I must find another self—a shadow self—neither man nor woman—Emily but not-Emily—

And then speak—

Charlotte

The next morning, Emily appeared in my bedroom before I had even got out of bed. Anne, her shadow, hovered at her elbow. Emily was at her most high-handed.

"We've thought about it," she said, "and we're going to go ahead with it."

It was almost choking her to agree to a plan of mine.

"Do you mean it?" I asked. I had expected more of a struggle.

"We wouldn't say it if we didn't," Emily said coolly.

"Splendid," I replied.

"There is one condition."

"What?"

"We will none of us use our real names."

I could see no difficulty with that.

"I won't pretend to be a man," Anne said. "It doesn't seem right."

"We've decided to use ambiguous names, not obviously male or female," Emily said.

"What are you to be called?" I asked.

"Ellis," said Emily.

"Acton," said Anne.

And after some discussion, I hit upon Currer as my nom de plume. For a surname, we eventually chose Waters, keeping our true initials. Still waters run deep, as they say.

So as soon as breakfast was out of the way, Anne and I sat down at the table together as Emily sifted and weighed and stirred and hummed and tasted in the background (for it was baking day and the baking still had to be done, after all) and the two of us took out our ink and pens and paper, and started to write.

There is something tremendously exciting about the beginning of this imaginary journey; for while the words remain unwritten, the idea in your head remains perfect, pristine, an object whose apparent harmony of form disguises the technical mastery which lies beneath. Once you begin, the whole thing starts to collapse, like that tower in Pisa which began tilting even as it was being constructed. What was melodious, simple, and beautiful in the abstract is painfully disappointing in practice: metaphors don't hang together, story strands lead nowhere, main characters turn out to be tedious, and supporting characters drag you off on tangents. What you end up with is always an approximation of the thing you originally envisaged. But even so, there are moments where the prose sings, and you know that you've done something remarkable, and I suppose that's why you keep going.

Four

A new arrival

Charlotte

That night at supper, Father made an announcement.

"We are receiving a new shipment of prisoners tomorrow."

Caught by surprise, I slurped my tea noisily. "Really?" Suddenly the morrow looked more interesting. New prisoners meant news from the mainland; the possibility of letters, books, newspapers; bulletins from the outside world, a reminder that we were not, after all, adrift in a primeval landscape, displaced in time.

"Six men," Father said, "fresh off the boat from England."

"What manner of men are they?" I asked.

"Two of them are incorrigibly violent. They would not submit to authority during the voyage out, and there seems little possibility of making useful labourers of them. I suspect they have been sent to me to keep out of harm's way, for they are quite mad."

This was no more than typical—many of father's prisoners seemed to be simply deranged, unable to live within normal human society without causing harm.

"Three others were caught stealing on the voyage over. Some of these fellows really do seem incapable of learning from their experiences."

I knew that Father was saving the most interesting prisoner for last. "That's only five," I said. "Who is the sixth?"

"An Irishman who caused all kinds of trouble during the voyage out."

"What kind of trouble?" I asked.

"He's an agitator, it would seem, a troublemaker. Hates the English, and every kind of authority. Tried to jump ship in Barbados, and then, when that was unsuccessful, was involved in an attempt to start an uprising on board the ship. The curious thing is, he comes highly recommended by the ship's surgeon, who seems to have taken quite a shine to him. It was the surgeon's intercession that saved him from the noose."

"What will you do with him, Father?" asked Emily.

"I don't know yet," Father said thoughtfully. "I shan't make up my mind until I've spoken to him and assessed his character. These fellows are often much more intelligent than they are given credit for, and it may be possible to harness his energies for some useful purpose. We shall see."

Extract from An Account of an Australian Penal Settlement, including some suggestions for the reform of the penal system, *by Captain Edward Wolf*

"*The Botany Bay of Botany Bay*"

The colonial administration has found it necessary over the years to set up a number of separate penal colonies within the larger colony to deal with refractory convicts. These places of secondary punishment (or "the Botany Bay of Botany Bay") have two purposes: one, to prevent convicts from absconding; and two, to provide a deterrent against further offences.

Absconding: Some prisoners have proven themselves unable to be controlled by the usual methods (irons, flogging, road gangs, &c.) and have become persistent bolters. While most are quickly recaptured (or turn themselves in when starvation threatens) some turn to theft, or "bushranging" (i.e., robbery with violence) to survive. These men pose a very real threat to settlers, particularly in outlying areas. In order to control these men and prevent them from absconding, it has over time become necessary to build prisons further and further from settled areas, so that even if these men do escape, they cannot find their way back to town.

The first of these settlements was established at Newcastle, seventy miles north of Sydney, where convicts worked at coal mining, lime burning, and cedar cutting. Escape attempts were frequent, although the Aborigines in the area proved both willing and able to catch absconding convicts and return them to the authorities. Unfortunately, Newcastle proved to be insufficiently remote, for settlers soon began to arrive in the area, attracted by the abundance of fertile land. Consequently, the worst prisoners had to be moved on to other prisons further north. Port Macquarie and Moreton Bay were both set up for this purpose, but their importance as places of secondary punishment soon waned, as the tropical climate made living too easy. Absconders, too, found they could live a very pleasant life outside the settlement, as food was plentiful and easily obtained.

The focus then shifted to island colonies, such as Norfolk Island, Coldwater, and Port Arthur (which is not, in fact, an island, but a promontory attached to the mainland of Van Diemen's Land by an extremely narrow, and therefore easily guarded, natural causeway). An island prison has many advantages over a land-based prison. There is generally no question of the land being required by settlers, and provided one keeps close control of shipping, there is little chance of absconding, as the vast majority of convicts are unable to swim. Norfolk Island, a thousand miles off the coast of New South Wales and four hundred miles from New Zealand, is in many ways a perfect prison. It is small, perfectly isolated, and very difficult to access. The only defect of

Norfolk is that its geographical isolation is perhaps a little *too* perfect: provisioning and maintaining a settlement in such a remote location is troublesome, and in the event of a disaster, help cannot readily be summoned. Coldwater, which is much closer to the mainland, is perhaps a more practical site in terms of administration.

Deterrence: For felons at home in England, the greatest threat we have (after hanging) is transportation. But once a felon has been transported, what do we have left in our arsenal to prevent him from offending again? We must have other places, names of terror, to stand in place of Botany Bay. For the hardened convict who is used to ill-treatment, or the man on a life sentence with no hope of returning home, only the grimmest of places can hold any terror for him. Thus, hard labour must be of the harshest kind, and discipline must be severe. It is not enough for a prison to be a dumping ground for unmanageable prisoners; a secondary penal colony must also have an exemplary, symbolic function. It must be a warning and a threat; a living hell. To some, this may seem cruel; but if a prisoner has nothing to fear, and nothing to lose, then there is nothing he will not do.

Charlotte

It was a fine, brisk, glaring autumn day, with a hard blue sky, high scudding clouds, and a vigorously cold wind that snapped at our faces and hands like a fox terrier. We walked in procession with Father and a detachment of soldiers from our house to the cliff top, and from there we picked our way precariously down the cliff. There was a path, but it was a difficult descent, especially for one as inactive as myself. Once on the beach, we arranged ourselves as a guard of honour and waited for the ship to arrive. This ceremony was not for the benefit of the convicts— Father preferred to keep us as far away from them as possible. We were there to wave off the departing batch of troopers, and to greet the new ones who were arriving. Father still harboured fond hopes that one day he might muster up some marriage partners from among his men, although, sadly, it had not happened yet.

"There!" cried one of the men, and pointed. We all turned to look, and saw a longboat being rowed toward the reef. The approach was, as I have mentioned, perilous, and I always watched boats arrive with a shrivelling, shrinking feeling in my stomach, for the boats did not always make it ashore intact. I had witnessed one such attempted landing where an unlucky wave had swept a boat sideways onto rocks, where it had caught with a terrible tearing sound. Some of the men were pitched into the water and dashed against the rocks; the water boiled like a cauldron, and even a strong swimmer would have been in difficulties. These men were for the most part unable to swim, and were soon lost beneath the waves. A rescue was mounted for those who had managed, somehow, to cling to the crippled boat, and those men were brought safely to shore. But even experienced oarsmen disliked the approach to Coldwater, and I certainly could not blame them for it. Emily had once expressed a fear that if anything should ever go terribly wrong, the people on the mainland might not send anyone to fetch us.

The oarsmen strained and bent their backs, and I held my breath as the swell rose and fell, tipping the boat up and down, but this time all was well, and the boat landed safely on the shore. The young officer in charge of the party marched crisply forward and saluted.

"Lieutenant Spufford, at your service, sir," he barked.

"How do you do, Lieutenant. I am Captain Wolf. Welcome to Coldwater."

"Thank you, sir."

"I believe you have some prisoners for me?"

"Yes, sir. All present and accounted for."

The six prisoners sat in a huddle together in the middle of the boat. Their hands and feet were shackled; had they fallen overboard, they would surely have drowned. All of them had the rough, pale, pinched look of the poor; they had spent the last six months at sea and I fancied they had probably spent much of that time without decent food or exercise or so much as a glimpse of the sky. It was easy to pick out the men Father had described as deranged—one twitched and muttered ceaselessly, his eyes darting about suspiciously; the other, a huge lantern-jawed fellow, seemed to exude an air of violence, although he sat quite still. It was harder to tell who were the thieves and who was the Irish revolutionary.

I stole a glance at my sisters. Anne was looking demurely at the ground, aware of the eyes of the soldiers upon her. Emily was gazing, as I had been, at the prisoners. Had one of them caught her eye? Her expression was unfathomable.

As we watched, the prisoners were hustled out of the boat and into the custody of a small detachment of soldiers. The shackles were removed from their feet (though not their hands) as their names were ticked off on a list. Then they began their stumbling ascent up the cliff face. I watched them as they slipped and slithered on their way up, knowing that if they should lose their footing they would probably fall to their deaths. Had no one realised what a dangerous practice this was? I determined to mention it to Father later.

"Lieutenant Spufford, I'd like you to meet my daughters."

I dragged my attention away from the prisoners. It was time to meet the new detachment of officers.

"This is my eldest daughter, Miss Wolf. This is Lieutenant Spufford."

"How do you do, Miss Wolf?"

I nodded politely to Lieutenant Spufford, a very upright, very proper young officer, then repeated the performance with Lieutenant Argent, Lieutenant Faulkner, and Lieutenant Jones. I lived in hope that one day a man would step ashore with all the qualities I was searching for in a husband—intellect, spirit, passion, &c. &c.—but I doubted very much whether I'd find him amongst this lot. The reception line moved on to Emily, who was distant, and Anne, who was coy. Then the new officers headed off up the cliff face and the old officers clambered into the boat and set out for the mainland. I watched them as they set out through the swell.

One day, I thought, that will be me.

Emily

I knew him at once—

His upright carriage, the look of defiance in his eye—all marked him out as a Man among men—He was wild, untamed, unbowed, yet somehow noble —He stood out from the others like an eagle amongst pigeons—

He is looking at me—

Oh dear God what shall I do? I cannot turn away—I am staring— he stares back—what does he mean by it? And why cannot I look away? My heart racing, I grow flushed—then pale—my confusion must be obvious to all—

The guard orders them to move—he turns his head to look up at the cliff—then walks away, a beast in chains—

Freed from his gaze, a dread feeling of Foreboding creeps over me— *This man means to do us harm*—

From An Account of an Australian Penal Settlement

The importance of interviewing prisoners

Some prison governors make no attempt at all to become acquainted with the character of the individual prisoners under their control. No doubt they feel that it is unnecessary, since each prisoner will be treated by the system in exactly the same manner (i.e., they will live under the same set of rules, to be applied disinterestedly to everyone). Prisons are designed to stamp out individuality, and induce a state of docile tractability. The machinery of a prison is geared towards that process. So why should one bother to inquire into the character of a prisoner, when that character is shortly to be stamped out?

In order to control a prisoner you must first determine his strengths and weaknesses. The prison governor's guiding principle should always be "know your enemy." A prison is a complex social organism, and it is necessary to invest some time and thought into proper planning if you want to ensure that the organisation runs smoothly. A prison is possibly the most volatile social arrangement in existence; keeping men in this situation under control is a ceaseless struggle. The one thing which all prisoners have in common is their desperate desire for liberty; second only to that is their desire for revenge. Close watch must be kept on them at all times in order to prevent violent uprisings, and the closest watch of all must be kept on the men of strong will and forceful character who are the natural leaders of the criminal classes. It is a simple matter to identify these men if one is a reasonable judge of character; once identified, it is vital to find some means of keeping them under control. This may be done directly, by keeping them away from others (in solitary confinement or isolated labour); through highly focused disciplinary action (punishing every infraction, however minor, with the utmost severity, in order to crush the rebellious spirit out of them); or indirectly, by reducing their ability to influence others. The prison rumour mill can be put to good use here: if one allows the rumour to spread that the "new chum" is intent on upsetting already existing hierarchies of power within the prison population, his companions can generally be relied upon to crush him for you.

But if the aim of a prison system is to produce better outcomes for society at large, is it really advisable to break the spirits of able men, even if they are from the criminal classes? Necessity has shown that in this colony, where able men are scarce, men with a criminal past can rise to become valued and respected members of society. However, there is little chance that men who have been tormented and brutalised for long periods, refused all opportunities for advancement, and never encouraged to explore their strengths or use their abilities, will emerge from prison willing or able to engage in productive labour.

In a young colony, it seems wasteful to throw away the lives of men who still show some potential, or worse, to allow their good qualities to be so warped and brutalised that they become outlaws. When such men are let loose upon the colony at the end of their sentences, we all bear the cost of their furious vengeance. Therefore, it has been my practice to identify certain outstanding individuals from the prison population, separate them from the mob, and attempt to rehabilitate them. A man who has been well-treated by the system will soon learn to identify with the aims and goals of that system; thus swiftly neutralising him as an oppositional force.

Register of prisoners

Number: 25/4/5
Name: Finn O'Connell
Ship: *Mary Elizabeth*
Year: 1847
Native place: Galway, Ireland
Trade or calling: Labourer
Offence: Arson
Place of trial: Galway
Date of trial: 12 November 1846
Sentence: 14 years
Secondary sentence: 7 years
Year of birth: 1817
Height: 5′ 11″
Complexion: Dark
Hair: Black
Eyes: Grey

Journal. 12th April

I have interviewed Finn O'Connell. He is a curious creature. I can understand now why he was sent so swiftly to me; I can also

understand why the surgeon on board the *Mary Elizabeth* was so drawn
to him. His manner in telling his tale was so eloquent, so touching,
that it stirred me deeply, in spite of myself. I cannot say what it is that
makes him so compelling, yet I cannot deny the effect of his charisma.
He is a common man, and his story, in these hard times, is not
unusual; and yet I found myself inspired, most uncharacteristically, to
offer him every available aid and assistance. He is, without a doubt, a
dangerous man.

Record of interview: Finn O'Connell

Q: *How did you come to be here?*
A: The blight brought me here.
Q: *The blight?*
A: You haven't heard of it? The blight is a disease that kills potatoes:
the flowers turn black, the potatoes rot in the ground, the whole harvest
goes bad overnight. We'd heard about it, but we never believed it could
strike us. It didn't seem possible—our crops looked so healthy. I think it
was around October that it reached us, October 1845. The potato stalks
turned black and our livelihood rotted in the ground. It all happened so
quick, there was nothing anyone could do about it. At first we tried to
eat the potatoes anyway, but that just made us sick. Everyone had the
runs. One child started bleeding from his arse, then got sicker and sicker
till he died of it. He was the first.

Those with money tried to buy grain, but there was none to be had,
and even if you could find it, the prices were sky-high. Those without
money—well, they did whatever they could. Ate nettles and sorrel and
dock. Killed rats. No one wanted to go to the workhouse—it was a matter of pride, you see. Better to starve than go on the parish. Of course
there was Peel's brimstone—a kind of corn, although you'd never know
it. Terrible stuff it was—if you didn't cook it right, it made you sick in
your guts. Some said they were trying to hurry us off quicker by feeding
us poisoned grain.

Fever came to our village towards the end of the winter. It was terrible—everyone was falling sick. Not just the poor, but the doctors and
the priests—everyone. Whole families were dropping, and so fast there
was barely time to bury them.

Then the summer came, and those that could drag themselves from
their beds found work with the government. Funny sort of work it was,
too. We moved a hill. Dug it down to nothing, put it in wheelbarrows,
moved it a hundred yards and built it up again. A make-work scheme, it
was, so we'd know it was charity we were receiving. There were people
sick with fever trying to support whole families on the wages from that
terrible work, and they felt lucky to get it too. But still there was precious little to eat. The seed potatoes were spoilt or eaten, so most didn't
get their crops in the ground. Wouldn't have made any difference if they
had, for at the end of the summer the crop failed again.

We began to think we'd been singled out for God's vengeance, truly
we did. The English said it was God's punishment upon us for over-
breeding and laziness—and for Papacy, too, I daresay. So a second winter
came and there was no food and no money and no hope. That second
winter was a hard winter too: bitter cold, with mountains of snow. The
fever came back, worse than before. The fever wasn't the worst of it
though; no. The worst thing was what it did to people's souls. At the beginning, things were hard, but people still had their pride, and their faith
that things would get better. They had a sense of belonging to something,
to families and to villages. That first winter, we all did whatever we could
to help those who were worse off than ourselves. Perhaps that wasn't
much, but it was something. But that second year, after hunger had been
gnawing at us for a whole year, those who were left had seen too much
suffering and were too close to the end to care any more about anyone
else. There was a family in a cottage just up the road from us—two brothers, a sister, and their mother. The father was in jail. The mother took ill
with the fever around Christmastime, and died in a week. Then the sister
who nursed her took ill as well. Her brothers locked her into the house,
and once a day they'd send in a little food and water on the end of a pole.

Eventually she stopped taking the food and water and they knew she was dead. So they tumbled the cottage and burnt it down, with their own sister inside it. I saw a woman from my village, a woman I'd known all my life, lying dead outside her cottage with her three little children dead beside her. No one dared to bury her for fear of the fever, and the dogs had been at her. But I did nothing myself. I didn't want to catch it either.

My family did alright for a while. Our crop failed, along with all the others, but for anyone with an enterprising spirit and a heart inside his chest, there were ways of finding food. We lived not far from the river, you see. There were convoys of food being shipped up and down it all the time, and it was easy enough to steal a little as it went by.

They called us bandits and ribbonmen, as if there were armed gangs of us roving the highways terrorising people, but it wasn't really like that. It was a lot of desperate men, some with families, some without, trying to keep body and soul together. That's all it was. I could have been nabbed a thousand times for stealing off the barges, but as it was, they got me for the barn. They'd put more men on the barges to guard them, so we went to the barn instead, me, my brother, and a friend of ours. When we got there, the place was under guard, but we were desperate, so we tried it anyway. There was a scuffle and a light got knocked over and that was it. Barn went up and we were nabbed. But when there's no food and no help, you have to help yourself.

Q: *Do you believe your actions were justified then?*

A: I believe what I did was understandable. If you're asking me whether I think what I did was *right,* well . . . The Bible says that stealing is wrong, and so does the magistrate. So there you are, I suppose it's pretty clear, what I did was wrong. But it also says that you should take care of your mother and your family and that you have responsibilities to the people around you. Is it right that you should let them starve, when there's food going past your door every day? And is it right that all our crops were being exported when people were starving? Is it right that landlords should use a disaster like this to clear tenants from their land, evicting starving people? Did you know, sir, there's more money to be made from sheep and cattle than from renting your land out to tenant farmers, so to some landowners the blight was like a blessing in disguise. All those dead tenants! What a stroke of luck! But of course it wasn't luck, was it, sir? Malthus said it was inevitable. Overpopulation causes these disasters. It's a law of nature.

Q: *Malthus?*

A: He's a writer, sir.

Q: *I am familiar with his work. I'm surprised to hear that you are.*

A: I haven't read it all, sir. Just enough to get the gist of it.

Q: *You can read?*

Charlotte

That night over the dinner table Father was pondering the Irishman.

"Quite a fascinating man," he mused. "His background is exceedingly humble, but he's had quite an education. He's read Malthus."

"I can't imagine what he made of it," I sniggered, for the very idea of a poor Irish croppy reading such a dense and complex work struck me as quite absurd.

"What was his crime?" asked Emily.

"He was convicted for burning a barn," Father said, "but his real crime was stirring up anti-English sentiment. The fire was an accident—the barn was full of grain, intended for export to Britain. O'Connell and his friends stormed the place so that they could steal the grain and distribute it among their people, who were starving."

"What happened to the people?" asked Anne irrelevantly.

"I don't know," Father said.

"But did they burn the barn before or after they got the grain?" Anne persisted.

"I really don't know," Father said. "But I do think O'Connell was very lucky. Men have been hanged for that kind of crime, but he was transported instead. He really is most intriguing. I believe he could go far if he was given the right opportunities."

"What sort of opportunity could he have?" I asked.

"I think I shall take him on as a special prisoner, and we shall see how he behaves himself. If he does well, who knows where he might end up."

I saw Emily's eyes open wide, but she said nothing, and started to clear the plates instead.

"Do you think it's wise to let him have so much freedom?" asked Anne. "What if he tries to burn the house down?"

"Then he shall be flogged," Father said coolly.

From An Account of an Australian Penal Settlement

On rehabilitation

On Coldwater, the majority of prisoners are incarcerated in the usual way, performing hard labour under the most rigorous discipline. But a small number of prisoners are siphoned off upon arrival and kept in a separate facility, where I have taken steps to produce in them a moral renewal, so that they will not sink into the degradation which is, regrettably, the lot of most prisoners.

The special prisoners, as they are known, live in a separate barracks and eat in a separate mess, so they do not come into contact with the regular prisoners. They labour for only eight hours a day (the regular convicts work a twelve-hour day); the remainder is spent in education and religious instruction. The special prisoners are taught reading, writing, and simple arithmetic; they also study passages from the Bible. Once a convict has progressed sufficiently in his studies, and proven himself worthy of my trust, some of the special prisoners move on to become members of my household staff. Their tasks are generally menial—cutting wood, fetching water, &c.—but they all understand the very great privilege which is being bestowed upon them, and vie for the honour of working in my house.

Not every convict will respond well to such a system. Some are so debased and so habituated to a life of crime that no amount of moral instruction will ever convince them of the benefits of honest labour. But an exceptional man is capable of transcending his origins and shedding himself of the convict taint, if he is given opportunity and encouragement to do so.

For an example, I turn to Ebenezer Green, one of my earliest experimental subjects. Green, a clerk by trade, was transported for forgery. Only eleven months after arriving in the colony he was caught committing the same offence, and sent to Coldwater. Most would no doubt have dismissed him as a hopeless recidivist, but when I interviewed him, I discovered that there was more to him than was immediately obvious. A devoted family man, he had left his wife and five children in a situation of extreme desperation back home. In both cases, he had committed crimes only in order to obtain funds to help support his family and pay the substantial medical bills accrued during the illness of his youngest son. While such a tale of hardship is scarcely uncommon, I saw in him an earnestness, an assiduity, that impressed me immediately. I employed him as my personal secretary, a position in which he quickly became indispensable (although of course I did not allow him to deal with matters to do with security, or anything that might be deemed confidential). After several years in that post, although I was loath to lose him, I secured him an early release and a clerical position in the colonial administration, where he now occupies a senior position. His family, I am delighted to relate, joined him in New South Wales, and all are now doing well.

Emily

I saw him yesterday, dragging stone from the quarry—

He is taller than I remembered—He has thrown off the miasma of Sickness which hung about him when first I saw him and he seems to have *grown*—or rather *expanded*—as if the island life somehow agreed with him, God forbid—

There is a Strange Energy on Coldwater which affects some people in this manner—Father himself responded to it—Some people thrive here, while others rapidly sink—

There is a firmness, a decision in all his gestures, a quick, sure look in his eye—as if no one has explained to him that this is a place of Subjection—he has not yet learned to bow his head, to hide the fierce light of his undimm'd eyes—Does he not realise that his defiant look could yet ruin him?

Can it be that Father is going to bring him here among us? Let him walk freely through our house? This man who burns barns?

My earlier Fears return—Can Father truly not see that there is something Demonic about him? I long to warn him—to cry out—But he has made up his mind—

This man has woven some sort of a spell on Father and nothing I could say will set him free—But what Mischief does he mean to do? I cannot imagine—Only time will tell—

What is to be done? I must be on my guard against him—

All would be well, I think, if he were not so Beautiful—

Journal. 22nd May

My delight in O'Connell grows daily. He has shown a quick intelligence and a real aptitude for learning. He is reading politics, philosophy, and science, and is always eager for more. He is clearly a mind starved for matter, for he falls on every new book I give him with an eagerness and energy which is most gratifying to behold.

"Are all convicts taught to read?" he asked me today.

I explained that they were not.

"And why is that?"

I explained that it was assumed that if convicts could read, they might get their hands on tracts which would give them dangerous ideas, and if they could write, they might then disseminate those dangerous ideas and foment revolution.

"An ignorant man can start a revolution," he said.

"But it takes an educated man to *organise* a revolution," I replied.

He thought about that for some few moments.

"You're taking quite a chance, putting me in the way of dangerous ideas, aren't you, sir?" he said, in that direct way of his, which in any other man might have been insulting; but looking into his fine, splendid gaze, I could not doubt the sincerity of his question.

"Yes, I am," I replied. "But I believe that even the most dangerous ideas can be handled safely, if they are considered in a thoughtful and intelligent manner."

He seemed content with this answer. And indeed, I am very much looking forward to the discussions we may have in the future, for he does have a most perceptive and unusual mind for a man of his station. All he needs is someone to mould him, to direct his learning and instruct him in his reading, and I very much hope that he will eventually mature into a remarkable man, ready to take his place as an equal amongst the best of colonial society.

If Branwell had lived, he would be almost of an age with O'Connell.

Five

Branwell

Charlotte

My life would have been very different if my brother had lived. If my brother had lived, he would have carried the torch for all of us. If my brother had lived to fulfil the magnificent promise he showed in youth, there would have been no need for me to stretch my wings. I believe it is quite possible that I would have been content to bask in his reflected glory, rather than shedding my own light. But my brother did not live. So it was all left up to me.

When I remember my childhood, it seems like an endless summer. The house at Haworth stood like a tiny island in a vast ocean of cleared land. Its verandahs were the only shade for miles around, as the assigned men had cleared every tree, every bush and shrub to turn the land into pasture. In the summer the sun beat down upon the land, blinding us, as the very air shimmered in the dust and heat. We'd lie around moaning in our English clothes as the sound of cicadas drilled our ears and the birds sat limply in the far-off trees, too hot to move or sing, and the sheep huddled miserably together, panting, their heads hanging. On Coldwater it is always cool and the wind always blows, even in summer; but at Haworth, on those vast baking plains, we dreamed of cool breezes without respite. And when the winds came—baking northerlies that sucked the life from your skin—they often brought with them the smell of burning, and great flakes of ash that spoiled the washing.

On those days when it was too hot to move, or think, we would lie on the verandah, looking at the trees, far off on the uncleared edge of the property, and Branwell would tell us stories. Branwell was a year younger than me. He was the brightest and the best of us—so quick and funny, full of jokes and games. Even though I was the eldest, it was always Branwell who took the lead. (He would sulk and throw tantrums if we didn't do what he said, but he always had the most amusing ideas, so we couldn't help but follow him.) Branwell wanted to be a soldier when he grew up, and Father had given him a set of toy soldiers as a present. These became our favourite toys and the heroes of all our games. At first we were content to reenact the adventures of Lord Wellington in his battles against Napoleon's army. But in time we invented our own heroes, then our own land, and our own battles. Branwell's land was called Angria. Later, Emily would invent Gondal, and everything would be different, but then, there were four of us and we all played together.

Although we were a foursome, Branwell was my special companion. He understood me best, and loved me best. We thought alike and had the same sense of humour. We were only a year apart, but there seemed no distance at all. I'm not saying it was idyllic; we were competitive and we fought and squabbled like a couple of cats. But beneath it all was an understanding that he and I were two peas in a pod; we were the same.

In all but one respect. I was always a cautious child; he was reckless, fearless. We were warned ceaselessly of the danger which surrounded us: snakes, spiders, blackfellows, escaped convicts, the dangerous tracklessness of the bush all around us. We were clinging tenaciously to the very edge of a world which was entirely inimical to us, and without extraordinary care, so we were told, we would never survive.

Branwell never believed a word of it.

On those hot, hot days we longed to go roaming in the bush we could see, far off in the distance. Out there it looked cool, and shady, and green. There was certain to be a creek where we could bathe our hot, dusty feet. We dreamed of it, longed for it. We talked and talked about mounting an expedition to see what lay out there in the cool green bush. And finally, one day, the temptation grew too great for Branwell. I was thirteen; he was twelve. The four of us were sprawled on the verandah, gasping in the heat.

"Today's the day," he said. "Today's the day we explore the bush."

"It's too hot," said Emily.

"It will be cooler in the shade."

"We're not allowed to go into the bush," I said. As far as I was concerned, that settled it.

"We won't go far," said Branwell. "We'll just go a little way. I have a compass. We shan't get lost."

"Where did you get a compass?" asked Emily curiously.

"Father lent it to me," Branwell said, rather shiftily.

"No he didn't," I said.

"Yes he did."

"No he didn't."

"Yes he did. Anyway, you girls can stay here if you want. I'm going whether you're coming or not."

"You can't," I said. "Father will be furious."

"How will he know? Are you going to tell him? I'll make you sorry if you do."

I glared at Branwell and he glared right back at me. He knew perfectly well I wouldn't tell on him.

"Well *I'm* not going," I said, folding my arms obstinately in front of me. "I think it's a stupid idea. It's too hot and you'll probably get lost."

"Fine. Then I'll go by myself."

And he gathered up the compass he had stolen from Father and a little flask of water and a piece of bread, and headed out for the scrub. "He's going to be in so much trouble," I said, annoyed that he was going without me. The three of us watched as his small, thin frame, bouncing jauntily along, grew smaller and smaller, moving further and further away, obscured by shimmering heat waves, and finally disappeared from view.

I've gone over that day a thousand times in my mind. In retrospect it seems perfectly clear what I should have done. I should have gone with him and protected him; I should have stopped him from going; I should have told Father where he'd gone and sought help straightaway. But I did none of those things. Was it laziness? Did I let him go because I couldn't be bothered chasing after him in all that heat? Couldn't be bothered accompanying him and keeping him safe? Or was it a kind of smug desire to be the good child, obeying orders even though Branwell was being naughty?

I know now it was a terrible shortsightedness. Branwell went to his fate because I was careless. I had heeded all the warnings, but I did not genuinely believe in the danger. I let him go because it never occurred to me that anything could *really* happen to him. He was so full of fun and life. I had never seen anything bad happen to a child. It did not occur to me that this day would be any different.

I played with my sisters through the long afternoon, eventually becoming so absorbed in our game that I quite forgot about Branwell. It was not until Father came home on his horse at the end of the day that I realised Branwell had not come home.

I was in a state of terror. What should I do? Although Branwell had been gone for hours, and the sun was starting to set, it still had not quite occurred to me that something might be wrong. While Father watered his horse, and washed his face and hands for supper, I wrestled with my conscience. Branwell had made me promise not to tell, but Father was going to notice his absence soon. Could I lie to Father?

Of course I couldn't. The moment his eye lighted on me when he came to fetch us for supper, I blurted the whole story out and then burst into tears. Father was furious when he realised what had happened, but the afternoon light was swiftly fading into evening, and he had no time to chide us. He collected the overseer and went riding off after Branwell.

Left alone in the house with my sisters, I finally realised the magnitude of what was happening. I had never seen Father look frightened before. The terror of it gripped my heart, combined with a tormenting sense of my own guilt. What if Branwell never came back? It would all be my fault. I alternated between blaming him for his obstinacy and begging his forgiveness for my thoughtlessness in failing to stop him.

"Father will find Branwell, won't he?" asked a red-eyed Emily. I assured her that Branwell was just playing a trick on us, and Father would certainly find him, or that he would soon come home of his own accord and laugh at us.

But Father did not find Branwell, and he did not come home of his own accord. Father came back well after dark, anxious and silent. I could tell he was angry, but was holding on to his temper. The next day he rode off at dawn to continue the search, sending his overseer to the nearest settlement, fifteen miles away, to get help. As the men rode away from the house, Emily, Anne, and I watched from the verandah, silent, fearful, guilt-stricken.

The long day crawled by, and I sent up prayer after prayer to God to send Branwell back to us. I promised anything and everything I could think of, senseless vows of self-denial: I would be a perfect daughter, I would do all my household chores without ever having to be asked, I would work twice as hard at my lessons, and never let myself be distracted by games. I promised never to be sharp with Emily, and never to despise Anne for being stupid. I promised never to antagonise Branwell ever again—if he would only come back to us.

As afternoon turned to evening, I thought my prayers had been answered. Word came back that they had found a piece of his blue shirt snagged on a branch. Emily and Anne hugged each other. I felt some of the weight lift from my heart. Surely, surely, they must be close to him? Surely he would soon be found? But the men rode back to the house that night without finding any further sign of him.

The third day of the search produced nothing new. On the fourth day, two men from the town turned up with a black tracker in tow. This man was famed for his abilities to find people in the bush (although his talents were usually reserved for finding runaway convicts) and everyone seemed certain he would find my brother alive.

I had never seen a black man close up before, and I watched him with a mixture of wonder and fear. He was partially dressed in a policeman's jacket and breeches, but he wore no shirt and his feet were bare. He seemed shy in company, gazing at the ground and talking in a low murmur. I had always imagined the natives as fierce, spear-brandishing savages, but this man seemed reserved, self-contained, withdrawn, waiting quietly until he should be called upon to do his job.

Watching him, I wondered about his special powers. How was it possible that he could see what was invisible to the rest of us? Was it a kind of magic? Almost as if he knew what I was thinking, he glanced in my direction. I hid, in a panic. I did not want those eyes, which could see so much, looking into mine. I was afraid of what he might find there.

After a good deal of discussion and argument, the party finally moved off, with the black man, who they called Jacky, in the lead. They were to go to the place where the scrap of shirt had been found; then Jacky would work his magic.

As the morning of the fourth day wore on, I found myself wondering what I would say to Branwell when at last he returned. Should I scold him for going off like that? But he must by now have learnt his lesson. Should I fall on his neck, weeping in gladness that he had returned? There was no doubt I would be glad to see him, but I didn't want to give him a swelled head. Perhaps I should feign indifference: *Ah, so you're back.* But that was not quite right either. Eventually I decided that as soon as I saw his dear face again, I would know what to say.

It was almost lunchtime when we saw the distant shape of riders moving against the trees. The three of us stood on the verandah, quivering with impatience and excitement, straining our eyes to see if our brother was amongst them. The party grew closer and closer, but still I could not tell. Finally, the group parted, and I could see Father riding along with something in his arms.

I think I realised he was dead from that first moment, but I hoped somehow to shield my sisters from the blow. "I see them," I said, "I think he is alive!"

But as they drew nearer and nearer we could see from the bleak, sorrowful faces of the men that they had found my brother too late. We watched, wide-eyed and disbelieving, as the party came all the way up to the house. My father dismounted, and then, carrying my brother's body in his arms, walked slowly up the verandah steps, and went into the house. We followed on tiptoe, as my father walked down the hallway and laid my brother's body down on his little cot. I told myself he was sleeping, he would wake up tomorrow; but I knew it was not true. Then Father rose and went back out to the front door. Gravely, he shook the hand of each man who had helped search for my brother, and into the hand of the black tracker, Jacky, he placed a one-pound note. Then he turned and walked back into the house, to sit at Branwell's bedside, and weep.

It all would have been different if my brother had lived, for Branwell was the one on whom all our hopes and dreams depended. Branwell hoped for a career in the army, but Father dreamed he would become one of the great men of the land, running a great estate and growing rich. But it was not just wealth that Father dreamed of; it was the heady freedom of a clean start in a fresh, new, unspoilt country. He hoped that one day Branwell might play a part in the building of a glorious nation; that he might be the first of a new breed of men.

But when Branwell died of thirst in the dusty bush, two miles from our property, all Father's dreams died too. Father despaired. He talked of giving up, of going home to England. He cursed the land which had claimed his wife, and two baby daughters, and now his only son. He lost interest in the management of the property, and our lessons ceased entirely, as he spent his days riding around the perimeter, or sitting beside Branwell's grave. It broke my heart to see his suffering, and to know that I was the cause of it.

As the weeks went by, and our lives went on, and then the rains came, I realised what I must do.

Sneaking into Branwell's room, which was still just as he had left it, I took a book that Father had given my brother, thinking it too difficult for me or my sisters to understand, and I read it from cover to cover, looking up every word I didn't understand, and then I read it again, just to make sure. And then I went to see Father.

"I have been reading an interesting book, Father," I said.

"Have you, my dear?" he replied. He was always kind to me, even though he blamed me for what happened (or so I thought then).

I showed him the book. "I know you thought it would be too difficult for me, but it wasn't. I'm sure I understood it all."

Father took the book from me. He knew it at once, and he frowned. "Where did you get this?"

"I took it from his room," I said. "I hope that wasn't wrong."

Father seemed at a loss to know how to reply. Frowning deeply, he seemed almost on the verge of tears.

"I know it's not the same," I blurted, my own eyes starting to swim with tears, "but you still have us, Father."

I hoped, with those few words, to express all that I was feeling: my unspeakable regret at the loss of someone so dear, my own dreadful awareness that I could never live up to his wonderful promise, the blight that his death would always cast on my life, and the knowledge that whatever I did, it could not make up for the fact that my negligence had led to his death; my desire to do everything in my power to dry up the well of my father's grief, to mend the hole in the family, to make everything better; to prove to him that the loss of his son need not, after all, be the death of all his hopes. And when Father finally started to sob, and took me into his arms, and hugged all the breath out of me, I realised that something momentous had taken place. Branwell was gone, but I could take his place.

Everything changed after that. Father was still distant—he was a busy man, after all. But he gave us free rein of his library, and answered all of our questions, and, since we were girls with inquiring minds, we received an education such as most young women could scarcely dream of. (It was not until we went to school—briefly—that I discovered how unusual our education was. The other girls were imbeciles compared to us, and were jealous of our superior intellects. The teachers themselves didn't know as much as we did. Only our hazy grasp of such feminine pursuits as needlework and knitting let us down.) And as I grew up, basking in the sunshine of Father's praise, I knew I was fulfilling my promise to him: my promise to become someone extraordinary, someone who was capable of taking my extraordinary brother's place. I owed it to them both to succeed. I *would* succeed.

Six

Beginnings

Emily

I saw him again today—

I was bringing in the sheets—and the prop which holds up the washing line suddenly gave way so that the line fell down in the dirt and my washing dragged on the ground—He was, I think, chopping wood somewhere nearby, although it seemed he was there suddenly out of nowhere—and he helped fix up my line again before too much damage was done to the sheets—and he helped me to carry them inside—

And then the two of us faced each other in the kitchen and he helped me to fold every one of the sheets—

I could not look at him, and we did not speak one word to each other—but as we folded, our bodies seemed to find a simple Rhythm of their own accord, so that we worked in Harmony, stretching the sheets, straightening them, folding them, moving together, drawing apart, like the steps of some homely Quadrille, the dance of domesticity—I found myself wishing that we might do this forever—

But we swiftly ran out of sheets, and with a nod, unsmiling, he was gone—

And all the time we folded the sheets, it seemed to me that a Strange, Wordless Communication passed between us—I was seized by the Certainty that I had seen his face somewhere before, I had *known* him before—so Familiar, suddenly, was his face to me—Yet it is impossible that we could have known each other—except in a Dream—Yet his Visage is imprinted on my Soul—

And as soon as he was gone I wanted nothing more but to chase after him—to gaze into his eyes—to ask him a thousand questions in perfect silence, to know all there is to know about him and to spill out all my secrets so that he may know the darkest and ugliest parts of my soul—

Not a word has passed between us—and yet some part of me, some wiser part, breathes the knowledge that my Feelings are Reciprocated, that his Gaze is as full of longing as my own—but I cannot tell whether this is a Dream or a Fancy or a Nightmare—

Charlotte

"I'm going for my walk," Anne announced, and pushed back her stool. We were all seated round the kitchen table, where we now seemed to spend every spare hour of the day. Emily glanced up and gave her a warm smile of farewell.

"Don't forget your bonnet," I reminded her, as Anne skipped out the door. She heaved a sigh, grabbed her bonnet with a sidelong glance at Emily, and slipped out the door.

For the hundredth time I felt the pang of exclusion. It wasn't fair that I should be the one cast in the role of nagging sister, but Emily didn't seem to care if Anne ruined her complexion, and someone had to take an interest. I knew they rolled their eyes at me, and I knew there was a secret dialogue that went on behind my back. I knew, too, that there was no point trying to become involved in it, for much of its piquancy was derived, I am sure, from the fact that it excluded me. And besides, I was too proud to let them know that I wanted to be part of their tiny circle of two.

Yet I still thought often, and fondly, of our childhood days, when we were still close, before Anne replaced me in Emily's affections. I did not resent it—how could I?—but I did sometimes wonder what Anne brought to their play other than an audience (something Emily had always craved). After Branwell, Emily and I had been collaborators for a time; I missed the sense of partnership, the absorbing pleasure of a shared project that we had once enjoyed together. It was true that we were back around the table, writing together as we used to; but the work proceeded in absolute silence, and I had no notion of what either of them were up to. Anne worked diligently in her neat and perfect hand; Emily sat in brooding silence, reading or mending. She had not, so far as I could see, taken up the challenge and begun to write anything new since we had decided to try and become published authors. And yet at night, in their room, after they had gone to bed, I could hear the whisper of their voices through the wall as they talked, and I felt sure they were talking about their work. How I yearned to be part of that conversation! But I was standing in front of a locked gate, and could not get into the garden, no matter how I tried. I longed to ask my sisters' opinions, to share my ideas and feel that I was not so entirely alone in my endeavours, but they had not asked to see what I was writing, and I was too proud to ask.

As I chewed my pen and brooded, Emily rose abruptly to her feet and left the room without a word. *Where is she off to?* I wondered. After a moment I heard the sound of a door opening, and then closing, and then, as I held my breath to listen, I heard a key turn in a lock. Emily had shut herself into Father's study, and experience had shown that she tended to remain there for some time (and who knew what it was she did in there?).

I was all alone with Emily's writing case. It was my chance to find out what she was up to.

I knew I should not give in to temptation. But my curiosity was too great.

I reached across the table and drew Emily's papers across the table, turned to the first page, and began to read.

I gazed across the water at the black isle rising from the deep. A thin plume of smoke drifting up into the sky was the only hint that the place was inhabited. From the shore, no dwellings could be seen, and no distant figure toiled upon those harsh cliffs.

"Come, sir," came a hearty voice, "let's be 'avin' 'ee."

The moment of my departure had come—a crew of brawny sailors were waiting to take me across the water.

How peaceful it looks, I reflected as we bounced across the choppy bay. The casual visitor would never guess at its foul and terrible reputation. Once more I began to wonder about the man I was to meet: Captain Thorn, the prison governor. He had ruled the island for ten years; a reign, I had heard, which was unsurpassed in its effectiveness—and its cruelty. And here was I, newly an officer and newly arrived in this strange and perplexing colony, come to write a report on him. Who was I, a stranger to these shores, to pass judgement on so formidable a man? Yet that was what I was here to do.

"I beg you, sirs," I said to the men as they rowed, "tell me what you know of Captain Thorn. What manner of man is he?"

The men looked at each other uneasily. "I don't rightly know how to answer you, sir," one of them said at last, "for we have little enough to do with him."

"Does he never come over to the mainland?" I asked.

"Not that I can recall, sir," said one.

"No, sir," said another. "He works very 'ard, Cap'n Thorn does. Keeps 'imself to 'imself the rest of the time."

"Is there," I hesitated to ask it, "any gossip about him? I am curious to find out anything I can about him."

"His men don't talk about him," said one of the sailors, "they wouldn't dare. They reckon he's got eyes in the back of his head—and maybe he does, 'cos not much gets past him. You know there's never been an escape while he's been in command?"

I murmured that I was aware of this.

My interlocutor glanced uneasily at his fellows, and then confided. "But I have heard it rumoured, sir, that he's gone mad."

"Mad? In what way?"

"I don't rightly know, sir. It's only a rumour."

At this the sailors lapsed into silence, and I was left alone with my uneasy reflections.

This was no Gondal tale. With a shock I realised that Emily was writing about Coldwater. But I could not recognise Father in her description at all. Cruel? Mad? This was not the man I knew. And what about us? Would we appear in this novel? And if Father had been so unkindly caricatured in this manner, what would she have to say about me?

I began to read again, and the tale gripped me immediately. It was the story of a young officer who is sent out to investigate the master of a prison who, it seems, is running wild in his isolated fiefdom. I had only just begun to get into the real meat of the tale—a tragic love triangle between a convict, a gentleman, and a woman—when suddenly Emily was there. She looked flustered as she came into the kitchen, but when she saw what I was doing, her look turned to fury.

"What are you doing?" she said.

I knew there was nothing I could really say in my own defence, but I had to say something. "I'm sorry. I was curious."

"You had no right to go reading my work."

"It's very good. If I hadn't been so absorbed I would have heard you coming, and you never would have caught me."

Emily was not amused. "If I wanted you to read it I would have shown it to you," she snapped, and whipped her manuscript off the table. She started to sweep out of the room, then thought again, grabbed up Anne's letter case, and made a dramatic exit in a swirl of skirts and slamming of doors.

"Why did you do it, Charlotte?" demanded Anne, in a low voice, as we did the washing-up. Father had vanished to read in his study, and Emily was off sulking in her room. "You know how fussy she is about privacy."

"Oh, for goodness' sake," I said, exasperated, "she left it out on the table in plain view. What was I supposed to do, pretend I couldn't see it?"

"She assumed you'd have the good manners not to read it," Anne said. She paused. "Did you read mine too?"

"No."

"Why not?"

I suspected she already knew the answer to that question. Her eyes dared me to say it out loud. I was not going to oblige her.

"I didn't have time. Why? Did you want me to?"

Anne spent a moment polishing a plate that was already dry, then looked up. "Yes."

I was a little taken aback by this. "You want me to read your novel?"

"Emily and I know each other's work too well. I think she's too kind to me. I need someone who will point out my flaws—something I'm sure you'll have no trouble doing, Charlotte."

She darted a look at me, daring me to take offence. But I took it in the spirit in which it was intended. "Alright then," I said lightly, "I shall be as rigorous as I can. When shall we start?"

"How about now?" she said.

So I read over Anne's work, and then found myself lying awake half the night worrying about it as I tried to work out what to tell her. The next morning, once breakfast had been dealt with, Anne and I sat down at the table together. Anne was nervous; Emily hovered in the background, disapproving, trying not to look like she was interested in what I had to say.

"I think your novel is very promising," I began.

"Only promising?"

I gave her a warning look to indicate *no interruptions please.* "Very promising indeed, but obviously it's hard to make pronouncements on a work that's at such an early stage. Your central character is interesting—a headstrong young lady will always drive a story forward. But I would be wary of making her *too* headstrong—it is potentially alienating for the reader."

"Only if the reader's a fool," interrupted Emily.

"Did you want to say something, Emily?" I asked coolly.

"No."

"Then can I go on please?"

She shrugged.

I turned back to Anne. "The sense of place is not particularly strong. I'd throw in some descriptions of the landscape, and make it clear where the novel is set. At the moment I don't know if it's England or Gondal or somewhere entirely different."

Anne turned to Emily and said, "I thought it needed more of that kind of thing."

Emily just shrugged diffidently.

Anne turned back to me. "I knew it was lacking, but I haven't quite made up my mind where to set it yet. Here, or at home."

"You'd better make up your mind then, for you won't get any further until you do."

"I didn't think setting was particularly important in this story, since the action all takes place indoors," Emily said, still trying to sound as if she wasn't particularly interested in the conversation. "The story is all about the characters and how they think and feel and how they behave when they're together. You don't really need long descriptions of the decor and the countryside, do you?"

"No," I said, "but you need to know where it's taking place, and where these people live, and why they live there. It's all a part of who they are."

"Very well," said Anne, "more landscape. What else?"

And for the next half an hour we talked, the three of us, about landscape and character and narrative devices, about Anne's manuscript, and about fiction writing in general, until we were all quite flushed with the excitement of it. And then, when I sensed that the moment was right, I turned the discussion round to Emily's manuscript.

"And you've decided to set your book here on Coldwater," I said, innocently enough.

Emily flushed, and Anne's face grew wary as she looked to see how Emily would respond.

"Not really," Emily said defensively. "It's similar, but it's not Coldwater."

"It sounds an awful lot like it. And the people in it are somewhat familiar too."

"Do you think so?"

"Captain Thorn for instance. Cruel, mad Captain Thorn who runs a prison and has a wilful daughter?"

"What about him?" The colour was rising in her cheeks.

"He's not based on Father?"

"No."

"Why did you decide to set the book here?" I asked curiously. "Or rather, somewhere very like here. It seems rather an odd choice."

"Why? I happen to think it's a very dramatic location. And besides, I don't really know anywhere else. How could I describe a life and landscape I don't know?"

I said nothing to this, for the novel I was writing was set in England, a country I had never seen.

"How far did you get into it?" she asked.

"I've only read the first chapter."

"You liked it then?"

"Oh yes. I particularly liked the bit with the ghost. I can't wait to see what happens."

"You won't like it."

"Why not?"

But Emily just shrugged at this and wouldn't answer.

"Would you mind if I read some more?" I asked. My casual tone sounded forced to me, but Emily seemed not to notice that I was hanging on her answer.

"You can read the first volume when it's finished," Emily said carelessly. I was thrilled, but one thing still remained, and this I could not ask. She eyed my papers. "Perhaps we could swap."

A warm flush of pleasure swept through me, and I think there was even a prickle of tears in my eyes.

"I'd like that," I said.

Over the next few weeks we established a new way of working. We sat together as before at the kitchen table and, as soon as the day's household tasks were done, we would write. We gave our evenings over to readings and discussion of one another's work. Emily was a spirited performer, doing voices and producing effects which made her prose sound even more ringing than it actually was. And quite unexpectedly, little Anne turned out to have a wry, almost acidic sense of humour which her customary reserve had quite hidden from me. The sardonic delights of her prose were a revelation to me. I cannot say what they truly thought of my work, although they were generous enough in their praise. Together we made up a little salon of three, and I thrilled to the feeling that we were kindred spirits working in unison to produce fiction the likes of which the world had not seen before. We were in accord once again, as we had been before, when we were all girls together. I had been readmitted to the charmed circle.

Seven

An unexpected proposal

Charlotte

"Lieutenant Bates—you wished to see me?"

He was standing in front of a fitful drawing-room fire with his back to me, displaying a fine wide pair of shoulders and a somewhat wider waist. His plump hands twisted together nervously. *This is a man with something on his mind,* I thought. He turned towards me with an amiable smile. "Yes, Miss Wolf."

He paused, seeking for words, and I reflected that everything about him, with the exception of his uniform and his boots, looked soft. He had soft, round features, a soft, spongy figure, and soft, sparse hair of a nondescript light brown. Although he was probably only two or three and thirty he looked like a great middle-aged baby. "How is your health?" he asked, finally.

"Excellent, thank you," I replied. "And yours?"

"Also excellent, I'm glad to say."

"I am glad to hear it. Do sit down."

He lowered himself onto the very edge of the horsehair sofa, almost missing it entirely. He clenched his buttocks and hung on grimly. I pretended not to notice.

"You look very well today, Miss Wolf. That gown becomes you."

It was a serviceable gown, rather plain, in a military shade of dark blue. "It is the gown I wear every day, Lieutenant," I observed.

I saw a brief look of panic cross his face. "Just as well it's so becoming then."

I smiled in assent and waited to see what would come next.

Lieutenant Bates took a deep breath and planted his hands on his knees. I sensed that we'd had sufficient pleasantries and it was time to get on to the business at hand.

"As you know, I have been a guest at your table many times, and I always look forward to the Captain's invitations with great delight. You and your sisters make delightful company and—stationed here—well—it's always a welcome diversion to spend time with ladies."

"Thank you," I said, though I wasn't quite sure this was a compliment.

"I believe that a man should marry," he continued. "It is by far the best thing."

"Society would concur, Lieutenant."

"For myself, I need a wife who's accustomed to the military life—a woman who knows how to make the best of things in adverse circumstances—a woman who's always amiable and easy to talk to, even in assorted company."

I was giving him my most interested expression but I didn't like where this was heading.

"You should know," he continued, "that your father holds me in the highest esteem and I come from a very respectable family. I haven't much money but I've been told by my senior officers that my prospects for advancement are excellent." He looked at me earnestly. "Miss Wolf, would you do me the very great honour of consenting to be my wife?"

I was astonished.

"Sir," I said, "I am amazed."

The awkwardness of proposing over with, Bates started to relax a little. "I realise that this may come as something of a surprise to you, since there hasn't been any particular sympathy between us before now."

No particular sympathy? When I was told Lieutenant Bates wanted to speak to me, I had a hard time remembering who he was. As far as I could recall, we had barely exchanged more than two words (greetings and requests to pass the plum duff aside) in all the time he had been with us.

"But I felt that, having decided on a course of action, namely to make you my wife, I should come and inform you of my intentions. If you aren't ready to make a decision straightaway—"

It was time to nip this fantasy in the bud. "Lieutenant," I interrupted, "this is most precipitous. Marriage is a serious business and should not be entered into lightly."

He hastened to reassure me on that point, as his colour rose. "I know that, Miss Wolf. Let me assure you, I've given it very serious thought, and I'm sure you're the most suitable candidate."

"Who made up the field?"

"Why, you and your two sisters, of course."

"Indeed? And what swayed you in my favour?"

"You are by far the most solid, capable, and pleasant lady of the family, Miss Wolf," he said warmly, "and already very experienced at running a military household, a task you undertake wonderfully well, if I may say so."

I looked at him indignantly. "Lieutenant Bates. If you had come and thrown yourself at my feet and professed your undying love for me, I might have been prepared to give the matter some thought. Unbridled passion can be very persuasive. But this earnest and businesslike proposal—Sir, it would be far more honest to advertise for a housekeeper."

He realised he had blundered, but he was not a man easily turned from his path, once he was set upon a particular course. He looked at me severely. "Marrying for love seems a foolish practice to me, and one that is doomed to failure. You need some time to think about the idea. I'm sure you will come around to it in time."

I regarded him with composure. "I'm sure I shall not. Please, Lieutenant. Let us not speak of this again."

This was clearly not the answer he had expected. He gave me a look of mild displeasure, mingled with perplexity, then rose to his feet.

"Thank you for your time, Miss Wolf. I can see myself out." And with that he walked stiffly to the door and departed.

I flopped down into Father's armchair, awash with contradictory feelings, as the door closed behind him. A girl does not get proposed to every day, and even when you have no interest in the proposer it is a disturbing event nonetheless.

It was true that, at the ripe age of thirty-one, I was no longer in the first flush of youth, and therefore could not afford to be choosy. I liked to think I was something of a realist, and I knew that my expectations were perhaps a little high. But while I was a realist, I was not a fatalist, and I was sure that I deserved better than this. "Solid and capable," was I? What about all my other qualities: my passionate and affectionate nature, my shrewdness, my intelligence, my abundant hair, and my rather fine eyes? (I knew I was not a beauty, but I thought I could be called handsome in the right light.) I was a gentlewoman in a country where gentlewomen are exceedingly thin on the ground, and I knew I could do better than Lieutenant Bates, but I was thirty-one and I had never actually been asked before. Doubt gnawed at me. *Perhaps he has his own hidden qualities, as I do? Perhaps I've just made a diabolical blunder? What if no one else asks me?*

But the fact remained that he did not love me, and I certainly did not love him, and the idea of marrying him seemed like a ghastly travesty. I tried to be pragmatic, to tell myself that there was more to a marriage than passion, and that I must think of my future. But the truth was, I was in love once, and I could not forget it. If I could not have the man I loved, I would have no one.

He was a lieutenant, and his name was Glade, Thomas Glade. He was Father's second-in-command, back in the early days, when Father was new to Coldwater and still finding his feet. He was about ten years older than myself; tall, like Father, craggy and dark, with a high brow and deep, piercing dark eyes, an aquiline profile, a sensuous mouth. He did not delight my sisters, for he had the kind of looks that lay somewhere between ruggedly handsome and ugly. That is to say, I thought him handsome, but Emily always thought he was ugly. Anne did not venture an opinion.

We met in the usual manner, at a dinner for the newly arrived officers. Over the years I have learnt to dread these events, but then I looked forward to them with great excitement. Lieutenant Glade was everything I had imagined an officer to be: cultivated, polite, well groomed. He did not explain at length about how he wished to make his fortune via this or that surefire scheme, or rail about the intransigence of convict labour. Instead, he remarked that he had recently been rereading Milton and had found it endlessly stimulating. This piqued my curiosity at once, for I had not yet encountered an officer who would confess to having read anything at all.

"His language is magisterial," Glade said, "the wonderful stately rhythm of it."

"He is the greatest English poet since Shakespeare," Father said.

"Now, Father," I chided, "what about Byron? What about Wordsworth and Shelley?"

"They are diverting enough but I do not think any of them has the lasting greatness of Milton," Father said, giving me a slight smile, for it was not the first time we had had this conversation.

"I cannot agree with you about Wordsworth," Glade said. "His profound spiritual awareness of landscape is very moving. But *Paradise Lost*, in its formal perfection, its conceptual greatness, belongs to a higher order entirely."

"My point exactly," said Father.

"But don't you think it's a pity that Satan is the most interesting character in it?" I asked, mischievously.

Glade shot me a rather startled look.

"Most of the characters are so grand and lofty and indifferent," I continued. "They're not like people, they're like mountain ranges, or galaxies. Satan is the only character who behaves like a real human being."

"Except that he's the embodiment of all evil," said Glade.

"Well, yes, but at least evil has energy, don't you think? Satan is full to overflowing with life and exuberance. I shouldn't like to meet Milton's God, or his Jesus, and I certainly wouldn't want a bar of his Adam. But I would very much like to meet Satan. I think he'd probably be very entertaining."

Glade could not think of a reply. I caught Father smiling at me approvingly.

"Who'd like some more claret?" I asked brightly.

The next day, to my great surprise, Glade came to call on me. Emily and Anne were agog, and came to sit with me in the drawing room as I entertained him. He had brought with him a copy of *Othello* to give me. I was doubly surprised—first, that of all the things he could have brought with him to Coldwater, he had seen fit to bring a copy of *Othello*, and second, that he would then give it to me.

"I thought you might like it, since you're so fond of evil," he said with a wicked smile, and I saw that he had a sense of humour after all. So we spent a delightful afternoon discussing wickedness—the wickedness of Richard the Third, of Lady Macbeth, of the more extravagant Greeks (Medea and so forth). I cannot tell you how delightful it was after so many years of familiar company to finally have someone new to talk to, someone who shared my passion for literature and who had read as much as we had. I had not quite realised until then how starved I was for company.

Emily teased me mercilessly afterwards. "Lord, Charlotte, you should be ashamed!" she said, as she poured cup after cup of sugar into the rhubarb she was stewing. "You were making eyes at that poor man in the most shocking manner."

"I was not," I said.

"*You* don't know, *you* couldn't see yourself. I was sitting opposite, I had an excellent view, and I promise you, you were making sheep's eyes at that officer."

"I thought he was engaging company, that's all."

Emily nodded, as if she knew better.

"The question is, does he feel the same way about you?" she mused.

"I think there was a certain admiration in his eye," Anne piped up.

"You thought so? I thought so too," said Emily.

"This is all utter nonsense."

"What did he write in the book?" asked Emily. "Is there a dedication?"

"I didn't look."

Anne seized the book and opened it to the flyleaf. "There is!" she crowed. Emily leaned her head in to read it.

"What does it say?" I asked.

"To my darling Charlotte—" Emily began. I grabbed the book from her and read:

> *To Miss Charlotte Wolf,*
> *Another evil gentleman for you to meet.*
> *Lieutenant Thomas Glade, April 1840.*

"You've made quite an impression there," said Emily.

Autumn turned to winter; the nights grew longer. Lieutenant Glade and I exchanged books and talked about literature. Our tastes did not quite coincide—I loved thrilling tales of passion, he had a taste for classicism, order, and structure—but we shared a love of reading, and that was enough. Father had taught us to appreciate literature through a process of questioning and argument; Glade found my combative approach a little confronting at first, but eventually he came to enjoy our engagements with the novels we had read. Our arguments over books felt, to me, like the battle of wits you found in the more mature of Shakespeare's comedies—*Much Ado, As You Like It*. I fancied myself as one of Shakespeare's boyish heroines, a woman in disguise, riddling with the man she secretly loved.

And perhaps he wasn't the most handsome man in the world, and perhaps he was the first man apart from Father who'd ever paid attention to me, but I thought he was magnificent. I woke up every day with my head buzzing, hoping to manufacture an excuse to see him. I felt more fully alive than I ever had before, incandescent with the light of my love. Emily stopped laughing at me and began to regard me with a kind of fascinated awe, for I think it was clear to her that I had fallen in very deep, and would not willingly swim out again.

Father knew nothing of our attachment. I believe we all shared the feeling that such matters had nothing to do with him, and were best not discussed; in fact, as far as possible, they were best conducted entirely without his knowledge or consent. If we reached the point of an engagement, then, and only then, would Father be consulted.

And in the meantime I dreamed of Glade every night with a fervour and intensity that shamed and thrilled me, for I had never felt like this before, awake or asleep. My whole body felt like it was conducting electricity, giving off sparks at a touch. They say that love is an emotion of the heart, but to me it was a whole-body experience, radiating through my skin, fizzing through my viscera, throwing my very being into a state of extraordinary disarray, chaotic, but delightful. The sight of him made my heart beat faster, and when I parted from him I felt as if my weight had doubled and I dragged my feet as I walked away from him. My body was flaming, but our relationship was truly a creature of the mind, for whenever we met the talk was of books, books, and more books. This was all I had ever hoped for; this was how I imagined true adult life would be. The prospect of physical love remained utterly remote, for he was a perfect gentleman and however many words and thoughts and glances we might have exchanged—and oh, those looks, those sighs!—I had not so much as brushed his fingertips since the moment we were first introduced—how long ago it seemed—and we shook hands. Every morsel of flesh quivered and shouted and sang for his touch, but in vain. There was not so much as a fervent press of the hand.

My moment came at last when Emily discovered, in the middle of cooking supper, that she was out of milk. I was sent off to fetch some from the quartermaster, and on my way I happened to spy Glade, standing alone amidst the wind-sculpted scrub, gazing out to sea. Forgetting the milk, I wandered over to join him.

"Good evening, Mr. Glade," I said.

"Good evening, Miss Wolf," he replied.

"What are you doing here?"

"Admiring the view."

I looked out at it critically. The ocean stretched, vast and empty, before us. No boat relieved the huge expanse with some human detail. But the sky was quite fine, dusky and ribbed with bands of golden cloud as the sun slipped behind the mountains to the west.

"I fear we are quite alone together," I said hopefully.

"Indeed. And what errand brings you out here at this time of the evening, Miss Wolf?"

"I had to get some milk."

"Allow me to escort you to the store then."

This was frustrating. At last we were alone together and he seemed annoyingly eager to deliver me back to my family.

"I'm in no hurry," I said.

I saw his eyebrows lift slightly, and a faint shiver of something seemed to go down his spine, for the atmosphere between us changed suddenly, and he was looking at me through quite new eyes.

"If you're in no hurry, then perhaps we may both linger a little longer," he said.

"The twilight is held to be the most romantic time of the day," I remarked, aware that I sounded a little shriller than usual. "Do you find it so?"

"Yes," said Glade. "But I think my favourite time of all is the first night of a full moon, when the moon is just beginning to rise like a great orange lantern in the sky. The harvest moon is so evocative."

"Will there be a full moon tonight?" I asked.

"I believe so," he replied.

And then words melted into nothing as our eyes met and then our lips met and he kissed me. Oh, the unspeakable bliss of that moment! How long I had waited for it, and how unutterably sweet it was when it came!

And oh, how brief, for as soon as the kiss was over he drew away, with a rather shocked look on his face, as if some uncontrollable part of him had suddenly taken over and done something he knew he should not have done. I did not mind—I was impatient for more and would quite happily have stood in that forest nook kissing him until the sun burnt away to a cinder—but I could see that he had frightened himself.

"Forgive me, Miss Wolf," he stammered, the picture of the proper officer covered in confusion, "I don't know what came over me. I hope you can forgive me for my shocking impertinence."

"Of course I forgive you—" I began, but he was still apologising.

"I should not have taken the liberty—I would not offend you for the world—"

"I am not offended, sir—"

"Please, let me take you home."

I had embarrassed him. Suddenly embarrassed myself, I allowed him to hustle me home, and could not quite bring myself to mention that I had not yet got the milk.

Emily was not pleased about the milk, but when I told her what had happened she was thrilled.

"He will propose to you shortly, I'm sure of it!"

She swept away all my misgivings with her certainty, and indeed, I

could not imagine any other way this story might end. So I held my
breath and waited for his proposal.

But it did not come.

Glade did not drop in on Father that evening, or on any subsequent
evening. He made himself all but invisible to me, and if he should
chance to see me at a distance he made himself scarce. I was in a frenzy
of terror. Had I been too forward that night? Had I frightened him
away somehow? I was convinced I had made some dreadful error of
judgement, but try as I might, I could not determine what it could have
been. But there could be no doubt—Emily agreed with me—Glade was
avoiding me. I made myself so sick with worry that I could no longer
eat. Father asked me if I was sickening for something. I told him I was
not.

This went on for a week. Then one night at supper, Father looked
up and said, "By the way, Glade is going back to Sydney tomorrow."

I dropped my teacup in shock, splashing tea all over my skirt and
smashing the teacup on the floor. Emily gazed at me, stricken.

"Are you alright, Charlotte?" asked Father curiously.

I attempted to cover my confusion. "Yes, of course. I don't know
what came over me."

"Why are you sending him back?" asked Emily, so that I should not
seem too interested.

"He asked to be transferred," Father said. "He wishes to return to
the mainland, I didn't inquire into the reason. I will be sorry to lose him.
He's a good officer."

"I think I need to change my dress," I said, for it was spattered with
tea. Glad of an excuse, I hurried to my room. Once alone, I flung myself
on the bed and succumbed to desperate sobs, my face pressed deep into
the pillow.

What could be the meaning of this? It was obvious he was leaving
to get away from me. Was I so hideous? What had I done wrong? And if
this was how he truly felt about me, why had he kissed me? Disappointment, fear, love, rage, swirled intolerably inside me. I would not bear this

disappointment without knowing the reason for it, I decided. I would confront him and make him explain himself to me.

It took me some time to stop the tears and get the hiccups under control, but as soon as I had, I changed my dress, washed my face, and put on my bonnet.

"I'm going for a walk," I said to the assembled family, although the night was closing in outside. I could not bear the look of pity on Emily's face, and I did not want to give Father a chance to stop me, so I marched as quickly as I could out the back door.

A late autumn storm was building up off the coast, and the sun was setting through livid clouds that boiled and threatened. The weather suited my mood perfectly, and I stamped through gusts of wind, my skirts flapping and billowing about me, heading for the officers' barracks.

When I reached it I rapped smartly on the door before I could think about the propriety of what I was doing. Eventually, an officer opened the door.

"Is Mr. Glade in?" I demanded, as if this was a perfectly ordinary thing for me to be asking at this time of the evening.

He raised his eyebrows at me, then turned his head and called, "Glade! Miss Wolf's here to see you." Then he turned back to me. "Would you like to come in, Miss Wolf?"

"No thank you," I said. "I'll wait here."

So I stood on the doorstep and waited. Inside, I could see officers milling about, looking out at me curiously, and whispering. I held on to my dignity and ignored them. Finally Glade appeared.

"Miss Wolf," he said awkwardly, "what are you doing here?"

"I think you know," I said tartly.

He looked pained. "Not here," he said.

I heard ribald laughter as he stepped outside and pulled the door shut. He drew me some distance away from the barracks, where there could be no chance of our being overheard.

"I've just been informed you're leaving tomorrow," I said, trying to sound commanding, although my voice quavered.

"That's right."

"Did you intend to leave without saying good-bye?"

"I had thought to say good-bye to you when I said good-bye to the rest of your family tomorrow."

"Don't I deserve more than that?" I asked. "Do I mean so little to you?"

"Miss Wolf—Charlotte—there is something I must tell you."

I waited, feeling my chin quivering.

"I'm married."

If he'd kicked me the shock would have been less. I looked wildly at his hands. He didn't wear a ring.

"I don't believe you!" I cried. "Where's your wedding ring?"

He scrabbled about inside his collar and drew out a ring on a chain. "I keep it here for safekeeping."

I felt as if the ground had suddenly collapsed beneath my feet and I was plummeting into an abyss.

"I should have told you the truth—I was a fool—I'm sorry."

"You kissed me!"

"It was a moment of weakness—"

"I thought you loved me!"

He looked at me helplessly. "I have no right to love you. I already have a wife."

Suddenly I saw a tiny flare of hope in the tunnel of despair that was rapidly closing around me. "You do care for me! It is only duty that holds you back."

"Without duty, I am nothing."

"But if you love me, surely that's the most important thing?"

"I have a wife already. I can never marry you."

"I don't care about that, as long as we can be together. We'll go away somewhere, where no one knows us. If we tell them we're man and wife, who will know any different?"

"We will know. God will know. And besides, I have a duty to my wife and child," he said.

"You have a child too?"

The first drops of rain were falling around us with fat, audible plops on the ground.

"You deserve a husband who will marry you and give you the decent life you deserve."

"I don't want a husband!" I wailed. "I want you! I don't care where we go, or what happens to us, I just want to be with you. We'll have our love. Love is enough."

"No it isn't," he said gently. "You should go back to the house. It's about to pour."

"What do I care? I can't live without you!"

"Don't say that."

"Why not? It's true. Let me come with you, or I'll try to swim after you."

He was doing his best to be kind, but I could see he was eager to get back inside. "Stop it, Charlotte. This is madness. It cannot be. I am sorry for it. But there is an end to it."

And he turned away from me then, abruptly, and walked away, leaving me with a thousand things unsaid.

"But I love you!" I howled, as the sky erupted around me.

I stood there for a long time, thinking, as the rain beat down on me. One part of me was all for running straight for the cliff and throwing myself off. At least it would prove to him that I was serious, for I felt that, at some level, he did not take me entirely seriously. And it would put an end to all my troubles, my misery smashed to smithereens on the rocks. But I could not quite bring myself to take that first step, to go to the edge of the cliff, to look over, to launch myself out beyond any hope of recovery, to take that leap into oblivion. Perhaps I still hoped that he might change his mind. Perhaps I lacked the courage of my convictions. Whichever it was, I did not kill myself that night, but instead, turned and walked slowly back to the house.

My soaking left me laid up with a heavy cold, and so I retreated to my bed and let Emily treat me like an invalid. I was not really that ill, but I felt that I had been savagely wounded, for the more I thought about what had happened, the more I was forced to see that Glade had been offered a choice, and he had not chosen me. Emily tried to reassure me that when a man has a wife and a child, he would be a bounder and a cad if he ran off with another woman. But I knew she did not really believe it and was only saying it to comfort me, for deep down she believed, as I did, that the only real law was the law of the heart, and that that law must take precedence over all others. If he really loved me—and I clung onto the belief that he did—he should have been willing to throw it all away and give himself up to love completely. I was ready to do that. Why wasn't he?

Either he did not love me enough, or he was not the man I thought he was. Both possibilities made me cry, for I did not want to believe that I had been deceived, or that he was a lesser man than I thought, or that he had found me wanting. Could it be I was not worth throwing everything away for?

Or had I never been any more than a passing fancy for him? Had he just been dallying with me while he waited out his time on Coldwater? But if I meant nothing to him, why had he been in such a hurry to get away from me? To escape the wrath of Father perhaps? But he had not even seduced me. Was I not even worth attempting?

I wrote him long, excruciatingly long letters, full of self-abasement and threats and promises—it embarrasses me to think of them now. But I don't know if he ever read them or even received them, for I never had a reply.

The day that Bates proposed, we all tried to return to work as usual, but the conversation kept lurching towards the subject of marriage. It seemed to exert an irresistible force upon us; however much we tried, we couldn't keep away from it.

"Let me guess," Emily said. "It'll be wedded bliss all round and the villains seen to in a suitably unpleasant way."

We were talking about happy endings.

"Of course," I said indifferently. "Why not?"

"I'm not sure that I find that sort of ending terribly satisfying," Emily mused. "Wedded bliss, I mean."

"Why ever not? How else should a story about a man and a woman end?"

"Sometimes obstacles can't be overcome," Emily said. "And it's dishonest to pretend that they can. In that case, the only way to end it is with a death."

"It's a bit grim though, isn't it?" Anne said.

"It's kept the Gondals going for the last decade," I observed tartly. Emily looked mildly offended, but Anne was amused.

"It's called tragedy," Emily said haughtily. "Life is tragic. In a way I think tragedy is less dishonest, as a form."

"You're such a pessimist!" I retorted. "And what you're describing sounds just as dishonest to me. You can't have the person you want, so you die? If you really wanted to create something honest, you'd have all your characters surviving their misfortunes and learning to live with disappointment, as generally one must."

Emily just cocked an eyebrow at me, smiling slightly. "So this ending of yours," she said, changing the subject, "where they all live happily ever after. Does it truly represent what you want out of life?"

"Isn't it what everyone wants?" I hedged.

"I don't care about what everyone wants, I want to know what you want," Emily said. "If you were given a choice tomorrow between marrying the man of your dreams or being a successful novelist, which would you choose?"

I hesitated just long enough for her to know what my choice would be.

"I knew it!" Emily crowed. "So why don't you write about that? Why not tell people the truth?"

"People don't want to hear the truth," I said stoutly. "They want love. They want undying passion. They want obstacles and then a wedding."

"Why should a reader be satisfied with a wedding if it wouldn't satisfy you?"

"Most readers aren't like me," I said. "If you want to succeed as a novelist you have to think about the reading public, you have to show a proper adherence to literary tradition. They want to believe in true love and happy marriages, and if you toss that out the window and tell them it's not possible they're hardly going to come back and read your next book, are they?"

"That's not the point."

"Of course it's the point! I intend to make books my bread and butter. You've got to know what people want or you'll never get anywhere."

"How can you write that sort of ending if you don't believe in it?" Emily asked.

"I do believe in it," I explained. "I mean, I'd *like* to believe in it. And I think some people really do manage it. I'm just not sure that I'd be one of them. But that doesn't mean it's not true—happily ever after, that is. So I think I'm quite justified in writing novels in which love eventually triumphs, for it is, after all, the most desirable outcome. Even if it's desperately unlikely."

That evening, Father called me into his study. It was a cold night, and outside the wind was shrieking, but Father's study was cosy and warm.

"I'm surprised that you rejected Bates out of hand." Father made a steeple of his fingers and levelled a quizzical gaze at me from beneath his heavy brows. "Surprised, and not entirely pleased. You could at least have agreed to think about it."

"You can't be serious," I said. "Me? Marry him?"

We were sitting in our customary positions in Father's study—he was sprawled at his ease in his chair, turned away from the desk to face me; I was curled on the little settle next to the fire. The desk was the best piece of furniture we owned, old and massive, made of good plain oak, unadorned and polished to a soft satin sheen, and the light from the fire made the wood seem to glow, as points of light danced on the polished brass of the handles.

"His prospects are good," Father observed neutrally.

I began to wonder if this was some kind of test. "I know that," I replied, "he told me so himself."

"You are very saucy, miss," Father said. "You haven't been besieged with offers."

"It's very kind of you to point that out, Father."

"I'm sorry, Charlotte, but it's preying on my mind. I have three fine daughters and they're all unmarried. I don't know what's to be done about you. I would like to see you settled and secure."

"I am settled and secure where I am."

"But you don't want to end up a spinster, keeping house for your poor old father, do you?" There was a glint in his eye.

"Would that be such a terrible thing?"

"You know I would like nothing better than to have you to myself for always. But what about you, Charlotte? Shouldn't you like a husband of your own? A house of your own?"

"Of course," I said offhand, "but my standards are so terribly high I may never find anyone who will do." Father smiled, taking this as a loving daughter's pretty compliment, but I wasn't quite finished. "So I suppose I'll have to make do with you."

I love him, but I am not above teasing him for his vanity.

But Father was not in a lighthearted mood. "You should not be so quick to judge, Charlotte," he said soberly.

I frowned. "What do you mean?"

"As you said, you have set your sights very high. Perhaps Bates is not exactly what you had in mind. But you must be realistic, my dear. We cannot always have what we want. Sometimes we must make do with what we can get. It is better to have a husband, any husband, than to have none at all."

My heart skipped a beat, and I looked at him with horror. "What do you mean, Father?" I asked. "Should I marry the first man who asks me, and be grateful for the offer? Am I so ugly and unappealing?"

"Of course not," he soothed. "Any man would be lucky to have you. All I'm saying is, the next time someone asks you to marry him, perhaps you should take a little more time to think it through. Get to know the gentleman better; talk things over with me. There is no greater happiness than marriage, Charlotte," he continued gravely. "I would be very sorry to see you lose the opportunity to know that happiness for yourself."

"Of course I'd like to be happily married," I said. "A *happy* marriage is the most wonderful thing in the world. But there are many *un*happy marriages, and I would hate to rush into anything out of desperation or necessity. To be stuck in an unhappy marriage seems to me to be the most wretched of circumstances. I would rather be dead."

Father sighed at my dramatic tone. "There is no need for that," he said. "You will never be forced to marry, Charlotte. You need not worry about that."

When Glade swept into my life, all my great ambitions melted away. I no longer had any desire to become a brilliant woman, to shatter the mould, to redefine forever what a woman was capable of. All I wanted was *him*, nothing else would do, nothing else was necessary. I wanted to live on love, to surrender the life of the mind and leap, shrieking, into the realm of the senses, to be his wife, his love, the mother of his children. Oh, the syrupy fantasies I had about living in a cottage with roses around the door and a tribe of bouncing, bonny babes!

But then he left me, and broke my heart. I still long for him, but only in the way that one longs to return to a happy dream when the morning comes and it vanishes forever. I still long to be chosen, to be the one and only. It frightens me to think that I may end up alone. But I have lost my faith in love, the love of romantic fiction. Until I lost Glade, I had always believed that one day I would meet a nice man and I would marry him and live happily ever after. After Glade, I no longer felt confident that that would happen. Glade had exposed the precariousness of human relationships: the possibility that love might not find a way, that the one person for you might not be available, that love might not be sufficient, or might grow tepid, or be contradicted by circumstance or duty. This was not the way things worked in the books I read. There, love had its own momentum; it was a force of nature, like gravity, and could not be resisted or denied.

Of course, once he was gone, common sense reasserted itself, and I realised what I had always known, but in the frenzy of love had conveniently forgotten: that I am not the motherly type, that I do not enjoy domestic tasks, that I really only like reading and writing, and that if I really were a wife and mother I would have precious little time for either activity. We are taught, in myriad subtle ways, that to be a spinster is to be a failure: it is a kind of invisibility, a social death, to be the one not chosen. You are a burden on your family, an embarrassment to your sex, not beautiful or agreeable enough to be plucked from the sidelines and asked to take your place in the dance of adult life.

But there is also a kind of protection in that invisibility. In my unmarried state, a perpetual daughter, there is a freedom to live a subterranean life of my own. Once my work is complete, I may do as I please. There are few claims on me and my time. And if I wish to pursue my dreams, to create fictional worlds, to write, to think, to speak in forbidden voices, who is there to tell me I may not do so?

Surely there can be no better life than this?

Eight

Father appoints a valet

Informer's Report

Information received from Finn O'Connell on the 2nd day of July, 1847

Prisoner *O'Connell* informed me that he overheard three men discussing a plot to take my life. Their preferred method was glass, ground to a powder and put into my food or drink. The men were debating how best to befoul my food and drink without placing my daughters at risk. When they realised they were being overheard, they ceased conversation. *O'Connell* did not know the names of the men, but believes that one of them was called *Grady* or *O'Grady*. An investigation has been ordered.

From An Account of an Australian Penal Settlement

Informers

The role of the informer is a vital one in the management of a prison, not because of the information to be gleaned—it is rarely of any use—but because it prevents the development of any sense of group identity or tribal loyalty amongst the prisoners. The use of an extensive network of informers allows one to "divide and rule" with wonderful efficiency, especially if all information is acted upon. (While it is often very difficult to ascertain whether the specific information given is true or false, it can be assumed that much of the information is *likely* to be true: a prison colony is always a hotbed of mutinous plans, and so it is more likely than not that the person or persons informed against *have* been plotting in some form or another.) Once prisoners learn that there are rewards to be had for informing, the majority of them turn swiftly on their fellows, and are quite content to sell out any man for extra rations or lighter labour. As the identity of the informant is never kept secret, the men quickly learn that they cannot rely upon one another, and although this does not stop them from plotting, it generally prevents those plots from coming to fruition.

Of course, the use of informers does have an unfortunate side effect: it tempts some men to invent things in order to gain favours or indulgences. While I do not believe it is desirable to encourage this sort of deceitful conduct, the advantages of the system outweigh its moral flaws; its usefulness in maintaining order cannot be denied. While the convicts are busy at one another's throats, *our* throats stay untouched.

Journal, 2nd July

Was there ever such a fellow as this? When O'Connell came to me and informed me of the plot he had discovered, he gave every impression of being dreadfully torn between his sense of duty to me and his loyalty to his fellows. While it should come as no surprise to me that most convicts are ready informers, interested only in what their information will buy (such, after all, is the system I have fostered), I must confess that I sometimes find it depressing and disheartening to look into those cruel, grasping, hardened faces and see in them no trace of fellow feeling, concern for others, or any sense of their moral duties. They are all intent on only one thing: saving their own skins and improving their own lot, and do not care one jot for the consequences.

O'Connell is quite different. Like many of these Irish fellows, he has a powerful sense of loyalty to his comrades, combined with a tendency to resent authority figures. Yet beneath this tribal loyalty, he has a good heart, and an honourable spirit; he knows that an assault on me would be both cruel and pointless (for it would make no difference in terms of the management of the prison; indeed, it would probably make things worse); he also has reason to feel some personal loyalty towards me, for all the effort I have put into helping him since he arrived here; so he made the difficult decision to come to me and inform on his fellows. He did not come to this decision lightly, and agonised over it for some time. But he decided in the end that he could not be a party to the plot, however indirectly, and must take steps to prevent it, for it would be a great wrong to do nothing when his words might prevent a murder.

I have seen other prisoners with eloquent tongues make great protestations over their reluctance to inform on their fellows. I am not a fool; such performances are familiar to me, and I am quite capable of seeing through them. This man is quite different. He is as open, as transparent in his emotions as a child. Whatever he thinks, it is immediately translated onto his face. If he told a lie, it would be apparent immediately. Having now dealt with him on a number of occasions, I believe that I have found in Finn O'Connell a man I can trust.

Charlotte

I woke suddenly, my heart racing, with the knowledge that there was someone in the room with me. Moonlight filtered through the curtains; and in the dim light I gradually made out a pale blur in the corner of the room. Dread gripped me, as of a supernatural visitation. Blood thudded in my ears. I could not move, or think. Frozen, I gazed at the figure in the corner, convinced it was something demonic, staring back at me. Then suddenly it was as if night turned to day, black to white, and I realised that it was, in fact, only Emily, sleepwalking. Once I understood this, the fear began to drain away; but the feeling that I was in the presence of something malign, something *other*, took some minutes to pass.

Once I was able to move again I clambered reluctantly out of bed, huddled against the cold, and took her arm. "Back to bed, Emily," I said. She turned a blank face to me; her eyes were open but seemed not to see me. Wordlessly she walked with me back to her room, pulled back the covers, and climbed into the bed she shared with Anne, whereupon Anne woke, belatedly, asking muddily what the matter was.

"I found Emily in my room again," I said.

Anne struggled for coherence. "I didn't hear her get up," she said.

"Well, she's back in bed now," I replied. "Try and keep an eye on her, can't you?" I was cold and out of sorts.

"I will," Anne said meekly.

Emily sighed and snuggled deeper into the eiderdown. I hoped this would be the only disturbance we'd see this night.

"I'm going back to bed," I said, and stumped back to my room. My feet were freezing, and it was some time before I could turn my bed back into the warm cocoon it had been before Emily's intrusion. But even once I had warmed up again I found it was some time before I could sleep.

Emily

I dreamed of him last night—

In my dream I was lost, wandering in the night—it was so cold—and I found *him* wandering too—I knew not what had drawn me to that place and he, too, seemed adrift, carried thither by some Tidal Force—

But he was not a figment of my imagination, some random dream-spectre—it was as if my Dreaming Self met his Dreaming Self on that strange plain—

And I could not tell whether his intentions were Affectionate or

Malign—whether he would cut my Throat and slice me open with a great hook—or touch his lips tenderly upon mine—Was he good, was he evil?—

But at the same time as I wondered these things, I also saw myself through his eyes—part angel, part wraith—how strange to see myself from the wrong side of the mirror—and knew he was wondering the very same thing about me—*is she a Succubus, will she destroy me, is she everything I ever sought, what does she mean to do to me?*

I reached out my hand—hoping to reassure him that I meant him no harm—his hard brown hand reached out for mine—

And I feel sure if our fingers had touched, something astonishing would have taken place—

But suddenly I am awake—home in the cold, draughty hallway—and Charlotte has me by the hand and is returning me to my bed—It was nothing but a dream—

But his presence was so tangible—so *real*—

We all live two lives—in two worlds—the Empire of Day and the Kingdom of Night—

The daylight world is bluff and honest and straightforward, like a farmer in his field—We can all describe its contours—its laws are immutable—Objects remain themselves—We are who we are, and cannot swap faces, names, positions, slithering from one subjectivity to another—This world is solid, describable, dense as granite, and we all inhabit it equally—

Whereas the night—

The very fortunate carry with them only the most fleeting traces of their nightly forays into the Kingdom of Night—They live blessedly untroubled by the memory of their visitations there, and say that they do not dream at all—

When nightly I am troubled by the bewitching, bewildering, bestial profusion of the glinting, glancing night, its weird creatures and inde-

finable locales, its myriad Disguises where one thing stands in for another, where the Dead mix with the Living disguised as figments of the
past, this strange, distressing phantom land—I long for the comfortable
certainties of these people who do not dream. They say that ignorance
is bliss, and I imagine it must be so—

Yet sometimes I wonder what Mysteries lie unglimpsed, unsus-
pected, in the inner coils of the Imagination where that shadowy country is located—For those who do not Dream have never asked
themselves the fearful question: Who is that Creature who rages in
dreams against slights and injustices which, awake, I would suffer in
silence? Who is the lascivious Beast wallowing in pleasures I would
shudder to contemplate when awake? Who is that liar, that trickster,
that creature composed so flammably of passions and madness? Is
that strange, slippery, many-faced creature who scuttles through my
dreams—the creature who can only be seen in the dark, inverted mirror
world of the Kingdom of Night—is that really me?

Which version of me is the real one—the Daytime one, all hard
work and duty and secrets and silences? Or the Nighttime one, so abundant, overspilling all boundaries?

Or does the real me lie somewhere in between, and the day-creature
and the night-beast are nothing but two different Shadows cast by the
real, true Self, which cannot be seen by any ordinary light (sunlight or
moonlight)—can be seen, perhaps, only by Divine light—or perhaps
cannot be seen at all—

So I cannot regret my dreams, for all that they torment me—Without them I am reduced to the hard-edged humble me of daylight—and
that would be intolerable—

Charlotte

The morning dawned frosty and clear. Emily looked bright, sharp,
and alert as she stirred the porridge vigorously, showing no ill effects
from her nocturnal wanderings. I, however, looked and felt like death.

"Good morning, Charlotte," Father said.

"Good morning, Father," I replied. "And how are you this morning, Emily?"

Anne shot me a warning look over the teapot as Emily replied that she was very well. Father was not to know about this latest adventure, then.

I settled in my place and accepted tea and porridge. The morning routine rolled on as always. I struggled to remember what day it was. Monday—washing day.

Father had an announcement to make. "I have decided to take on a valet," he said, looking rather pleased with himself. Suddenly he had our complete attention.

"I suppose you mean a convict?" I asked warily.

"Yes. Finn O'Connell."

I was appalled. "The barn-burner?"

"Yes," said Father evenly. "I believe he will do me excellent service in the position."

"Does that mean he'll be spending a lot of time in the house?" asked Anne. Emily, who had not uttered a word, was looking rather pale.

"He will often be about the house during the day, but he will return to the barracks at night. He will be working for me, so I will make sure that he is properly supervised."

Emily looked like she was about to faint. While I was not quite as distressed as Emily, I couldn't help feeling anxious about this rash suggestion.

"But, Father," I said, trying not to sound too confrontational, "why have you decided after all this time to take on a convict assistant? It's been some years since you last employed a personal secretary. And you've never had a valet."

The look of pleasure faded from Father's face. "A man of my station should have a valet. It is the right and proper thing. And besides, I believe it will do the fellow good to have a position of responsibility."

"Will he take his meals with us?" asked Emily faintly. Cooking was never far from her mind.

"I don't think it would be appropriate for a servant to eat with us," Father said gently. "He will eat in the mess with the other prisoners."

"Of course," Emily murmured, embarrassed.

"I understand your concerns," Father said, "but I assure you that this fellow is perfectly trustworthy. He will make a fine addition to the household. You'll see."

There were advantages to having a valet. He would take on responsibility for some of the domestic tasks, leaving us with more time to ourselves. But I had never become accustomed to the idea of having convicts about the house. I could never feel entirely at ease, knowing that there was someone in the house who did not belong there. Despite all Father's assurances, and my faith in his judgement, I could never trust a convict.

Journal. 28th July

O'Connell was not pleased by my decision. He failed to see the honour I had bestowed on him and scowled most dreadfully when I told him he was to be my valet. Seeing his unhappiness, I asked him to explain himself, and he told me that he had never thought to go into service, and that it would not suit him to be a servant. At once it became clear to me that the idea of service, although generally considered quite appropriate to a man of his station, does not suit his temperament. As I have noted before, he has a positive mania for liberty, and the thought of being a servant—that is, deferring to another—is deeply repugnant to him. He lacks the willing submissiveness which we have decreed most suitable for his class, and I know that I should be trying to beat his insubordination out of him. Yet I cannot, for his situation reminds me rather painfully of my own. True, I never committed a crime; but I was once poor and humble and refused to know my place, and I was not content to stay at home and live in the manner of all my people, in drudgery and ignorance. I sought an education and found patronage and was given my start in the army, and now here I am, my humble origins forgotten, rich in land, an important man. Men of enterprise *should* be able to rise, if they deserve it; and I am not one to stand in a man's way.

And yet I had to learn how to work hard, and to endure, and to suffer for what I wanted, to go without, to do what was uncongenial for the sake of getting ahead. I learnt discipline, and endurance, and he must learn these things too, or he will never get anywhere.

Informer's Report

Information received from Thomas Edmonds on the 14th day of August, 1847

Special Prisoner *Edmonds* has informed me that he overheard Finn *O'Connell* cursing and abusing me, and threatening to "make me pay" for making a servant of him, saying that he was "no man's servant" and "better than that." While there were no specific threats made, *Edmonds* insists that *O'Connell* is not to be trusted, and is "only waiting for a chance to have his revenge."

Journal, 14th August

I have always got on well with Edmonds and do not believe him to have a particularly vicious disposition. Yet what am I to make of the information he brought me today? Could I be wrong about O'Connell? Every instinct tells me I can trust him; and it is certainly possible that Edmonds, envious of O'Connell's swift rise (how ironic that O'Connell does not see it so!), has invented this story to damage him, and to attempt to win my favour. Yet it has never been my practice to ignore this sort of information; and if I am honest, there is a small, a very *small* element of doubt in my mind. If I am wrong about him, the consequences could be disastrous. But I am not wrong. It isn't possible.

But perhaps I should devise some means of testing him?

Nine

A dinner party

Charlotte

Father decided to throw his new valet in at the deep end by having a dinner for ten—the four of us, Father's second-in-command, Mr. Fry, four junior officers, and the surgeon. To my intense dismay, my would-be suitor, Bates, was among the officers. He bid me good evening with a pink tremulous dignity, and I accorded him the same courtesy, neither of us referring by look, word, or gesture to our awkward interview some weeks earlier. I had not seen him since that day, and looking at him again, I could not regret that I had not accepted him. There was something about the quivering pinkness of his flesh that repulsed me—I feared that under that uniform he resembled a white-haired, pink-fleshed, wriggling little piglet. Struggling to banish such horrid thoughts from my mind I steeled myself for the long, trying evening ahead.

Father's dinners were not, on the whole, enlivening affairs, for we were all of us at our worst in company. My sisters and I could only talk about books and poetry, and the officers could only talk about guns, convicts, and land prices. Father would discourse on politics and we would all listen politely, and I would pass round the claret and the officers would get drunk, and Emily would stare ferociously at her plate refusing to eat anything, but trying to disguise it by jumping up and down all night to serve things while Anne smiled distantly at the officers like a gorgeous automaton. And as the night wore on, Father would develop a lecturing tone and pontificate, and I would chatter ever more aggressively in an attempt to make up for the boundless silences of my sisters, who were always struck dumb in the presence of men they were not related to.

Tonight promised to be even more trying than usual, for Father had decreed that O'Connell, in his new role as valet, should wait on us instead of Emily. Emily had taken this news very ill, for she would now have no way of hiding the fact that she wasn't eating, nor could she avoid her conversational responsibilities by hiding in the kitchen. Anne, who always did whatever Emily did, had fallen into a sulk. And when I saw O'Connell looking awkward and resentful in his new uniform, without the first clue what to do with the serving spoons, I knew we were in for a night of unremitting torture.

The talk, as ever, turned swiftly to land: how much it cost, where one should buy, what to do with it once you had it. One of the younger officers, a fair-haired fellow with thrusting teeth and prominent ears, was lamenting the fact that he had not been posted here sooner, so that he might have been on hand to take advantage of the crash. (The early 1840s had seen intense speculation in land which sent prices soaring; when, around 1843, the crash came, the price of land, but also stock, horses, houses, carriages, and luxury goods, came tumbling down.) There was, this young man said ferociously, a killing to be made if you had capital to spare.

Try as I might, I could not find land or land prices interesting, although I understood that every man in the colony found them enthralling. The land itself was so featureless, so depressing and so hostile, it was neither comfortingly homely nor thrillingly picturesque. And the obsession with speculation and wealth struck me as simply vulgar. But I did my part to keep up the flow of talk as we slurped our way through the soup, and did my best to sound interested as the gentlemen tried to outdo each other with tales of astonishing bargains snapped up, cunning deals pulled off, and all kinds of sharp practice, double-dealing, and out-and-out cheating which, bizarrely, they seemed to find quite admirable.

Meanwhile, of course, neither of my sisters had spoken a single word, and Emily, who had made not eating into an art form, had not so much as tasted the soup.

Anne

She was sure Emily was sickening for something. There was a high-pitched whine in the air that no one else could hear, which got between her ears and inside her skull and vibrated there until she thought she would go mad. Emily was sitting opposite her in a state of high alarm, her eyes riveted on her plate, her back painfully straight. When Charlotte asked Emily a question in a vain attempt to draw her into the conversation she jumped as if she had been jabbed with a fork, but could scarcely murmur an answer. Anne tried to keep her head, to follow the conversation, to do her duty (Charlotte had warned her in a fierce whisper as they were getting ready that *she had better pull her weight tonight or else!*), but the disturbance surrounding Emily was too much for her. And still there were three courses to go. It was unendurable.

Charlotte

There was a disaster when the fish arrived, as O'Connell, cack-handedly serving, dropped one of the delicate little soles with a splat onto the floor. I saw him glance at Father, attempting to gauge his response, and I wondered at that look, for there was nothing of subservience in it, or fear of chastisement, or any sense of remorse for having failed his master. No; his look was almost a challenge, as if to say *there now, what are you going to do about that?*

But Father, showing his good breeding, pretended not to have noticed, and when O'Connell reached me, I whispered to him that I would go without. This earned me a horrible look from Emily, but I ignored her. I would not be a party to her ridiculous whims and fancies.

The conversation now moved on to horses, another subject about which I knew nothing, and the difficulty of finding a decent mount in the colony. Story upon story unfolded, all equally uninteresting to me: a magnificent horse left behind in England, a magnificent horse ruined by the long journey to the colony, a magnificent racehorse seen in Sydney, in London, in Edinburgh; racing generally, then steeplechasing, then hunting.

"Have you been to the races, Miss Wolf?"

"No, I'm afraid not."

"It is marvellous fun, Miss Wolf. If you ever get a chance you should go."

Riveting stuff.

Meanwhile, Emily's ill temper was growing and expanding until it was almost visible, hanging like a black cloud over the table. I wondered that Father did not seem to have noticed it. Emily had been known to let her temper get the better of her in the past, and I feared we might be in for some inappropriate behaviour. My fears were realised when she jumped up, before Father had even signalled O'Connell to start clearing the plates away, and started removing them herself. O'Connell, rushing to intercept her, managed to get somehow entangled with her. They jerked apart in panic and confusion, staring at each other like frightened animals; Emily lost her grip on the plate she was holding, and it crashed to the ground, splitting neatly into two pieces, spilling lemon butter sauce down the back of Mr. Fry's jacket. I looked at the plate in dismay, knowing that we were already missing two pieces from the service, and fervently hoping that it could be mended without the join being too obvious.

"Emily," Father said, in a quiet but dangerous voice. She looked at him wildly, and I thought she had momentarily lost any sense of what she was doing. "O'Connell can take care of that."

She blushed, and sat down again, the picture of confusion. O'Connell hurried round the table, removing the plates with a rattle and clatter that made me fear for the crockery, and disappeared into the kitchen at high speed. As soon as he was gone I felt some of the tension in the room dissipate, and wondered if I was the only one conscious of it. Into the silence I joked rather awkwardly that it was so terribly difficult to find decent servants, at which the gentlemen laughed, and Emily scowled, and the conversation rolled freely onto the second most popular topic after *land*, which was *labour*.

"There's no future in convict labour," said Mr. Fry, who I knew had profited handsomely from his long stay in the colony. He was a hard man; I had never liked him. "You can't get a decent day's work out of them. Convict labour will never be as profitable as free labour."

"That's all very well for you," grumbled the big-eared young officer who had earlier been talking of the bargains to be had amongst the financially distressed, "you've already made your pile from convict labour. What about the rest of us who came too late? Why should we pay for the labour you had for free?"

"It's time this colony grew up," said another officer. "Convict labour was useful enough in the beginning. There wasn't any other choice then. But now we do have a choice, and I'd much rather see an end to convict labour."

"But while there *are* convicts," Fitzwilliam mused, "we'd do better to put 'em to work. It's the best way we know to reform them."

"Exactly!" the young officer added, glad someone was taking his side.

"It hasn't done much for the convicts we've got here," drawled Mr. Fry. "I never saw a worse bunch of villains in my life. If I had my way, I'd never let them out among decent people. Don't you agree, Miss Wolf?" he added suddenly, turning to me, and I wondered why his thoughts had suddenly tended in my direction.

"I'm not sure," I said, taken by surprise, "it doesn't seem kind to lock them all up and throw away the key."

"But I'm sure you'd feel safer knowing that such men weren't roaming loose, though, wouldn't you?" he persisted.

"Well—yes," I said, "but I should hate to think that my personal comfort was the cause of another's misery."

Some of the officers laughed, although I didn't think I had said anything particularly amusing.

"I can't see anything wrong with using convict labour provided one can keep them in line," said the young officer, who I suspect was growing a little belligerent with wine. "In fact, I think they're far better than free labourers. You say you get a better day's work out of a free man, but from what I've heard, the opposite is the case. Wages are so high now, and people are so desperate for any sort of labour, that a working man can pick and choose where he wants to work, and will never go outside the towns, and if you try to discipline him he'll just run off and work for someone else. Whereas an assigned man can't run away, and if he loses your stock you can flog him."

O'Connell returned during this tirade, and placed the joint in front of Father to carve. I could not help feeling a twinge of misgiving as I saw him hand the carving knife to Father, and reflected that he had been left alone out there in the kitchen, where there were any number of sharp knives. It seemed a greater act of trust than any convict deserved. How easy it would have been to dash in while the gentlemen were at their ease and plunge that knife into Father's back, right between the shoulder blades. But Father began to carve the meat as if the thought had never crossed his mind, while O'Connell stood at his shoulder, watching with a hungry intensity as the knife cleaved the pink tender flesh, his eyes never leaving that long deadly blade. And I wondered what sort of game Father was playing: Was it a test? Was he teasing his new valet? Father liked to outface the most dangerous men by going amongst them unarmed and then daring them to attack him. Something in his manner, his bearing, always cowed them; they never dared to take up the challenge.

But watching them tonight, master and slave, I felt that something was afoot, that at any moment O'Connell might snatch the knife from his hand, and that Father knew it; and in this battle of wills, no one could be sure of the outcome. The slices of meat dropped away from the bone. Still O'Connell watched; still I waited, scarcely breathing. Death was circling.

Deliberately, calmly, Father handed the knife back to O'Connell. "You may serve the guests," he said.

Standing there like a creature enchanted, O'Connell made no attempt to move, holding the knife in his hand. He seemed to be feeling its weight, thinking something through; behind his flat, blank visage, you could see the slow machinery beginning to turn. He looked at Father, and with a weird inevitability, the arm holding the knife began to rise. Anne caught her breath, suddenly noticing what was going on. Father sipped his wine, with studied obliviousness. Almost as if he was willing O'Connell to strike, I thought, watching the tableau, wondering if this time my father's luck would hold, or whether he had finally gambled on the wrong man.

But the hand that held the knife trembled in midair. O'Connell blinked, and swayed slightly. Then he picked up the serving plate and began to move, serving the slices of delicate roast meat onto the plates as if nothing had happened. And I realised that the gentlemen all around me were still talking about convict labour as if nothing had happened. Was it possible that they hadn't noticed?

"I say we've got convicts enough," Mr. Fry was saying, "we don't want any more. They are far more trouble than they're worth, and anyone who doesn't think so has obviously never tried to get a proper day's work out of them."

The young officer was by now looking very red in the face. "Well if we can't have convict labour, we should bring in coolies from somewhere. At least they know how to work."

"The working men won't like that," chortled Fitzwilliam.

"I don't care whether they like it or not," said the irascible young officer. "We must have labour if we are to progress and I know every one of you here agrees with me."

"Of course we must have progress, by which I understand you to mean profit. And who cares if that profit is built on slavery?"

Emily had leapt into the fray. I looked at her in disbelief. Her eyes were blazing with a febrile intensity; she was in a fury.

"Why, madam," the young officer blustered, rather put out, "no one said anything about slavery. Slavery is abominable."

"A convict cannot choose where he works, nor is he paid for his labour. He cannot leave if he is ill-treated, and he is almost certain to be ill-treated from what I have seen. What is this, if it is not slavery?"

"A slave is a piece of property which can be bought or sold, while a convict is only required to work for the duration of his sentence," the young officer said stiffly. "There is no similarity between the two systems."

"They say that slavery is degrading both to slave and master," Emily said, looking down her nose at him with all the fury and scorn she could muster. "It is degrading to the slave because it deprives him of his humanity, but it is just as degrading to the slave owner, because it encourages him in all the vices of tyranny, arrogance, cruelty, and the indulgence of degrading passions. It teaches him that some human lives have no value, which tends to devalue all human life in his eyes, reducing all that is good and true and civilised to the question of profit."

"And where do you think your own family's wealth comes from, Miss Wolf?" snarled the young officer.

"I believe my daughter is not quite herself." Father's voice, calm and firm, but with an edge like steel, cut through their quarrel, silencing them both. "Emily, perhaps you should go and rest."

Crimson, Emily got up from the table and hurried out without a word. The young officer, belatedly realising he had caused a scene and insulted his senior officer into the bargain, started scrambling for apologies.

"Please forgive me, sir—I didn't mean—that is—"

"Think nothing of it," Father said smoothly, making it perfectly clear that the young officer had a great deal of ground to make up. "Now please, if you'd like some more of the roast meat, you need only ask."

The rest of the meal was conducted in almost total silence.

Anne

Anne fled as soon as the meal was over. She found Emily in their bedroom, pacing angrily and muttering to herself, very overexcited.

"How could they carry on like that?" she burst out as soon as Anne walked in. "Talking about him as if he wasn't even there, talking in such a degrading fashion about him, as if he was a thing and not a person. It's disgusting—disgusting!"

After a moment, Anne realised that Emily must be talking about the new valet.

"It is inhuman! They treat them like beasts, not people. How can they live with themselves—call themselves Christians—gentlemen—when they lack any sense of common human decency—"

Emily was in a frenzy. Alarmed, Anne tried to do everything in her power to soothe her, offering warm milk, trying to change the subject, but nothing worked. As soon as she thought the flames had started to die down, Emily would spring up from the bed and start pacing again, gesticulating and ranting about the cruelties of transportation.

Father looked in on them. "I realise that young man was being provoking," he said, rather sternly, "but I would very much appreciate it if you would refrain in future from making a spectacle of yourself."

Emily cast her eyes to the floor. "I'm sorry if I embarrassed you, Father. I'm not sure what came over me."

But Father did not seem inclined to chide further. He left them alone again and closed the door. Emily erupted.

"Father agrees with me. He agrees with every word I said. He hates the convict system and would like to see an end to it, but did he defend me? No! Did he agree with me? No! How can he be so hypocritical? It's beyond all comprehension!" And so on and so forth, until Anne was weary beyond endurance.

"I'm tired," she said. "I'm going to bed. You may do as you please."

Exhausted and irritable, Anne put on her nightgown, unpinned her hair, brushed it out and braided it, while Emily ranted, growing ever more incoherent, neither noticing nor caring that Anne was no longer listening.

Why does she do this to herself? Anne wondered. For she knew that this could only end one way.

Emily

My Body huge and pulpy, aching where it comes into contact with the bed, an ache that courses around my body like a pack of hounds when I move—Every movement makes my Brain thunder with pain, but my body too tender to stay in one place for too long—the pressure of mattress on hip or shoulder or thigh or stomach seems to draw pain irresistibly so it builds up and collects—

I lie still for as long as I can—rationing the discomfort against the great shrieking blows inside my head—

Nausea punches its way around my stomach and my organs leap sickeningly up into my throat—I retch, my whole body jerking, but nothing comes—

Wondering if I might possibly faint, I lie still, concentrating on getting from one breath to the next—*in* two three *out* two three—Sometimes I can hypnotise myself into a kind of sleep—but not this time—

My hipbone feels as heavy as lead, bruising the flesh between hip and bed—Time to move again—

Trying to keep my head still, I shift ever so slightly—The inside of my skull lurches horribly, but not unbearably, as the blood moves sluggishly through my leg—Relief—at least for a minute or two—

A Voice speaks my name.

I open swollen eyes—Through a mist of fine black dots which

merge here and there into splodges, I see O'Connell looking down at me—

How Beautiful he is—

And how terrifying, with his face like a jungle Beast—a Tiger, or Jaguar—some lithe, muscular, night stalker with eyes like jewels and cruel, reeking claws—What does he intend? What is he doing here? Will he kill me? I can do nothing to prevent him, I cannot move—He reaches out a hand, and places it against my forehead—

O! how cool his hand!

I feel a jolt, a spark of energy, that courses through his palm and into my head—And almost at once I feel the intensity of the pain start to blur and recede as the magic elixir of his touch moves down my spine and spreads out through my limbs—I have a vision of my own body, translucent and dark, and the fire from his fingers coursing downward and outward, spreading through veins and arteries and capillaries in ribbons of light, bringing illumination to the dark, pain-soaked flesh, washing it clean, burning away the horror and gloom, leaving only shining perfection—I raise a hand to my face and am unsurprised to see that my fingertips leave Ghostly luminescent trails in the air—My skin has turned to mother-of-pearl—Ariel's song comes to mind—*but doth suffer a sea change / into something rich and strange*—This is exactly how I feel—Rich and Strange—

I smile at O'Connell and he smiles back.

I see you're feeling better.

What did you do?

I have healing hands.

Over his shoulder I can see water rising up the walls—has the tide come up several hundred feet? Or has the island sunk? *I can't swim*, I think, but that doesn't seem terribly important either, as I seem to be breathing underwater with no difficulty—

I believe I'm hallucinating—

What can you see?

The room is full of water. We are both floating in it.

He looks around him, and raises an eyebrow—

A kingdom under the sea?

Yes.

Sounds like a nice place to be.

And I know at once that it is some magic of his own that has sped me to this marvellous place, this Airy Sea-green Palace beneath the waves—

And I know too that come what may I must keep this man by me, for he is my saviour—Destiny has a twisted logic indeed to bring him here under such extreme circumstances—Yet he was always meant to be here and I was meant to be here too—We were fated—doomed—to meet—Both our lives have been converging on this moment—And now nothing will be the same again—

Ten

A disturbance

Anne

Anne woke, feeling dazed and stupefied. She was sleeping in the easy chair beside the bed so she wouldn't disturb Emily in her illness. Had Emily woken and called out to her? Anne peered through the darkness, her eyes aching. Outside the night was dark and moonless, and the wind keened over the roof. Dimly she could make out Emily, lying on her back, tendrils of hair clinging wetly to her skin, fast asleep.

The she heard it. "Help! Help! Fire!"

She jumped to her feet and ran out into the corridor, not stopping to think that the voice which had cried out was quite unfamiliar. A dull flickering glow came from the end of the corridor—Father's room—and Anne could see now that the hall was already wreathed in smoke. Her heart in her mouth, she ran down the corridor, and into Father's room. The curtains were aflame, and the bed—with Father still in it—was starting to scorch and smoke.

"Father!" she screamed, but he didn't stir, didn't move. And then, to her astonishment, a figure appeared as if out of nowhere: O'Connell.

"Fetch some water," he said. "I'll get him out of there."

Anne grabbed the pitcher of water from the washstand and flung it over the curtains. But the pitcher was barely half full and the flames continued leaping towards the ceiling. The bedclothes had started to burn in earnest now, but as Anne watched in horror, O'Connell darted forward, grabbed Father, and dragged him clear. With Father out of immediate danger, Anne ran to get water from the kitchen, and almost collided with Charlotte, who had been wakened by the commotion.

"Father's room's on fire," she explained, but she did not have time to stop and listen to the hysterics which ensued.

Anne grabbed up a bucket of water from the kitchen and ran back into the room, hurling the water at the seat of the fire. O'Connell was hard at work, beating at the flames with a blanket, and between the two of them, with much darting about and hurling of water, they managed to put out the fire.

With the emergency over, Anne went out into the hall, which was now almost pitch-black, stumbling over Father, who was still lying on the floor, cradled in Charlotte's arms.

"He hasn't woken up," Charlotte said anxiously.

"He'll be alright once he gets some fresh air in his lungs," said O'Connell. "It's just the smoke."

Charlotte almost jumped out of her skin. "Who's that?"

"O'Connell. The valet."

"I'll get a candle," Anne said. It was ridiculous trying to get anything done in the dark. She went off to the kitchen and managed to get a light from the fire.

When she returned she found Charlotte huddled suspiciously against the wall, while O'Connell, covered in smuts, waited patiently in the doorway of Father's room. Anne found a little water left in the bottom of a bucket, and splashed it onto Father's face. He woke, and started coughing.

"Oh, Father!" gasped Charlotte. "Thank God!"

"What—happened?" Father wheezed.

"There was a fire in your room," Anne said. "Mr. O'Connell saved your life."

"Is—" His question was interrupted by another fit of coughing, but Anne knew what he meant to ask.

"The fire's out and everyone's safe."

O'Connell turned to her. "If you don't need me for anything else, I'll be getting back to bed."

"Of course," said Anne.

O'Connell slipped away, and they turned their attention to the business of finding spare bedding for Father, and setting it up on the floor of his study.

It was not until the next morning that Anne thought to wonder how O'Connell had come to be in the house in the first place.

Journal. 21st August

I do not know if I was asleep or awake; it seemed that I woke; I was lying in my own bed, and a strange vision rose before me, tall and wraithlike. It was a phantom, a woman, robed in white, with a pale face, and weird, dark, burning eyes. As I looked at her, immobilised with fear, she came and gazed down upon me for a long moment. "Who are you?" I asked, but she did not reply. Then she began to drift about the room, as if blown by a wind, picking up my things and looking at them, and putting them down again. And everything that she touched began to burn with a pale, eerie fire, until the whole room was aglow with an unearthly greenish light.

That is all I remember of the dream; for such it must have been. When I truly awoke, my room was ruined, and I had been pulled from the flames by O'Connell.

Charlotte

The morning dawned dull and overcast, with rain threatening. We all went to examine the damage to Father's room, and the leaden light showed us a dismal scene indeed. The curtains were gone, with only a few scorched and tattered rags clinging to the rails. The walls were filthy and blackened with smoke and the rug on the floor had been ruined by soot and water. Father's bed was a charred mess; only one pillow remained untouched. Of the rest, sheets, blankets, quilts, mattress, all were too damaged by fire to be saved.

The question in all our minds, of course, was how the fire had started.

"It seems fairly clear what happened," said Anne, stooping to pick up a candle from the floor. "Father must have left this burning, and it somehow set light to the curtains while he was asleep."

"I never go to sleep without putting my candle out," said Father.

Anne frowned, worried. "Are you sure you put it out last night?"

Father thought about it for a moment, stroking his chin. "No," he admitted. "I don't remember actually putting it out. But I'm usually very careful about it."

Anne went to the window, which was slightly ajar (Father was a great believer in fresh air). "If the windows were open, the curtains might have blown out and caught the candle," she suggested. Father nodded, but he still looked doubtful.

Personally I couldn't understand why Anne was going to such pains to make it look like an accident when it was quite obvious what had happened. "I think we all know what happened here. The convict set the room alight himself."

Anne and Father turned to look at me. Anne was alarmed, Father unaccountably angry.

"Why do you say that, Charlotte?" he demanded.

A little taken aback, I explained. "Anne said he was already in the room when she came in. It was he who raised the alarm. If the window was open he could easily have climbed in and set the fire himself."

"So he started the fire and then risked his own life to rescue me?" said Father sarcastically.

"Yes," I said. "So you'll think he's a hero and ask the governor to give him a free pardon."

Anne was looking uneasy. "It does seem like a bit of a coincidence that he happened to be awake, and happened to see the fire, and arrived just in time to rescue you."

"And waited until there was a witness to the rescue," I added.

"This is all idle speculation," Father snapped. "I will speak to O'Connell myself."

I should have realised that Father would not be willing to hear ill of his new favourite. Nonetheless, it needed to be said.

"Father," I reminded him, "he broke into our house. He was roaming around here in the middle of the night. It's not something I think we should encourage." The thought of it made my blood run cold. Bad enough that he should be allowed into our house in the daytime, but the thought of him climbing in a window at night while we all slept . . . Horrid imaginings crept into my mind and it took all my powers of self-control to chase them out again.

Father took the point, I think, although he was not at all pleased.

"Thank you, Charlotte," he said testily, "but I believe I can deal with this without any advice from you."

Incident Report

Involvement of Prisoner O'Connell in a fire in Captain Wolf's quarters on the 22nd day of August, 1847

On the night of the 21st August, Prisoner *O'Connell* reports that he was unable to sleep, and happening to glance out his window, noticed what appeared to be the light from a fire at one of the windows of the governor's residence. Fearing for the safety of myself and my family, he escaped from his barracks by forcing the door, and made his way up to the house. There he discovered that there was indeed a fire burning in one of the rooms—mine. As the window was fortuitously open, he gained entry through it, awoke the household, and endeavoured to put out the fire. He was assisted in this by two of my daughters, I myself being rendered insensible by smoke. *O'Connell* was himself burnt on the hands and face while effecting a rescue, although the wounds are not serious.

When asked why he did not attempt to raise the alarm, he explained that he did not wish to alert the other prisoners to the fire, for fear that they might take advantage of the confusion. Nor did he attempt to raise the troopers so that they might help him fight the fire. As their barracks are situated at some distance from the governor's residence, *O'Connell* felt that it would waste too much time to go all the way over there and come back with help. His first instinct was to go into the burning house, help the inhabitants, and attempt to put out the fire. Prisoner *O'Connell* has shown by his actions a degree of gallantry which is virtually unknown in a convict, and has earned my highest esteem, as well as my gratitude.

Journal. 23rd August

I have turned the matter over and over in my mind, and despite the doubts and concerns of Mr. Fry, and Charlotte, I am convinced that O'Connell played no part in starting the fire. Anne's first surmise was correct; the fire began when my curtains were set alight by the candle. I have questioned O'Connell closely, paying the minutest attention to his voice and demeanour. There are certain infallible signs which give away the liar; none of these signs were visible to me. O'Connell is the same truehearted, stout and honest fellow I have gradually come to know and trust. I cannot believe he would play me so false as to attempt to murder me in my bed by letting me burn to death. Nor can I accept Charlotte's wilder conjectures: that perhaps the incident was staged for the purposes of gaining my favour. I would not put it past some of the men here to try such a thing, but not O'Connell. It would be beneath him. He is a man of action, and not so calculating as to attempt to curry favour in such an underhand way.

There does remain the question of how he got out of his barracks at night. The barracks door was locked; but it is imperfectly made and he demonstrated that it is possible to force a way out. I have had the door fixed; escape is no longer possible. And yet I am uneasy; there was only one point in my interview with him when I did detect a note of falsehood in his voice, and that was when I pressed him for details on this matter. What was he doing in the middle of the night looking out his window at my house? How did he get out without waking anyone else? Did he, in fact, get out without waking anyone else? Was he involved in some sort of plot or scheme? None has been discovered. This warrants further investigation, I think.

My daughters are rightly alarmed by the thought of a prisoner wandering the island by night, unguarded. I will speak to him on the morrow and impress upon him that on no account is he to be out of the barracks without permission. I am willing to give him some leeway, but I will not permit liberties.

I am in two minds as to what I should do next. His actions deserve some sort of recognition—but what? I am half tempted to write to the Governor and petition him for a ticket-of-leave for O'Connell. It would be a highly unusual request. O'Connell has served only a short portion of his sentence, and there is a good chance the Governor would refuse on those grounds. Nonetheless, something must be done. Perhaps there is no harm in making the request. It cannot hurt. Or perhaps some sort of monetary reward might be suitable? But no—he would be more grateful for a taste of liberty, I think. And indeed, I believe he has almost earned it.

Yet I would be sorry to lose him. I have come to look upon him almost as a son.

Charlotte

It is worse than I thought.

This afternoon, as I was clearing the tea things from Father's desk, my eye happened to light upon his journal, which was lying open on the table. I did not intentionally read what was there, but before I even realised what I was doing, my eye had swiftly scanned several lines which spoke of his intention to seek a pardon for this man!

When Father took up O'Connell as a special case, I was alarmed by his enthusiasm, which seemed to me misplaced, but I did not argue against it with any real vehemence, for of course it was not my place to do so. Prison business is Father's concern, not mine, and I had no business meddling. So I held my tongue. When Father took him into our home, I was concerned—as we all were—about the wisdom of such an action, given Father's short acquaintance with the man. The incident at dinner with the knife, followed closely by the fire, have convinced me that my father's faith in this man is deeply misguided. It seems obvious to me that he is a ruffian and a villain and is merely biding his time. But for reasons known only to himself, Father's faith in this man is unshakable, and he will not listen to reason.

What strange power does he wield, to have so entranced my Father? If Father writes to the governor with this bizarre request, it cannot help but reflect badly upon him, calling his judgement into question and possibly damaging his reputation, even his whole career. This whole ugly business is distressing in the extreme. Something must be done. But what?

Eleven

After Branwell

Charlotte

The day that we buried Branwell was desperately hot. The sun shone down with a blistering intensity out of a sky that was barren of clouds, hot and blue and dry. The air shimmered over the ground, so that it looked like floodwaters were creeping towards us from all directions. But the ground, baked dry, was as hard as iron, and I knew the assigned men had dug my poor brother's grave only with the greatest difficulty. The grave lay some distance from the house, beneath the sheltering branches of a great lemon-scented gum tree. As I stood beside the grave and listened to the words of the service, the delicate citrus fragrance seemed to fill my nose and chest, robbing me of breath, so that I gasped in the heat like a fish out of water. I had always loved that scent, but ever afterwards I could not smell it without feeling a tightness in my chest and a sense of rising hysteria.

Emily and Anne wept copiously at my side. I was dry-eyed, although I could not determine why. A voice in my head whispered, *You are a hard-hearted girl, and a horrible sister. You didn't love your brother enough. If you really loved him, you'd be crying for him now. Obviously you didn't love him enough. Perhaps you wanted him dead. Perhaps you're glad he is dead.*

Half fainting in the heat, I struggled to silence that wicked voice by listening to the droning words of Father Graham, but I could not follow what he was saying: it all sounded like gibberish. And still the voices in my head grew ever more insistent. *You wanted him dead. You wanted to be the special one. You hated him because Father loved him best of all. That's why you let him die.* I shook my head in furious denial, but I could not resist the creeping, filthy feeling that the truth was coming out. *But it was all for nothing. He will never love you best. You were the one who let Branwell go. You are responsible. He will never love you. You are a murderer.*

I clapped a hand to my mouth to prevent a howl of denial escaping from my lips, and the horror of this idea—*I am hateful, I am a murderer*—forced the tears to flow. At last I sobbed as if my heart would break. Father glanced at me, and I felt some slight relief that at last I was acting like a proper loving sister should. But deep down, I knew that I was a terrible, hateful fraud, for I was only crying for myself. I had no tears to shed for my brother. I could not deny what the voice in my head had told me. It must all be true.

Time seemed to stop after we buried Branwell. At night Father sat on the verandah, smoking, endlessly smoking, staring into the darkness. During the day he would disappear without a word, and not return until evening. Anne was tormented by the possibility that he might get lost like Branwell, and never come back at all. When he was home he hardly seemed to notice us at all. Our days had no structure, no order. Emily took it upon herself to feed us, for if she had not, we would have starved. I regarded this with a confused, angry bafflement, for Father made it quite clear to me that, without Branwell, he could see little point in carrying on. Had he then forgotten his three living daughters? Did we mean so little to him?

The wicked voice in my head was almost a constant refrain: *See? He does not love you. He has turned against you. He knows what a wicked girl you are.*

Tormented by that voice, tortured by guilt, I could not escape from the feeling that Father had turned away from us forever. I tried to devise ways of bringing him back to us, of absolving myself of guilt, and atoning for the wrong that had been done. I could not tell anyone how I felt; Emily and Anne had not the slightest idea. They clung together through this trying time, but I was alone, alone with the certainty of my sin. I knew they could never begin to understand what I had done, the monstrous feelings that lived in my heart. One phrase began to drum in my head: *An eye for an eye, a tooth for a tooth.* I had to offer myself in Branwell's place. It would not bring him back, but it would expunge my guilt. I who had caused his death must now be made to suffer for it. And lurking at the back of my mind was the feeling that if this was what it would take to make Father notice me, then by God I would do it. I could see my own grave beside Branwell's, with Father weeping beside it, bitterly regretting that he had not realised what a treasure he had had until he lost me; and with all my sins wiped clean by my act of self-sacrifice I would rise to Heaven as a little angel and join dear Mama and Branwell and the two baby sisters who had gone before me. I imagined with pleasure the gratitude of Emily and Anne, when Father was forced to return to his senses and resume his family responsibilities. The only thing to be determined was the method, and it did not take me long to realise what that should be.

I found myself returning day after day to the site of my brother's grave. Sometimes Father was there, but he was always so immersed in his own sorrow that he never noticed my approach, and I could slip away unseen. My attention focused on the great tree which sheltered the grave, that tree which had troubled me so much during the funeral. I knew exactly what I had to do: one morning as the sun was rising, I would slip out with a sturdy rope, I would walk to this tree, I would tie the rope to a branch and wait until I saw Father approaching, whereupon I would hang myself. Then, when Father came to visit the grave, he would be greeted by the pathetic spectacle of his daughter hanging over the grave of his son. The thought of this tableau pleased me immensely, and I knew it was the only way to proceed. But certain technical difficulties presented themselves. Climbing the tree was going to be difficult, for the lowest branches were out of my reach, and the trunk was silver-smooth, providing no footholds for a small and not very agile girl.

I spent a number of days pondering this problem. We did not have a ladder, so that was not a possibility. I thought at first of making off with a horse, climbing on its back, and from there climbing into the tree. But I was not sure I could make off with a horse, nor that it would obey me even if I could, for I was a little frightened of horses, and they knew it. To make matters still more complicated, the only way I could see myself getting onto the horse's back was with the aid of a saddle and stirrups (for I was not a tall girl), but I had never saddled a horse, and was not sure how it was done. So I was forced to abandon that idea. I considered carrying a chair up from the house, but could not find one that was tall enough. Eventually, recalling various seafaring books I had read, I realised that all I really needed was the rope. I could tie a series of knots in it, toss it over a tree branch, and climb up the resulting rope ladder. There was something so pleasing, so simple in this idea, that I could not resist it. I rushed to steal some rope, carried it off with me to the tree, and laboriously tied a series of knots in it. It took me several tries before I could get it lashed firmly enough around the branch so that it would take my weight, but eventually I managed it. Taking off my shoes and stockings, I went very solemnly to my rope ladder, grasped it firmly in both hands, and began to climb.

It was not as easy as I had expected. My arms had no strength to pull me up, and as soon as my feet left the ground the rope began to swing wildly, so that I could not move at all. I clung for a moment to the yawing rope, then jumped down again, disappointed. Would all my hopes and plans come to nothing, defeated by the feebleness of my arms? A kind of rage blazed through me: I would not let it beat me. And so with a grim determination I jumped up once again, and I grabbed, and I pushed, and I swung, and I clung, and I scrabbled my way up, despite the burn of the rope and the stinging drip of sweat in my eyes and the clinging, confining trouble of skirts and petticoats, and I wished with all my heart that I had thought to steal some breeches from my dead brother (alas, the thought came too late—what a picturesque tableau that would have made!), until finally, I slung one arm over the branch, then the other, and perilously, painfully, with the last of my strength, dragged myself up onto the branch.

I had climbed ten feet into the air, and now I sat astride the branch, looking down, my chest heaving as I struggled to catch my breath, my face fiery, but my heart filled with a sense of elation that I was finally so close to my goal. Once I had caught my breath sufficiently, I hauled the rope up (with difficulty—it was very heavy) and began to fashion a noose. I knew little of knots, and nothing I tried looked convincingly like a hangman's knot. So eventually I decided to fashion a noose around my neck and secure it with a double knot. I felt sure that once I launched myself at the ground below, the effect would be the same.

So I sat on the branch, and I waited, and as I felt my last minutes go ticking by, a strange sense of calm crept over me for the first time since Branwell's death. The clamour in my head grew still. The ceaseless thrashing of emotions—remorse, grief, anger, resentment, pain, fear, all tumbling one after the other in an exhausting rush—ebbed, and slowed, and stopped. Soon, all the frustration and fear would be over. I would be with the angels, and Branwell's angry ghost would be appeased, and Father would be sorry, and all would be done with.

Then I saw, far away across the open paddock, the unmistakable shape of Father coming towards me. Panic spiked. Suddenly I wasn't sure. Was I ready to do this? Was it really what I wanted to do? What would it feel like to die? Would it hurt? They said death was instantaneous, but how did they know? There must surely be a little moment of knowledge after your neck broke, before you died? Imagine the terror of that moment! And there was the drop, that long moment of anticipation as you waited to hit the end of the rope. My flesh screamed out in terror, so that I thought I would jump out of my skin, but then something within me took over. I brought my leg round so that I was ready to drop off the branch, smoothed my skirts, and tidied my hair. A stern voice said, *You must do this. It's the only way.* And as soon as I saw Father look up, and notice me in the tree, I launched myself into space.

The fall was quicker than I expected. I felt no fear as I was dropping, but as soon as the rope grabbed at my neck, with a horrid jolt, I was filled with a desperate, scrabbling terror. I did not want to die, but this realisation had come much too late. Despair, horrible despair, shot through me, but I fought and struggled nonetheless. The pain in my neck was excruciating; the rope bit into my tender skin; I dangled, kicking, gasping, unable to breathe; my head began to fill with pressure as if it was about to explode; my eyes went red and I could see nothing; faintness stole into my limbs, which kicked more feebly; I could not breathe, I could not breathe, and my whole system panicked and revolted, deprived of the breath of life. I have only the vaguest memory of Father, his eyes starting from his head, running towards me, shouting something, and grasping me around the waist, and holding on to me. I was told afterwards that Father supported my weight at the end of that rope for half an hour, screaming at the top of his lungs for help, until someone heard him and came to see what the matter was, and cut me down.

When at last I came to myself, my madness was gone, and I was filled with remorse, and my neck hurt, but I was as happy as I could have hoped to be, for Father was leaning over me with the tenderest expression on his face, so confused and so full of love.

"Why, Charlotte? Why?"

"It should have been me and not him," I rasped, through sadly bruised vocal cords.

"You know that you can't bring him back," Father said, his eyes filling with tears.

"But it was my fault he went away. I wanted to suffer for it. I wanted to be punished." As I said it, I felt it to be absolutely true, and the tears welled up in my eyes, and I started to cry.

"Oh, Charlotte, it was not your fault. I am the only one to blame. I did not look after you all properly. If I had been a proper father to you, we would not have lost him."

And I realised that this, in fact, was what I had wanted to say to him all along: I *am not to blame,* you *are to blame.* But in the general flood of emotion, and in the warm light of his regard, which was trained so intensively on me, I could happily let this pass. For at last, at long last, I had his full attention. "I thought that you blamed me," I said.

"Of course not, of course not," Father said.

Words tumbled out of me. I no longer knew what I felt, what I wanted. "You have been so cold, so distant. I thought you hated me." My tears masked the accusing note I could not keep out of my voice. Father went pale.

"I could never hate you," he said. "I love you. You girls are all I have."

And you'd do well to remember that, said the little voice in my head.

It was about two weeks after this that I stole the book from Branwell's room. Looking back, I suspect that this act of defiance would not have had such a dramatic effect if I had not, a fortnight before, proved my seriousness by trying to hang myself from a tree.

Sometimes, only extreme measures will suffice.

Twelve

Night walk

Charlotte

Emily was sleepwalking again.

Over a period of several nights, Anne managed to wake up and catch her as she blundered blind from the bed, but on the night in question, exhausted by several nights of broken sleep, she did not wake.

The night is another country, and Emily journeyed through it alone. Fast asleep, she got out of her bed, went to the door, passed down the hallway and into the kitchen. There, through some dreadful oversight, the kitchen door was unlocked and unbolted, and Emily, wraithlike in a nightgown, opened it and passed through it into the dark. As the rest of us slept, Emily walked through the soaking grass, the freezing blast of the wintry air roaring off the ocean failing to shake her from sleep. Where was she going as she followed the geography of dreams? What strange internal narrative was she caught up in? What was so compelling that neither the cold nor the danger nor the fear of falling could conspire to wake her? Afterwards, Emily could not or would not say, but something had her in its grip, some scaled, clawed, green-glinting night-beast that would not set her free, and so she walked across the valley under a night sky burning with stars. And what happened there, she could not, or would not, say.

I was awakened by a cannonade of banging doors as a sudden gust of wind blew through the open kitchen door and sent every door in the house slamming shut. I woke, fearful and cold, and listened for the sound of movement in the house. In the room next door I heard the stretcher (which had replaced his scorched bed) creak as Father got up and went to investigate. A sudden cry from my sister's room brought him running.

"She's gone!" I heard Anne cry. "Emily's gone!"

All three of us hurried to the kitchen and found the door swinging open, while a cold wind bumped round the room.

"She must be sleepwalking again," Anne said.

"Do you think she's gone outside?" I asked doubtfully. "It's freezing out there."

"She's not in here. She must be out there somewhere."

Childish night terrors flickered through my mind as I looked out at the cold dark rectangle of night. But these terrors were real; the night was a dangerous place. Who knew who (or what) might be lurking out there in the wintry darkness?

"I'll call out the troops," Father said shortly. "We have to find her. You get the fire started."

So the alarm was raised and the sleepy troopers were dragged from their beds and sent out with lanterns to hunt for Emily, while we kindled the fire and put on the kettle and listened to them calling her name. I feared the worst. Looking at Anne's pinched, anxious face I knew she blamed herself for not preventing her escape. How long had Emily been out there? I wondered. It was a very cold night. How long did it take to die of exposure?

It felt like hours that we waited, but it cannot have been more than an hour before she was found, dazed and shivering, wandering in the grass. A trooper brought her inside, and for the next five minutes we could hear them bawling the news to one another like goats calling on a mountaintop.

We wrapped Emily in a blanket and planted her in front of the fire to warm up. She seemed to be in shock, unable to give coherent answers to our questions. Father came tumbling in the door, deeply distressed, and leaned over her anxiously.

"What happened?" he asked. "Are you alright?"

But Emily was speechless, and stared fixedly into the fire, shivering violently.

"Did you meet anyone out there? Did anyone hurt you?"

Emily would not look at him, which only made Father even more alarmed.

"Tell me what happened, Emily. Did you meet someone? Did you know him? Did you see his face?"

"Don't, Father," interjected Anne.

"Was he a convict or a trooper?"

Anne leaned towards Father and murmured in his ear. "Even if there was someone, this is not the time to be asking."

But Father would not be put off. "Tell me what happened!"

At last Emily dragged her eyes away from the fire and looked at Father. "I can't remember," she said, in a frostbitten whisper, and then turned back to gaze once more into the fire.

I watched Father crouching beside her in an agony of conflicting emotions, his hands clenching into fists, desperate to act, unable to do anything. He obviously felt sure that something horrible had befallen Emily, but he could do nothing about it until she sanctioned it, and she had just refused to do so.

He got to his feet. "I'll send the men out to check the barracks," he said. "If there's anyone who's not where he should be, I want to know about it."

He grabbed his greatcoat and stormed off into the night, pausing only to warn us to lock the kitchen door behind him. And then, in a swirl of rage, he was gone.

"I'll get the brandy," I offered, since I thought brandy was usually offered in such situations. I hurried off to fetch it from Father's study, pondering what had occurred. Had Emily been so deeply entranced that she didn't know what had happened to her, if indeed something had happened to her? But seeing her distracted state, I felt sure *something* had occurred. Whether she knew what had befallen her and wasn't saying, or genuinely didn't know, I could not tell.

I returned with the brandy, poured some into a glass, and gave it to Emily. She took a tiny sip, and gagged, but when Anne tried to take the glass from her, she gripped it tightly and would not let it go.

"Are you hurt?" asked Anne softly. "Is there anything I can do?"

But Emily still would not speak. So we sat there in a weird wordless state, in the dread early hours of the morning, suspended in silence, waiting for I knew not what. And gradually I began to feel that there was some wordless dialogue taking place between Emily and Anne which I could not be part of. I itched to break in upon their silence, but it walled me out and excluded me. I could not enter their world.

Instead, my mind began to drift over possible scenarios. I imagined some vile brutish convict, with his foul body and fouler breath, encountering her, wandering asleep on the wet grass; grabbing her and throwing her upon the ground, dragging her nightgown up and wrapping it tightly about her face, so that she could not see or scream or scarcely even breathe; taking her there upon the ground, hurriedly, and when he was finished striking her a heavy blow to the head before melting away once more into the night. It would explain why she was so dazed. *He could be any one of them,* I thought. A convict who had got loose somehow from the barracks (although they were locked in at night). Or maybe a trooper (but surely not an officer, surely not one of those ambitious young men who sat at our table?). Or it could have been one of the special prisoners, the trusted few, who were not under guard. There were no other possibilities—he must be here among one of those groups of men, for there was no easy way off the island. We would not be safe until he was found. And even then, could we ever be sure they had found the right man?

I watched Anne and Emily awkwardly, feeling sure that I should be doing something to participate in the business of offering comfort. I wished I knew what to say, how to respond. But extreme emotional situations like this one paralysed me. What if I said the wrong thing and caused further hurt? I could scarcely imagine how Emily must be feeling, and I had no idea what she might want or need me to say. So I did nothing at all, merely stood there and watched, because to leave—even though I was superfluous—might look uncaring. But by staying I only managed to make myself feel angry and resentful at my own uselessness, as if Anne's simple emotional connection with Emily was some sort of rebuke. I was the eldest sister, shouldn't I be the strong one in times of crisis?

I understood Father's need for action perfectly. At least, running around out there, waving his gun and shouting orders, he could feel like he was contributing something useful to the situation.

"I'll put the kettle on for tea, shall I?" I said.

Anne

Later, when the commotion had died down, Anne rigged up a screen out of sheets, and put it up in the kitchen. Then she used every vessel she could find to boil up enough water to fill the hip-bath, undressed Emily, and bathed her.

She wasn't quite sure what she expected to find—some visible mark of difference, perhaps? Cuts, bruises, blood? But there was nothing. Emily's long white body, her transparent skin laced with blue veins, was the same body she saw every night and every morning. It was as if nothing had changed—even though everything had changed.

Anne and her sisters had a much clearer idea about the human body than most young women their age, as their father had given them a grounding in human anatomy. She knew that, seen from a physiological perspective, the loss of virginity involved the rupture of a fairly delicate membrane, and that was all. She knew the mechanics of procreation, and also of birth, but it all seemed so impossibly remote, so unlikely, so far from her own experiences and anything that she might personally *do*, that she had shied away from thinking about it altogether. Even when she thought, vaguely and shiveringly, about marriage and children and what it would mean for her, it seemed like something that would eventually happen to someone else.

Now, suddenly, she was forced to confront the idea that she, like Emily, like Charlotte too, was an adult woman, and that this had some surprising and unappetising consequences. There was an aspect of human life, a most intimate and crucial one, that she knew nothing about. But Emily had found out about it, in the most shocking and cruel way—she was almost certain of it. Emily had crossed a bridge and Anne could not follow. A gulf had opened up between them, and it was this that Anne had half expected to see as she washed Emily's body. But there was nothing to see.

Anne took a jug of hot water and poured it over Emily's head, soaking her hair, loosening the tangles, and then began to wash it, working it up into a great foaming mass while Emily screwed her eyes tight shut. Emily was vain about her hair, and washed it frequently—it was one of her few luxuries. But now she gave no sign of pleasure in the process as Anne rinsed and massaged, washing the soap away.

Anne's mind boiled with questions, but she knew she could not ask them. She had to wait until Emily was ready to speak, and then she would listen. But she doubted whether Emily would ever tell her the things she wanted to know; nor could she imagine ever framing them as questions. What had it felt like, that moment of invasion? Apart from the shock, the fear, the horror of the particular situation—what was the physical sensation *actually like?* Married women obviously had to submit to this practice all the time. Was it always repulsive? Or might it be tolerable in more controlled circumstances, such as in the marriage bed? It was clearly not painful for men—quite the opposite—since even an innocent young woman could not help but be aware that many men seemed to spend a large portion of their lives in hot pursuit of physical pleasure. But what was it like for a woman?

Anne dipped the cloth into the water and sloshed it onto Emily's back so the water rolled in rivulets, and goose pimples appeared on Emily's flesh. She took the soap in her hands and worked it up into a fine lather, smoothing it across the expanses of skin, across Emily's back, her shoulders, her arms, washing her hands and fingers, and then her décolletage, her breasts and her stomach. Anne dipped the cloth and worked the soap up again into a good lather and moved on to wash her legs and her feet. Through all this, Emily sat still, doing what she was told, saying nothing, and when Anne tried to look into her eyes, she saw that Emily had gone somewhere far away inside her head.

"That water must be getting cold," Anne said. "Let's rinse you off, and then you can get dry."

Anne took the last kettle of hot water from the stove and poured it over Emily. Emily tipped her head back so her coiled hair tumbled down her back. The water spilled over her face, and she let out a sigh. But still she said nothing.

And Anne began to wonder if, perhaps, just possibly, they had misread this situation. Was it possible that Emily had not been sleepwalking, had not fallen victim to foul play, but had been doing something quite different, and had done it quite consciously? The feeling that was coming from Emily now was not at all what Anne would have expected if she had indeed been assaulted. When Emily was ill it felt dark, jagged, roiling, like a scream, with a texture to it, thick, like matted fur; but all she was sensing now was a strange, electric hum, a resonance like the sound of a cello, almost too low for human hearing. Something had happened, that much was clear. But what?

Emily stood up and stepped out of the bath. Anne helped her to dry off, wrapped her up warmly, and then sat her down again by the fire so she could comb the tangles from her hair. And as the two of them fell into the rhythm of it, lulled by the warmth of the fire, Emily took a breath and began to speak.

"There is something I need to tell you," she said. "I have fallen in love."

"Who is he?" asked Anne, in a low, calm voice, although her mind was racing. Surely it was not one of the new officers? They had seemed, at dinner, much like every other batch of officers—agreeable enough, but undistinguished, with that special brand of cultivated loutishness that one often found in young men from the ruling classes.

"His name is O'Connell."

Anne was bewildered for a moment. Had there been an O'Connell among them? Then the penny dropped.

"The convict?"

Emily kindled defensively "What if he is a convict? He has hands and arms and legs, like any other man. It just so happens that the law has passed sentence on him. But he is still a man like any other."

"You are teasing me," Anne hazarded. "You don't really mean it, do you?"

"Of course I mean it," said Emily. "I never joke about love."

"So—tonight—"

"I was with him."

Anne was stunned into silence. Shock, embarrassment, disappoint-ment, disgust, envy, surged about her heart. The scale of Emily's trans-gression thrilled and repulsed her; and it filled her with a dreadful sense of foreboding. No good would come of this, she felt sure of it.

"I dreamed he was calling to me," Emily said. "I had no choice, I had to follow. I don't know if I was sleeping or waking, but I followed. I found him in the barn, among the beasts; their breath was warm and smelt of hay. It was dark in there, but we could see each other well enough. His eyes—his hands—I've never been so frightened, or so fully alive. All my life I've felt like a mind stranded in this strange, mysterious cage of flesh; I never truly felt it belonged to me. But now I feel like I own my own skin; mind and body are fused together; I know now how to put my thoughts aside and just live."

Anne had a thousand questions she wanted to ask; she felt as if she were poised on the brink of wondrous revelations; but all those won-derful and exciting and forbidden questions melted away in the face of one awful and inescapable truth. Anne could not look at Emily's shining face, could scarcely bear to frame the words, but she had to say, "You know that this relationship is impossible, don't you?"

Emily's face clouded with acute, sudden distress. "Don't say that."

"Father will never permit this. Never."

"He doesn't have to know."

"He'll find out, and it'll be the end of everything."

"He won't find out. I won't let him."

"You'll never be able to keep a thing like that secret. And besides, he's got a long sentence to serve; he won't be able to marry you."

"A convict can marry if he has permission."

"Do you really think Father's going to give permission for this man to marry *you*?"

Emily was silent for a moment. "But Father likes him. He's a special case," she protested.

"Not that special."

"Why are you determined to cross me?" Emily wailed.

"I'm only pointing out what you should know yourself."

"But don't you see, I think Father might approve, once he gets used to the idea. He has decided to make a project of him. And given time, if all goes well, don't you think it's possible he might permit us to marry?"

Anne thought about it. It was true that Father had taken a particular fancy to the Irishman and had taken him under his wing. He had high hopes for him, if he could just be kept out of trouble. But surely seducing the gaoler's daughter was the worst kind of trouble he could have got himself into? A betrayal like that would send Father into a murderous rage. Emily was living in a dreamworld. This could never be. A lady and an Irish convict was too grotesque a proposition for even the most liberal of prison administrators to cope with.

"Father will never agree to it," Anne said gently.

Emily frowned, a shimmer of tears in her eyes. "Then I can't let him know," she said.

Anne's heart sank. "I wish you'd think about this," she said. "It will surely end badly. Better to end it now, before you get in too deep."

"It's much too late for that," said Emily. "He is mine and I am his and there's nothing more to be done."

Anne thought she recognised a Gondal quote, but couldn't quite place it. She said nothing more.

Journal. 30th August

All my efforts to get to the bottom of the incident with Emily have failed. She will tell me nothing about what occurred; nor has she confided in her sisters. Anne is clinging to the belief that nothing happened, but I cannot believe it is so. Emily is strangely altered; I am sure she met with some foul play. Of course I am sympathetic to her modesty, but she must understand, I cannot avenge this vile act without more information. But I am entirely in the dark as to what happened; it is intolerable.

Incident Report

Prisoners refusing to work in the quarry on the 30th day of August, 1847

Trooper *Greville* came to inform me that a work gang had downed tools and were refusing to work their assigned task in the quarry. Upon arrival at the site, I found one man had been injured, and the rest were refusing to work, saying the site was too dangerous. They maintained that the injured man had been struck by falling rock, and that the cliff face had been destabilised by heavy rain. They pointed to some rubble lying about as evidence, but as it is a quarry, there is no shortage of rubble lying about! I told them I did not believe their tale and that I insisted they return to work. They refused; the ringleader, Prisoner *Robertson*, menaced me with his pickaxe, and the others did likewise. Trooper *Greville* became alarmed, and would have fired upon them; but I judged this to be unnecessary. I remonstrated with them, and when I ordered them a second time to return to work, they all did as they were told.

The injured party, Prisoner *Barker*, is making a good recovery. While he corroborates the story of a rockfall due to heavy rain, I remain unconvinced.

The working party has been assigned to the wet quarry as a disciplinary measure.

From An Account of an Australian Penal Settlement

The wet quarry

The cliffs of Coldwater provide us with quantities of useful stone for building. The business of quarrying the stone, and then transporting it up the cliff face, is arduous and exhausting, making it ideal labour for convicts in ordinary work gangs. For the more refractory prisoner, the wet quarry is recommended. The wet quarry consists of stone which lies beneath the waterline. The prisoners working the wet quarry must work in salt water, usually no more than waist-deep, without shoes, while resisting the effects of the tide and waves as they break across the rocks. The excessive arduousness of such labour, and the great risk of physical injury, makes it an excellent punishment for the wilful.

Journal. 30th August (cont.)

Why did I do it? I could have ordered up more troopers and made those men work at gunpoint; I could have slapped them all in chains and had them flogged for their disobedience. But no: I needs must go amongst them, and risk danger, and *force* them to bend to my will. As I walked towards them I felt like a gladiator walking onto the field to face an archrival, knowing I was properly prepared, knowing I was the better man, but still tingling all over with fearful anticipation, the anxiety that accompanies any great test where the outcome is uncertain

and must be fought for. And when I realised that they were determined
to oppose me, my anxiety turned to exhilaration, so that I could barely
restrain myself from laughing aloud. All my doubts and worries
seemed to fall away in the certainty of action: here was a situation
where I could act, where I could prove my mastery. A sense of
confidence in my own powers welled up within me, filling me with a
vitality I can scarcely begin to describe, but which is something like the
reckless delight that comes sometimes in battle. Unarmed, I walked
among them, knowing that if I faltered I could end up dead (for
although Greville had his musket trained on them, he could not have
killed them all, should they have acted in concert). I faced them, those
eight men armed with pickaxes, and I dared them to take a swing at
me; and indeed, I really did long for one of them to lunge at me, so
that I might have the pleasure of striking him down. But they all saw
the look in my eye. None dared to attack me, and for a moment I
knew what it was to feel invincible. Once I had forced them to
concede, it did not take much to drive them all back to work,
muttering and cursing and shooting me looks of impotent hatred.

O, how I despise them! They are so vengeful, yet so timid; so full
of hate, and yet so lacking in resolve. They are all cowards, for all their
brave talk. And as I walked away, my victory over them swiftly lost its
sweetness; for indeed, they are worthless opponents. Yet it gave me a
sense of satisfaction for the rest of the day to know that this situation,
at least, was firmly under my control.

Charlotte

I walked in on them that evening in time to hear Anne say, *Such a pity
you won't be able to have a trousseau.* I think I must have made some sound,
for they both spun round to look at me guiltily.

"Trousseau?" I echoed.

They looked at each other, and I saw them deciding in that look
whether or not to tell me the truth.

"I am engaged," Emily said finally.

"To be married?" I asked stupidly.

Emily nodded warily.

"To whom?"

Another one of those looks. How I hated those looks!

"The convict O'Connell," Emily said.

The shock hit me with the force of a blow. "Does Father know?"

"No, and you mustn't tell him," said Emily quickly.

I was annoyed—what did she take me for? "Of course I won't. But you have to tell him."

"I will. When the time is right."

"And when will that be, pray?" I asked, trying to calculate what the Irishman's sentence must be.

"Soon."

I was still trying to come to grips with this news, thinking through the implications. "But you know you can't marry."

"Why not?"

"He is not free—he cannot support you."

"I will wait for him."

"Did you discuss how many years of his sentence he still has to serve?"

"There may be ways around that."

My skin prickled. "What do you mean?"

"He may be granted a ticket-of-leave."

"I thought for a minute you meant to abscond."

Emily went very still. "Why of course not," she said evenly. "You know such a thing is impossible."

I stared at her, trying to read her intentions. "Don't try it," I said. "They'll shoot you both on sight."

"Why, Charlotte, I said I had no intention of running off with him. What an idea!" But her lighthearted tone did not fool me for an instant.

"You cannot help a prisoner escape," I said, "it would be unforgivable."

"Oh, Charlotte, will you please stop harping," Emily said irritably, for she knew I was right. "I'm not going anywhere. I will live at home as I have always done, until he is free and we can marry and live as man and wife."

I regarded her suspiciously for a moment more. "And you're really sure this is what you want? You hardly even know him."

"I know him well enough. I have seen into his soul."

There was no arguing with this sort of remark, so I withdrew to examine my feelings.

The whole affair seemed reckless and bizarre to me. The convict O'Connell was certainly handsome, in a rough sort of way, even I could see that; but he was a convict, a man who had committed a serious crime and proven himself incapable of submitting to authority. There was a wild streak in him, and any potential wife would be well-advised to treat him with extreme caution, for surely a man who was so disrespectful of the bonds of society would have a similar disregard for the ties and responsibilities of marriage. As far as I was concerned, his character would have been enough to frighten me off. But it also seemed likely that this man had intentions which were not romantic. It had probably not occurred to my heart-struck sister that he could be using her to help him escape. I determined to speak to Anne as soon as possible and urge her to remonstrate with Emily, for I feared that some mischief was afoot, and we might all, eventually, be dragged down by it.

But lurking beneath my suspicions and fears was another tiny voice, which asked, *Why isn't it me? Why didn't he pick me?* Competing forces in my heart chased back and forth: *You're much more attractive than Emily. No, you're a dried-up cranky old maid, who'd want you? You're too argumentative, too fond of your own way, your nose is too beaky and your waist is too thick.*

Why does this upset me so? I wondered. For it was not just fears for Emily's safety that troubled me, nor even the revolting thought of taking a brute as a husband. It was not even jealousy that my younger sister was to marry before me (although there was certainly a modicum of hurt pride involved), for I am, as I have said, somewhat ambivalent about marriage. It was the realisation that my sister would no longer be alone, as I was alone. For despite all that had happened, despite Glade, and Bates, and the various disappointments I had been dealt in life, there was still a part of me that was conventional enough to be willing to give up all my hopes and ambitions for the sake of *a good match*. Somewhere in my treacherous heart, I longed to be *chosen*, to be loved and adored above all other women. It was pleasing to be regarded as exceptional for my intelligence and my sharp tongue; but in my darker moments—and oh!, this was one—I would have given it all away to be a beauty. I longed for love. It was the fire that burned within me, the insistent voice that screamed day after day: *Look at me, see me, know me.* Every word I wrote, everything I did was fuelled by that incoherent, indomitable drive. I would not be no one. I would not disappear. I wanted someone to tell me I mattered.

And what stung me to the quick was the recognition that my sister, for all her frailty and her craziness, for all her timidity in her retreat from the world, had somehow, quite unaccountably, seized for herself the kind of mad love we had all spent our whole lives dreaming about. I poured my soul out in books, but Emily had put down her pen and paper and gone out the door and grabbed something which I would never have dared to claim for myself. She had shown a boldness, and a willingness to take a chance on love, which I found both admirable and terrifying. Her bravery threw my own cowardice and lack of vision into sharp relief; for however much I disliked O'Connell, I could not fail to realise that Emily saw things in him that I had never dreamt of. Looking into her eyes, I could not help but see myself reflected there; and I could not avoid seeing how small my reflection truly was.

I cornered Anne as she headed out for her walk the following day. A harsh wind was working steadily up into a gale, and I could not imagine why she wanted to go out, but she was quite insistent, so I walked some of the way with her.

"You do realise this attachment of Emily's is quite impossible, don't you?" I demanded.

Anne gave the impression of someone trying to hold in strong conflicting feelings. "She loves him."

"But it's complete madness!"

"Love is not always rational."

I was in no mood for epigrams. "He's obviously using her for some purpose of his own. Has she learnt nothing in all the time she's been here?"

"She says he's not like the rest of them," Anne said uncomfortably.

"In what way?"

"She thinks he has the soul of a poet. She thinks he can save her."

"From what?"

"Her illness. Unhappiness. Everything."

"But isn't it obvious? He thinks with her help he'll be able to escape."

"I'm sure that's not all it is," Anne said unhappily. "Emily is no fool."

"She is a fool when it comes to love. She thinks men are like the characters in novels and poetry, but they aren't. You have to talk to her. Make her see sense."

"She won't listen."

"Then make her listen."

Anne's eyes were brimming with tears. "You don't know what she's like!" she cried. "If she thinks I've crossed her she'll never speak to me again. She loves him. She won't listen!"

"Then it'll all be on your head if it goes wrong," I said crossly. I'd had enough of this conversation, and the cold wind was giving me an earache. "I'm going back inside."

And with that I stumped off back to the house, leaving Anne to wrestle with her cowardice as best she could.

There was a story I heard, before I came to Coldwater, about a man who ran a prison. He was a man of liberal views, who believed that his prisoners could, perhaps, be convinced to give up crime if they were treated with kindness and consideration and given some incentive to work. He regarded his prison as a kind of laboratory where he could put his various ideas into practice, and one of his experiments involved installing prisoners in various positions of trust within his own household.

This governor had a daughter, and like us, she lived inside the prison with her father. Her father had no aptitude for education, however, and so he took the fateful step of installing one of his prisoners—an educated man, transported for forgery—as her tutor. Perhaps inevitably, this relationship moved in time beyond the pedagogical, but as the schoolroom was unsupervised, her father was not made aware of it until the unfortunate girl was discovered to be with child. (At least in one version of the story. I have also heard that the convict and the young woman's affections were ardent, but chaste. Somehow, I doubt it.) Needless to say, when the prison governor at last found out about the connexion, the convict was removed from the house, but this was very much a case of closing the stable door after the horse had bolted. Military life being what it is, the story of this young woman's disgrace was soon the talk of the town, and in despair, her father despatched her home to England to hide her shame with relatives. The father's credibility suffered a blow from which it never quite recovered, despite his otherwise distinguished record of service. This one lapse of judgement was sufficient to ruin forever his chances of advancement in the colonial administration.

This story always intrigued me because it seemed to describe someone whose life resembled mine in many ways. I always wanted to know more about this girl—what was she like? was she in love with this convict? how did it all begin? was it a terrible, tragic love match, or something rather less delightful?—but no one seemed to know much about her. She was not the subject of this story—it was the fate of the father, hoist with his own petard, which tickled the fancy of the general public. So in this absence of information I was forced back onto my own resources to imagine what must have taken place. When I was in a sunny temper, I liked to picture it as a love match—passions flaring as they read to each other from the pages of Donne and Shakespeare, her trembling delight as he introduced her to the works of Coleridge, Wordsworth, and the incomparable Byron. After all, he was a gentleman, or so the story goes, albeit one who had fallen upon hard times.

But I am not renowned for my sunny temper, and I had my suspicions that perhaps, after all, the man had ravished her; although, to the best of my (admittedly imperfect) knowledge, no such complaint had ever been laid (of course, this particular detail may have been left out in the retelling, since it turned a rather amusing story into a rather awful one). I had spent much of my life within spitting distance of convicts— generally convicts of the very worst kind, the twice-convicted—and they were, all in all, so hardened, vile, and degraded that they sometimes seemed to belong to a different race of people entirely. This is why I find the story, to this day, so difficult to comprehend. The hands, bodies, and faces of these men were so battered by hardship and cruel treatment that I could not imagine them ever inspiring tender thoughts in my breast, and their outward appearance only gave a taste of the degradation that lay within. These men, branded incorrigible by the state, existed now primarily as a warning to others: the horror of their fate was intended as a living example to other convicts to do as they were told. The gentler emotions had been hammered out of them, leaving only the basest feelings: anger, envy, hatred—and lust. Once these men were transported to Coldwater, or Van Diemen's Land or Norfolk Island or any one of the many secondary penal institutions, they were completely deprived of female company, and they seemed therefore to live in a perpetual state of lascivious frenzy. My sisters and I had long since learned to close our ears to the vile and hideous suggestions that were made whenever we came into the convicts' view; that is, we had learnt to ignore them, but despite my general ignorance of the terms and expressions they used, their meaning was all too clear to me. I was in no doubt about what my likely fate would be should I ever find myself alone and unprotected with any one of these men, even if only for a few minutes. I entertained no fond illusions; I lived in the lion's den, and I had no desire to put my head in his mouth.

Yet some other governor's daughter had not shared my feelings—had delivered herself into the hands of the beast. What had she been thinking? Was it helpless passion? Boredom, pure and simple? Or was it something else?

And more to the point, what was my sister thinking?

She had always been unstable—highly strung, as Father preferred to put it. Sensitive. Emotional. Erratic. Had it all finally become too much for her—had the strain tipped her over the edge?

Had my sister gone mad?

Thirteen

A bonfire

Charlotte

To this day I cannot say for sure how Father found out. Emily blamed me, of course, but I had nothing to do with it. The first I knew of it, Father came storming into the kitchen, slapped Emily so hard across the face she went reeling to the floor, then grabbed her by the arm and dragged her off to her bedroom, where he slammed the door on her and then wedged a chair in front of it so she couldn't get out. With Emily yelling and screaming and banging on the door to be let out, Father returned to the kitchen and confronted us.

"Did you know about this?" he roared.

I thought about lying. Perhaps it would have been better to do so. But I didn't think he'd believe me. "We had an inkling," I hedged.

"And you didn't see fit to tell me?"

"It was not our business to tell."

I had never seen Father in such a rage. "I have raised a pack of hyenas," he snarled. And then he turned and stormed out of the house, slamming the door so hard that all the crockery jangled in the sideboard.

Shaken, I turned to Anne. "How do you think he found out?" I asked.

Anne's eyes were wide and terrified, like a mouse who has just felt the shadow of the hawk pass over her. "I don't know," she said.

I heard booted feet outside the door, and thought that perhaps Father had returned. But when I went to see who it was, I discovered, to my astonishment, that Father had posted a sentry outside our door.

"Captain's orders, Miss Wolf," he said, poker-faced, "in case of trouble."

I closed the door, stunned, realising that the soldier was not there to keep people out—he was there to keep us in.

"Can't we let Emily out?" begged Anne, who was finding the hammering on the bedroom door more than she could bear.

"If Father comes back he'll be furious," I said. But the sentry on the door had made me rebellious—what did Father mean by locking me in? I had done nothing wrong! "But he's furious anyway. Open the door."

We pulled the chair away from the door and let Emily out. She was just as furious as Father, and came bursting forth to accuse me.

"You did this, didn't you?" she demanded.

"I never breathed a word!" I said.

"Who else knew?"

"Anne knew. O'Connell knew. He may have told others for all we know."

"If Father stops me from seeing him, I'll never forgive you," Emily said.

"But I didn't do it! This had nothing to do with me!" For I declare I was a little frightened by the strength of Emily's passion. As a child she had sometimes been gripped by fits of ungovernable rage, in which she overturned furniture and threw things on the floor, and I feared for my safety if she got a hand on one of the frying pans.

"Don't blame Charlotte," Anne begged, "the prison is full of informers. Someone might have seen you with him, and guessed something, and told Father."

"Why would anyone else care?" Emily demanded. "I know it was you, Charlotte."

"It could have been anyone," Anne insisted bravely. "The prisoners all trade in secrets. They hope to win privileges for themselves by informing on others."

I saw Emily absorb this and felt the force of her rage begin to subside—or at least, that part of it which was directed against me.

"Do you swear it wasn't you, Charlotte?" Emily asked, at last.

"I swear it wasn't," I said.

I don't think she entirely believed me, but Anne's intercession had done the trick. Silently I reflected that I really ought to be much nicer to Anne in future.

Incident Report

On an altercation between Captain Wolf and Prisoner
O'Connell on the 5th day of September, 1847
Report compiled by Lt. John Fry

Captain *Wolf* was observed to enter the special prisoners' barracks, where he found Prisoner *O'Connell* at his breakfast. According to the testimony of the other prisoners present, he grabbed *O'Connell* by his hair and yanked him from his seat, and then proceeded to drag him out into the yard (this evidence cannot be corroborated by independent witnesses). Once in the yard, Trooper *Greville* reports that Captain *Wolf*, who appeared to be in an agitated or excited state, pulled out a revolver, held it to *O'Connell's* head, and challenged him to a duel. *O'Connell* pointed out that he was unarmed and could not fight a duel. Captain *Wolf* then seized Trooper *Greville's* weapon and handed it to the prisoner, insisting that he defend himself. The prisoner refused to do so. Trooper *Greville* then intervened, at some risk to himself, and took back his weapon. Trooper *Greville* then asked the Captain if he wished him to place the prisoner under arrest. The Captain assented, and Trooper *Greville* arrested the prisoner.

Upon investigation, it has come to light that *O'Connell* has been guilty of the vilest crime imaginable against one of Captain *Wolf's* daughters. Although Captain *Wolf* acted inadvisably, he was clearly acting under the influence of powerful emotions and could not be held accountable for his actions.

Journal. 5th September

I have been deceived, cruelly deceived. How could he do this? To think I let him into my house, and treated him like a son, and this is how he repays me! My poor daughter, my poor, deluded daughter, seduced and tricked, just as I was. I cannot blame her, for he fooled me just as surely as he fooled her. It is her sisters I cannot forgive. They knew about it. They both knew about it. And yet they lied to my face when I asked them about it. Even Charlotte, my own Charlotte. Of all of them, I thought I could trust her. It is clear to me now there was no assault that night. The two of them intended a meeting. To think a daughter of mine could do such a thing. Such whorish, unnatural, unwomanly behaviour—But am I not to blame, after all? Did I not bring my daughters to this place, did I not surround them with these filthy, degraded scoundrels, burning with lust? Can I blame them for becoming warped and unnatural in a place so warped and unnatural as this? No! I am to blame! Let the punishment fit the crime—I am punished for my hubris with the corruption and ruin of my daughters, who I held most dear. I tried to build something here, something magnificent. I tried to take the dross, the refuse of society, and turn them by a kind of alchemy into gold. Now I see the corruption cannot be purged. Do all dreams of utopia founder upon the weakness and corruption of ordinary human beings? That he, of all people, should be the one who betrayed my trust, after all I did for him. I thought I was too clever for him, but in the end he was too clever for me. They were right. He is a dangerous man. Would that I had thrown him in a dumb cell and flogged him until he came apart at the seams before I let him loose upon my family. My mind is ablaze—I am adrift—all that I held to be true is false—my daughter a liar and a whore—and he, whom I thought to be the one true thing in this sea of villainy, turns out to be the worst of all. What do I do now? How do I continue? I can trust nothing, no one. The best turn out to be the worst and the ones I love the most turn silently against me. Oh God, I shall go mad—

I see what I must do. I have been too kind, too fond, too foolish fond. There will be no indulgence, no kindness. Only steel. The inflexible march of discipline. I will be deceived no more. My daughters, my officers, my prisoners, will feel the weight of my wrath. A sickness has spread through the island but I will root it out I will root out the weakness in my heart I will sear away the poison and wipe everything clean I will start afresh I will tumble the cottage on all our heads and I will burn it down to prevent the infection spreading it's the only way the only way burn it out this island's mine and by God I'll make sure they know it!

Charlotte

After a long afternoon spent simmering silently in his study, Father came bursting out his door as we were preparing for tea. We all looked up to see him cross the hall and go into Anne and Emily's bedroom with a dreadful sense of purpose. At first, none of us could work out what he was up to, but then he emerged suddenly with a spilling armful of pages. He came into the kitchen, thrust us out of the way, and pushed the paper into the fire. Emily howled like an animal, and lunged for the pages, careless of the flames, but Father grabbed her and threw her outside, slamming the kitchen door and locking it.

"What are you doing?" I asked, although it was obvious enough what he was doing. The question I really meant to ask was *why?*

Father went into the bedroom and came back with another armload of papers. "It's this pernicious rubbish that caused all this trouble," he said grimly, "these romances, filling your head with disgusting fancies." He stuffed his second load of paper into the fire, almost smothering it, but then the paper caught, and burned brightly. Floating ribbons of ash drifted up the chimney.

"That's our work," gasped Anne, "our life's work."

"The product of diseased minds," Father snapped, as he snatched up Anne's writing case. His eyes were very bright; he seemed almost hysterical. "The only way to get rid of this sort of infection is to burn it out. Destroy it at the source."

"Father, don't!"

Anne tugged at his arm, trying to drag her writing case free from his grasp, but his arms were like steel. She hung off him like a toy.

"You can't do this!" she begged. "Please don't destroy our work!"

But he would not listen; he flung the writing case into the fire, where it cracked and flew apart, spilling its contents into the flames. The pages caught and crisped merrily in a riot of flaring sparks; page after painstaking page blackened and burnt and there was nothing we could do but stand there and watch. Anne ran to me, the tears coursing down her face, and we clung together in a corner as Father stormed and raged about us. We did not try and intervene. Father was too far gone in his anger—he would have hurled us against the wall if we'd tried to stop him. But even as choking smoke billowed out into the kitchen and lacy sheets of black ash whirled and eddied about the room, events seemed to take on a weird unreality. He could not mean to stop us writing, could he? It was unthinkable. It made no sense. No, this tempest would pass and everything would go on as before.

Father continued to throw handfuls of paper into the fire until the flames were choked with ashes, and then abruptly he seemed to lose interest. Dull-eyed, he turned to look at the two of us, clinging together in a corner. "There will be no more writing," he said flatly. "From now on you will attend to your duties. I want to see discipline in this household. Discipline, not indulgence. Is that understood?"

"But, Father—" I began.

"Is there something you wish to say to me, Charlotte?"

Something in his look frightened me, and I backed down. "No," I said.

"Good." He took a deep breath then, and smoothed back his hair with hands that were blackened with soot. "I will have supper in my room, tonight. Charlotte, you will bring it in to me."

"Yes, Father."

A sudden calm had come over him. It seemed scarcely possible that this same man had been a whirling, seething avatar of vengeance mere moments before. He squared his shoulders, adjusted the sit of his jacket, and walked soberly from the room.

Anne burst from my side and went to open the kitchen door. Emily tumbled in, tearful but furious.

"Did he get everything?"

"He says we aren't allowed to write any more!"

"We'll see about *that*."

I thanked my lucky stars that for some reason Father had seen fit to leave my own papers intact, for I could not have borne to see them burnt up. But I could not determine what he meant by it. His words had seemed unequivocal enough—there was to be no more writing—but he had not touched my papers. Did he mean to punish me, along with my sisters? It seemed grossly unfair if he did. I had done nothing wrong, after all. No; it was impossible. Emily and Anne were to be punished for their deceitfulness, but surely I was not to be included in the prohibition?

"I will speak to him," I said, trying to spread a soothing balm on their jangled nerves. "He is angry, but I'm sure he'll get over it in time. I'll ask him to reconsider."

For a moment I saw myself in a saintly glow as my sisters' benefactor, preserver of family harmony, interceding on their behalf with a father worn out by emotion. I could already hear his weary admission that he had gone too far, and that he was only trying to do what was best for us. I could feel my sisters' eternal gratitude. . . .

"We don't need your help, Charlotte," Emily snarled, jolting me from my reverie. Her look was hard and unforgiving. "I don't know what part you played in all this, but I know you had some hand in it. I will never forgive you for what you've done. Never!"

I feared that Emily might actually spring at me. But Anne wrapped a restraining arm around her neck, shooting a warning look at me, and almost dragged her away.

"Come, maybe it isn't so bad," she murmured. "He may not have found all of it."

The two of them then disappeared into their room, from whence presently I heard Emily's bitter tears as she discovered the calamity Father had wrought upon the chronicles of Gondal.

It was left to me to brew the tea and cut the bread and butter and take a tray in to Father. As I waited for the kettle to boil, and looked at the mess the flakes of ash had made on the whitewash, I resolved I would not let myself be overwhelmed. I would not be caught up in all this hysteria. No; I would keep my head and I would do what I could to make the best of a disastrous situation. Alright: things had spun horribly out of control, and there had been some unforeseen consequences. But that could all be managed. All would yet be well.

It had long been apparent to me that if I hoped to succeed in my plan, I would have to leave Coldwater and return, not just to the mainland and Sydney, but to my true home, England. I had not yet discussed this with my sisters or my father, but it seemed obvious to me that the step must be taken at some time or other. Father, I was sure, would have no real objection to a return home. Why else did young men leave England and come to such far-flung colonies as these, if not to amass fortunes and then return triumphantly home? And as for my sisters, I felt quite certain that they longed for the whirl of society just as I did. I knew perfectly well that they disliked it here, and would be glad to leave. There was the awkward matter of Emily and her fellow, her dreadful fellow. But the thought of it made my gorge rise, and I could not quite bring myself to believe that she could really be serious about him. It was a kind of delusion, a marsh fire of the island; and once we sailed away from here and the island loosened its grip upon us, she would surely come to her senses. Then, I felt quite certain, she would recoil in horror from what she had done, and reject him utterly. But I would not be the one to chide her for it. We are not to be held accountable for the dreadful things we do or say when we are ill; we are not ourselves. That was all I would say to her on the matter, when the time came: *You were not yourself.*

We had been isolated here in this terrible place for so long. Surely, surely, our time had come to be recalled from the margins? Thinking of the gilded salons of London, the galleries, the music, the plays, the people, my heart swelled in my breast. Oh God, to be free at last of these vicious, cruel, narrow-minded, vulgar people, with their land deals and their whining over the cost of labour, these terrible, lucre-obsessed philistines! Knowing that I was finally getting close to achieving all that I had longed for, I felt as if my brain was about to explode with excitement, and the thought of spending even one more day in this vile, windswept place seemed almost more than I could bear.

But I mastered my excitement. Rome was not built in a day, and Father had yet to be convinced. But now that my goal was so close I could almost touch it. I was sure that I would not stumble.

With a confident heart, I picked up the tea tray and went into Father's room.

He was sitting at his desk, and a pen drooped from his fingers, but he was not writing. His eyes were hooded, fixed unseeing on some distant point, although they were turned towards the window; and in fact there was nothing to see there but the interior of the room, reflected waveringly in the darkening glass. I coughed to warn him I was there, and he revived with a start. He shot me a quick glance that did not quite reach my face, and then said, "Put the tray down there."

I put the tray down where he had indicated, watching him. He was composed now, but there was an instability in the air that should have warned me to keep my mouth shut. But I have never known when to back away, so I plunged right in.

"May I talk to you, Father?"

He sighed. "What is it, Charlotte?"

I folded my hands in front of me, like a schoolgirl about to recite. "I am very sorry if I deceived you about Emily."

He pressed his lips together tightly, and his nostrils flared as he took a deep breath. But he said nothing.

"I only just found out about it myself the other day. Anne and Emily kept it from me. I was endeavouring to convince Emily to tell you the truth, so that you could give her the benefit of your help and advice. I knew it was a mistake to keep it secret from you." He looked up at me, a glint of anger in his eye. "More than a mistake," I amended hastily. "It was wicked, and wilful, and wrong. But she was so very much in love, and so terribly confused, she did not know what to do for the best, and of course *he* was no help to her at all. It was in his interest to keep it a secret, and so he forced her to remain silent. But I think she might have told you everything, given a little time, I really do." This was a lie. But if it would help Emily, I was willing to throw it in.

Father was scrubbing at his brows with his thumb and forefinger. "Very well, Charlotte. I accept that you did your best."

He intended to dismiss me. But I had not finished.

"May I ask what you intend to do now?" I asked humbly.

"Now?"

"Now that you know the truth."

He looked at me uncomprehendingly, and not very pleasantly, either. "Are you asking me what I intend to do about *him*?"

The thought had not even crossed my mind. I could not care less what Father did with *him*. "No, Father. I meant about us. I wondered whether you intended to take us away from Coldwater."

Father's eyes found mine. A note of irritation crept into his voice "Take you away? Whatever for?"

"I thought that, after what happened, it might be best for all of us if we left Coldwater. Particularly for Emily. A change of scene will help her to get over this unnatural attachment." This made her love affair sound like an illness; but after all, how else should one describe it? "There is also," I added hesitantly, "the possibility of the damage to our reputations if the story should get out."

Father's jaw set, and his eyes, blazing with fury, were now riveted on me. "You did not seem to care for your reputations when you kept this disgusting liaison a secret from me."

I had an inkling that this interview was about to slip out of my control. "We did not intentionally deceive you, Father."

"Nonetheless, you did deceive me. Your sister is ruined, Charlotte, and the whole colony will know of it before the week is out, you can rest assured of that. She will be a laughing stock. She has brought disgrace upon us all."

My heart skipped a panicky beat. I could feel the colour rising in my face. "All the more reason to take us away from here."

"All the more reason to keep you here, away from gossip. I mean to keep you safe. And if that means putting locks on all the doors, by God I will do it."

Father no longer looked like the man I knew. There was a stranger speaking with his voice, looking out through his eyes. I could not tell if he was in earnest or not, but a terrible claustrophobic fear gripped me, a fear that he might really keep us here, buried alive, forever.

"Father, please—be reasonable. You must see that we cannot stay here!"

He stared at me for a long moment, and a look of dreadful realisation stole into his eyes. "So that's what you were hoping for," he whispered. "My God. You don't care what happens, do you? So long as you get your own way."

"I don't know what you mean, Father," I said, as the crimson blood flooded up my neck and into my face.

He was still staring into my eyes, and a terrible caressing tone crept into his voice. "Charlotte, my dear. So strong, so determined. Such a pity you were not born a man. You might have commanded armies.

"I see now what all this has been in aid of. This is all because you wish to go away and make your fame and fortune with that book you are writing, is it not?"

I started to demur, but he spoke over me. "I fear it is time I told you something I have not had the heart to tell you up until now."

Suddenly my heart was hammering. His voice was all reasonableness, but I knew that whatever it was he was about to say, I did not want to hear it. But I could not move. I could not drag my eyes from his face. I had to stay and listen.

"You would do well to give up your aspirations," he said. "I have hesitated to tell you the truth, for I didn't want to hurt your feelings. But this folly has gone on long enough, and I must put an end to it before any more harm is done. It is true, Charlotte, that you have a certain easy facility for writing—what is called 'a way with words.' You can construct a pleasing sentence; indeed, you can construct great strings of pleasing sentences. Your vocabulary is good, your grammar is strong, and you are clearly quite well-read for a woman of your age.

"But the fact remains, Charlotte, that all of this is not sufficient to make you a great writer. You have lived a very sheltered life, and while you have read widely, your understanding of the world is neither broad nor deep. You lack sophistication, and you have no insight into the workings of the real world. You have no understanding of contemporary politics and no notion of the pressures of business or public life. While this is entirely appropriate for a young woman of your station, it leaves you sadly ill-equipped to depict human society in any sort of satisfying way. And I am sorry to say it, but your self-absorption makes you unable to empathise with anyone, living or imaginary, who does not closely resemble yourself. The work you have pursued over these many years, while charming in its own facile way, is of no more interest to the general public than the children's tales it closely resembles. In short, Charlotte, while you have a talent—yes, I think it would be fair to call it a talent—for the written language, you have absolutely nothing of interest to say. Therefore, I think it would be best if you gave up your ambitions in that line forthwith, as they are only destined to bring you unhappiness, and concentrated on finding yourself a husband."

Father's eyes met mine, and a gentle smile curved his lips. And I knew that I had been punished for my treachery, punished most brutally. For Father's cruel words had turned all my hopes and dreams suddenly to ashes.

Two

I have done nothing but in care of thee,
of thee, my dear one

THE TEMPEST

One

Writer's block

From An Account of an Australian Penal Settlement

On discipline

It is a truth universally acknowledged that the sort of man who joins the army as a common soldier is generally the worst sort of man: a wilful and fanciful creature, idle, indulgent, thoughtless, and rash. He is accustomed to being his own master, and thinking of himself as entirely free; it goes against his own nature and inclinations to submit himself to the control of others. In order to turn him into that model of efficiency we call the soldier, it is necessary to break his spirit, so that he will learn to follow orders. His wilfulness must be beaten out of him, with harsh discipline and the lash, so that obedience becomes automatic and instinctive.

Should we then be surprised that a convict—who generally comes from an even worse stratum of society than the common soldier, and is even less inclined to obey orders that are not to his liking—must be brought to heel through frequent application of harsh discipline, threats of violence, and the lash?

Charlotte

I still loved Father as I had always loved him; but I could not forgive him for taking the one thing away from me which made life tolerable. Father had been in earnest when he told us we would not be allowed to write any more. He kept his own private supply of pens, ink, and paper in a trunk in his study—he had the only key—and issued an order that under no circumstances were we to be allocated any writing materials by the quartermaster. Emily tried to obtain some nonetheless, and when rejected, came storming home in a blazing fury. But it was not the lack of tools that I resented (although I thought it was both petty and irritating that Father kept them locked away). It was Father's attempt to strike at my very heart, to make it impossible for me to write, out of sheer pique at being deceived. For his words had most assuredly done their work; even though I had no paper and not so much as a pencil, and therefore could not attempt to sit down to work, I knew such an attempt would be impossible, for all my words had deserted me.

I had always had an inexhaustible store of tales and people and questions and ideas that welled up from nowhere, unbidden. Now, suddenly, I felt as if I had been felled by an unexpected blow, and awoke to discover I had lost one of my senses. Stunned, deafened, I looked out at a world drained of colour, a world without delight. My father had taken my heart and squeezed it in his great fist until it ceased beating, and then put the lifeless, bloodless thing back into my chest. A ghost, I walked through a phantom world, untouched by any joyful sensation. My outlines were amorphous; objects, words, emotions passed straight through me. Nothing mattered, now that the thing that had made my life worth living, the thing that made me *me*, had been taken away.

From time to time I tried to tell myself that Father was wrong; he had been angry, he had spoken in haste, he had not meant what he said. For he *had* been angry, and he *had* spoken in haste. But I could not dismiss what he said, for deep down, I suspected he had spoken the truth.

All my life I had wanted to believe I was exceptional; now I knew that I *was* exceptional, but only in my arrogance and self-deception.

This was a crueller blow than Glade had ever struck me, and this time there was no consolation. I could not write, I could not read, I could not think. All I could do was breathe, and sleep, and drift.

Emily

I feel as if a Tiger has taken up residence in my breast—a rage has kindled within me which cannot be Quenched—I will not let Father crush my spirit, as he would that of a rebellious Convict—whatever torments he can devise, I am equal to them—I will endure—I will endure—

Gondal is gone—lost in the fire—Anne was very worried about how I would bear it—and indeed it is a Blow—but Gondal lived in our Hearts and our Heads before it was ever set down on paper—we can write it out again if we need to—but strangely, I no longer feel the need—it is as if a Chapter in my Life has closed and another has begun—it was Dear to me, and Essential, and without it I would not be Myself—but the loss of it now is not so great that it cannot be overcome—

The loss of my other manuscript, however—

The tale on those pages was so much more Dear to me because it seemed to tell the tale of my life even as it was unfolding before me—I am in it, and he is in it, and Father is in it—

I feel that in some way—unknowing—I Conjured up the Disaster which has befallen us all, through the Spell of my words—

How strange it seems to me that Father should uncover the truth—and tear us asunder—just as I began to describe my hero and heroine being torn asunder upon the page—it is uncanny and I do not like it—yet I cannot ignore it—If there is some Strange Force at work here, I must allow it to work through me—I must rise to the Challenge—Father's prohibitions be damned!—If I have to sing him up from the deep with my song, I will do so—I will find him, and I will bring him back, and we will be together—and no one, not Father, not Charlotte, will stop me!

Charlotte

Emily found paper and pens. I didn't ask where she got them from. I didn't care. The work began again, as they tried to replace what had been lost, piecing two half-finished novels together from scraps of torn and disordered paper. At first Emily and Anne worked only at night, in their room, with a blanket hung over the door to hide the light. But as the weeks went by, it became clear that such secrecy was unnecessary. Father did not care what we did; we rarely saw him. I was worried about him, but Emily just smiled her new, hard smile, and took to working quite openly at the kitchen table. Anne, more cautious, liked to keep a workbox at her side, so that if Father should appear she could hide her papers and whip out the stocking she was knitting, which never seemed to grow any longer; but Father never did appear. Emily had become so brazen she did not even bother pretending. I think she was hoping for a confrontation. But none came.

Emily seemed to be possessed by some new spirit, a devouring flame that burned intensely, driving her on, not letting her sleep or rest. We had seen her like this before, of course; her attacks often seemed to feed these subsequent periods of frenzy. But I had never seen anything quite as extreme as this before. She was always awake before anyone else in the morning, with a fire blazing in the hearth and breakfast cooking; she flew through the housework at such a pace that Anne and I struggled to keep up with her, and she flung herself into her work as soon as the chores were done, writing like a creature possessed until it was time to cook the dinner, and sometimes even then she would stop in the middle of the preparations to jot something down. Once dinner was eaten and the dishes were cleared away, it was back to the pen until suppertime. Even after supper she would not stop, bending closer and closer over the page until she threatened to ruin her eyesight, scribbling away in writing that grew ever tinier and more cramped, exchanging papers with Anne so they could read over the day's work and discuss it late into the night. There was something alarming about her febrile energy, but at least it was keeping her going. I did not dare to speculate about what might happen when her will, or her energy, faltered.

As for me, I listened and watched, but did not participate. I was on the outside once more, looking in, but this time I knew there was no hope of return. The power of incantation had left me when I lost my words. That part of me was dead.

two

The Diver

Anne

Anne left Emily writing and Charlotte ironing Father's shirts. The afternoon beckoned. It was a crisp, cold, sunny day, with an occasional tracing of clouds high up in the sky. The wind blew as strongly as ever, bending the grass in silvery waves, so it seemed like the whole earth was in motion.

On a whim, Anne decided to clamber down the cliff to look at the water. Avoiding the path down to the main beach, she picked her way down to a spot where the soldiers sometimes fished off the rocks in their spare time. But it was deserted now, and surprisingly balmy, as a rocky outcrop provided some shelter from the wind, and the angle of the cliff scooped up the afternoon sun like a spoon. Anne jumped from rock to rock, toasty warm, enjoying the sting of spray as it misted off the rocks. Finally she found what she was looking for—a rock formation which they'd named Nature's Eye. At some distant point in the past, a huge round piece of white quartz, the size of a giant pumpkin, had been lifted up out of the ocean and landed in a nest of black rock which, by curious chance, happened to be shaped rather like an eye. The white stone formed the colourless iris of the eye, and at high tide water trickled in to fill the surrounding space, so that it seemed the very spirit of the island, huge and ancient, gazed placidly up at you. When she was younger, and Father had taken them all out for walks, it had always been Anne's favourite spot. When it was her turn to choose the destination of their walk, this is where she always chose, until Emily and Charlotte eventually rebelled at the lengthy climb over rocks and cliffs, and refused to go there anymore. Now Nature's Eye was hers alone, and she made regular visits to gaze into it, and think.

But there would be no reverie today. As she stood gazing at the eye filling and emptying with clear seawater, as if it were caught in an unquenchable cycle of grief, she was startled by a sudden splash, and looked up to see a man clambering out of the waves and onto the rocks. Her gasp of surprise caught his attention, and for a moment they froze, staring at each other.

He was young, and thin as a reed, wearing only a pair of old breeches. The muscles in his arms were like knotted rope. His hair curled in wet tendrils around his face and his lips were full and sensuous. *O brave new world that has such people in't*, thought Anne, as she stared. The moment held, suspended, and then he broke into a smile.

"Hello," he said. His eyes, a shifting oceanic blue, enveloped her.

"Hello," she replied. "Where did you come from?"

"From the water."

"I can see that. But how did you get here?"

He grinned lazily. "I swam, how'd you think?"

Anne goggled at him. "From the mainland?"

He shrugged, as if it was all in a day's work to him. Perplexed by his calm, Anne asked: "Don't you know what this place is?"

"It's a prison," he replied readily.

"You shouldn't be here, you know," Anne said.

"Neither should you, so far as I can see. But here you are."

Anne gazed at him for a moment, wondering if he was an escaped convict. But if he was, what was he doing landing on the island?

As if he had read her mind, the young man asked: "So are you an escaped convict?"

"Not as such," she replied pertly, a little pleased by her own quickness.

"What's your name?"

"Anne."

He nodded. "You're one of his daughters then."

"Yes." So he did know something about Coldwater. She waited for him to complete the introductions, but as he said nothing she was forced to ask him his name.

"They call me the Diver."

For the first time she noticed he was carrying a rough sack. "Is that your name or your occupation?"

"Both." The Diver reached into his sack and pulled out an oyster, still in the shell, which he cracked open with a fierce-looking knife, and then offered to her.

Anne recoiled. "What's that?"

"What do you think? It's a rock oyster."

"You want me to eat it?"

"What else would you do with an oyster?"

"But it's not cooked."

He gave her a quizzical look, then, with a faint shrug, tilted his head back and let it slip down his throat.

Feeling like this had been a test, and she had failed it, Anne sought desperately for further topics of conversation, unwilling to let him leave just yet. That he seemed in no hurry to go did not, at that stage, occur to her.

"How could you have swum here?" she asked. "That water looks freezing."

He turned to look at it, as if the question had not occurred to him before. "It's not so bad once you're in," he said thoughtfully.

"But they say there's a current that comes up directly from the South Pole and if you get caught in it you'll get sucked all the way back down there," Anne said. One of the soldiers had told her this on a very hot day when she'd been thinking of going in for a paddle. It had sounded reasonable enough to her. But the Diver was cocking an eyebrow at her, and she realised she must have been misinformed.

"Sounds unlikely," he drawled, "but you could be right."

Flustered, Anne blundered on. "But there are sharks, and stingrays. And a special kind of long seaweed that wraps round your legs and pulls you under so you drown."

"You don't say."

"You're laughing at me," Anne accused.

He straightened his face. "For someone who lives on an island you don't know much about the sea."

Irked, Anne decided to put him in his place. "You shouldn't be here, you know. If anyone saw you they'd think you were trying to break into the prison and they'd probably shoot you on sight."

But this didn't seem to upset him in the slightest. "Why would any-one break into a prison?"

"To help someone get out."

"Ah." He mulled this over. "Why didn't you raise the alarm?"

Caught out, Anne hedged. "I still might."

The Diver hoisted his sack more comfortably onto his shoulder. "Give us a chance to get away, then."

"I didn't say I *would*—" Anne began, then, fearing that she had said too much, fell silent. He looked like he was ready to leave, and she tried one last time to detain him.

"I never learnt to swim," she said.

"No?"

"Is it difficult?"

"Easiest thing in the world. You should learn. Living where you do."

He gave her a wink, then turned and moved down to the water's edge. He dived in, his body slicing the water apart without so much as a splash, and then he was gone, as if his natural element had reclaimed him, leaving Anne, dry-footed, on the shore.

When eventually she started to walk back towards the house, Anne found that she could not get the smile off her face.

Emily

Anne is full of Secrets today—she came back from her walk brimming over with Excitement but would not say a word about what she had
seen—It is quite unaccountable and I cannot remember the last time she
kept a secret from me—

But I will not pry—

Washing day—excellent day for drying—I find that the Gondals do
not trouble me so insistently today for I am Full of thoughts of Cather-
ine and Blackheath (not sure about that name) and their strange, gnarled,
windswept home—

Anne's Behaviour really is most troubling—

Anne

Every day for a week, except for two days when it rained, Anne lingered as long as she dared on the rocks near Nature's Eye, hoping to
meet once more with the Diver. She could not tell what drove her to it,
and she knew that she was doing something very wrong. But her curiosity, and her desire to see him again, was too strong to be ignored, so she
pushed all the prohibitions aside, brushed her hair until it fell down her
back like half a yard of running water, and waited for him.

Finally her patience was rewarded. He appeared, ten days later, step-
ping streaming from the water, with his sack on his back. He put it
down, and she watched in horrified fascination as the sack started surging and squirming about by itself.

"What have you got in there?"

"Crabs. Good eating."

"Don't tell me you eat those raw."

"Not them, no." He watched her with a candid, intimate gaze. "I
wondered if I'd see you again."

"I've been waiting for you." There seemed little point in dissembling, since it must be obvious that she was waiting for him; and besides, Anne couldn't really see the point in playing coy and feigning indifference. He would only see through it, and she didn't want to seem like a ninny.

He smiled, pleased, and his smile made her heart lift.

"Brought you something."

He crouched down and peered into the sack, gingerly put his hand in, and drew out an irregularly shaped fruit, not quite oval, smooth-skinned, the colour of a peach, and rather bruised from being pummelled by crabs.

"What is it?"

He did not answer, but pulled out his knife, cut a piece off, and handed it to her. "Don't eat the skin," he advised, "it's not very nice."

Anne lifted the piece of fruit doubtfully to her lips and nibbled at it. Her mouth exploded with an intense sweetness, and she looked up at him, startled, delighted, in time to see his answering smile of pleasure.

"I've never tasted anything like it!" she exclaimed. "What is it?"

"It's a mango. They grow up north."

She raised her eyebrows momentarily—he'd been up north?—then quickly forgot about it as she finished the piece of fruit she'd been given and looked for another. "Is there any more?"

He laughed as he cut off another piece for her. "Like your tucker, don't you?"

She was too busy eating to answer.

The Diver explained that he lived just across the water in the settlement that had sprung up around the bay. This settlement had once been little more than a place where troops and convicts stopped before the last leg across to Coldwater; but now, as new land was opened to the north and settlers spread out over the country, it was a rapidly growing town. He made his living, he said, fishing the abundant waters of the bay, and this frequently brought him across to the island.

"I usually come in the afternoons," he said. "And I always land here."

"I'll look for you here then," Anne said.

"I'd like that," said the Diver.

Three

Malaise

Cancellation of Special Prisoner Program
12 September 1847

The category of Special Prisoner has now been cancelled. All prisoners previously receiving special privileges of any kind (special freedoms, shorter work hours, education, extra indoor duties, extra rations, &c.) have had these privileges revoked. They will be returned to ordinary work gangs and set to work along with their fellows. They will be quartered along with the rest of the men. The special prisoners' barracks will remain empty until a suitable alternative purpose can be found for them.

Journal. 12th September

I have asked Mr. Fry to take over my duties for the time being; I have let him know that I am unwell.

And how should I describe this malaise, after all? I am not physically ill; I suffer no pain, no nausea, no headaches; they passed quickly and have not returned. But I have not been able to regain my strength. It is as much as I can do to drag myself from my bed in the morning, not because I am weary—although I am afflicted by a certain lethargy—but because to do so seems utterly pointless. Yet to remain in bed fills me with a weary disgust at my own weakness and idleness. My work seems loathsome and meaningless—the endless scheming and plotting as I tried to devise new and better ways to torment my prisoners; the building projects and engineering projects as I sought to expand my fiefdom, this verminous pile of rock. What an act of futility it was to hack this place out of the hillside! This will never be anything other than a prison, and like all the others it will soon be abandoned. Why did I go to such lengths to build handsome buildings here in stone? Once we leave, all my labours will be tumbled by the saltbush and the wind, and in a few years only a heap of stone will be left to mark my passing.

I can hardly bring myself to move my hand across this page; everything I do swamps me with the loathsome certainty that my life is a savage and futile joke.

Informer's Report

Information received from Prisoner William Briggs on the 14th day of September, 1847

Prisoner *Briggs* reports that there is serious dissension among the prisoners now that the Specials have been returned to the main barracks. *Briggs* reports that a group of "common" prisoners, led by John *Collins* (who is well-known to us), has been tormenting the Specials and calling them "soft," teasing and tormenting them beyond endurance. The Specials, as a consequence, have formed their own group, led by William *Davis*. Fights between the rival camps are common, and there have already been some serious injuries. *Briggs* fears there may soon be a death, as the rivalry shows no sign of dissipating.

Informer's Report

Information received from Prisoner Graham Skate on the 15th day of September, 1847

Prisoner *Skate* reports that William *Davis* (formerly a Special) was heard expressing a desire to have the head of Captain *Wolf* on a silver platter.

Informer's Report

Information received from Prisoner Thomas Edmonds on the 16th day of September, 1847

Prisoner *Edmonds* reports that William *Davis* is plotting to "knock John *Collins* from his perch." *Collins* has long been an unofficial leader among the prisoners, and has lately been using his position to abuse those former Specials who have now returned to his domain. *Edmonds* believes that *Davis* plans to kill *Collins* and take his place as master of the prison.

Journal, 17th September

Fry came to me today demanding that we take action to control the prisoners. He handed me a sheaf of reports showing that Prisoner A wants to kill Prisoner B, Prisoner C wants to kill Prisoner D, &c, &c. Naturally enough all the prisoners want to see me dead, and I must say, there are times when I share their feelings. Fry was very concerned that we should not lose Collins, since we can control him; he reminded me that no understanding has been reached with Davis, who has a grievance against me for removing him from his cosy situation. I told Mr. Fry to do nothing at all; if the lazy dogs tear each other apart, they will save us the trouble of hanging them.

Informer's Report

Information received from Prisoner Samuel Cumberland on the 22nd day of September, 1847

Prisoner *Cumberland* reports that John *Willis*, Samuel *Taber*, and Lance *O'Donohue* are planning to break out of their barracks in dead of night, steal into the governor's residence, string the governor up by the neck and hang him until he is dead, and then carry off his daughters, who are to be distributed one to each man. The daughters are then to be used as hostages to negotiate a safe passage back to shore.

Incident Report

On the death of Prisoner John Collins on the 24th day of September, 1847

Prisoners report that while eating his dinner in the mess, Prisoner *Collins* got into an argument with several men, one of whom was Prisoner *Davis*. This argument quickly became violent and came to blows. A general riot then ensued. Hearing the noise, the troopers went in to restore order. When they had done so, it was found that Prisoner *Collins* had been stabbed with a knife. He was taken to the infirmary, but his wounds were severe, and he has since died. A thorough search was made of the prisoners' mess, and the murder weapon was discovered. The knife appears to have been fashioned out of some scrap metal, possibly obtained from a pickaxe. Attempts to determine who wielded this blade have proved less than successful, for the eyewitness reports differ wildly. Many prisoners have named Prisoner (formerly Special Prisoner) *Davis* as the assailant, but as they are men from *Collins'* own faction, who hate *Davis*, this information cannot be trusted. However, Prisoner *Davis* has been placed in custody until a proper trial can be held.

Memorandum

Re: Investigation and Trial of Prisoner Davis
25th September 1847

Mr. *Fry* will be taking full responsibility for the investigation into the death of *Collins* and the trial of *Davis* (and/or others, as necessary). All questions on the matter should be referred to him.

Journal. 25th September

I do not know what I would do without Mr. Fry, for since my illness, all my mental powers have deserted me. I can no longer look at a man and read his guilt or innocence in his eyes. Once I had a sixth sense for mutiny, an instinct for deception. It has deserted me. True or false, I cannot tell; to me, everything seems false.

Mr. Fry is untroubled by such concerns. He is not a subtle man, and has his own methods for getting at the truth.

Charlotte

Father was in retreat. He took all his meals on a tray, and left the day-to-day management of the prison to Mr. Fry. Father had told Mr. Fry he was ill; and perhaps he was; when I took the tray in to him he was pale, and did not look at all himself. Where once he had been im- maculately turned out—clean-shaven, well-brushed and groomed—he languished now in his shirtsleeves, his hair uncombed, his pale face smeared with stubble that darkened with every day that passed. He kept his windows shut, and no air freshened that close and sickly room.

This was not the first time I had seen Father like this. It had been many years, of course, but those far-off days were seared upon my memory like a brand; how could I forget? This was the Father I had known after Branwell died: remote, careless, blank-eyed. Then, he had taken to going on long, long rides around the property; now, he stayed in his room. Then, it had taken drastic action to shake him from his malaise; I hoped that this time I need not use such a risky stratagem.

One evening, as I arrived to collect his supper tray, I decided to speak to him.

"Father, I'm worried about you," I said.

He lifted his eyes to me with infinite weariness. "I beg your pardon?"

"You have been shut up in here like a hermit for weeks. Are you ill?"

"No."

"But if you are not ill, what is the meaning of this? It is not like you to be so retiring, to take so little interest in your work."

"I don't see that it's any of your concern," Father replied haughtily.

I was cut to the quick by his rejection; how could he speak to me like that, I who had once been his favourite? "How can you say such a cruel thing?" I cried passionately. "If my own dear father is unwell, whose concern is it, if not mine?"

"I am perfectly well, Charlotte," Father replied, shrinking away from me, as if he feared some contagion. "Please do not upset yourself."

"I can't help it!" I replied. "I am very worried about you. It seems to me that you have some great grief or trouble weighing upon you, a trouble which oppresses you so greatly you cannot work or rest. Will you not tell me what afflicts you?"

Father sighed. "I am very tired, Charlotte. That is all."

And he would say no more, asking me so insistently to leave that I was forced to obey.

But the following day, when I took his supper tray in to him, he was a little more forthcoming.

"I have been giving the matter some thought," he said solemnly, "and I believe I have discovered the cause of my illness."

"You have?" I said, reflecting that yesterday he had denied being ill.

"I was afraid it was merely melancholia," Father said with a shudder, for he had a morbid fear of mental weakness, "but on further thought, I have realised that I am suffering from a physical illness; a contagion brought into my house by that Irishman."

Father did not utter his name, but it was clear from the way he spat out the word "Irishman" that he meant O'Connell.

"Is it not possible," Father continued, growing gradually more animated, "that the blight which is currently afflicting Ireland could be more wide-ranging in its effects than has hitherto been realised? This blight destroys the potato by withering the stalk and making the tuber rot in the ground. He told me that those who tried to eat the blighted potatoes became ill. Could it be that this illness which afflicts potatoes can also affect humans? The epidemics of illness and death which have accompanied the spread of the blight have been widely reported. Isn't it possible that some evil variant of this illness has been brought to this country by the Irishman and his compatriots?"

"It's possible," I said, although the idea sounded far-fetched to me. But then, I was no scientist.

Encouraged, Father went on, grabbing me eagerly by the wrist as if to ensure my attention. "It seems quite clear to me now that all our trouble started when Emily took up with that man. She caught the contagion from him, and passed it on to me. If we are to prevent the spread of this illness we must take drastic measures."

"What kind of measures?"

"In Ireland they tumble the house and burn it to the ground."

"That seems extreme, Father. And not very safe. Where would we live?"

Father frowned, rather irritated by these niggling details. "I am only thinking of your welfare, Charlotte."

"But I'm not ill, Father, and neither is Anne."

He frowned, looking at me searchingly, as if trying to discover some sign of infection. "You may be immune, or the illness may be slower to develop in you. I pray you will not be afflicted."

"Have you discussed this with Mr. Fitzwilliam?"

Father snorted dismissively. "Fitzwilliam's an idiot. All he knows how to do is cut. He wouldn't have the faintest idea how to deal with something like this."

"And what precisely is the nature of your illness, Father?" I asked.

Father sighed, massaging his brow with his fingertips. "An acute stage of illness—that passes quickly—followed by an extended period of—what I can only describe as a malaise. I feel as if I am shrouded in a fog. I cannot think, I cannot work. It is almost like a paralysis—but a paralysis of the will, rather than the body."

"And have you noticed any improvement in your condition, Father?"

"None. I fear this may afflict me for the rest of my life."

His haunted look frightened me, and I groped for solutions.

"What if we consulted a doctor, a proper doctor? He might know how to cure you."

"Perhaps."

"There must be good doctors in Sydney."

"I cannot go to Sydney."

"Why not?"

"I dare not leave the island unguarded."

I frowned. "It would not be unguarded. Mr. Fry could run things in your absence."

"No."

"But he is running things for you now."

"The convicts don't know that."

I could not quite understand why Father was being so difficult about this. "Alright then. If you won't go to the doctor, why not bring the doctor here?"

"Impossible."

"But why?" I cried.

"If they knew I was ill, it would be disastrous," Father said, his eyes blazing. "If they suspect, even for a moment, that I am losing my grip, it will be the end. The prisoners will rise, I'm sure of it."

"But, Father, you're ill," I said, frustrated. "You're not doing anyone any good by refusing to seek treatment!"

"I am the only governor—the *only* governor—who has never had one mutiny or escape. I will not let my record be blemished by this temporary weakness."

"You said it might be permanent."

He scowled angrily at me, and the fear was plain to see in his eyes. "I will not let this illness defeat me. If I can't leave here in triumph, I will not leave at all."

My heart flipped over in my chest. "I beg you to reconsider," I said. "If you were to leave now, no one would think less of you. Everyone knows you've done an admirable job here. Your record is perfect. This is the ideal time to leave, when everything is shipshape."

"Everything is not shipshape," he said softly. "Look at what happened to your sister." He paused. "Before *he* came to my island, I had every prisoner under my control, every man jack of them. But he brought a contagion to the island, and now this place isn't mine anymore. It's slipping through my fingers. I cannot rest until I've purged the contagion. I cannot leave until then."

The sound of obsession was in his voice, and it chilled me. "How will you know when you've purged the contagion?"

"I will know," he said flatly.

He would never leave. That was the long and the short of it.

I sat at my sewing that night, watching Emily read her work aloud, but I did not hear one word she said. Thoughts of Father filled my head. He didn't seem to care if he dashed his career, his life, and his family all to pieces on the rocks of Coldwater. His stubbornness and pride would not allow him to make a strategic retreat. This was more than just an illness; it was a kind of mania. *Paralysis of the will,* he had called it. As if the power of his will alone had held everything in balance here, and not the military apparatus of guns, the lash, and the noose. Had he actually believed he was omnipotent?

Twice now I had begged him to take us away from Coldwater, and both times he had refused. Admittedly the first time I had been thinking mostly of myself. But now I was thinking of him, only of him. Father was ill; he needed to be removed from the pernicious atmosphere of the island as quickly as possible.

I got up and shut the door so the sound wouldn't travel down to Father's study, then planted myself at the table. "We need to have a talk about Father," I said.

Anne and Emily looked up at me, surprised, like a pair of foxes interrupted at dinner. "What about him?" asked Emily, not bothering to disguise her hostility.

"He's not well," I said.

"We know," said Emily.

"You do?"

"He's been behaving like a lunatic for weeks," Emily said shortly. "Have you only just noticed?"

I ignored this. "He's gone into a decline. We have to try and convince him it's time for him to leave."

"Why?"

"Because something terrible may happen if we don't."

"Like?"

Emily's recalcitrant attitude was starting to get on my nerves. "Like an uprising, or a mutiny. If we can't convince Father to leave voluntarily, I shouldn't be at all surprised if the officers wrote to the governor and had him dismissed."

"I think we should let them," snapped Emily. "He deserves to be dismissed for what he's done."

"And then what happens to us?"

"I suppose then we'll have to go back to London. Wasn't that the plan, Charlotte?"

I looked at her, exasperated. "We've got to do something to help Father."

"Let Father save himself," said Emily.

"How can you be so unfeeling?" I cried.

"I obviously get it from him," Emily said. "He doesn't seem to care how much suffering he inflicts upon me. I am worn out, Charlotte, and I don't care how he feels."

"You're not going to help me?"

"No, I'm not," said Emily.

"Anne?"

"I don't see what we can do," Anne said. "He never listens to us. The only one who can convince him to leave is you."

I glared at the pair of them, filled with contempt. "You're like Goneril and Regan. I'm ashamed of you both."

Shaking with anger, I stalked out.

Now what am I going to do? I thought.

For days I brooded. No course of action suggested itself to me. And then one morning I happened to look out the window and saw Mr. Fry in the distance, supervising a working party, and my own words came back to me: *I shouldn't be at all surprised if the officers wrote to the governor and had him dismissed.*

Mr. Fry had been Father's second-in-command for several years. He was, I guessed, about forty, with a massive square head set on an equally square and massive frame. He was known for his prodigious feats of strength, and sometimes, at dinner, he could be convinced to demonstrate his powers by lifting up chairs containing several junior officers at once. He did not possess, as far as I was aware, a sense of humour. He was a tough, stern, dour, hardworking career officer who despised convicts and hated laxity of any sort, and beneath his flinty exterior raged an all-consuming lust for power. He wanted my father's job more than life itself.

I intercepted him as he made for the officers' mess.

"Mr. Fry," I said, "I have come to seek your advice."

It was the first time I had ever sought him out. He looked, to say the least, surprised. "My advice? On what?"

"My father's illness."

His eyes lit with cunning, and he smiled a smile that showed all his teeth.

"You are aware, of course," I said, endeavouring to sound like the naïve young lady he no doubt thought I was, "that my father is ill."

"I am very well aware of it, Miss Wolf," he replied. "Most regrettable. Is he any better?"

"Quite the contrary," I sighed, "I believe he is worse."

"I am sorry to hear that," said Mr. Fry, attempting to arrange his features in an expression of sympathy.

"As you can imagine, I am very worried about him."

"As we all are, Miss Wolf."

"I am eager to determine what the best course of action would be to ensure his speedy recovery. I am inexperienced in these matters and am unsure how to proceed."

"Well, in my opinion, the Captain should certainly begin by consulting a physician. Or several physicians. So that they can determine what's wrong with him."

"Yes, I thought so too," I said brightly.

"And then he should follow whatever course of action the physicians recommend. In my opinion—and of course I am not a medical man—they are likely to recommend a rest cure."

"Do you think so?"

"I am almost sure of it. This is a very arduous post. The nature of the work here is no doubt contributing to the length and severity of the Captain's illness."

"It is a very arduous post, this one, isn't it?"

"Very arduous."

"Then I see we are in agreement. I, too, feel that Father would be best to leave the island as soon as possible."

Mr. Fry's cunning smile appeared again, exposing his teeth all the way back to the molars.

"Unfortunately, Father does not agree."

The smile abruptly faded.

"You have discussed it with the Captain?" Mr. Fry asked sharply.

"Of course," I said, gazing up at him guilelessly.

"And he has expressed a reluctance to leave the island and seek medical help?"

"He categorically refused. You see, he doesn't believe that there's anything wrong with him. Nothing to speak of, anyway. He is really quite immovable on the subject."

Mr. Fry frowned. "If he doesn't think there's anything wrong with him, why is he leaving me to run the prison?"

I gave Mr. Fry a reproachful look. "I didn't say his position made sense."

Mr. Fry's eyes narrowed. "So the Captain isn't making sense?"

"I wouldn't put it like that," I said delicately.

"How would you put it?"

I took a deep breath. "Father has always obeyed the dictates of his conscience and done his duty. He believes it is his duty to remain on Coldwater and carry out his work as best he can, whatever the cost may be to his own health and well-being. It is my opinion that Father is letting his sense of duty blind him to what is necessary."

Mr. Fry eyed me thoughtfully. "And you were hoping I might be able to help you . . . see about getting him removed?"

I did not wish to seem too eager. "Father has given many years of exemplary service here on Coldwater. I believe he has earned the right to a dignified retirement. He is too aware of his duty to seek it on his own behalf. But I believe that we who love him have a duty too, and that is to save him from himself." Dizzy with my own rhetoric, I was starting to choke with emotion.

Mr. Fry shifted uneasily from one foot to the other. "Quite right, Miss Wolf. Quite right."

"I would hate to see my father removed from his post," I continued. "That would be unconscionable, given his magnificent record of service. But if it could be done quietly, and privately, I feel that it may be possible to convince him to go. I do not see any easy way of removing him otherwise."

Mr. Fry took the warning. "No one wants to see him removed from his post. That is the last thing anyone wants. But if the Captain's health is at stake, I don't see that we have any alternative but to intervene."

I smiled at Mr. Fry. "Then I can leave it in your hands?"

He bared his teeth at me once more. "I will see what I can do."

Four

Suspicion

Letter, 2nd October 1847

Dear Captain Wolf,

It has been brought to His Excellency's attention that you have been suffering for some weeks now from a persistent illness which has prevented you from performing your duties. His Excellency was most surprised that you did not see fit to inform him of your illness. If you are too ill to write, please send word immediately, and we will make arrangements for someone to be sent out to assist you.

His Excellency eagerly awaits your reply.

Yours sincerely,

J. P. Simpson for

His Excellency Governor Fitzroy

Charlotte

The effect of this letter upon Father was both immediate and dramatic. He came charging into the kitchen—the first time he had ventured there in weeks—and was so excited that he did not even notice that the table was covered in contraband writing materials.

"I knew it," he said. "There is a plot afoot."

I froze. We were discovered. I was undone.

"What do you mean, Father?" piped Anne.

"My own men are trying to undermine me."

My life was over. Emily's crime was nothing compared to mine. He would kill me for sure.

"How do you know?" Emily drawled. Anne shot her a warning look, but Father didn't seem to notice.

"I've been opening their mail."

Emily made a noise of protest. I could scarcely breathe. Was this the moment he would turn on me?

Father turned to Emily haughtily. "I have a right to open any mail coming in or out of this prison if I believe the security of the prison is at risk. I think a mutiny counts as a risk to security, don't you?"

Emily shrugged.

Father started pacing, gesticulating with one long index finger. It was not a mannerism I had ever seen in him before. "But I knew anyway. I have a sixth sense about this sort of thing. When mutiny's in the air you can smell it. I've been here too long not to know how to read the signs. They think they can get rid of me, but they can't. This is my island, my prison, my system. I built it. I won't let them take it away from me."

Gradually it was dawning on me that Father knew nothing of my part in the affair. I felt a queasy sense of relief.

"Treachery," he continued, "is the one thing I can't abide. It makes a mockery of everything we're trying to do here. This colony must live by the rule of law, and that means building a society with structures that everyone can respect. If people start ignoring chains of command and acting for themselves, we'll end up with chaos. Some may see our colony as nothing more than a sinkhole, a pit in which to throw away England's human waste. But we have a chance to be so much more than that. We can be the purifying crucible where we burn off the convict taint. But first we must root out selfishness, and lawlessness, and anarchy. Otherwise all is lost."

He went into a reverie. He seemed to have forgotten that we were there.

"What do you intend to do, Father?" asked Anne, reminding him of where he was.

"I intend to stop them, of course," Father said, with a gleeful smile. "But I must not rush things. They don't know that I'm onto them. I shall bide my time, and see what they do next."

Consumed with plots and plans, he turned and disappeared back into his study, slamming the door.

Journal, 5th October

At last I feel the black clouds lifting from my head! I have been lost at sea for so many weeks, uncertain of my path, not sure how to direct my energies. Everything seemed so futile, but now, at last, I know what it is I must do. My island is under attack. I must defend it to the best of my ability. They will not destroy me. This island's mine, and they will not take it from me.

Charlotte

Father's malaise vanished as if by magic, only to be replaced by a horrible energy, full of volatility and suspicion. The cruel man I had glimpsed as he raged and stormed and burnt my sisters' papers seemed to have taken over, displacing the gentle and disciplined man I knew. The new Father was disdainful and haughty and endlessly suspicious, given to listening at doors and demanding to know what we were talking about.

I had always known, although I had never really given it much thought, that we, and Father in particular, had been surrounded by plots since the moment we set foot on the island. Father lived in an atmosphere of suspense at all times, wondering when the next attempt might be made on his life. But despite the terrors ranged outside our cottage walls, we had somehow contrived to maintain an illusion of tranquillity in our family life. Now, it was as if the walls between Father's professional life and his personal life had broken down. The threat, which had always been outside, had somehow got inside; suddenly *we* were the threat. Suspicion was everywhere; it seeped from the walls and peeped in the windows. It tapped inside the walls at night and broke open the embers in the grate. It was the stuff we breathed; it hung about us like a sickening miasma.

Now that I was living in the daily searchlight of my father's suspicion I began to realise what I had never realised before; that his long tenure on this island had given rein to an authoritarian streak in his nature, so that it expanded into a positive mania. He had built a world for himself on Coldwater. It was his Gondal, only it was real; he set its boundaries, its rules and conditions. Its population were his characters, and he controlled their actions through a multitude of different means, both overt and covert. He had thought we, too, were under his control; the discovery that we were not came as an enormous shock to him, because suddenly he was forced to realise that we were not part of his story anymore; we were trying to write our own. It had not been the fact of Emily's affair that Father objected to; it was that it had been conducted on the margins, in secret. What the rest of us saw as an unfortunate and inadvisable affair of the heart, Father saw as a monstrous challenge to his authority, an attempt to dethrone him in the very heart of his kingdom. The very fabric of the universe which he himself had created had come apart at the seams, and he had never even seen it coming.

And now that he had uncovered a plot among his officers it was as if all his worst nightmares were coming true. His trusted valet and his beloved daughters had betrayed him; of course, it naturally followed that his officers would betray him too. All the world was a nest of traitors and spies, all bent on his destruction. But Father was not crushed by this—far from it! The discovery that *everyone* was against him seemed to set him free, releasing in him a boundless stream of pure energy as he rose to the challenge. I had not seen Father so excited, so full of enthusiasm and exuberance, in years. He was fizzing, crackling, glowing, so that I almost feared to get too close in case he burnt me.

There could no longer be any doubt. Father was quite mad.

The ring in the wall

Anne

October came, bringing rain and storms, and much to her frustration, Anne found herself confined indoors for days on end. On the days when she could get away, the Diver did not come; and so she began to fear that some accident had befallen him, or he had gone away, and would never be coming back. The thought that she might never see him again distressed her deeply, for she had come to look on the stolen moments she spent with him as the only bright point in her days. What his feelings on the subject were she could not tell, for she was very fearful that perhaps, after all, he was merely trifling with her. She did not dare to trust him too much; and as days turned into weeks and she did not see him, her thoughts began to take on a darker hue. It had occurred to her that, however big the town across the bay might be (and it did not look particularly large glimpsed from Coldwater), it was somewhat unlikely that a purveyor of seafood would have sufficient custom among that transient population to make a decent living. While the seafood itself could not be denied, Anne suspected that there was probably some other reason for the

Diver's frequent visits to Coldwater. She would like to hope he was there to see her, but she doubted very much whether this was the case.

But at last the weather turned, and a belated spring arrived. The winds that roared and buffeted across the island lost their savage edge, becoming soft and sweet and mild; there was a new warmth that made Anne prickle to throw off her heavy winter garments and run around in the open air, feeling the new grass beneath her feet, and the sun, which grew warmer and richer every day, on her skin. The sky opened out from a leaden grey into an ever more lustrous blue, and the days grew longer and longer. In spite of herself, Anne felt her spirits lift, even though nothing at home had changed—Charlotte was still sulking, Emily was utterly distracted, immersed in a world of her own making, while Father ... well, who knew what was wrong with Father? But outside, the birds were hurling themselves gleefully into the mating season, and the trees were full of possums which barked and howled and fought in the night, and the air was scented with sticky sap as the trees shook out their leaves, as the return of the sun woke everything from the long, miserable, wind-lashed torpor of winter.

And so it was in a spirit of renewed optimism that Anne took to climbing down the rocks each day and waiting to see if the Diver would reappear; but she was not so giddy with the arrival of spring that she would welcome him with open arms, and forget all the questions which had occurred to her while the weather was still bleak. She was sure he had been less than truthful with her, and she was determined to get certain matters straight.

But when she actually laid eyes on him again, after so many weeks of separation, her resolve almost died, for his eyes were so blue and his smile so wide despite the goose bumps all over his arms, that her heart fluttered madly in her chest, and he looked so pleased to see her, and she was so pleased to see him, that she could hardly bring herself to risk affronting him by questioning him too closely. But she had to know the truth.

"Tell me," she said, "what are you really doing here?"

He blinked. The question had come quite unexpectedly. "I come here to fish. I told you that."

"Are there no fish left on the mainland?" asked Anne, keeping her tone polite, but letting him know she would not be lied to. "Is that why you have to swim such large distances at such personal risk? Or is there another reason?"

The smile on his face was frozen in place as he racked his brains for an answer. She could see the thoughts chasing one another across his face as he tried to decide whether to keep lying, come up with a new lie, or tell the truth.

"There is another reason," he said, finally.

"Well?"

"I have a brother here."

This was unexpected.

"I've been keeping an eye on him. If I could come over here openly and honestly I would, but it's not allowed, the prisoners here can't have visitors. So I have to sneak in."

It did not occur to Anne to doubt him. And in spite of herself, she was touched. It was very easy to forget that all those much-maligned men her father kept locked up all came from somewhere, and had families who wondered where they were, and how they fared.

"What happened?" she asked.

The Diver hesitated, then took her arm and led her to a slightly more secluded spot, where he could warm up out of the wind. They sat down together in the lee of the rock, and after a moment, the Diver began.

"I was only a lad when I first went to sea," he said. "We were poor. There wasn't any work back home. It was the best I could get, and I'll admit, I thought it would be a fine adventure. My brother wanted to come away with me—Robert, his name is—but he was too young, and I wouldn't let him come. Told him to stay home and mind his ma and I'd be home again when I'd made my fortune.

"I was away for about five years, what with one thing and another, and I went to all sorts of places, and when I finally found myself back at Southampton, my first thought was to make my way home and see how everyone was doing. But imagine my surprise: before I'd even had a chance to leave the docks, I spied my own brother, chained up, going aboard a ship bound for Botany Bay. He was very much changed. When I last saw him he was a happy, healthy, bonny boy; now he was skinny and sick, half-grown and rough-looking. He said our mother was dead, and one of our sisters too—the others were in service, or married—our father was long gone—and he told me he'd fallen into bad company, and been pinched for swiping a gentleman's handkerchief. It was very hard to hear that my mother and sister were dead, for I hadn't known a thing about it and had thought them all to be just as happy and healthy as I left 'em. But it was hardest of all to think that if I'd let my brother sign on with me all those years ago I might have kept him safe, and he wouldn't be in such a pickle now. So I signed on to the ship which was to be carrying him to Botany Bay, so that I could keep an eye out for him, and maybe make things a little easier for him, if I could."

The Diver stopped for a moment, gathering his thoughts. "He survived the passage alright. We had a good ship's surgeon on board who saw to it that the convicts were well looked after. When we reached Sydney I left my ship—New South Wales was as good a place as any for making my fortune, I thought—and planned to stick by my brother, wherever he might go. He was lucky at first. He was assigned to a good master, who gave them enough to eat and didn't treat them too harshly. His sentence was seven years, and everyone said if he didn't muck up he could expect to have his ticket-of-leave in four. And once he had that, he could start over—clean slate. He'd be ready to start making something of himself, and what better place to do it than here? There are far more opportunities for a working lad here than there ever were back home.

"I took a job nearby so I might be able to visit him whenever his master allowed, and for a time we did very well. But then I got restless, and decided the job I had didn't suit—I wasn't accustomed to landlubbers' work—and nothing else thereabouts seemed to suit me either, so when I was offered a place on a whaling boat, I decided to take it. Robbie seemed to be doing well where he was, and he urged me to go, so I went.

"There's good money to be made from whaling. We'd made a lot of plans, you see, about what we'd do when he got his ticket-of-leave, but they all took money, and neither of us had much of that, so I thought I'd set to and earn as much as I could while I waited for him. Anyway, I was away for a season, and made myself a tidy sum, but when I came back to see how he was getting on, Robbie was gone.

"They told me he'd stolen a pig from his master and sold it, keeping the money for himself. He swears it wasn't him that took it, one of the others fitted him up, but the judge didn't believe him. And so they sent him here.

"You wouldn't believe the trouble it caused me to find out where he was. Everybody seemed very suspicious of me and were loath to tell me anything about where he'd been sent. But eventually someone took pity on me and told me where he was to be found. 'Not that it'll do you any good,' the fellow told me, 'for you can't visit him where he's gone. Best forget all about him.' But I couldn't do that, so I followed him here.

"It's not easy, working out how to break into a prison. There's a lot to work out—how to get across the bay without being spotted, where's the best place to land without being shot or smashed on the rocks, and once I'd made it, there was the question of how to find Robbie and get word to him without either of us getting into trouble. I had a stroke of luck early on, when I found him working in the quarry. He wasn't far from the water's edge, and it was easy enough for him to sneak away—as if to make a call of nature, if you take my meaning—and at last we had a chance to speak.

"He was in a dreadful way. He'd only been here four months, but already he looked like an old man, and he's only young—just turned twenty. He's had two hundred cuts since he came here—cuts of the lash, I mean. And the work's terrible hard. They treat them like slaves, and there's never enough to eat, and what food there is gets taken by the stone men, who share it out depending on who's in favour this week."

"Stone men?"

"It means a hard man, someone who'll kill you soon as look at you and care nothing for the consequences. Someone who doesn't feel hurt or pain, or anything, and will laugh as you hold a torch against his ribs, and ask you to make it hotter."

Anne was appalled—she could not even imagine a world where such traits were considered virtues.

"That's how it works, you see: there are these gangs, and you have to be protected by one, or you're for it. Loyalty, that's what it's about. Loyalty and terror. I'd heard about what went on in these places—the torment of the damned—but from what Robbie's told me, it's much, much worse than people say. I can't mention some of the things he said in front of a lady like you, but it's enough to break your heart."

He was silent for a moment, looking out to sea, collecting himself. "Robert was never a bad lad," he continued, "and I think he would've done his time fair and square and waited for his ticket-of-leave if he hadn't been done wrong. But now I don't know what's to become of him. Whenever I see him he's more downcast, more desperate, more eager to escape."

"There's never been an escape in all the time Father's been here," Anne said, without thinking. Father was very proud of his unblemished record, and never hesitated to remind them of it.

"Doesn't mean they can't think about it," said the Diver. "Escape is the only thing that gives them hope—escape, or death."

Now that he had brought up the subject himself, Anne felt she could ask him the obvious question.

"And do you intend to help him escape?"

The Diver was silent, gazing at her. "After all I've just told you I'd be a pretty poor brother if I left him here to rot, wouldn't I?"

Anne felt the sting of tears in her eyes, as disappointment wrestled with fear in her heart. The Diver, watching her, seemed to read the confusion in her eyes.

"Come with me," he said, getting to his feet and holding out a hand to her. "There's something I need to show you."

"Where?" asked Anne warily.

"Along the rocks."

"Tell me what it is first."

"No. You need to see it for yourself."

Anne hesitated, suddenly aware that she did not, after all, know him very well. Where was he taking her? Could he possibly mean her harm? He had taken a great risk in revealing his true intentions to her. What if he pushed her off the rocks into the water? She would surely drown. But she wanted to believe she could trust him. And besides, she was curious.

So she took his hand—his skin was sticky with salt—and allowed him to assist her along the rocks. They scrambled across the rocks and around a headland.

"There," said the Diver, and pointed.

Before them was a cave in the rock, streaked black with weed. Looking up, she noticed what appeared to be a path winding down from the top of the cliff, marked here and there with some ragged ribbons of red cloth. Curious, thought Anne, she had never noticed the path before. She thought she knew her island better than that.

"It's a cave," she said. An idea struck her. "You're a smuggler?"

He laughed. "No. Come on."

He led the way. The final approach to the cave was a difficult one—she watched with dismay as he vaulted across a gap more than a yard wide between two rocks. Deep green water boiled beneath.

Looking back at her from the other side, he called out to her encouragingly. "Come on, you can do it. I'll catch you."

Anne measured the distance doubtfully. She thought she could probably make it, but there was also a chance she might fall into the water and get sucked out to sea. She took a deep breath, trying to steady her nerves, and readied herself to jump.

"You might want to hitch those up," the Diver called, indicating her skirts. Anne blushed at the suggestion, but she could see he had a point.

"Turn your back," she called.

"No. I might need to catch you," he called back.

Reluctantly, she decided she would have to forgo decency, and, conscious of his gaze, she hitched her skirts up out of harm's way. With the breeze caressing her stockings she felt brazen and bold and deliciously wicked.

"Now jump!" called the Diver. "Don't worry. I'll catch you if you fall."

Anne clamped down on her fears, balanced for a moment on the balls of her feet, then leapt with all her might across the gap. She barely had time to feel frightened before she found herself landing squarely on the other side.

"Well done," he said, grinning at her, as she hastily untucked her skirts and let them cover her legs once again.

"Well, let's get on," she said, briskly, filled with a contrary mixture of embarrassment and excitement.

They clambered across to the mouth of the cave. It smelt dankly of trapped seawater, weed, and rotting marine life. The tide was low, but at high tide, the cave clearly filled with water.

"Well?" she said.

"Come and look at this."

He led her to the back of the cave, and showed her an iron ring bolted to the wall. The sound of the surf clanged in the confined space.

"What is it?" she asked. "A mooring for boats?"

"There's no water in here for a boat," he observed neutrally.

"There is when the tide's up."

"That ring'd be underwater when the tide came up."

Anne frowned, perplexed. "Well, what's it for then?"

"Took me a while to work that out myself," the Diver said. "Then one day I happened to see two soldiers coming down that path from the top of the cliff. They had a convict with them, in chains. The three of them came in here, and then the two soldiers came out and climbed back up the cliff again, leaving the convict behind."

"They left him here?"

"Chained to this ring."

Anne's skin prickled with claustrophobic terror at the thought of being confined in this dank, stinking place. Suddenly the weight of the cliff above her head seemed overwhelmingly oppressive.

"Once they were gone I crept in and spoke to the fellow. He said he'd been reported for insolence and this was his punishment."

Suddenly it dawned on Anne. "But this cave is underwater at high tide."

"So it is," said the Diver grimly.

"But surely—surely they wouldn't put a man in here to drown, would they?" The horror of it crawled into her head and would not go away—a helpless man, chained to a rock, watching as the waves washed in and out of the mouth of the cave, gradually getting closer and closer to his feet as the tide rose, the water rolling higher and higher, the remorseless push and pull of the waves sucking at his body, battering him against the rocks, as he tried to hold his head above the water. . . .

"There's a little ledge up there," the Diver said, breaking in on her thoughts. "I helped him climb up. I told him if he held on, and kept his head, he'd probably be alright."

"And was he?" Anne breathed.

"I don't know. When I came back there was no sign of him."

Anne was silent for a moment, engulfed with horror. She could not understand why someone would do such a thing, why such things were allowed to go on, why no one had stopped it, or why she was now being confronted with this excessive cruelty. "Why are you showing me this?" she asked angrily.

"I wanted you to understand what kind of a place this really is," he said. "The other prisoners aren't the worst of it—not by half. The real monsters are the ones who run the place."

In spite of herself, Anne's temper kindled. Didn't the Diver realise he was maligning her father, and all the men he commanded, men she knew personally and had eaten dinner with? They were not the most refined of men, and they were rather boorish and grasping, certainly, but to call them monsters was simply outrageous.

"I suppose you think there shouldn't be prisons like this," Anne said.

Hearing the note of criticism in her voice, the Diver's face hardened. "If a man commits a crime, he should be punished for it, that's only fair. But he shouldn't be locked in a cave full of water until he's half dead of fright. He shouldn't have the back ripped off him by the cat for nothing at all. He shouldn't be used for target practice by soldiers with nothing to do."

"I don't believe that such things go on here."

"I've seen it with my own eyes."

"You don't know what happened to that man. They might have come and let him out before the water came up."

"They didn't."

"But I'm sure this was just an isolated incident."

"That ring looks like it's been there a while."

"That doesn't mean they use it." Anne could feel the ground slipping from beneath her feet. "I know that my father runs a tight ship—"

"A tight ship? Do you know how many prisoners died here last year?"

Anne was silent.

"They're buried all over the cliffs up there. Unmarked graves."

"My father is not a cruel man. He's strict, but he's fair."

"They call him Cerberus. The three-headed dog who guards the gates of hell."

"I didn't realise you were so well educated," she said nastily, without thinking. His face darkened.

"I know you don't want to think ill of your father," he said, "but I'll tell you something, you don't know the half of what goes on here. Ask him about this cave and see what he says. Go on. Ask him."

"I will," snapped Anne, "and when he finds out what's been going on here he'll put a stop to it."

"Well, we'll just see, won't we," the Diver snapped back.

Upset and angry, Anne turned and hurried out of the cave into the sunlight. But once she was out on the rocks, she was no longer sure of exactly which way they had come. Desperate to get away from the Diver, she went weaving through the rocks, looking for the place where they had jumped across. Finally she came to what looked like the same channel. If anything, the crossing looked more difficult from this side, but she refused to let that stop her. Not willing to give him the satisfaction of peeking at her ankles a second time, she left her skirts where they were, and jumped.

But she had not calculated for the angle of the rock she was landing on. It sloped down towards the water, and she had landed with one foot on her skirts. Off balance and hobbled, she slipped, scrabbled, and then fell, skinning her hands, banging and bruising her knee and her ribs as she hit the rock on the way down. Shocked, she did not have time to catch herself. Suddenly she was immersed.

Cold water came at her in waves—instantly as it soaked through her stockings, more slowly as it soaked through her bodice. She kicked and floundered, trapped in a cocoon of clothes that grew heavier and more restrictive with every moment that passed. The shock of the cold drove the breath from her body and a wave smacked her in the face, so that her eyes and nose stung with the salt and her mouth filled with water. The surf dragged her several yards out to sea, then rushed in and dashed her against a rock, and Anne had the sudden thought that she was mortal, she might die, she might die right here. The immediacy and terror of this discovery almost made her sob. Frantically she clawed at the rocks around her, struggling to keep her head above the water, desperate for a handhold, but the rocks were slick with seaweed and her fingers slithered across them uselessly.

Then she felt a pressure on the back of her dress. The Diver was lying flat on the rock above, arm outstretched, and was attempting to pull her in.

"Grab hold," he gasped. "I'll try and pull you up, but you're going to have to help me."

His assistance gave her a new burst of desperate strength. The tide was trying to tug her out to sea once more, but she kicked and floundered, reaching up to grab at the rock. She found a dry handhold, and kicked frantically with her legs in an effort to propel herself upwards. One foot found some purchase on the rock, and she tried to lever herself up. But the rock was slippery, and she slipped back down into the water. She started to go under, but the Diver still had a hand on her.

"I'll count to three," said the Diver, "and when I get to three, you push and I'll pull. One—two—three!"

And with a great concerted effort, she pushed and he hauled, and the tide rushed back in and lifted her up, and somehow she got herself far enough out of the water so that he could pull her all the way out. For several moments she lay, exhausted and shocked, on the rock, catching her breath, aware that the Diver, too, was gasping for breath beside her. The wind blew over her skin, chilling her to the bone. For a moment, neither of them spoke.

"Thank you," Anne said finally.

"Couldn't leave you to drown," the Diver replied.

"You must be dedicated to go into that water voluntarily," she said. "It really is freezing."

Another silence fell.

"I suppose you'll have to tell your father about me," the Diver said, feigning indifference.

Anne hesitated. "I don't have to," she said. "I could tell him I found the cave all by myself."

"I'd be much obliged," he said stiffly.

"After all, if Father ever found out I'd been meeting you, he'd never let me out again."

The Diver smiled slightly.

"Whatever happens," Anne said, aware that what she was about to say was treasonous, "I'd hate to think I was never going to see you again."

He smiled at last. "No fear of that. I'm like a bad penny. Keep turning up. You'd better get home before you catch your death."

She arrived home soaked and shivering.

"What happened?" gasped Emily when she saw her.

"I fell in the water."

"But how?"

"I was jumping between two rocks and I missed my footing and fell in."

"But *why* were you jumping between two rocks?"

"I went to look at something."

"What?"

"Does it matter?"

"Why won't you tell me what happened?"

"I did tell you."

"No you didn't. There's something you're leaving out."

"There's not."

Emily drew in a deep exasperated breath and let it out again. "Alright. What was it you went to look at?"

"A cave."

"And what was in the cave?" asked Emily sarcastically. "A pirate's treasure?"

Anne wondered whether she should tell Emily what she had seen, and the Diver's explanation for it. She was reluctant to do it, for she knew it would upset her sister, and possibly bring on another attack. But worse than that, it would give her another reason to hate Father. And although Anne could not yet bring herself to believe that Father knew anything of this, she knew instinctively that Emily would seize on this information. And her resentment, already festering, would grow.

But she needed to talk over the events of the afternoon with someone, and Emily was the one she had always confided in. Her brush with death had left her profoundly shaken, for she had never quite understood, on a visceral level, that she herself would die, until that moment when she discovered that her little body was suddenly in the grip of something powerful and indifferent which could easily consume her, and that there was nothing at all she could do about it. There was no real way to discuss how she was feeling without explaining about the Diver, but Emily did not know about him yet. Perhaps the time had come, she thought.

"Let me get into some dry things," Anne said, to postpone the conversation a little longer. For she was not exactly sure how to tell Emily that she had been secretly meeting a man on the beach for weeks and had not said a word.

They retired to the bedroom, and Anne pulled off her wet clothes and got into her warmest dress and wrapped herself in a shawl. But still the shivering would not subside. Her feet were purple and felt twice their normal size, numb with cold.

"Get into bed and warm up," Emily suggested. Anne did as she was told, and Emily perched beside her, wielding a comb on her wet, salty, tangled hair. "You might want to wash it later," she suggested as the comb immediately snarled in tangles.

Anne tucked her freezing feet up beneath her. "There is something I didn't tell you," she began.

This came as no surprise to Emily.

"I met someone down by the water."

"Who?"

"He's called the Diver."

"That's a name?"

"He's a kind of fisherman, I suppose."

"A fisherman? What was he doing on Coldwater, was he lost?"

"Oh no." Anne paused. "It wasn't the first time I've seen him there."

Emily's eyes, which were already wide, widened further. "I knew you'd been sneaking out to see someone. I thought it must be an officer."

"You knew?"

"Well, I guessed it must be something like that."

"And you didn't say anything?"

"I didn't want to pry. I knew you'd tell me eventually." Emily gave her a wry, dark-eyed look. "So tell me about him—what's he like? Is he handsome?"

Anne picked at her fingernails. "I don't know exactly. I think he is. You might not agree."

"And he's a fisherman?"

"Yes."

Something stirred behind Emily's eyes. "So he has a boat then?"

"He swims across."

"What? You can't be serious."

"It's true. I was down by Nature's Eye one day and he climbed up out of the water right in front of me."

"Really?" Emily was very impressed with the picture she saw in her mind's eye. "Are you sure he's real? He's not some kind of water spirit trying to snatch you away?"

"He's real enough."

"I'm shocked," Emily crowed, not sounding shocked at all. "What a hussy you are! But I can't believe you've kept it a secret for so long."

Anne shrugged.

"So what happened today?"

"We went to look at a cave. Then afterward we had a row, and I fell into the water. If he hadn't been there I probably would have drowned."

Emily's look grew serious. "He saved your life?"

"Yes." Anne frowned. "It is a very singular thing to know that you are about to die. It's very lonely."

Emily reached for Anne's hand and squeezed it. "You didn't die," she said. "You're safe here with me, and I'm very glad of it." She planted a kiss on Anne's hair, and then resumed her combing.

"We argued," Anne continued, pushing aside the residual remnants of her fear, "because I asked him the real reason he came to the island so often. Because I didn't believe it was really to catch crabs or oysters. It turns out he has a brother here."

Emily raised an eyebrow, interested.

"He showed me a cave. He said they take prisoners there and chain them up while the tide comes in."

Emily's hand and the comb stopped moving. "I don't understand."

"The cave's underwater at high tide—or at least partially. I think."

"They drown prisoners?" asked Emily sharply.

"I hope they only do it to frighten them."

"I hope it's a damned lie," Emily said savagely. "What did this fellow mean by it? Why would he tell you something like that?"

"So I'd understand why he has to help his brother escape."

Emily stopped and looked at her, and Anne knew that her thoughts had jumped from the Diver's brother to another prisoner, who had also been badly treated, and who also dreamed of escape. "But I don't believe it's true," Anne said hastily. "Father isn't cruel. He's an enlightened man. He wants to reform the men."

"The men who he thinks are worth reforming. The rest he couldn't care less about."

"Father wouldn't treat anyone like that," Anne insisted. "I'm sure the problem is the men. There are one or two rotten apples, that's all. Once they've been found, they can be thrown out."

"You know what they say about rotten apples spoiling the whole barrel. It may be too late," Emily said wryly. "So what are you going to do?"

"I must speak to Father about the cave."

"You're not going to tell him about your Diver, are you?"

"Certainly not. But I have to ask about the cave. I want to see how he reacts. I want to know if he knows about it. If he does—" Anne broke off.

"If he does?" Emily prompted.

"I've got some serious thinking to do," said Anne.

That night she went to see Father in his study. The door was ajar, and she stood for a moment in the doorway, watching him. He was sitting quietly in his big leather chair, reading by the light of a candle. He had spectacles perched on his nose, and Anne was struck by how grey his hair was getting. He suddenly became aware of her, and whipped the glasses off his nose. Anne was touched by the vulnerability of the gesture as she took a step into the room.

"Forgive me, Father," she said, "I hope I'm not disturbing you."

"Not at all," he said. "Come in."

He offered her a seat on the settle, and she perched there, wondering how to begin.

"To what do I owe the pleasure?" Father queried.

As she gazed at him—her own dear father—Anne longed more than anything to be able to run away and forget those questions she had to ask. But she could not forget; the questions had to be asked. Even though, as she now fatalistically expected, they would ruin everything. Father had been so suspicious lately.

"I saw a curious thing on my walk today," she began, feeling like Judas approaching Gethsemane. "I came upon a cave at the foot of the cliff, just on the waterline."

Father went very still, but his look did not betray the slightest quiver of emotion. "A cave?"

"Do you know it? It's not far from Nature's Eye."

"I believe I know where it is," he said evenly.

"I went inside, for curiosity's sake." She tried a light laugh. It came out sounding like a hysterical giggle. "Looking for pirate's treasure."

He smiled warily back.

"And I found an iron ring bolted to the wall. Now here's an odd thing, I thought. What could this possibly have been used for?"

"An iron ring?"

"Yes. Do you have any idea what it might have been put there for?"

"None at all," Father said.

"But it must have been put there by someone. The island was uninhabited before the prison was built, was it not?"

"I believe so."

"So it must have been put there by your predecessors. Or perhaps one of the men?"

"I can only imagine it must have been," Father said blandly.

"Do you have any idea who it would have been?"

"I'm sorry, my dear, but I don't."

Unsure what to do next, Anne fell silent. A vague feeling of dread was fingering her spine. Were they really the signs of guilt she read in her father's bearing? She knew he prided himself on always knowing when he was being lied to, but Anne did not share his talent.

"I'm a little concerned to hear you've been wandering around down there by yourself," Father said. "I thought I'd made it quite clear which areas you're permitted to go to."

"You told me I wasn't to go anywhere near the prisoners."

"You're not to go anywhere dangerous," Father corrected gently.

"That leaves me with nowhere to go, Father," Anne tried to joke. "The whole island's dangerous."

"Yes, well, that is a difficulty," Father said. His voice was mild, but there was a glint of steel in his eye.

Aware that the moment for subtlety had passed, Anne decided to ask him directly. "You would never permit a prisoner to be chained up in that cave, would you, Father?"

Father's face was suddenly blank. "No. What would be the point of that?" He studied her. "Who have you been talking to?"

Chilled, Anne tried to look brave. "No one."

"You've never concerned yourself with prison business before. Why start now?"

"I was concerned."

"Were you?"

Father was staring at her with the eyes of a jungle predator. The words of the Diver came into her mind: *They call him Cerberus, the three-headed dog who guards the gates of hell.* . . . And suddenly she could glimpse what others might see when they looked at Father: the military man, the gaoler, with his eight years on Coldwater. No trouble, no escapes. Did it take a monster to control an island full of devils?

"In future, I suggest you choose a more prudent course for your walks," Father said. "I would not want to have to stop you; I know you are very fond of walking. This is not a safe place, my dearest. You should be more careful."

It was a warning—the only one she would get. "Yes, Father. I'm sorry."

"Was there anything else?"

"No."

"Good night then."

Her vision of the other Father, the bloody gaoler, Cerberus, wavered and vanished, and in an instant he was Father again—the man who had tucked her up at night and told her stories and tied her bootlaces—dear Father, bowing his head as he went back to his book, straining his eyes to read the print, and then giving up the pretence and putting his spectacles back on his nose. Anne withdrew, closing the door behind her.

Torn between her desire to believe in him and the insistent feeling that the Diver might be right, Anne went back to the kitchen, where Emily was writing and Charlotte was frowning over a book. Emily raised her eyebrows at her as she entered. Anne just shrugged in reply. If anything, her sense of confusion had increased.

Journal, 7th October

Anne is lost to me. She is in league with my enemies. I do not know who she is plotting with, but evil has entered her heart. Oh, Anne, my sweet girl—

Anne

That night she dreamed about drowning. She was swimming down, down, towards a door on the bottom of the sea, hoping that it would release her from the close grasp of the water into a place of light and safety. But as she got closer she realised that there was nothing down there but another expanse of murkier water, and no way out. She woke up in a panic, to a room bathed in moonlight.

Six

Endings

Charlotte

It had never occurred to me that I might have to take responsibility for the welfare of my sisters while Father was still alive. But I could no longer ignore the evidence of my eyes. Father was lost to reason, lost in a dark tunnel, and every day took him further from us. The moment was close at hand when we would be thrown back on our own resources; and I was terrified, because I was not ready. I had hoped at the very least to have a novel written and ready to go when the moment finally arrived; but I had nothing. I was still wordless; struck dumb like poor Lavinia.

I had waited forlornly for some hint, some stirring of my old fire; but none came. And as the weeks went by, and Father fell deeper and deeper into madness, and still no help arrived from the mainland, I decided that enough was enough. Only the lazy sat and waited for the muse to descend. Inspiration will only come, I told myself, if you invite it in and set a place for it. Father's words had dealt my confidence a dreadful blow, but was I so feeble that I gave up at the first whiff of criticism? I liked to think I was made of sterner stuff than that. So I picked up a pen and forced myself to write.

It is a cold enough start in life to come into the world an orphan, but I believe that mine was colder than most.

How can you come into life an orphan? I wondered, looking at the words I had just written. No one is *born* an orphan, unless their mother dies at the moment of birth, or just before. Visions of babes hacked from the wombs of their deceased mothers rose before me. It was an unprepossessing way to start a novel. I crossed the line out and started again.

There was no possibility of taking a walk that day.

That seemed more promising; more immediate and active. But whatever I had intended to write next was wiped instantly from my mind as I heard footsteps in the hall. Was it Father returning unexpectedly? I hastily sat on my papers and dropped my shawl over the inkwell. But the footsteps kept going; no head appeared round the door. I retrieved my papers and discovered that a corner of my shawl had got into the ink. This was a bad omen, but I refused to heed it, and went back to the page to examine what I had written.

There was no possibility of taking a walk that day.

What had I meant by that? What came next? I had no idea. Inspiration had vanished. So I crossed that out too and started again.

The weather was foul
The weather was exceedingly foul
The wind was
The rain
It was hopeless.

That night, Father called me into his study.

"I have lately been giving some thought to what you asked me," Father said, sounding for all the world like a rational man. "And I'm beginning to think there might be some merit in the idea."

"What idea, Father?" I asked cautiously.

"Returning to town," he said impatiently. "Obviously I cannot go. I have too much work to do. But I feel that it might be best if I sent you girls away."

My jaw dropped. After all this time, could it really be so easy?

"You are nearly thirty-two, and still unmarried. Emily is a hopeless case, of course. No one would have her now. But I think there is still hope for Anne. She is pretty enough to make a good match, even at her age. Don't you think?"

I stammered something approximating agreement.

"But it's you I'm most concerned about, Charlotte," he said. "Do you intend to marry at some time in the future? Or have you quite set your mind against it?"

"I remain open to the possibility," I said.

"I had begun to wonder," Father said. "I accept that Bates was not to your taste. Are you, perhaps, still hoping that Glade will come back for you?"

"No, Father," I said, surprised by the suggestion. The bitter nip of disappointment still tormented me, but I had given up hope long ago.

"It has lately been brought home to me that I know very little about my daughters' lives, your hopes, aspirations, and so forth. I thought perhaps I should take the time to sound you out. Is there anything—or any-one—I should know about?"

"No, Father, there is not."

"You would not lie to me?"

"No, Father. If I had tender feelings for anyone I would tell you. But I don't, I swear."

He nodded, satisfied, at least on that point, and fell silent.

"If that's all—" I began, hoping I might get back to my mending, but Father was not finished.

"Tell me something," he said. "When you turned down Bates, was it because of this book-writing business?"

"No," I said, "I turned him down because I didn't like him."

"But what if you were asked by someone you did like?"

"That hasn't happened yet."

"And do you anticipate that it ever will?"

There was a combative note in Father's voice that worried me.

"I would certainly like to marry some day," I said carefully.

"I am relieved to hear it," Father said. "For a girl should marry, if she possibly can. Marriage is a marvellous institution. I'm sure you would be much happier if you were married."

"I'm not unhappy now, Father." Well, that was an out-and-out lie. But I don't think my lack of a husband was the cause of it.

"I don't think we really come into our own until we experience true love, the mature love of two adults coming together in marriage. I was a boy until I married your mother; her love made a man of me. Marriage and family force you to grow up; you can no longer be selfish when you've got the well-being of others to think about."

Is he calling me selfish? I wondered.

"It was a great sorrow to me that my married life was brought to such an abrupt and early end." He paused, and I noticed his eye travel to the miniature of my mother which he kept on his desk. "You are very like your mother in many ways."

"I thought Anne was the one who resembled her."

"I meant your personality. She had a very eager mind. And she could be very stubborn."

I could have sworn that was a quality I inherited from Father.

"You are very like her. Very like," he mused. "She was taken from me too soon."

I looked at the face of the mother I did not remember. I had never quite been able to make the leap of imagination which would allow me to see the flat, pink face in the miniature as a real woman, a woman who had died younger than I was now. Yet for Father, that tiny image, as conventional and generic as a child's drawing, represented all that was left of the woman he had loved. All, that is, except the three daughters she left behind. Not for the first time, I wondered who she was, this woman who had given me life. And I wondered what it had been like for my father to lose her.

"Did you ever think of marrying again?" I asked.

For a moment I thought he wasn't going to answer. But then he spoke. "For a time I thought perhaps I should find another wife to help me look after you. But in the end I could not bring myself to do it. I loved your mother. I could not replace her so easily, just because it suited me."

And I glimpsed, as I never had before, just how lonely it must have been for him, missing his wife, surrounded by screaming brats, in this rude, brutish, uncivilised place. "Poor Father," I said softly.

"Try to find yourself a husband," Father said. "One who's worthy of you. Forget this business of writing books. It will not make you happy."

"I rather suspect that you're right, Father."

He smiled at me. "I know I'm right."

He seemed so relaxed, so amiable, that I decided to push the issue. "And when," I asked carefully, "had you thought of sending us back to the mainland?"

The smile faded. "Did I say that my mind was made up?" he said coolly. "This is not the sort of thing to be undertaken lightly. There is much to consider. First of all, I would have to find a house for you to live in and then have it made ready. That could take some time."

"Of course, Father."

"And then, one of you would have to remain here on Coldwater with me."

I looked at him, horrified.

"I cannot run the household by myself," he said, looking at me with something like satisfaction. "One of you would have to stay here with me."

Who would he choose? Me, his former favourite, for companionship? Or would he choose Emily, the household genius who knew how everyone liked their meals cooked? Or would he choose Anne, since it was traditionally the youngest child upon whom these responsibilities fell? I dreaded the thought of being left alone on the island with Father; but I was even more alarmed at the thought of what might happen if

Emily was separated from Anne. I felt like the unfortunate farmer in the riddle who must transport a fox, a chicken, and a bag of grain across a river, carrying only two items at a time, and must somehow contrive to prevent the chicken from eating the grain and the fox from eating the chicken. Father was watching me keenly, his teeth slightly bared, and I realised that his suggestion had been a threat, not a promise.

"You are quite right, Father," I said reluctantly. "This is not something we should rush into. When the time is right, we can all return to the mainland, and in the meantime, we are all very cosy here together."

He smiled, very pleased with himself. "To be quite truthful, Charlotte," he said gleefully, "I am in two minds about what I want for you. On the one hand, I believe that you would be happiest with a husband and a family of your own, and I do want what's best for you. You know that, don't you?"

I nodded.

"But on the other hand, I do greatly enjoy your company. I will be very sorry to lose you."

"Every parent must endure that loss eventually," I said.

"I know," he said, "but I think I'll feel the loss of you most keenly."

It should have been a touching thing for him to say, but everything he said now seemed to come freighted with a secret significance, as if he was speaking in a code that only he could understand, and I wondered what he was thinking about as he gave me an unnerving smile.

"But I must bear it," he said finally, without taking his eyes off me, "for I would hate to see you miss out on your great chance at happiness."

The interview was at an end.

Anne

The clock ticked. The coals fell apart in the grate, and Charlotte got up to fuss over the fire. Emily was bent over the page, writing, writing. Anne watched her dispassionately, wondering whether, if she took herself off to bed, Emily would even notice she had gone.

Over the past few weeks, Emily had become so immersed in what she was doing that she scarcely even noticed Anne anymore. Her mind was somewhere else entirely, and ordinary discourse was more than she could manage. As for the exchange of papers and ideas, that had more or less ceased, for Emily no longer needed her opinion, and Anne had stopped writing entirely.

Ever since she met the Diver, the words on the page had begun to seem like a pale substitute for the real thing. She did not quite dare to speak the word "love," even to herself, but she had begun to live for her glimpses of the Diver, frustrating and exhilarating and terrifying as they were. At last she was able to understand the compulsion Emily had felt; she knew why Emily could not possibly break things off with O'Connell, just as she could not stop seeing the Diver. There was a part of herself, a very noisy and compelling part, which had been caged up for a great many years, and every day, at sunrise and sunset, the creature that lay within would howl and yowl and cry to be let out, battering itself against the bars until it was bruised and bloody. This creature was a great, powerful, rangy thing, built for speed and vast open spaces, and to keep it caged up was a barbaric cruelty. But at last the cage door was open, and Anne could not begin to imagine how she might go about putting the creature, which was perhaps the boldest and truest part of herself, back inside the cage. Writing about love had been a kind of soothing balm that they spread upon the wounds, but it could not compare with the real thing.

She felt that she was standing on a precipice. There were two possibilities she could see before her: to turn back, or to leap off. She was facing a choice between two lives: a life lived vicariously, on the page; or a life lived for real, with all its uncertainties and dangers. For a long time she had believed that there was a kind of satisfaction to be found in living in the immaculately crafted narrative worlds of their own making, where everyone was beautiful and articulate and the stories had a satisfying shape and texture, and beginnings, middles, and endings. There were no unresolvable messes which dragged on for year after year in the house of fiction. So what if they didn't really exist? Their perfection made up for that. And, for all that her sisters drove her to distraction sometimes, they were the dearest companions of her heart, and she loved them, and could not imagine life without them. The thought of waking up beside someone other than Emily was terrifying.

Terrifying, but also exciting. For she was beginning to see, oh so clearly, that the house of fiction was a pale, powdery substitute for the real world. In the space of a moment, the paper knights of her imagination had been blown away by the salty, sinewy arms and oceanic eyes of the Diver, so mysterious, so intriguing, and so unknowable. The pallid, dust-covered pleasures of a life lived inside books suddenly seemed unbearable when she compared it with the boundless promise he seemed to offer. And who could tell whether she would end up happy or miserable? At least she would know she was alive.

She was not sure what dragged her back from her reverie. A sound? Or the absence of sound? It took her a moment to realise that the scratch of the pen had ceased; the room had fallen silent. Charlotte turned slowly to face Emily. Anne looked down at the page, and read:

I lingered round them, under that benign sky; watched the moths fluttering among the saltbush, and scrub; listened to the soft wind breathing through the grass; and wondered how any one could ever imagine unquiet slumbers for the sleepers in that quiet earth.

And under that, in emphatic letters, she had scrawled:

THE END.

Emily lifted her eyes and gazed at Anne. She seemed dazed, as if she'd been asleep for a long time. "It's finished," she said.

Emily

It ends with a great storm—a Tempest—

It begins with a rising Wind, keening at first, then whistling, gusting stronger and stronger, blowing until the Trees are pressed hard against the ground, their leaves stripped away, with a sound like a great Cry, a cry of Protest, as Nature rises up—

Then come the Waves, driven by the gale—the ocean, grey as grit, green as bile, grey as ashes—waves hurl themselves in a fury against the cliffs, the Water piles up against the Rocks, rising up, climbing higher—while unseen, far below, Boulders Grind one on another beneath the water, tearing at the footing of the Island, carving it away, threatening to Topple it—

And then the Rain comes—at first a distant Hiss barely audible over the keen of the wind—coming closer, ever closer, until the Hiss becomes a Growl, and the Growl becomes a Roar—and then it is upon us, and the water comes in sheets, in torrents, raindrops the size of fists, a moving mass of water, and every drop pouring down as if hurled by the gods, shafted and aimed to find out every chink and nook and cranny in walls and roofs and windows and doors—and the wind weaves through, seeking out every Weakness, every Rotten spot, every bent Nail and uneven Join, every crack and split, driving water in at every turn, until the storm has picked apart every roof and wall and is opening every dwelling to the fury of the sky—a torrent of Hail rattles destruction on every bare naked head, for the wind has done its work and all shelter is gone—and still the Tide washes further and further up the cliffs, boiling and seething and o'erleaping until it crests the cliff top—and then a great wave, the Greatest wave, comes sweeping in from far away, a mighty uprising from the unglimpsed deep, and pours over all—rushing in the windows and doors in a foaming green-and-grey mass, rushing into the barracks and the cells and the storehouses and the barn, picking up the chicken coop and bearing it squawking away, drowning the vegetable gardens and tearing the trees up by the roots and sweeping them up in the great surging, weed-strewn wall of water as it surfs across the island, sweeping up convicts and troopers and governors and daughters and cats and cows and possums, and the birds go screaming up into the sky, to be swept out to sea, there to perish—and still the water surfs on and on, tumbling rocks and filling cells, so that the men locked within are suddenly afloat in those dreadful dark subterranean places—and the wave passes over, carrying all before it—until the whole island is swept clean—and the waters run cascading down the cliffs in a thousand waterfalls—carrying with them a thousand jugs and spoons and petticoats and leg irons—

And soon the wind stops its keening and the rain passes over to pour devastation on other places—and the waves pull back from the cliffs and the island emerges from the water—

And lo, it is as if the island is washed clean—where once there had been prisoners and buildings and a gallows tree, now there is a sea of mud—with here and there pristine rock emerging, scrubbed bare by the floodwaters as they rose and fell again—the island is reborn—Nature has taken her revenge—

Some consummation is approaching—it is very near—soon I will know what all this has been for—

I pray that it will be the ending I have longed for—

Blow, winds, and crack your cheeks!

Anne

Emily came running after her as she went out for her walk. It was the kind of windy day that makes dogs run around yipping and whining and makes small children excitable, and Emily seemed to have caught the feverish mood. Her dark-circled eyes were shining, and her cheeks had a wind-burnt flush which looked startling against her extreme pallor. She was so thin now that she looked like a bundle of sticks wrapped in parchment, but she radiated an intense energy, even as she gasped for breath from the exertion of her very short run.

"Let's go to the prow of the ship," she said, between gasps.

Anne just nodded, as if this was not a very strange occurrence indeed. She noticed that Emily was clutching a bundle wrapped in a shawl tightly against her chest, but did not ask her what it was.

It took them half an hour to reach the prow of the ship—a lookout, so named because of the way it jutted out into the sea—for Emily was very weak, and often had to stop and rest. The sea, when they reached it, was wide and grey-blue, shimmering in the sun, as a great flock of seagulls circled frenziedly around a school of fish far below. The wind ripped their hair back from their faces and sent it streaming out in a straight line behind them, and Emily stood for a long moment, gazing out at the water, gathering herself, making Anne wonder if she meant to throw herself off. But then Emily unwrapped the shawl from the bundle she carried, giving Anne just enough time to realise that this was Emily's completed novel, before she peeled off the first page and tossed it over the cliff. But the wind was so strong that it had barely left her hand before it was snatched up and blown in the opposite direction, back onto the island, to tumble and dance among the scrub. For a moment, Emily was dismayed, but then she started to laugh. She threw another page up into the air, then another.

"What are you doing?" Anne cried.

But Emily didn't answer. Laughing, she began a kind of mad dance, peeling off sheets of paper and letting them fly where they would; perilously she danced along the cliff edge, hopping and skipping, scattering her words to the winds, as if she hoped, by setting them free, to open all the doors, to release the helpless prisoners of passion confined within the pages and all the captives on the island, to crack open the authority of the author and eject everyone from the narrative, characters and prisoners and daughters and troopers all, to begin their own journeys and engineer their own endings. Some of the pages blew away and got caught in the trees; some tumbled over the cliff edge, caught by contrary gusts, and drifted down to land in the sea and mingle their ink with the ocean; every page, ripped and torn and tumbled and dispersed, until Emily was left empty-handed, her bosom heaving with the effort, her hair witchily tangled, her face stretched into a ghastly grin of triumph.

"Soon it will all be over," she said.

Charlotte

I was speechless when I learned what Emily had done.

I could not believe that she had done such a foolish and destructive thing when at last we were so close to our goal. Emily's novel could have been an instant sensation, but now it was only food for fish, lost forever to the waves. She had never wanted to be a part of my plans; now she had her revenge.

"It was a sacrificial act," Anne said doubtfully, but she would not explain further.

I should have known it would all depend on me.

The answer came to me quite suddenly. Once again I picked up my pen, and began to write:

Dear Governor Fitzroy,

I write to you as a daughter who holds grave fears for the health and well-being of her father.

My father, Captain Edward Wolf, is the governor of the prison at Cold-water, and for some weeks now he has been afflicted by a terrible illness, which he calls a malaise or blight. I am afraid he is deceiving himself, for those who love him can see quite clearly that my father is no longer in his right mind. In short, he is mad.

I am loath to reveal this terrible secret to you, for it is dreadful to see a great man laid low; but as my father is refusing all treatment, and will not (out of a sense of duty) abandon his post, I am forced, in desperation, to turn to you. Please, sir, I beg you, for his own sake, and ours, you must recall my father at once. I am convinced that he will return to his senses if he is removed from the pernicious environment of this island; but it must be done quickly, and without prior warning. In his infirmity, my father believes his men are plotting against him, and that a mutiny is imminent. Were he to receive word that he is being replaced, he may act rashly.

Mr. Fry can be trusted: I suggest you direct any communication to him, and arrange to have any letters conducted to him privately, rather than through the normal mail service.

Finally, sir, I pray you will consider my father's dignity. He has done you good service during his time here, and if, at the last, the great strain of life on Coldwater has become too much for him, he should not be treated too harshly because of it. There has never been so much as a hint of madness in him, or in his family, until today; and I repeat, I am convinced he will quickly recover himself once he is returned safely to civilian life. I trust that you will treat him honourably.

Please help us——there is no one else I can turn to.

Your obedient servant,

Charlotte Wolf

Seven

The dumb cell

Emily

I fear that I am going mad—

I don't know where he is or what Father has done with him and I cannot find out—Father would not tell me even if I was speaking to him—

I wish now I had made more of an Effort to become friendly with the officers (but I did make Enormous efforts, all of which came to nothing, for I cannot be Bright and Easy in men's company as some women can), for if I had a friend amongst them I could at least find out where he is hid—and if he is still alive—

Anne's revelations have struck me dumb with fear—for I cannot doubt that they are true—I fear that he is dead already and I will never see him again—

I wait every day for a Message from him but nothing comes—surely there must be ways? Father would not go on so about the Underhandedness of Convicts if they did not have ways of going behind his back—But there is Nothing, and his Silence only feeds my Fear, for surely if he lived he would send some word?

He cannot have stopped Loving me?

My head buzzes with plans—all Foolhardy—but I can do nothing until I know his Mind—

Perhaps it is up to me to find the truth—

I have to squeeze out the bedroom window to avoid the guard on the door—I will make my way to the cells and there try to seek him out—

A great Variety of people abroad—I am forced to take the Longest route imaginable, through the Scrub—I am not accustomed to the exercise and soon out of breath—even the scrub is a risky strategy—I almost stumble upon a party of convicts chopping down trees and must describe a wide arc to avoid them—a lone man is pissing in the bushes—the sound of me crashing through the undergrowth nearly frightens him out of his Wits—

After much stopping and starting and ducking behind bushes at last I reach the cells—only to discover that the cells are guarded—how to express my Frustration!—Furious that I had not thought of this, although of course it seems Obvious to me now—

But I have come this far and I am not ready to give up yet—

I creep around to the back of the cells, and spy the tiny windows, high up in the walls, that let in light and air—They are much too high to look through but I might get a message to him even if I cannot see him—

O'Connell!

No answer—I dare not raise my voice much above a Whisper—I cannot be sure whether he would hear me, even if he is within—

Finn O'Connell!

No answer—

Are you there, O'Connell?

Still no answer—Perhaps this cell is empty—or he's sleeping?—but I cannot call any louder for risk of alerting the guard—I move on to the next window—

Finn O'Connell?

This time I hear a stir—my heart leaps in my breast—but the voice that answers is not his—

Who's that then?

O'Connell?

No, but come in 'ere and I'll give you a better ride than 'e ever gave ya!

I back away—

There is one more window to try—I call as before—On the instant, the man inside the cell starts thrashing about and crying out: *Mary? Is that you? Have you come to take me home? Mary? Take me away from here! Please help me!*—and sundry other Pleadings that are Piteous to hear—

But he is not O'Connell either, just a poor madman—and the noise he makes soon brings the guards—He manages to convince them there is someone outside the window—and I am Caught—

Father Livid when he discovers what I've done—calls me a Whore and all sorts of names—It is all one to me, I do not care what he thinks of me—

I ask him what he has done with O'Connell—

You will never see him again.

Is he dead?

No.

But I cannot trust him—I know he does not trust me—

Father threatens to lock me in my room if I will not behave—he says he will put a Bolt on the bedroom door and bars over the windows and make me stay there—*Who will cook the dinner?* I wonder—

I would be reluctant to keep you under lock and key. But I will do it, if necessary.

He is quite serious—I refuse to be browbeaten—But could I bear to be locked in?—I'm not sure I have the fortitude—

And after all my efforts I am still in the same dreadful situation—knowing nothing, fearing everything—

Journal, 10th October

And now Emily is lost to me too. But I cannot say it comes as a great surprise. I knew there was little hope for her. The infection has done its work. It can only be a matter of time before she moves in open rebellion against me. But I cannot worry about that. The most important thing is to make sure that Charlotte remains untouched. Charlotte is my only hope now.

Anne

"I wasn't sure what to expect, coming back here," the Diver said. "A guard waiting on the rocks with a rifle."

"I haven't told anyone about you," Anne said. It was close to the truth—telling secrets to Emily was like telling secrets to herself.

He was silent for a moment, eyeing her, chewing on his lip. "There's something I need to ask you. Well—tell you. And ask you," he said finally, uncharacteristically awkward.

She looked up at him expectantly.

"My brother and I have decided the time's come. I'm going to help him escape."

Anne sucked in a great breath, shocked by the suddenness of it. It had been at the back of her mind for some time that this day must be coming, but she had hoped against hope that it could be put off. Now, hope was at an end.

"How soon?"

"I'm not sure exactly. But soon."

"Oh."

She turned her head away, so that he would not see the tears in her eyes. And then she remembered what Charlotte had said about O'Connell: *He's obviously using her for some purpose of his own, and she's letting it happen.* Had she been an even bigger fool?

"Tell me," she said slowly. "What did you think, that first time, when you saw me standing on the beach?"

"What did I think?"

"Did you think, This girl may yet be of some use to me?" Once it was put into words, she felt certain she had finally hit upon the dismal truth.

"Is that why you think I've been coming here?"

She looked at him defiantly, although she could barely see him through the tears in her eyes. "Well, isn't it?"

"No!" he cried. And his face was as sober, as truthful, as resolute as she could have wished. "I don't care whether you help me or not. To tell you the truth, I haven't had any reason to come here so often, except to see you."

"Really?"

"Really." Feeling himself on surer ground, he grinned at her. "You may not have noticed, love, but I've been courting you."

Anne blushed, as an unstoppable smile spread across her face. It was as if the sun had come out. Weeks of fears and doubts were melting away as if they had never existed. "You've never called me *love* before," she said.

"If you don't like it—"

"Oh no, I like it very well."

"Do you, love?"

He was moving closer. Anne was so choked with anticipation and desire she could barely breathe.

"You're an officer's daughter and a lady and I'm—well, I'm no one at all. But if you'll have me, I'm all yours."

"Will you take me away from here?"

He grinned. "Don't reckon I'd have much choice in the matter. Your father'd hunt me down and horsewhip me for stealing one of his precious daughters."

"Where would we go?"

"Anywhere you want to go. I bet you'd be a town kind of a girl."

"Not necessarily."

He thought about it for a moment. "We'll follow the sun up north, then. I know some beautiful places. What do you say?"

Now that the moment had come, there was no hesitation. "Yes."

Emily was peeling potatoes for dinner when Anne told her the news. She had been worrying about how Emily would take it, but to her great relief, Emily dropped the paring knife and threw her arms around her neck. "Thank God one of us is going to be happy," she said, and kissed Anne's ear.

Relieved, Anne pushed Emily's wet hands away. "You're all potatoey," she said.

"When will you go?"

"I don't know yet. He is going to help his brother escape. I'll go with them then."

"It will be dangerous," Emily warned. "Bad enough that he's taking you away. But with an escaped prisoner . . . You'll be fugitives."

"I want to go with him," Anne said. "I couldn't bear it if he left without me. Waiting for him to come back. I couldn't bear it."

Emily squeezed her hand. "I know," she said softly, and her face clouded with the memory of her own trouble. "How does he plan to do it?"

"He's going to bring a boat at dead of night."

"Surely someone will see?"

"We'll go when there's no moon."

Emily picked up her paring knife again. Strips of potato skin dropped smoothly from her hands. "They say that there are no secrets inside a prison," she said. "Do you think—is there a chance—his brother might know where O'Connell is?"

"I don't know if—"

"Please," interrupted Emily passionately, "I don't know where he is. It's as if he's disappeared."

"He can't have disappeared," Anne said. "He must still be here somewhere." But she remembered what the Diver had said about un-marked graves all over the cliff tops.

"I went into Father's study," Emily said, "and checked the rolls. O'Connell's still listed. He hasn't been reported dead or missing. But I've been looking and looking for him, and I haven't seen him anywhere."

"Looking?"

Emily blushed an ugly crimson. "You can see a great deal through Father's telescope."

"I'll ask him to find out whatever he can," Anne said. She hesitated. "You can come with me, you know. When we leave here."

"Without him?"

Emily turned on her a look so full of pain, and longing, and frus-tration, and anger, and misery, that Anne felt her own eyes fill with tears. The pang of imminent separation gripped her, and for a moment she wanted nothing more than to stay right here, in this one room, and cling onto Emily forever and ever. Adventure, true love, real life, all seemed to fade into insignificance against the one person who had been the polestar of her existence, her sister, her life.

"But I can't leave you behind!" Anne cried.

"Not so loud," said Emily. "Charlotte'll hear."

"I couldn't bear to be parted from you," Anne said, a little more qui-etly. "And I'm sure the Diver will be glad to take you with us once he understands the situation."

"Perhaps he can find a little room for me and O'Connell in his boat. Of course I'll have to find out where he is first." And she sighed, dis-couraged.

"And when you do," Anne said, hoping to cheer her up, "we'll stage a breakout, and be the only people ever to escape from Coldwater."

Emily smiled. But Anne could see her heart wasn't in it.

When she told the Diver of Emily's request she was rather troubled to realise that the whole matter was well-known to him. Had everyone heard the shameful story of Emily's secret passion? But the Diver didn't seem to consider it at all shameful, and promised to find out what he could about O'Connell's present location. His grave look made Anne fear the worst.

But some days later, when they were able to meet again, he had some heartening news.

"He's not dead," the Diver said, "although by now he probably wishes he was."

"Why?" asked Anne nervously, "what have they done to him?"

"There are a set of cells your father had built as an experiment, called the dumb cells. They're underground, with no windows. Once they shut the doors on you, it's totally dark, and totally silent. It's been known to send men out of their wits."

"Has he been there all this time?" Anne asked, stunned.

"That I couldn't say, but it's where he is now."

Anne digested this news. "It'd be like being buried alive," she murmured.

"Very like," agreed the Diver.

"What would be the purpose of such a cell?" she wondered.

"To drive men mad. To break their wills."

"There must have been a scientific reason," Anne said, trying to convince herself. "Father believes in applying scientific principles to his work."

"Does he indeed?" said the Diver, not impressed.

"Is there—" Anne faltered, not sure whether to ask this, "—is there anything you can do for him?"

"To get him out? No. It's heavily guarded, and there's only one door."

"But you're getting your brother out," Anne said.

"He's not locked up under special guard," the Diver said. "My brother's sleeping in barracks; he says it's not that difficult for him to get out at night, as long as he's careful. What you're talking about—you'd need men and guns. I'm sorry, but I can't help you with that."

"But there must be something you can do," Anne said, with a sinking heart.

"I'm sorry," the Diver said.

Informer's Report

Information received from Prisoner Graham Skate on the 19th of October, 1847

Prisoner *Skate* reports that the Specials are planning an escape. They mean to seize the supply ship when it lands, and flee to New Zealand. Only the Specials are to be allowed on board. Any Common men who should attempt to join the group will be thrown overboard.

Informer's Report

Information received from Prisoner Thomas Edmonds on the 20th day of October, 1847

Prisoner *Edmonds* reports that a group of Commons are planning an escape. They mean to seize a ship and flee up the coast, before possibly sailing to America. They have begun spreading a false story that the Specials are planning such an escape in an effort to divert suspicion from themselves.

Anne

She awoke to the sound of tapping on the glass.

Anne froze, but Emily had already leapt from her bed and thrown open the window, her face radiant with sudden hope. But the face she saw was not the face she had hoped—dreamed—of seeing.

"Anne?"

It was the Diver. He was tense and nervous, far from the water, out of his element. Anne took a moment to wind a shawl around herself before coming to the window.

"What are you doing here?" she hissed.

"I've had some news," the Diver said, his eyes darting suspiciously about, as if he expected at any moment to feel the heavy hand of a trooper landing on his shoulder. "Are you going to let me in?"

Anne exchanged a look with Emily, then stepped back. He climbed in the window with all the alacrity of a housebreaker.

"What news?" asked Anne, after she had performed the briefest of introductions.

"I saw my brother today," the Diver said, his voice low and agitated. "I was hoping to make final arrangements for our escape. He told me there is a breakout planned."

Anne and Emily gasped.

"There is a supply ship due here the day after tomorrow. Some of the convicts are planning to stage an uprising, overpower the guards, and seize the ship. Any crew who won't join them will be thrown overboard; once the ship is taken, they plan to sail to New Zealand and either settle there, or find a passage home to England."

Anne's heart started to beat faster. "They must know they cannot succeed," she said.

"They mean to try. But don't you see? If there is to be a rising the day after tomorrow, it means we'll have to make our escape tomorrow night."

Anne felt the room begin to spin. "Why?"

"Because once there's been a breakout they're sure to tighten security. Better to do it when they're not expecting it." He hesitated. "I wouldn't like to leave you here, knowing there's a breakout planned. Anything could happen."

"Tomorrow night then," Anne said faintly.

"I've got a place on the mainland we can hide. There's room for both of you."

"And one more?" asked Emily.

He eyed her unwillingly. "Perhaps. But only one."

"Alright," said Emily decisively. "We'll come."

"Wait a minute!" said Anne. "I need time to think." Everything was moving too fast.

"There's no time. I'll wait for you on the beach at midnight tomorrow. If you're not there, I'll know you're not coming."

Anne stared at him helplessly, paralysed. The Diver brought her fingers to his lips, and kissed them. "Midnight tomorrow."

Quick as a wink, he was out the window again, slippery as a fish.

Once he was gone, panic started to rise in Anne's chest. "What am I going to do?" she whispered.

"Go with him," said Emily simply.

"Just like that?"

"It's what you were planning, isn't it?"

"But not like this."

"What's changed?"

Anne looked at Emily in disbelief. "There's going to be a breakout. We can't go and leave Father and Charlotte behind."

Emily's jaw set obstinately. "They'll be alright."

Anne realised that she was shaking. She sat down on the bed and clamped her hands together between her knees. "It's my duty to tell Father about this."

Emily was appalled. "How can you even consider doing such a thing?"

"It's my duty," Anne repeated.

"If you tell Father what you know, they'll be waiting for the Diver, and if they catch him, he'll be thrown in jail, or shot and killed."

Anne knew Emily was right. But all her instincts told her it would be wicked, utterly wicked, to keep this knowledge secret. If the guards knew a revolt was planned, perhaps it could all be stopped before it had begun, and there need be no chaos, no disaster, no bloodshed. Stumblingly she tried to explain herself, but Emily was having none of it.

"The Diver will never forgive you if you betray him. And neither will I. You have to choose, Anne."

Anne looked at Emily, and thought that she no longer recognised her sister. There was a ferocity in her that had never been present before. This long winter had changed her.

"Think about all Father's done here," Emily said. "Think about what he's done to me. To all of us. This could be your only chance to escape."

"He's our father," Anne insisted, her voice thick with tears.

Emily hesitated for a moment, then took a new tack. Her voice, thrilling, caressing, murmured in Anne's ear, worming its way into her heart, lulling her conscience to sleep.

"What's the worst that can happen?" she said. "Maybe the prisoners will try to rise when the supply ship comes. Who's to say they will? You know what cowards they are. Probably nothing will happen at all. But let's just say they do rise up. A few prisoners might get away. They probably won't. But if they do, Father's perfect record is spoilt, and the governor will be forced to replace him, which means Father gets sent home where he can't do any more harm to anyone. Charlotte might even make him take her home to England, which would make everyone happy. So you see? Where's the harm?"

"What if the mutiny's successful and they kill all the troopers? What happens to Father and Charlotte then?"

"You're very melodramatic all of a sudden," Emily said teasingly, as if there was nothing very important at stake. "The prisoners are always threatening to break out and kill us all. Has it ever happened? No. Do I think it will happen the day after tomorrow? No."

"The Diver thinks it will."

"He is being overcautious. He does not know the convicts as well as we do. They are all talk. He doesn't realise that."

Anne looked at Emily doubtfully. She could feel her defences crumbling. All her life she had followed Emily's lead. The habit of obedience was too strong for her to resist; but it was more than obedience, it was a deep-seated belief that love began and ended with loyalty to Emily, her opinions and feelings and actions, and that loyalty was more important than any other set of rules or beliefs. And even though she knew Emily was trying to persuade her for reasons of her own, she could not resist the force of Emily's will. And so, despite her terrible misgivings, she found herself agreeing that she would keep silent, she would say nothing to Father, and she would make herself ready for flight.

Eight

Bertha

From An Account of an Australian Penal Settlement

Treadwheels

The treadwheel is a device resembling a paddle wheel or mill wheel. It consists of a great revolving wheel or drum, with a series of steps radiating out from it. The prisoner stands on these steps, and as the cylinder turns, the prisoner must step onto each successive step so as to avoid falling. The speed is adjustable; while it is most common for the treadwheel to turn at a brisk walking pace, it is possible to operate the machinery more quickly, so the prisoner is obliged to run. While this device can be used for pumping water or grinding corn, it is more commonly used simply for "grinding the air"—that is, prisoners are obliged to walk ceaselessly upon it for no useful purpose at all. The exhaustion produced by this activity, combined with the demoralising effects of its utter futility, are said to result in highly quiescent prisoners.

Charlotte

Father called me into his study as I was thinking of heading off to bed.

"I owe you an apology, Charlotte," he said, as I came warily into the room.

"For what, Father?"

"I have ruined everything I've touched," he said. "But please believe me, I did it with the best of intentions."

I had no idea what he was talking about. "I have no cause for complaint, Father."

"Haven't you?" he said, morosely. "When I have blighted your life and made you into a kind of monster, unfit for anything?"

The unexpected insult brought tears to my eyes. But his mood seemed tranquil, almost sad, and in no way accusing.

"Look at you! You're plain, you're aggressive, you're wilful. If you could find a man weak or foolish enough to marry you, you'd make his life a misery, and he yours, until the time you eventually tore him to pieces with your wilful stubbornness."

He took my hand, and drew me down to sit beside him. Reluctantly, I let myself be drawn. "I do not blame you, Charlotte," he said, so close I could feel his hot breath upon my cheek. "This is all my fault. I am entirely to blame. When you came to me all those years ago and demanded those opportunities which fate had denied your brother, I—"

Even now, he could not bring himself to say Branwell's name, and I felt language shrivel up and blow away, a lifeless husk, in the face of that terrible and unassuageable grief, the grief that had marked his life.

"Your brother was irreplaceable—but I thought—I thought—It was madness, I know, but I hoped that you could—not take his place, exactly—"

He swallowed, then continued, more evenly. "In time, I came to see it almost as an experiment. How would you turn out if I pretended you were boys instead of girls? I knew what science said about the inferiority of the female mind—too much stimulation of the brain drives a woman mad, weakens her constitution, makes her ill, and eventually kills her." Father paused thoughtfully, eyeing me, considering, perhaps, my obvious robustness. "There are sound scientific reasons for believing this to be the case. But stupidly, I thought you might be different."

"And we *are* different," I said. "When we went to school, all our teachers were amazed at how advanced we were."

Father pursed his lips. "They say an educated woman is rather like a dog walking on his hind legs: it is not done well, but one is surprised to see it done at all. But as I say, I do not blame you, Charlotte. You are what I have made you. It pleased my vanity to see my precocious little girls writing books and answering back. *What wonderful, bright, wicked daughters I have, so witty and so amusing!* I thought. It never occurred to me that you would grow up to defy me."

I stared at him dumbly. The barrage of insult, delivered in the tenderest fashion, with the sweetest look of high-minded compassion, had rendered me speechless.

He reached out to stroke my face kindly. "Poor Charlotte. I tried to produce a genius, and have only succeeded in making a shrew."

Would this never cease? And all the time, his bright eye was fixed upon me, waiting and expectant. I could not understand what he wanted of me. Was he exploring new depths of cruelty by insulting me thus? Or could it be—I was staggered by the thought—that he was asking my forgiveness for what he had done?

"Thanks to me, you are fit for nothing. You have already made it clear that you do not wish to marry. I hoped you would change your mind, but I fear that you would never be happy in marriage. You are too wilful to marry a strong man, and you would hate anyone who tried to control you. But if you married a weak man, you would soon come to despise him. What am I to do with you, Charlotte?"

It seemed obvious to me that if I was indeed so utterly ill-suited to marriage, I had no course open to me other than to earn my own living; but it did not seem sensible to say so.

I started as he reached out and captured my hand again. "I thought with you I could strike the perfect balance, that I could bring you up to be a completely well-rounded woman: loving, compassionate, but intelligent too; a spirited companion, with a mind of your own. . . ."

"I'm a companion?" I said. "That's what all this was for? So I wouldn't be a dull wife?"

His voice changed, raw, cracking. "If I could have a wife like you . . ."

Something stirred in me, something hot and beastly and incoherent, and I became scorchingly and horridly aware that Father was not just the man who gave me life, he was a *man*. He stared at me with a strange, confused hunger that found a momentary echo in me, an echo which was almost immediately swamped beneath an avalanche of fear.

"Father," I said shrilly, jumping up, "if you'll excuse me, I think it's time I said good night."

"Charlotte—"

"Good night, Father."

I ran from the room, bumping into the door frame in my haste, skidded into my bedroom, and shut the door. My heart was hammering.

How strange, I thought, staring into the looking glass at my face, that square, peevish, plain face I looked at every day, *that for all that time I was trying to be a son to him, and I thought he was trying to make a daughter out of me, he was actually trying to turn me into a wife.* It was so funny and so horrible all at once that I started to laugh. And then I started to cry. And then I couldn't seem to stop.

I woke in the small hours of the morning to the sound of Father hissing my name in the darkness.

"Father?" I murmured, my mouth thick with sleep.

"Charlotte, I need to tell you something."

I gradually made out a figure sitting at the end of the bed—Father, in his shirtsleeves. My heart lurched—*what was he doing in my room in the middle of the night?*—but he seemed to want nothing more than to talk, so I did not cry out. And even if I had, who would have come running?

"What is it, Father?"

"I was not entirely truthful when I talked to you tonight. There's something I was leaving out. Something I've always left out." He paused. "When I was a young man, I met and married a young woman called Bertha—"

"Bertha?" I interrupted. "But my mother's name was Maria."

"I'm well aware of that, Charlotte. Your mother was not my first wife."

"*What?*"

"I had another wife before your mother."

"And what happened to her?"

He did not immediately answer my question.

"When I met Bertha I was barely twenty-one years old; she was nineteen. It was a whirlwind romance. We married quickly—too quickly, some said—but we were madly in love. And for a while we were very happy.

"Bertha was a lovely girl, quick, energetic, very clever, and so witty. I loved her very much, but I knew she was sensitive, very changeable in her moods. She'd be in the heights of ecstasy one moment, in the depths of despair the next. Anything could set her off—you had to be very careful what you said or did, or she could wind up in tears.

"She was a writer—just like you and your sisters, Charlotte. Bertha mostly wrote poetry, but she also wrote prose—she started a novel after we were married. She hadn't attempted to have any of her work published. She kept insisting it wasn't good enough yet, but one day, one day she'd do something worth showing to the world. And I believed her, I had faith in her, so I let her continue. I admit, I prided myself on my unconventionality. I found it charming that she was spending her days scribbling away at a novel. But after we'd been married for a year or so, and she still wasn't pregnant, I started to worry.

"I don't know who first put the idea in my head, but eventually I came to the conclusion that it was the writing that prevented Bertha from conceiving. All that nervous energy she was expending on the page must somehow be interfering with the normal functions of her body. The solution to me seemed quite simple: she must stop writing immediately.

"Well, Bertha loved me, so she agreed to stop, but it was a very bitter thing for her. I was often away, so she was frequently alone in the house with no company and nothing much to do, and she was forbidden from doing the one thing she most dearly loved. She quickly became very melancholy, so melancholy she could not get out of bed. I was desperate about her, and called all sorts of doctors in to see her, but none of them could do anything for her."

And did it never occur to you, I wondered, *to let her begin writing again?* But I said nothing.

"Then at last I found a doctor who claimed to have the answer. He showed me testimonials from ladies and their husbands who had been cured by his methods. He assured me he knew exactly how to make Bertha well again. He advised me that any sort of stimulation would be disastrous for her and would only make matters worse, and I should make her rest as much as possible and eat a good fattening diet of milk, cream, and beef. He also insisted I should remove all stimulating material from the house—she was not to write letters or read books or even newspapers, and she was certainly not to pick up a pen and write fiction. So I put her to bed and took her books away, and because she was a loving wife she acquiesced, but she grew more and more unhappy.

"Your aunt came round to visit me. She took Bertha's side against me, and told me I was only making her fat and miserable. She told me I should end the treatment, but I wouldn't listen. The doctor had said Bertha would probably get worse before she got better, and I just had to be patient and persevere. So I waited, and Bertha did get worse. She began to wander in her mind. I was beside myself, but I didn't know what to do except follow the doctor's orders.

"Then Bertha tried to take her life by leaping from the bedroom window. Luckily or unluckily, the drop was not high enough, and she was unharmed. But after that, I refused to take any chances with her safety. In the room that was to have been the nursery, I had bars put on the windows and a lock put on the outside of the door, and I put her in there, to keep her safe, until her wits returned and she was well again.

"But still she did not get better. I struggled on alone, waiting and hoping that my wife would eventually come back to me, but there was no improvement. At first she was wild, and would scream and shout, begging to be let out, hammering on the walls. I tried to explain that it was all for her own good, but I could not make her understand. Gradually, she grew quieter, until she did not even acknowledge me when I came into the room. She sat there, still as a stone, staring at nothing, and nothing I could say or do would move her. I found this too distressing, so eventually I stopped visiting, except to bring her meals.

"This went on for two more months. Then one day, there was an accident in the kitchen, which started a fire."

"She was burned?" I breathed in horror.

"The servant unlocked the door and let her out. She ran away before they could catch her. They pulled her from the river two weeks later."

For a moment, he was silent. His voice, when it spoke again, was ragged. "I blame myself for what happened. I know I drove her mad. I was trying to do the right thing, but I knew nothing. I was only a foolish child. I took the thing I loved most, and I ruined it.

"But I thought—with you—I could right the wrongs I had done. Poor Bertha had a fatal weakness in her mind, but I thought I could breed you up to be stronger. I dreamed that one day, through my girls, she might live again, and have the life that should have been hers."

"But, Father," I whispered, "we're not her. We're just us."

"Of course you are, dear one. Of course you are," he said, patting my foot through the eiderdown. I drew it back as if I'd been stung. "But you don't know how very like her you are."

"I thought you said I was like my mother—Maria."

"Maria gave birth to you. But Bertha was your real mother. A light went out of the world when she died—but it returned with you."

"I'm not Bertha," I said, agitated, "I'm Charlotte!"

"That doesn't really matter now, does it?" he said.

He reached for my hand and pressed it to his lips. I experienced a dizzying loss of self—who was I after all? Was I Charlotte? Or was I Bertha? The world cracked and time slipped and I felt like I was there, trapped in that room; I felt that I knew her, I *was* her, locked up and silenced, confined in the nursery by the man who loved me best of all. I wrenched my hand away from him and scrambled backwards over the bed. The room was filled with ghosts. The blood pounded in my ears. I thought I was about to faint. Could it be true? All my life, had I been a player in a drama which had begun and ended before I was born, a drama I had never suspected? Had she ever existed, this mad, lost first wife? In the delirium of the night I could not tell.

"Get out of here, Father!" I said, trying to sound as stern as I could while struggling not to burst into tears. "You are not well. Go back to bed!"

"But you have not heard what I came to tell you. I have a plan, Bertha!" he said eagerly. "Soon, when all this is over, you and I will leave here and set up house together. We can go anywhere you like—it could even be London—yes, why not? We will set up house together, just the two of us, and I will let you write as you did before."

The hairs on the back of my neck rose. *Soon, when all this is over? Just the two of us?*

"I never wanted to punish you. I should have known you would never plot against me, not really. Your sisters can't be trusted. But once we leave here, they can go their own way—it's what they want, after all."

"You'd turn them out?" I breathed, horrified.

"It's what they deserve," Father said mildly. He reached out in the darkness, groping for my hand, and, finding it, he held it in a crushing grip. "I know I can trust you, Charlotte," he said, in a fierce whisper, "you're the only one I can trust. Come with me, and I'll give you everything you ever wanted."

Suddenly I wondered whether that great heavy weight sitting on the end of my bed, with his alluring voice and his hot breath, was my poor mad father, or the Devil himself. "What do you ask of me in return?" I managed to croak. In the darkness, I could feel him smile.

"Obedience," he said simply.

And at once I could see the life he had mapped out for me. An endless childhood, stretching out to the end of my days. Father and I, a little world of two; the whole of Coldwater shrunk down to a duo, where Father ruled and I obeyed. An endless childhood, stretching out for year after year, with Father making all of my choices for me, sapping my will until I no longer knew what I thought or what I wanted, wearing me down like a convict on a treadwheel, and all in the name of love. I had lived this nursery life for thirty years. I could not endure it for another thirty.

"Father," I said. "There is something I need to tell you."

And then I told him everything, everything I had done. I told him how much I'd hated O'Connell, how appalled and delighted I'd been when I discovered Emily was in love with him. I told him who it was that had seen to it he found out about their relationship. I told him about Mr. Fry. I told him I had written a personal letter to the governor, asking to have him dismissed. I told him everything.

When I had finished at last, a dreadful silence fell. My heart was thumping with the dreadful exhilaration of what I had done, the fear, the relief, the giddy delight of unburdening myself at last from the weight of my hideous deceit. The dutiful daughter had been cast aside, once and for all, and the monster of ambition stood naked before him. I waited for the space of three heartbeats to see what he would do. And then suddenly I felt a great pressure around my throat. He had seized me by the neck and was throttling the life out of me. The scent of lemon and eucalyptus rose in my nostrils and I was back at Haworth, kicking and struggling, as the blood pounded in my eyes and ears and tiny lights swarmed in the darkness. Father's fingers bore inexorably down upon my tender flesh, squeezing the life from me; and it was as if all those years between that day and this, those twenty years, had been nothing but a dream, the flickering figment of my dying fancy.

But then suddenly he released me. I sucked the sweet air into my lungs through hideously bruised tissues, and heard my breath rattling and gasping as it passed through my throat. I felt the mattress give as he leapt off the bed.

"You are no daughter of mine," I heard him say, his voice shaking in the darkness. "I have no children. When the supply ship comes, the three of you will be on it. I will have no more to do with you."

"But where will we go?" I managed to gasp.

"That is no longer my concern." And with great ironic courtliness, he added, "Your wish is granted, Charlotte."

And then he was gone.

Father had cast me out. The day after tomorrow I would be boarding a ship and heading off to Sydney. There would be no one there to meet me; I had no money, no friends, and nowhere to go. I should have been terrified, but there was no room left in my heart for fear. I had escaped death for the second time. I was as calm and serene as a millpond. My life was in ruins, but at last the torment and the fear were over. Father had granted my wish. He had set me free.

I lay awake for most of the night, but shortly before dawn, I drifted off to sleep and into an intense, troubling nightmare. I was walking through a town, which in the dream I knew to be London. I was both myself and not myself—I was at once Charlotte and Bertha, Charlotte knowing herself to be Bertha. Crowds bustled everywhere, malign, indifferent, obstructing my path. I was running away from my husband's house, the house that was on fire. I was trying to get to the beach (Coldwater fused with London in the dream) where a boat was waiting to take me away, but first I had to cross the river. I knew the river was perilous, but I could not go any other way, so I stepped onto the bridge and began to cross. And then I heard a great uproar somewhere ahead of me— a neighing and a shouting and a rattle of chains and a rumble of wheels. The crowd opened before me and I saw there was a runaway horse on the bridge, dragging a cart behind it. The cart was banging and crashing about as the shrieking horse charged towards me, its eyes rolling, hooves striking sparks, flailing dangerously at the screaming pedestrians, and the noise they made served only to terrify the horse further. The traffic on the bridge was reduced to a milling frenzy as horses trampled people and men tried to seize reins and bridles, and carts and cabs and carriages overturned, and I cowered against the railing as the heaving, thrashing beast rushed towards me, and then the runaway horse charged the railing and smashed through it and went screaming over, and suddenly there was nothing holding me up and I went toppling backwards into the foul, turgid water. I had jumbled impressions of being struck on the head, of being in the water, of a vile taste in my mouth, of the appalling sight somewhere overhead of the runaway horse, thrashing and writhing, caught in the traces, suspended between the bridge and the water, slowly strangling as the leather straps bit deeper and deeper into its flesh, until finally its desperate struggles pulled it loose, and it fell with a mighty splash into the water where, horribly entangled, still screaming its plight, it sank like a stone.

My chest constricted with terror, I woke, the screams of the horse dying away in my ear, the vivid edge of my fear only gradually fading. I lay awake as darkness turned to dawn, turning over the strange events of the previous night. As the grey light of day moved into my room I realised that the story Father had told me was almost certainly not true: it was the product of his disordered imagination, nothing more. He had never known a young poet called Bertha, or been married to her, or gradually smothered the life out of her, except in his dreams. But while I knew the story had no basis in fact, I could not forget this woman, the wasted life she represented, and I could not help speculating about what had prompted Father to tell me that strange tale in the middle of the night. What had he been trying to tell me?

And then I remembered the curse he had laid upon me. I was to be cast out. And my heart stopped in terror.

Journal, 21st October

This will be my final entry.

The contagion has done its work. Charlotte is infected. All hope is lost. The only thing I can do now is contain this blight as best I can. All must be tumbled. Nothing is to be spared.

May God have mercy on me.

Nine

Escape

Emily

Tonight we venture to cross the terrible waters that keep us from freedom—

I dare not think about it for Fear that I place a curse on the whole proceedings—

So I will think only about tomorrow—

Tomorrow the men will rise up and take over this dreadful place— they will open up the prison gates and storm the ship and set sail for freedom—and I too will be free for the first time—free to live, free to love—tomorrow we will be together again—

Perhaps he will be greatly changed from his time in the cells—it's said they drive men mad— But I cannot believe anything would drive him from his wits—his spirit is too supple, too strong to break, even under that enormous pressure—

No, he has spent a time in the Underworld, and soon, so soon, he will be free—I will be his Orpheus, he my Eurydice—but no, that's an ill-starred comparison—

He will be my Persephone, destined to spend a time underground—
but soon he will be set free, and returned to me—

Oh my beloved, I want to take you in my arms and kiss your blind
eyes and teach them how to see, whisper in your ears until you learn how
to hear again, and caress you and hold you until you know I will never
let us be parted more—

Charlotte

Father was up at first light. I could hear the customary sounds from
the room across the hall as he washed, dressed, and went out. I waited
until he was gone, for I did not wish to face him again after last night.
Once I was certain he was gone I hurried out to the kitchen to pass on
the news to my sisters.

Emily was kindling the fire as I entered and Anne was taking the
teacups down from the sideboard.

"Did Father speak to you before he left?" I asked.

Emily shook her head. "Should he have?"

"Father came to my room last night. He was quite mad—raving—
and we quarrelled." I did not think I needed to tell them the reasons
why we had quarrelled. "He has decided we are all in league against
him, and he plans to put us on the supply ship tomorrow. He is turning us out!"

Anne's eyes widened, but Emily just smiled darkly. "Congratula-
tions, Charlotte. At last you've got your wish."

"This isn't funny!" I cried. "Tomorrow we will be entirely on our
own. We have no money, no friends, nothing! What are we going to do?"

Emily just looked at me with the flat, carnivorous gaze of a tiger.
"You were always a great one for plots and plans, Charlotte," she said.
"I'm sure you'll think of something."

"But you don't understand! He's putting us *all* on the supply ship tomorrow," I insisted. "We have to do something. We have to prepare."

"We won't be here tomorrow, Charlotte."

Anne shot Emily an accusing glance, but Emily would not be silenced. "We're leaving here tonight."

It took me a moment to fully comprehend what she was saying. "You're leaving? Without me?"

Of all the betrayals I had ever suffered, this was the cruellest. *They mean to abandon me.* What had I done to deserve this? Did they not know, could they not see, that everything I had done had been for them? All my struggles, all my plots and plans, as Emily put it, had all been for *their* independence, to secure *their* future.

"How could you do this to me?" I whispered.

"I know what you did, Charlotte," Emily said simply.

And for a moment, just a moment, I felt something in me waver and sag, as if the bright, hard light which illuminated my path had flickered and begun to go out; and my adamantine sense of purpose, formerly so strong and true, suddenly began to seem brittle, mazed with cracks and flaws. I could glimpse the wreckage which lay strewn in my path.

But then the words came to me, and I knew what to say.

"Father has disowned me," I said, as plainly and humbly as I knew how. "I am all alone, and I'm frightened, and I don't know what I'm going to do."

Emily gazed at me for a long moment, and from the corner of my eye I saw Anne wince, as if she was bracing herself for the final recriminations, the hatred, the bile that Emily had stored up in her heart for month after month. Breathless, I waited to see what Emily would do. Would this be the moment in which she took her revenge upon me at last?

"Look for us when you come ashore," Emily said finally. "We'll be waiting."

I watched them go about their daily business in a sort of daze, not quite able to grasp that they were actually leaving. It was Emily's baking day, and so she made a batch of shortbread, just as if she was planning to wake up in her own bed tomorrow. To look at her, you would never have known that anything unusual was afoot: she was perfectly serene as she went about her duties, her face as mild and abstract as a Madonna; although this in itself was something of a change—she had been brittle and short-tempered for months, abrupt in her movements, hasty and short in her speech, her brow set permanently in a frown. It seemed not so much a transformation, but a reversion to an earlier time, when she had been happy and contented, keeping house and playing at Gondals with Anne. Indeed, it gave me a guilty pang to realise that Emily had not looked genuinely contented since that time—only a few months ago, although it seemed so much longer—when Father was shot, and I had suggested we should write novels. As for Anne, it was lucky for her that Father was nowhere to be seen, for even in his distracted state, he would surely have noticed that something was amiss. Her rosebud mouth was compressed into a tight knot, her face had set into grim lines—suddenly she looked much older—and her eyes looked swollen, though whether from tears or lack of sleep I could not tell.

After a long day's absence, Father came in to tea. At first, I thought he had been restored to his old self, for he was calm, quiet, and deliberate, and his old economy of movement and speech had returned. But as I watched him eat I realised that there was something else, a brooding threat, lurking behind his eyes. Something was afoot: but what?

The silence in the room, broken only by the tinkle of china, the scrape of a teaspoon, the creak of a chair, seemed to thrum with anticipation. Wordless messages were passing between Anne and Emily. Father sipped his tea and buttered slices of bread, and I thought of Saturn devouring his children.

We waited like hungry wolves, watching Father eat, waiting for our chance. The plan was already set, but all depended on him. What would he do next? I hoped desperately that he wouldn't go out again, or disappear into his study. I thought he would never stop eating, but finally he swilled down his last mouthful of tea, wiped his mouth, pushed back his chair, and got to his feet.

"Oh, before you go, Father," I said, "could you help me with something in my room?"

"Certainly," he said, all unsuspecting.

He went up the hall to my bedroom, and I followed him, Anne and Emily trailing silently.

He stepped inside and turned to look at me. And in that moment I grabbed the door and slammed it shut on him. The look of betrayal on his face as he realised what I was doing will stay with me forever. I grabbed the handle and threw my not inconsiderable weight into keeping it closed until Emily could turn the key in the lock, but it took all my efforts to keep the door closed as he tugged vigorously from the other side, trying to force his way out.

"What is the meaning of this?" he roared. "Let me out at once!"

"It's for your own good, Father," I called forlornly. "Please try to be patient."

"Let me out this instant, damn your eyes!" he roared.

But of course all his bellowing was pointless, for I was not going to let him out.

As the banging and hammering continued, Anne, Emily, and I looked at each other, a little shocked by what we had done. Emily was the first to break the silence.

"That's that then," said Emily. "We must get on."

"Yes," said Anne.

Emily turned to me, and I knew that the moment I had been dreading was at hand. "Look for us when you come ashore. We'll be waiting."

"Good luck," I said.

She hugged me tight, an intense embrace, and then, all too quickly, she was gone.

"I'll be back in a few minutes for the bags. Keep an eye on Father," Anne said. She gave me a tense smile, and then she, too, was gone.

I sank down on the floor with my back to the bedroom door and dissolved into tears. I was exhausted, and now I was alone with Father. I was glad the door kept us apart.

Anne

It was a dark night, with a sliver of moon appearing and disappearing behind scudding clouds. Rain threatened, but had not yet struck. Anne and Emily hurried in silence across the night-smelling grass, heading for the tree line, and thence to the guards waiting outside the dumb cells. Emily carried with her a small bundle; Anne was empty-handed. As the low-roofed hut over the dumb cells drew into view, Emily halted. Anne went on, moving through the trees, until she had passed the buildings. Her guts swam with nerves; fear robbed her of breath. She had no idea if this was going to work, and if it was up to her they would not be attempting it. But Emily had insisted that she would not leave the island while her man was still in custody. So they were attempting a jailbreak. And while it was certainly true that no jailbreak had ever succeeded before under Father's regime, Father's regime was no longer what it had been; and it had never been tried by someone with access to Father's keys.

For a moment, Anne thought of giving up, of running straight down to the beach and waiting for the Diver. But they had come this far; she could not back out now. And how would she ever explain herself to a wrathful Emily? Anne tried to summon up the spirit of Lady Alexandrina, steeled herself for the performance ahead, and then went dashing headlong out of the cover of the trees, running for the dumb cells and the two troopers who guarded them.

"Oh, sirs, please help me!" she cried, as she headed towards them, discovering it wasn't at all difficult to sound suitably distraught.

The troopers, who had been looking cold and bored, snapped to attention, and peered at her through the gloom.

"That you, Miss Anne?" asked one.

"Yes," she gasped, "oh please come and help me. My sister is sleepwalking again. She's gone out of the house and I can't find her anywhere. I'm so frightened she'll walk right off the cliff if I don't find her."

The troopers looked at each other doubtfully, wondering whether to leave their posts.

"Please," she begged desperately, hoping that one wouldn't elect to stay behind, "we may not have much time."

"It'll be quicker if we split up," said one.

"Any idea which way she went?" asked the other.

"I'm not sure, but I thought I caught a glimpse of her back that way. I don't like to trouble you, but I'm afraid to go by myself."

"I'll come with you, miss. Don't you worry," said one.

"No, I'll come with you," said the other. "Why don't you go and look the other way."

"We'll all go together then," said Anne, eager to get them moving. "I think it was this way."

And she led them off towards the trees.

She had not spent much time out of doors at night, and even though she knew the island was quite benign, human inhabitants aside, it took on quite a different complexion once the sun went down. The air was heavy with the smell of salt, cold and chilly and wet, laced with the flavour of trees that only gave off their scent at night. Things shifted and rustled, twitched and snapped as they trampled noisily through the bush. The trunks of the ghost-gums were pale in the moonlight, and their feet snapping branches and crushing leaves released a thick cloudy perfume of eucalyptus. Her spirits sank uncontrollably, and she began to feel frightened. Although her sense of direction was usually excellent, Anne quickly lost her bearings in the dark, so that the scrub seemed to expand in every direction, becoming limitless. She began to feel, as she thrashed and stumbled on, that the bushland she had plunged into was not the bush she knew, but was some other, archetypal forest, the endless forest of fairy tales, where it is fatal to stray from the path, and all manner of malign things lie in wait, in caves and in trees and under logs. The presence of the two troopers crashing along beside her was only partially reassuring, for she began to have the uncanny feeling that they were being followed by something which used their own noisy passage to mask the sounds of its own progress, a scaled or furred beast which stopped when they stopped and marched when they marched, slithering through the night gardens of its own domain, drawing ever closer.

"Look out!" cried one of the troopers, grabbing her by the wrist. She caught a glimpse of open air between the trees and pulled up just short of a precipice. The wind off the sea hit her in the face and she looked out and down, in a kind of fascinated dread, at the vertical drop below. There was no path down this section of the cliffs. At some point in the past, the rock had sheared off and dropped into the water below. And she had nearly gone the same way.

One of the troopers peered reluctantly over.

"Do you see anything?"

Anne looked too, half expecting to see Emily lying like a broken toy on the rocks far below. But of course, there was nothing.

"No."

Anne was suddenly eager to get away from this place. She felt sure she had given Emily enough time.

"There's no sign of her," Anne said. "Would you escort me back to the house? Someone else may have found her."

"You're sure? We can keep looking."

"No. Let's go back."

So they turned and began to pick their way back through the scrub, which turned out to be not very deep at all, for it was only a matter of minutes before they emerged once more onto open grass. Anne looked about her anxiously for any sign of the fugitives, but they were nowhere in sight, and she prayed that they had made it safely down to the beach.

"Does she do this often?" asked one of the troopers. "Sleepwalking I mean?"

"I'm afraid so," Anne said. "But she doesn't often get out of the house."

"Must be a worry," said the other trooper.

"It is."

"We haven't been introduced," said the first trooper. "My name's Skeldale."

"Vauxhall," said the other.

"How do you do?" said Anne politely. "I'm Anne Wolf. But you already know that."

"Nice to finally make your acquaintance," said Skeldale.

"Same goes for me," said Vauxhall.

Aware of their eyes on her, Anne wondered just how long it had been since they last had any shore leave. "Do you like working here?" she asked.

"Not specially," said Skeldale, "but you've got to go where you're sent."

"I'll say one thing for it," said Vauxhall, "there's nothing to spend your money on. I've saved up a packet since I been here. I'm going to buy some property when I get back to Sydney."

"Really? Where?"

Anne was only half listening as Vauxhall started filling her in on the best land deals. Privately, she was marvelling at how simple it was to hold a conversation with men she didn't know. It had always seemed petrifyingly difficult before. What did one say? How did one respond? What did you do if you couldn't think of anything to say? But the answer was quite simple: keep asking them questions and they would talk about themselves all night. Suddenly the prospect of living in normal society again did not seem so daunting.

But the real world, she reminded herself, was still a very great distance away.

At last they reached the house. "Wait here," said Anne, and left them waiting by the front door. She slipped inside and found a pale, frightened-looking Charlotte guarding the door.

"Is he still in there?" she hissed.

Charlotte nodded. "All going to plan?"

"So far."

Anne went back outside. "Oh, good sirs," she bubbled. "Such a relief! My sister has been safely found and returned to her bed."

"Oh," said Skeldale, rather disappointed. "That's good news." He looked at Vauxhall. "S'pose we'd better get back to our posts."

"Yes," said Anne. "And thank you so much for all your help. I'm very grateful."

"No trouble at all, miss," said Vauxhall.

"Let us know if you ever need anything else," said Skeldale.

"I will," said Anne, giving them her sweetest smile. "Good night."

With great reluctance, Vauxhall and Skeldale turned and headed off into the darkness. Anne watched them go, a touch regretfully, wondering how they would fare tomorrow. Then she shut the door and went back into the house to collect the two carpetbags that contained everything she and Emily were taking with them. It was not much to show for a whole life, but they had little choice.

"Wait," said Charlotte, "I thought of something you should take."

From her pocket she took out a small green case and handed it to Anne. Anne knew it at once: it was a set of six very old silver teaspoons that had once belonged to their mother.

"We can't take these," Anne said.

"They're worth money," Charlotte said. "You might need them."

Anne felt a wave of guilt at leaving Charlotte behind. "Come with us," she said impulsively. She had rarely felt so tenderly towards her prickly older sister, but the thought of leaving her behind to deal with Father and face rioting convicts seemed too cruel for words.

"But I will see you tomorrow," Charlotte said, puzzled.

Anne drew Charlotte out the door and into the darkness. She could almost feel Father straining to hear them from behind the bedroom door.

"There's something you don't know."

As quickly as she could, Anne told Charlotte about the Diver, his brother, and the mutiny. "You must promise me," she finished, "that as soon as we're gone, you'll go somewhere and hide."

"But—but what about Father?" Charlotte asked, her voice almost disappearing as she tried not to cry.

"You must do as you see fit," Anne said. "We are leaving at midnight. If you must tell Father about this, at least give us a chance to get away."

"Of course," Charlotte said.

Anne put her arms around Charlotte, pressing her cheek against her sister's cheek, wishing, far too late, that things had been different between them.

"Be careful," she said.

Anne picked up her bags and headed out through the kitchen. She closed the door behind her and made for the beach, and she did not once look back.

Emily

As soon as they were gone I ran out from the edge of the trees and made my way to the dumb cells—

What appears at first to be a low hut or cottage is actually a sentry post and a long sloping corridor or Tunnel that leads down at a steep slope into the earth—I went down—it was quite dark—and felt a Chill as of the Grave strike me—I tried not to think of how my love had fared living in such a dreadful place for so long—if his wits were not Wrecked, I feared his Health would be, for the cold was deathly—

I prayed that the keys I had found were the correct ones—if they were not, all was lost—

At the bottom of the tunnel were three doors—

I felt like a Figure in a Quest whose fate hung upon the correct choice of door, although I knew this was Absurd—

I stood quite still for a moment—listening—and although there was no sound, but for the distant roaring of the waves and a faint whistle of the wind through a chink in the walls above—I knew that my love lay behind the middle door—

I put the key to the lock—I turned it—I opened it—

Finn?

Movement within—breathing—then his voice—

Emily?

I stepped into that cold, dank place—Death surrounded me at once

and I felt like I was falling—up and down, night and day meant nothing—my blood began to roar in my ears and I felt like I was spinning—
yet my feet were anchored to the ground and I took courage, knowing
that I could yet find my way out—

I have come to get you out.

I cannot stand.

I will help you.

Where are we going?

Away from this place.

I took a step forward—and my foot encountered some part of
him—I fell to my knees—oh longed-for moment!—and took him in my
arms again—how weak he felt! yet how tightly he held me—

I can't believe you're really here. You're not a ghost?

I'm as real as you.

I did not want to tarry—his captors could return at any moment—

Here, let me put this on you.

I had brought with me an old dress, a shawl, and a bonnet—feeling
for his arms in the darkness, I pulled the dress over his head, and dragged
his arms through the sleeves—it was a very tight fit and there would be
no hope of doing the dress up across that broad back—I wrapped him
up in the shawl, hoping it would keep the dress on him—tied on the
bonnet—and then I draped his arm around my neck—

In truth he could not stand at all and was weak as a Baby—but
somehow I managed to take his weight—and together we struggled—
agonisingly slowly—up the path to freedom—

At the top he stopped—and I saw him gaze wildly around him as
the night air struck his face—

It is night.

Yes, and a dark night, luckily for us.

I thought I had gone blind. Is that the moon?

It is.

It looks so blurry.

All will be well. But we must hurry.

He smelled of earth and sickness—but I knew that in time I could make him well again and give him back the gift he had given me—

You must love me a great deal to do this for me.

It seemed a curious thing to say—a dark chill feeling crept over me—something in his tone did not seem right—

Would you not do the same for me?

He did not answer—

We crept on slowly—and I fancied that he was recovering his strength a little—but still I dreaded the cliff that lay ahead of us—if he could not walk down himself, would I be able to manage us both?

Fears and doubts assailed me—we struggled on—at last we reached the path down the cliff to the beach—

Can you make it?

I'll try.

Fearfully, perilously, we began—But soon we began to slip and slither—the footing was loose and uncertain—he fell heavily and could not get up—finally he resorted to slithering down on his backside, and in this manner, with many groans and cries, he reached the sand—

I looked Anxiously for the man who would be our Rescuer—of him, no sign—we were alone—

I was more tired by that long anxious walk than I had anticipated—and I hoped there would be no more exertions on the other side of the bay—

I sat down beside O'Connell in the sand and gazed around me—the white surf shone in the moonlight—far above, the wind tore a hole in the clouds and I caught a glimpse of a rich, deep, splendid array of stars—Gazing up at those ageless eyes I felt myself shrinking to a single drop of water, a grain of sand on the beach—my earthly troubles retreated and for a moment I was no more, no less, than a stone being turned and ground in the churning surf—

You once made some promises to me.

I have not forgotten.

Do you intend to honour them?

I tried to read his answer in his face—but I could not—in the darkness his face was a savage mask—blank, featureless—his eyes two dark hollows, his mouth a wound—

I suppose you think, now you have rescued me, I am beholden to you?

I do not.

But you would lay claim to me?

I make no claims. But I asked you a question. And you have not answered it.

I will not be owned. Not by any man, and not by a woman either.

Why do you speak of ownership? I want to see into your heart. When you said you loved me, did you tell me true, or did you lie?

He was silent a moment—

I told you true.

And do you love me still?

Before I answer that question, tell me this. You fell in love with me when bars stood between us and there was no chance of us being together. You do not know me. You do not know what I am capable of, what I have done, what I still might do. Are you willing to risk all on me?

His eyes glittered in the dark as he fixed his gaze on me—was he trying to warn me?—was he testing me?—I could not guess his purpose— I could only tell him what I know to be true—

If you mean me harm I cannot stop you. But I do not think you do. I believe we were meant to be together, and that a bond was forged between us that goes beyond words. What does it matter that we have not spent any time sitting in a drawing room, taking tea and getting to know one another? The heart speaks its own language, and I believe that our hearts knew each other from the moment we first set eyes on one another. They are entangled, and cannot be separated. I must love you or die. I have no choice.

He leaned over and took my face in his strong hand—his fingers scorched their prints into my jaw like a brand—and then twined in my hair—he drew me to him—he kissed me—his face rough, his lips tender, sweet-salty—a taste of the sea—

Then we are doomed to love.

Ten

The waves

Charlotte

"Charlotte?"

Father's voice was intimately close. I fancied he must have his face pressed right up against the door.

"What is the meaning of this? Where's Anne going?"

His voice was calm—he sounded like the cool, rational father of old, and for a moment I let myself think that maybe things would be alright.

"She is eloping."

"With whom?"

"I'm not exactly sure. He has a boat."

"I take it Emily is going with her?"

"Yes."

"She never forgave me for putting a stop to that liaison with the convict."

"She hasn't given up on him either."

"What do you mean?"

"They're taking him with them."

There was a long silence.

He's taking this surprisingly well, I thought. But then I heard movement from the other side of the door: Father was getting to his feet. I listened, wondering what he was up to, and was almost stunned by the force of the blow as Father threw his weight against the door, slamming it into my head. My ear started to sing on the side where I'd been struck, and I was sufficiently disoriented that I was not able to stop Father from opening the door and shoving me out of the way. Dazed, I grabbed at him as he pushed past me, but he brushed me off as if I were a cobweb. He knew there was only one place a boat could land; he knew exactly where to find them. With my ears still ringing and my head aching from the blow, I set off after him.

A few fat drops of rain plopped around me as I chased Father through the darkness. He knew I was there, but he knew I could not stop him, so he didn't care whether I followed him or not. He was like a machine, steaming across the grassy slope towards the cliff and the path down to the beach. I wished I'd thought to disarm him, but the thought had not crossed my mind; and I did not know how I could have managed it in any case. I could not guess at what he intended. Would he drag Emily and Anne home and lock them in their rooms? Or would he take more drastic measures? In his passion, there was no knowing what he might do.

He took the path down the cliff in leaps and bounds, as if he feared nothing for his own safety, but some evil angel was guiding his footsteps. I slithered down more cautiously, searching the darkness for any sign of my sisters. Were they still here on the beach? It could not be midnight yet, the time Emily had nominated. I feared their ferryman would come too late.

But as I neared the bottom, I heard a ghastly cry spring from Father's throat, and, looking up, I saw that there was indeed a boat surfing towards us through the hissing swell, and four dark figures were splashing out to meet it. One seemed unsteady on its feet, and the others had to support that one, but I could not tell who it was. Father ran across the beach and went plunging after them. I struggled down the last few yards of cliff and watched helplessly from the sand. The first of the figures was dragged up into the boat, which rocked dangerously but did not quite tip over. Then a wave struck them and both occupants were almost thrown back into the water. The second figure climbed in, and then the third, as Father drew ever nearer. Then the four of them that were in the boat combined to pull in the last. As soon as all were safely in, the boatman took the oars and began to row as hard as he could, pushing out into the surf, but it seemed certain now that Father would catch them. As he lunged for the gunwale, my heart lurched with horror, for out of the darkness, a huge wave suddenly reared up above them. I saw the faint pale blur of the five faces looking upward as the water closed on them, and I feared that they would all be drowned in an instant, but then the boat slipped over the top of the wave, and I saw it come crashing down on Father. I ran down to the water's edge, hoping to catch a glimpse of Father, while the oarsman pulled frantically on his oars, trying desperately to get clear of the roil where the waves were breaking. To my relief, I saw Father stand up in the boiling white water, which was now only knee-high as the water sucked out again. He let out another cry of rage and despair as he saw that they had escaped him, and he took a few strides after them, but already they were pulling further and further away, and another wave was bearing down on him. He stood his ground, and the wave crashed around him. He staggered, but was not knocked off his feet. Then I heard his voice drift back to me, blown by the wind:

"I will find you, God damn you," he cried. "I will hunt you down and I will bring you back!"

But in the immensity of that churning water and those rearing cliffs, his voice was as thin as the cry of a seagull. The two of us stood alone together on the beach and watched as they rowed out over the reefs that guarded the island, the boat a tiny shape tossed by the water, now visible, now hidden by the waves, now visible again. So what happened next came to me as a discontinuous series of glimpses: first they were alright, rowing steadily for the mainland; then they were being tossed sideways by a sudden rearing swell; then the moonlight glinted off black rock, and I could have sworn I heard the tearing of wood; then there was only one figure in the boat; and what had become of the others, I could not tell.

Anne

With a shocking suddenness she was pitched headlong into the water. The Diver cried out; and she thought she heard Emily scream. *We are all drowned*, she thought, as gravity pulled her under the water. But she kicked up strongly and broke the surface of the water, and began looking frantically around her. There was the boat, with the Diver still in it. But where was Emily? Where was O'Connell, and the Diver's brother?

"Anne!" screamed the Diver, spotting her.

"Emily!" Anne called, twisting and floundering in the water, searching desperately for her head.

"Try and swim over!" shouted the Diver, frantic, although he knew she couldn't swim.

"I have to find Emily!"

"She's lost," said the Diver, "save yourself!"

"Help!" It was Emily's voice.

Anne swung around, straining to hold her head out of the water as she kicked and struggled, trying to find her sister. Then she spotted her, already some distance away.

"I can't hold him!" cried Emily. She was trying to support O'Connell, although she could not swim herself.

"There they are!" screamed Anne to the Diver, pointing. "Help them!"

But the tides were already dragging them apart. Emily and O'Connell were swept away by a rip, even as she struggled to reach them. A wave washed over them both, and when she looked again, she could not see them. Despair tore through her. She began to look around for the boat, but she could not see it.

"Help!" she called.

She heard his answering voice in reply, but already it was moving away. "Where are you? I can't find you! Anne! Robbie!"

"Help!"

But the water pulled them further and further apart, and when finally she glimpsed him, he was rowing away from her, and he was alone in the boat. She swallowed a huge mouthful of water and realised she was on her own.

Holding her head up high out of the water, she began a frantic, desperate dog paddle. The movements were unfamiliar and her waterlogged clothes held her as tight as a fish in a net. The current seemed to be dragging her out to sea and she remembered what she had been told about the tide that would take her to Antarctica, the seaweed that would grab her and take her down. The water smacked over her head, burying her beneath a sea of bubbles, and she kicked hysterically for the surface, her mouth full of water, wondering how long it would be before she could no longer hold up her head and she no longer had the strength to fight for the surface—but then suddenly a wave caught her and she found she was coasting back in to shore, back to Coldwater. For a few brief moments, she felt like she was in flight, and she was filled with a dizzying sense of hope—maybe there was a way out of this after all, maybe she was not for drowning. Then the wave passed beneath her and she was forced to dog-paddle again. When the next wave caught her she was not so lucky—suddenly she was among rocks and the water slapped her hard against them, dragging and tumbling her along, ripping skin off, bruising and battering, the intense cold of the water making the pain seem even more acute. But then she was clear of the rocks, and in open water, and the wave had passed over, and she struggled on, although her arms were scorching with an intense red pain and she was starting to shiver right down to her bones with the cold. Then her feet briefly touched bottom, and she knew she was almost home. With her last strength she floundered through the water, put her foot down experimentally, and discovered the water was now seven feet deep and she was submerged. Panicked, she kicked up to the surface again, and was carried by a last surge of surf into shallow water.

And then, astonishingly, Charlotte was there, helping her out of the water and onto the shore.

"Where's Emily?" Anne gasped, through a mouth puckered by salt.

"I don't know," said Charlotte.

"I lost her," said Anne. "I saw her—she was in the water—but then I lost her—"

"I couldn't see."

"We'll raise the guard—get them to take the boat out and look for her—"

"It's too late," said Charlotte.

"She'll be alright," Anne insisted, although a deep and terrible fear was spreading through her, the sickening blow of loss, "we just have to find her."

"It's too late," Charlotte repeated. "We've lost her."

Emily

Panic at first as you cannot take a breath—a deep, visceral animal feeling—you gasp and gasp but all that comes in is water, choking you— you are being smothered, surrounded, invaded, you fight for breath, fight for the surface, but it is gone—shattering fear—the knowledge that you are going to die—an immense sorrow for all that you've lost, all that you will not do—then the panic fades—and you start to drift and you think *I have been here before*—and I wonder if I am remembering a dream or something far earlier, those earliest moments of life—and I wonder if I have come back to the place where I started—liquidity, life—and then he is there, smiling at me—he takes my hand—*I have so much to show you*—

Eleven

Revolt

Charlotte

I forced Anne to return with me to the house, take off her wet things, and put on a change of clothes. The fire had not been banked and had gone out completely; the house was dark and cold. Already it felt curiously abandoned, as if the fight was already over, the battle lost, the island given up. But I was determined things would not end this way. The uprising would be stopped, Father would come back to me, the cottage would be our home again, and we would leave it formally and officially, with all our things packed up in boxes and trunks and shipped back to Sydney. There would be no scrambling, desperate flight off the island, like refugees fleeing a war. Perhaps today was the day the orders would come that would bring an end to Father's reign. Perhaps today was the day we would all start the long journey home.

As the sky in the east began to lighten, and the island emerged once more from darkness into a bleak grey half-light, Anne and I made our way back down the cliff once more. Father had not moved; he stood on the beach, gaunt, still, like an Easter Island statue, staring out at the water, daring it to give Emily back. But there was no sign of her; or of O'Connell; or of the boat, or the Diver.

"Father," I said, "there's something you should know. The prisoners are planning to rise today."

He did not move, did not stir. His expression did not change, and I wondered if he'd even heard me.

"There's going to be a revolt. The prisoners are planning to rise up and seize the supply ship. If they find us, they will kill us."

Still there was not a sign, not a word from Father.

"Do you hear me?" I screamed.

He let out a great sigh, and turned to look at me, his face as lined and craggy as the cliff face. "Let them come," he said. "What do I care?"

"You've got to do something," Anne said, "or we'll all be killed."

A ghastly smile spread across his features. "Last night before supper I locked all the officers in the mess. I barred the door so they couldn't get out. There was mutiny in the air. I could feel it. I'm never wrong."

I was aghast. "We've got to let them out," I said, "there's no time to lose!"

"It is already too late."

"Father, they're going to kill us," I shouted.

"It is my punishment," he said gravely, and turned his face out to sea again.

Panic fluttered in my chest. He was not going to lift a finger to help us. We were on our own.

Anne would have stayed with Father, I think—waiting, perhaps, for her man to return?—but I grabbed her and dragged her off. We had to let the officers out and warn them about what was coming, and then we had to find a safe place to hide.

"Do you know what time it's supposed to happen?" I gasped, as we struggled up the cliff path. Anne was bounding ahead of me like a young rabbit.

"Any time now," she called back. "I think it was planned for dawn."

The sun had not yet crept over the horizon but I was sure it could not be far off. *Dawn* was a very imprecise measure of time—were we already too late? When we reached the top of the cliff would we find hordes of convicts swarming over the island? Or was there still time?

Anne was already receiving instructions through the door when I reached the officers' mess. "Wake the troops," I heard a muffled voice say. "Get them to break down the door."

Anne rushed off to rouse the men, and I was left to keep a nervous lookout, expecting every moment to see rampaging convicts erupting onto the scene.

Soon the troopers arrived with axes and sledgehammers and set to work breaking down the door. It was quickly accomplished, and the officers emerged, filthy and unshaven, into the light. Mr. Fry took charge, despatching men to guard the armoury, and ordering another detachment to guard the approach to the beach. If anyone tried to get on or off the island, their orders were to shoot on sight. We were put into the care of a young officer, who was told to keep us safe (although how one man was supposed to do that against a determined mob I could not imagine). The men scattered, but I feared our efforts had come too late—a smell of smoke began to suffuse the air.

Plumes of smoke began to pour from the windows of the convicts' barracks, and the prison complex began to look like an ant nest stirred up by a malicious boy with a stick. Prisoners emerged and began surging about, waving firebrands and pickaxes and stones and anything else they could lay their hands on. I saw a lone trooper struck from behind by a rock, and then the mob surged over him, and I feared there would be nothing left of him when the seething scrum dispersed again.

Then I saw a head turn in our direction. A finger pointed. We had been seen.

"You've got to hide us somewhere," I insisted, tugging on the arm of the young officer who had been assigned to us. He gaped and dithered, not sure what to do.

"I'll take you back to the cottage," he said, trying to sound decisive. "You should be safe there."

"Nonsense," said Anne, "if the mob comes after us, it's the first place they'd look."

"Then I'll put you in the cell block."

"You'll do no such thing!" I snapped.

"I know a place," Anne said suddenly. "They'll never think of looking there."

"Where?"

"It's a cave, down by the waterline. Trust me. We'll be safe there."

"I'm not taking you down there," said the officer, staring. "Come on. We're going to the cell block. Now."

He grabbed each of us by the arm and started dragging us away. Anne wrenched herself free. "Come with me, Charlotte!"

"We've got to stay with him," I said.

She gave me one last imploring look and then ran off. I yelled at her to come back, but she did not look back.

"We haven't got time for this!" squeaked the officer. "Why can't you obey orders?"

So I allowed myself to be hustled off to the cell block, but I did not truly understand what I had agreed to until I reached the place. The cell block was the most sturdily built construction in the settlement, a squat, massive building with thick stone walls and tiny barred windows. The officer took the keys, pushed me into an empty cell, slammed the door on me, and locked me in. And so there I was forced to sit, shivering in the cold, waiting for the assault I felt sure would come at any moment. For there were other convicts around me in the other cells—I could hear them hooting and hullooing and demanding to be let out—and I felt sure that once the mob had killed all the troopers they would surely come and set their unfortunate fellows free. And then they would find me. And I had to struggle hard not to think about what would certainly happen next.

The smell of smoke grew ever stronger. I heard sporadic outbursts of gunfire, and much shouting. I could hear the ghastly sound of wounded men cursing and howling. And all around me, the air seemed filled with the roiling atmosphere of destruction. Fire had taken hold of the island—the roar of it gradually engulfed all other sound. I tried to climb up and look through my window to see if it threatened me, but I could not gain a foothold sufficient to drag myself up. The walls of the cell block were made of thick stone, but, looking up, I saw the roof was made of wood, and would surely burn. Of all the ways I had imagined I might die, it had never occurred to me I might burn to death, locked in one of my own father's prison cells.

And what of Father? He would almost certainly be cut down where he stood, down there on the beach, unless he suddenly came to his senses and defended himself. A detachment of troops had been sent to guard the approach to the beach, but would it be sufficient? Would they be able to stop the prisoners escaping on the supply ship?

A dreadful thought struck me then. What if they did abandon the island? What if the officer who had locked me in here had been killed? No one would know I was here. I would be left behind, forgotten, abandoned, caged. I could die here, locked in this cell, I could starve to death. But I did not dare cry for help, for fear of who might come to let me out.

And I did not dare to wonder what might have become of Anne.

Gradually, as the daylight brightened and the fires cracked and rumbled on, I realised a kind of quiet had fallen. There was no more gunfire, no more shouting. Where had everyone gone? I wondered. Was it all over? Had the convicts finally won? Would they be shortly coming to let us out? Or had they abandoned the imprisoned to their fate?

When, finally, I heard a key in the lock, I was close to collapsing in hysterical terror. I pressed myself into a corner of the cell, fearing myriad disasters—fire, rape, starvation, a quick bullet to the head. I could no longer determine which was worse—abandonment to a slow, solitary death, or the searing indignities that would surely follow discovery. But then I saw a uniform, and an anxious face. It was the young officer who had locked me in, coming to set me free.

"You can come out now," he said. "It's all over."

I rose to my feet and followed him tremblingly out into the morning. The island looked like a vision of hell, bathed in crisp spring sunlight. Here and there men lay, wounded, bleeding, some still living and twitching and moaning, others dead, turning livid, horribly still, twisted into the unnatural forms of death. A stink of blood, of stomachs, of the acrid steaming insides of people rose up in the still, cold, morning air. Most of the buildings were burning to the ground; the cell block was one of the few that remained untouched. No attempt was being made to put the fires out, for the troopers were too busy dealing with the prisoners to care. The bush that ringed our settlement had caught fire too, and was burning ferociously, flames rising high into the air as the eucalypts heated, caught, and then exploded, burning like torches. We were standing on a vast tract of cleared land, and so were probably safe from the flames, although I could not be entirely sure. The whole island, it seemed, was ablaze. Soon, there would be nothing left, and there was nothing to be done about it.

The young officer explained that the revolt had failed—they had never even reached the supply ship. He pointed to the parade ground in front of the dreaded triangle, where the remaining convicts had been herded into a group. They were being held at bay by troopers with rifles, but the troopers were greatly outnumbered, and I reflected that if the convicts had made an organised rush they could easily have overpowered them. But the convicts merely submitted sullenly as several troopers rushed around and chained them all together in one great rope of human misery.

"Where is Anne?" I asked. "Have you seen her?"

"Not since she ran off," said the officer. "But I'm sure we'll find her soon enough."

His assurances did not comfort me much.

"And what about Father?"

He hesitated. "I have not seen him either."

It was all too much. "I would like to go back to my house now," I said.

So he escorted me up the hill towards the cottage, but as we drew nearer I saw that it had not escaped the torch. A section of the roof was gone, and the windows had blown out. Smoke blackened the walls, and there were still wisps of smoke rising from it. I tried to comfort myself that it was not razed to the ground, but nonetheless it seemed clear that it was quite unliveable, and that all our things must surely be destroyed. In the face of all that I had lost, the thought that my manuscript had probably fuelled the fire reduced me, at last, to hopeless tears.

"I'll take you to the mess," the officer said awkwardly, "we'll get you a cup of tea."

For some reason the officers' mess had been left standing, and the cook was doling out a belated breakfast. Nearby, the quartermaster's store had been broken into and ransacked. Sugar, flour, tea was spilled everywhere, and the ground was crisscrossed with white footprints. The convicts, of course, had been after the rum stores.

I had never been inside the officers' mess before, and it was a pleasant enough room, with long tables and whitewashed walls, although there was a lingering feral smell of enclosed bodies after the lock-in. The officers all stared and murmured when they saw me walk in, and I felt distinctly uncomfortable as I thought about what my father had done to them. Would they blame me for all that had happened?

My officer found me a chair, and some tea, and some bread, and sat me down in a corner. The thought of food nauseated me, but I took a few bites out of politeness, and discovered as I did so that my body was very hungry indeed, even if my heart told me I was not.

Mr. Fry detached himself from a group of soldiers and came to join me, offering me a reassuring smile, although on that humourless face it looked rather ghastly.

"I'm glad to see you're alright, Miss Wolf," he said formally. "But where are your sisters?"

"I lost Anne in the melee," I said. "She said she knew of a hiding place. A cave?"

Mr. Fry frowned, then glanced at the officer who sat with me. The young officer nodded, and departed.

"And what about Emily?"

I could scarcely frame the words. "She escaped last night with the prisoner O'Connell. They were lost at sea."

"Escaped?" he repeated sharply.

"They did not succeed."

He did not push the point.

"Where is Father?"

He took a deep breath. My stomach plummeted; I already knew what his answer would be.

"I'm very sorry, Miss Wolf. He is dead."

Tears sprang to my eyes, and I scarcely heard the explanation he gave, as I was engulfed by the knowledge of shocking loss. I was quite, quite alone in the world, and Father, poor dear Father, was dead.

"He died heroically," Mr. Fry said. "A group of convicts headed for the beach, planning to overpower the crew of the supply ship and make their escape. Your father, despite being unarmed, was able to subdue the convicts and prevent an escape attempt being made. If it were not for your father's heroic actions, all might have been lost."

"How did he die then, if he subdued the convicts?" I asked.

"He was hit by a stray bullet as he came back up the cliff. Death would have been instantaneous."

"Where is he?" I asked. "I want to see him."

Mr. Fry looked at me dubiously. "I don't think that would be a good idea," he said.

But I insisted, and when I threatened to become hysterical, he gave in.

They had set up a temporary morgue in a tent, with a curtain to separate the officers from the enlisted men. There had been no arrangements made to house the bodies of the convicts. Mr. Fry conducted me silently to the officers' enclosure, and then discreetly withdrew, so that I might say my good-byes as best I could.

Some effort had been made, I think, to tidy Father up, for his face was unmarked, although there was a single splash of blood turning brown upon his cheek, and more of it matted in his salt-encrusted hair. His face was colourless, with the fixed, greyish pallor of death, and although his eyes were closed, he did not look like he slept. There was an unmoving rigidity to his face, a fixedness, which seemed to preclude the possibility of him ever waking up again. A blanket covered his body, and although I knew it must have been placed there to spare my feelings, I could not help myself. I had to peel it away, to see what terrible harm had turned my father from a man to a cold, colourless lump of clay.

His shirt, ripped and stuck to him in rags, was drenched in livid sworls of red and purple, drying to a crimson-brown, spotted here and there with thick, sticky blackish clots. That stray bullet had done its job spectacularly well. Father's chest no longer looked like skin stretched neatly over a compact network of organs. Now it was a horrible crater. The first time Father was shot the assassin had missed his heart, but the second time he had truly found his target.

I had been so impressed with myself, with my maturity, on that night, several months ago, when I sat down with my sisters and talked so matter-of-factly about what we would do if anything should happen to Father. I had never imagined anything like this. This was beyond my power to imagine; this was beyond everything.

I covered him up again and left the tent.

Mr. Fry was waiting for me.

"Your father was himself again when the call came," he said soberly, in the measured cadences of a dead march. "I don't deny that there were problems here—the governor has already been informed of them, and it's too late to do anything about that. But when it mattered most, the Captain rose to the occasion and was himself once more. I know it was he who sent you girls to let us out. And that it was he who uncovered the plot among the convicts. I intend to make it clear in my report that the Captain was a hero who died defending his men."

I very much wanted to believe this account of Father's last moments, even if it did not tally with his behaviour over the last few weeks of his life. Military discipline had given my father his contours; it was the rigour that had shaped his personality. Without it, he became amorphous, unfamiliar, a troubling and frightening figure I could not recognise. Now, in death, he had been given back to me in the shape I first knew him.

"Thank you, sir," I whispered. "I cannot tell you how grateful I am."

He nodded, brushing my gratitude aside. "The supply ship is standing by. I've signalled that you'll be returning to Sydney. Is there anyone there you can stay with?"

I shook my head dumbly.

"Not to worry. I'm sure we can sort out something."

"And what about Anne?"

"We'll find her."

But they did not find her. The officers returned from searching the cave, and said they had found no trace of her. The grim business of burying bodies began (proper graves for the troopers, a pit for the convicts), but her body was not among them. It was as if she had vanished.

Mr. Fry helped me put together a few belongings from the wreckage of our home, and then assisted me into the boat which would take me across the water. I was so hysterical with fear that I think they almost left me behind, but our trip across the bay was quite uneventful, and I was soon climbing up a ladder and standing on the deck of the ship that would take me back to Sydney.

How can I describe my feelings as I watched Coldwater moving away from me at last? As the boat slopped up and down in what felt, to me, like mountainous seas, but was probably only the gentlest of swells, I gripped the gunwale so tightly my knuckles turned purple, and I thought my heart would expire, it was hammering so hard. When we landed on Coldwater all those years ago the island had seemed enormous, rearing up out of the water like a subcontinent. Now, I could see it was only a rock in the ocean, not even a very big rock in the ocean, and it had probably once been a part of the mainland before the action of the tides cut it off. It had felt like a world in itself, a place so estranged from the natural world that Gulliver might have visited it. I half expected to see it sink into the sea as I left it behind, as if only the force of my father's will had kept it afloat all this time. But there was nothing uncanny about it. It was as it had always been, a small, rocky island, no longer a fortress of pain, an empire of suffering, but a smoking, burnt-out little settlement on the sea, which would shortly be returned to the gulls and penguins.

Anne

When she was certain that the tide was no longer sluicing in and out of the cave mouth, Anne stiffly and painfully unfolded herself from her hiding place in the narrow cleft of rock at the top of the cave. The Diver had been right—it was above the water at high tide, but only just. The more vigorous of the waves had washed seething and foaming over her head, so that she feared she would certainly be sucked out once more into the open water. But she clung on like a limpet, hour after hour, hardly daring to think about what might be going on up above, growing ever more weary and wet and cold, until all thought was driven from her head except the one, immediate imperative: to hang on tight. A rage to survive had been kindled in her heart and she never for a moment considered letting go, letting the tide take her where it would, giving up the fight. She would live to fight another day. She would live.

She made her way slowly to the mouth of the cave, hoping to catch some sun and warm up, for she was so cold she feared that exposure would snatch from her the life that the ocean could not. But the sun was not yet over the yardarm; this part of the island would not be in sunlight until the afternoon.

Now that the risk of drowning had receded, memories of the previous night began to bleed back into her thoughts. Emily's radiant happiness in the darkness on that silent beach as they waited for the Diver; the brief moment of euphoria as they believed they might succeed; desperation as Father came after them, driven by his obsession to prevent any and all escapes; terror as the boat tipped and they were thrown into the water. And then, a sea of unknowns. Emily. The Diver. The feeling of panic as she was washing through the water, but a panic that was larger than herself, doubled, the panic of two bodies, two minds. The old bond between them threatened to annihilate all reason as Emily's terror arced through her, overwhelming in its intensity. But as panic claimed her, there in the water, and peaked, then snapped, leaving her suddenly clear-headed and alone, she knew that she had lost her. And when, later, she was standing on the beach with Charlotte, crying for a boat, she knew that she was just trying to console herself, trying to pretend that she still believed there was a chance. She knew deep down there was no chance. She had felt the precise moment when the line between them was severed. And had Emily taken a leap into some unknown place of wonder, with her beloved beside her? She hoped that she had.

An unexpected movement caught her eye. Fearing the worst, Anne crouched behind a rock ledge and peered out suspiciously. Then a cry of joy burst from her lips. It was the Diver.

He looked up sharply at the sound, and when he saw her he started to laugh, a joyous, abandoned laugh, and started leaping across the rocks towards her. He caught her up in his arms and squeezed her tight, spinning her round and round, knocking the breath out of her, his face buried in her hair, and then he put her down on her feet and kissed her, avid and bruising.

"I wasn't sure if I'd find you here," he said finally. "Last night—when I lost you—"

"I made it ashore."

"And the others?"

She shook her head, unable to speak.

"I'm sorry, love." He stroked her face with a tough, callused finger.

"Where is your brother?"

He flinched at the question, and she knew what the answer was. "I lost him too."

The Diver fell silent. Anne pressed her face against his chest, inhaling his faintly briny scent. So this was how it ended, the two of them alone in the world. Emily was gone, and so was his Robbie, and the hole each left behind gaped hugely in their two aching hearts. How swiftly death moved.

"Take me away from here," she said.

"Don't you want to go up top, find your family?"

And she thought, *I want to be free from the past. I want to be a ghost. I want to disappear. I don't want to be Anne Wolf anymore. I want to dissolve and turn into something else. I want a transformation scene. I want to eat fruits with no names and swim in waters that aren't on maps. I want a new name and a new place. I want to be alive. I want to get out of the house of fiction and see the great world.*

"I just want to get away from here," she said.

He had anchored his boat off the rocks; they had to swim out. After all she had been through, the water held no more terrors for her. Her body was already numb with cold; once she was submerged again the water began to feel warmer than the air, although her teeth began to chatter so violently she felt as if they might shatter into pieces. He showed her how to float on her back, and then he towed her out to the boat. None of it seemed quite real. As the Diver started rowing her towards the mainland she began to wonder if this was really just a dream, one of those endless circling dreams where you try to get somewhere but however hard you try it just seems to get further and further away.

She was jolted sharply awake by a slap across the face. Pressing her palm to her stinging cheek, she stared up at him, outraged. "Don't go to sleep," he said.

Shocked, she struggled into a sitting position and watched the mainland coming closer. He was not aiming for the settlement, but headed instead for a sandy beach about half a mile to the south. The sand was beautifully white and clean, laced with seaweed, and above it was a seemingly impenetrable wall of scrub rising up to impossibly tall trees with glistening silver-white trunks.

"Is that where we're going?" she asked.

"Yes."

"But there's nothing there."

He smiled and said nothing.

Soon the boat was gliding in to shore. The Diver jumped out and waded through the water, then held a hand out to her. She took it, and jumped overboard. The water was waist-deep, and together they waded ashore. Anne flopped down on the sand as the Diver pulled the boat securely up onto the sand. He turned and grinned at her.

"No rest yet."

He hauled her to her feet and she followed him up the beach. There was a faint path through the scrub, and they followed this to a clearing. In the middle of the clearing was a tent made of canvas, stretched over a framework of green saplings. There was a cooking fire, extinguished now, in front of the tent, surrounded by a ring of rocks, with an old log drawn up beside it for a seat. A billy hung on a cradle of sticks, and a chestnut mare contemplatively cropped the grass under the trees.

"This is where you live?" she asked.

"This is it."

He led her up to the tent, and she peeked inside. The interior was sparsely furnished, with a swag on one side and a selection of boxes on the other. These boxes held some clothes, a tin cup and plate and some cutlery, and a few other essential bits and pieces—a map, a compass, a knife, a rifle. There was, she realised, not one book anywhere in the place. She could see a skink silhouetted against the wall of the tent, and brilliant specks of sunlight shone through pinpoint holes in the canvas. The thought of lying here in the night, with only that frail covering between the wind, the weather, and the wild things was a rather daunting thought. The thought that she would be lying there with *him* was an even more daunting thought.

She turned around and discovered him watching her, an anxious look on his face.

"It's not what you're used to, I know, but it's not so bad once you get used to it."

She realised he was ashamed of the poverty of the life he was offering her. It was the first time she had seen a chink in the armour of his irrepressible confidence.

"I'm sure I shall like it very well," she said.

A more impermanent dwelling could not be imagined, but the little tent was clean, and fresh, and new. There had been no dramas, no sorrows, no tragedies enacted within its canvas walls. There was no lingering savour, here, of madness or illness or death. It was fresh, raw, uncontaminated by sorrow. It was the clean slate she had been looking for.

She smiled at him, and saw an answering, rather relieved, smile spread across his face. And then she was in his arms, and kissing him as if she would never let him go.

Epilogue

My advice to any young Australian writer whose talents have been recognised would be to go steerage, stow away, swim and seek London, Yankeeland or Timbuctoo rather than stay in Australia till his genius turn to gall or beer. Or failing this, to study anatomy, especially as it applies to the cranium, and then shoot himself carefully with the aid of a looking glass.

HENRY LAWSON

"So, you're a colonial!" beamed Mr. Black. "You don't look half as wild as I expected. And you can read and write, too. Jolly good. So you want to be a novelist?"

"I am a novelist," I said.

"Quite," said Mr. Black, looking rather put out. "Not published though, eh, missy?" He tapped my manuscript, which was sitting on his desk. "I think I can do something with this but you'll have to make some changes."

"Such as?"

"Get rid of the gore. You finish up with a pile of corpses, it's positively Jacobean. And you'll have to change the location. Set it somewhere civilised. No one wants to read a romance set in Australia. There's no one there to admire. Just convicts and cannibals."

"There aren't any cannibals in Australia," I corrected, as politely as I could. Mr. Black did not take correction well at all.

"As far as the British reading public are concerned there are, and that's all anyone need care about."

Several rejection letters later, I received another invitation to make an appointment.

"It's alright I suppose," said Mr. Brewster, "but I'm not too keen on the ending. Never underestimate the power of the happy ending, my dear! Leave the punter with a rosy glow at the end and that's what they'll remember afterwards. Case in point: saw a production of *Romeo and Juliet* at Drury Lane the other week. Juliet woke up at just the right moment and everything was alright, it ended with a beautiful wedding and everybody walked out of the theatre smiling their heads off. Never had a nicer night in the theatre. Another example: *King Lear*. Original version's absolutely horrid. Everybody ends up dead, bereaved, or miserable, and you walk out of there wondering if you'd be better off smothering your children right now while you've still got the chance. Whereas in the new improved version, Cordelia is rescued in the nick of time, the loving father and daughter end up in each other's arms, Cordelia marries Edgar, and it all ends exquisitely. Do you think you could manage something like that?"

Persevere, said my aunt Jane, and persevere I did. But it was extremely disheartening and my manuscript was beginning to look horribly dog-eared. Then, finally, I received another invitation to come in and meet the publisher, a Mr. Smith.

He met me at the door, and against my own better judgement, I warmed to him. He did not seem as much of a charlatan as the others I had met; indeed, it seemed just possible he might actually be interested in books. But still, I dared not let myself hope.

Once he had introduced himself and we had sat down in his office, he began to speak, slowly and deliberately. "There are people who would say that a character with such naked ambition—I refer to the heroine of your book—is shocking and immoral. Such unladylike behaviour! Surely there cannot be such persons in civilised society?"

This sounded bad. But I had steeled my heart against disappointment. I would not cry. I would endure.

"However, my own experience would tend to suggest that people everywhere, men and women, can be cruel and greedy, just as they can be kind and loving. It's a slippery world we live in and people don't move in straight lines. We all want to be loved. We all want to be remembered. We all want to survive, in whatever way we can."

He paused, and his eyes met mine, as confusion turned to the dawning of wild, scarcely believing hope.

"I should like to publish your book, Miss Wolf."

I tend a garden in my dreams, a garden on an island, where a city of light is built upon the cliff face, a city on the water, where music plays every day and the sun shines and the ferns are rich and green, and red-and-blue parrots dart between the trees. It is a beautiful and civilised place, where the people discuss poetry and sit on their piazzas watching the lights change on the water until late into the night, where a man and his three daughters can live in harmony, a quartet of delight, where there is no anger, no cruelty, no madness, no revenge; only words, and love.

Historical Note

Charlotte (1816–1855), Branwell (1817–1848), Emily (1818–1848), and Anne (1820–1849) Brontë, four of the six children of the Reverend Patrick Brontë and Maria Branwell, grew up in the parsonage at Haworth in Yorkshire. All four children showed precocious talent, as artists and particularly as writers. Their voluminous juvenilia describes the history of two imaginary countries: Charlotte and Branwell's Angria, and Emily and Anne's Gondal. Between 1835 and 1845 the family were separated as the sisters took up positions as teachers and governesses. Branwell, despite showing early promise as a painter, failed to make any headway as an artist. He worked in a number of situations but failed in all of them, largely due to the problems brought on by his addiction to opium and alcohol. In 1842 Charlotte went to Brussels to study French at the Pensionnat Heger, where she formed a passionate attachment to M. Heger, the husband of the proprietor. Her feelings were not reciprocated, and in 1844 she returned to Haworth. In 1845, following Branwell's dismissal from his post as a tutor, all four siblings found themselves together again at home for the first time in ten years. At this time, with their financial future looking highly uncertain, Charlotte stumbled upon a collection of Emily's poems, and encouraged her to seek a publisher. *Poems* by Currer, Ellis, and Acton Bell appeared in 1846, and sold two copies. Undeterred by this failure, Charlotte began writing *The Professor*, Emily began *Wuthering Heights*, and Anne began *Agnes Grey*. *Wuthering Heights* was published with *Agnes Grey* in December 1847, and was attacked by critics for its savagery. Following her failure to find a publisher for *The Professor*, Charlotte began *Jane Eyre*, which was published in 1848 to immediate acclaim. Anne's second novel, *The Tenant of Wildfell Hall*, was also published in 1848. Branwell, weakened by the effects of opium and alcohol addiction, died suddenly in September 1848. Following his death, Emily became ill, and died of tuberculosis in December 1848. Anne followed, dying of the same illness in May 1849. Charlotte went on to publish *Shirley* (1849) and *Villette* (1853). In 1854, she married her father's curate, Arthur Bell Nicholls, and died in the early stages of pregnancy in March 1855. *The Professor* was published posthumously in 1857, the same year as Mrs. Gaskell's enormously popular and influential *Life of Charlotte Brontë*. The Reverend Patrick Brontë, having survived all his children, died in 1861 at the age of 84.

Lieutenant-Colonel James Morisset (1780–1852) was commandant of Norfolk Island from 1829 to 1834. A career officer, he had seen service in the Peninsular War, where he suffered massive and horrifying facial injuries when a shell exploded in his face. He was posted with his regiment to New South Wales in 1817. His enthusiasm for tormenting prisoners led to his appointment to Norfolk Island, with instructions to make the settlement a place of exemplary terror. He responded by constructing a regime of infamous brutality. Throughout 1833–34, Morisset suffered from migraines (the result of his head wound) which prevented him from performing his duties. The day-to-day running of the prison was left to his second-in-command, Mr. Fyans. On January 15, 1834, the prisoners mutinied. The uprising, although a failure, was the largest in Australian penal history, and ended Morisset's career.

Alexander Maconochie (1787–1860), a lawyer's son from Edinburgh, served in the Royal Navy during the Napoleonic wars. He was captured by the French and spent two years as a prisoner of war. Maconochie was appointed to run the penal colony of Norfolk Island in 1840, with authorisation to set up a new, experimental penal colony alongside the existing one. Maconochie introduced a system where new offenders would be given indefinite sentences. They would have the opportunity to earn "marks" for good behaviour and hard work; when they had accrued sufficient marks, they would be set free. Marks could also be used to buy luxuries, such as tobacco. Maconochie's radical ideas earned him many enemies, and he was recalled in 1844.

In his history *The Fatal Shore*, Robert Hughes offers this footnote to Maconochie's career:

> *Maconochie's critics especially relished, as light relief, the fate of his eldest daughter Mary Ann, or Minnie. It only showed how this Caledonian do-gooder, the felon's friend, could be hoist with his own petard: Minnie's education had been entrusted to an educated convict, a young and handsome Special transported for forgery. The nineteen-year-old girl (bored stiff, one may surmise, by the social horizons of Norfolk Island) had shown a tender and deep sentiment for her tutor. It is not known whether he actually seduced her. But when the story got out, it sent the colonial conservatives into fits of sniggering delight and filled the Sydney and Hobart papers with columns of innuendo. Minnie, bereft, was packed off to England and the care of an aunt; she died there, a spinster verging on old-maidhood, at the age of thirty-two.*

Coldwater

Mardi McConnochie

A Reader's Guide

A Conversation with Mardi McConnochie

James Bradley *is the author of* Wrack *and* The Deep Field.

James Bradley: What was your starting point for the novel?

Mardi McConnochie: I wanted to write something about the Brontës. It's a very crowded field—you only have to go into any university library to find that out. But it's crowded because they have a kind of mystique, a fascination which doesn't go away. It's the wonderful mesh between the books they wrote and the romantic gloom they lived in.

JB: What specifically did you want to explore?

MM: Funnily enough, it was the sibling rivalry. Being a writer is, for most people, a very solitary occupation. I suspect most of us prefer it that way—to be the lone wolf is in our nature.

JB: But you've written a novel about three Wolfs—not a lone wolf at all.

MM: Four Wolfs, if you count Father. So the book arose from a question: What was it like for them, these three writers living in such very close quarters, working together? And not just any writers, either—three of the greatest women writers working in English, all in one family.

JB: So why did you decide to set the book in Australia?

MM: A number of reasons. On a practical level, I needed to find a way of breaking them out of the biographical detail and liberating them as characters. I had to find a way to make the story my own. On another level, I am interested in exploring an Australian identity, and this seemed a good way of doing that.

JB: I'll come back to the second point, but tell me about liberating the Brontës as characters.

MM: Initially I tried writing about the "real" Brontës, but I found it quite frustrating. I'm not a historian, I'm a novelist. I prefer to make things up. But when you're dealing with historical figures it can be very easy to get bogged down in the fine detail. Eventually it occurred to me that if I could just move the story somewhere else, then I could use the elements I wanted to use, and treat them as fiction, rather than some uneasy mix of fiction and fact. At first I was going to update the story, but it didn't make sense moved into the present day. (Unless you were going to set it in, say, Iran, or some other place where women are still intensely controlled by their families—which I think would be interesting, but unfortunately quite beyond me.) So then it struck me that I could move the Brontës from England in the 1840s to Australia in the 1840s, which would allow me to kill two birds with one stone. I could re-imagine them as three writing sisters, who happened to be called Charlotte, Emily, and Anne, but displace them to the bottom of the world. It was a way of writing about the domestic, artistic, and emotional concerns of the characters, while placing them in a larger context—the development of a uniquely Australian literature.

JB: Does Australia have its own Brontë sisters?

MM: No. Australia's colonial history begins with the arrival of the First Fleet—a shipment of convicts—in 1788. Robert Hughes called Australia a "gulag without walls," and for a long time that was all it was. As time passed more settlers who saw a chance to get rich began to come, but even by 1848, when *Coldwater* is set (the year *Jane Eyre* and *The Tenant of Wildfell Hall* were published and Branwell and Emily Brontë died, amongst other tumultuous events), Australia was still a demanding and dangerous place. Getting here took six months on a ship through some of the most perilous waters in the world, the colonies were founded on convict labor, and the fact that messages and news took six months to arrive from England meant the colonies were isolated in a way that's very hard for those of us in the modern world to understand. Given all of this it's hardly surprising there was little or no cultural life here, and what there was tended to be imported. Certainly there was no local publishing industry. So even if there had been a Charlotte Brontë writing novels on an isolated NSW pastoral property, or in a prison colony, it would not have been possible for her to get them published. Unless she decided to shake the dust of home from her feet and move to the cultural center of the world—London—which is what my Charlotte eventually does.

JB: Do your imaginary sisters fill a gap then?

MM: Yes. The idea of literary ancestry is important to me, but I come from a place with fairly shallow cultural roots. (I'm not talking about indigenous culture, which has extremely deep roots indeed, but I wouldn't want to lay claim to them myself.) Australian literature didn't really hit its straps until the 1890s (of course there are important early figures before that, but I'm talking in general terms) and it's a very masculine culture. We don't have any George Eliots, any Jane Austens, any Brontës. We don't even have much in the way of a Romantic movement. So inventing some antipodean Brontës was a way, for me, of filling the gap. It's a way of imagining what might have been.

JB: A Shakespeare's sister for Australia?

MM: Exactly, although my predictions are a little less gloomy than Virginia Woolf's.

JB: On the subject of Virginia Woolf, is there any significance in your choice of name for your sisters?

MM. Of course. This is not really a Brontë book, or not *only* a Brontë book—it's a book about becoming a woman writer, and you can't really avoid Virginia Woolf when you're talking about that topic. Even today, her insights are so sharp and fresh and illuminating.

JB: If you started with the myth of the Brontës writing together at their kitchen table, is it fair to say you end with Virginia Woolf's suicide by drowning?

MM: Suicide does seem to be one of the iconic fates of the woman writer—think of Virginia Woolf, Sylvia Plath, Anne Sexton. There's something which the culture seems to find very alluring in the idea of a woman torn apart by her talent. I allude to it in the Bertha chapter, which is one of the most intensely literary chapters in the book. You'll find references to Jane Eyre, Virginia Woolf, *The Madwoman in the Attic*, and Charlotte Perkins Gilman's "The Yellow Wallpaper" embedded in that section. Personally, I prefer the triumphalist ending where the woman writer becomes very rich and famous and lives to a ripe old age to be feted and celebrated.

JB: There are a number of references to *Jane Eyre* in the book. Is *Jane Eyre* your favorite Brontë book?

MM: I've loved different Brontë books for different reasons at different times. When I read *Wuthering Heights* for the first time in my late teens I *just loved* it. It seemed like the wildest, most passionate, most exciting book I had ever read. It clearly has that effect on a lot of people. It's such a weird and marvelous object because it seems to spring from nowhere, and there was never a second book, and the life doesn't seem to provide any explanation for it. (Not that I think the life ever does. Novels, I think, come from some mysterious place and there's not usually a lot of point trying to explain where they come from.) I have a lot of time for *The Tenant of Wildfell Hall*, Anne's best book. It's like Ibsen's *A Doll's House*, only fifty years earlier. I love *Jane Eyre* for its fairy-tale qualities, and for the fact that it's been such a fertile text for so many women writers. And I love it because Jane is such a stunning creation, so strong and so angry and passionate and determined. Her charisma and her indomitable will just leap off the page.

JB: The epigraph to Part 2 is taken from *The Tempest*—it's one of many Shakespearean references throughout the book.

MM: The Wolfs are a highly literary family—they view the world through the prism of literature. They never stop reading, or writing, and the world they create for us in their various pages is a very literary one. Shakespeare deals frequently with fathers and daughters—especially in the late plays. The text is meant to echo with those other father-daughter relationships. Lear and his daughters, Prospero on his magic island. I always thought there was something a little bit creepy about Prospero—he's just a little bit too manipulative. You could say that in my text Miranda turns the tables on Prospero and makes off with the book of magic herself.

JB: In your book, Anne is the only character who's written in the third person. Why is that?

MM: When I was writing the book I tried very hard to make the voice of each character quite distinct. Charlotte's voice, which dominates the book, is quite personal and intimate, but also quite bullying in lots of ways. She wants you to see it her way, and she doesn't mind lying to you and manipulating you. Emily's voice was inspired in part by Emily Dickinson. She represents an alternative vision of the woman writer, as mystic. Anne is used to seeing everything through someone else's eyes, she is the most shy and retiring of the sisters, and she has not yet come into her own. But she is also the most rational and the most clear-sighted. While her sisters are both, to a certain extent, hysterics, Anne is the cool one who keeps her head in a crisis. For me, the third person is a cool, distant, and rational voice, and that was appropriate for Anne.

JB: So is that how you see the three Brontës? Charlotte as a bully, Emily as a mystic, and Anne as the cool-headed rationalist?

MM: I don't think I've created an accurate depiction of the three Brontës—if such a thing were possible, and I doubt it is. A number of reviewers have taken issue with my depictions of this or that sister, as if I were betraying some generally accepted truth about what they were "really like." But I think each generation re-invents the Brontës in their own image. The Victorians saw Charlotte as a model of filial piety, quietly tending her aged father, nursing her tragic sisters, etc. etc. To them she was the angel in the house, but to us she is something quite different. We see her rebellion, her rage, her creative powers, her determination to speak. Future generations will no doubt see something else—if they continue to read her.

JB: I'm interested in the picture you create of worlds within worlds. All four of your characters—the three girls, plus the father, Captain Wolf—create worlds for themselves, which they rule with fists of iron.

MM: Charlotte, Emily, and Father are all megalomaniacs, desperately striving to subdue the world to their will. Emily does it by creating an imaginary world called Gondal, Father has his apparatus of guns and soldiers, and his scholarly *Account of an Australian Penal Settlement.* Charlotte is a manipulator. And in the end, Charlotte wins the battle over who gets to rule the world, not only because she gets what she wants, but because she gets to tell her version of the story.

JB: Should we assume then that the book Charlotte takes to London is the book that we've just finished reading?

MM: Yes.

JB: It's obviously a very literary book. At one point Anne wonders if it's better to dwell in the house of fiction or to venture out into the unknown territory of the real world. Could you talk about that?

MM: I've been criticized for giving Anne a conventional romantic ending, but that's not how I see her choice at all. I think there are enough clues about the Diver's unreliability (he abandons his brother, he can't hold down a job for any length of time) to signal to the alert reader that this is not going to be happily ever after. What Anne opts for is a step into the unknown, into danger, and out of the comforting but stifling dreamworld of Gondal. It's about leaving childhood behind and becoming an adult.

JB: Do you think Emily ever becomes an adult?

MM: Emily finds a way of living her entire life at fever pitch, as it's lived in Gondal. I hope that the reader will stop and wonder how much of what Emily relates is true and how much is fantasy.

JB: So is Finn O'Connell real or imaginary?

MM: Finn is real. The nature of his relationship with Emily is questionable.

JB: This is a book that is very interested in the question of love. Charlotte tells us "the only real law was the law of the heart, and it was that law which must take precedence over all others." But it's not a conventional romance narrative, is it? There is no "Reader, I married him"—at least not for Charlotte.

MM: There are no weddings at all.

The traditional romance plot offers the chance of perfect happiness through union with another. In Charlotte's story, the love object is not a man: it's an idea. She's pinned all her hopes for happiness on getting to London and getting published, which I think is just as conventionally romantic as the idea of living happily ever after with Prince Charming.

If you look past the surface of what the sisters tell you there's quite a lot of ambivalence in it about love and about men. Anne is never sure if she can trust the Diver, even though she throws her lot in with him at the end.

Emily insists on seeing Finn O'Connell as demonic. All the men in this novel, including Father, turn out in the end to be unreliable, dangerous, and even mad.

JB: They are all Heathcliff or Rochester figures.

MM: Exactly.

JB: Early in the book, the characters discuss endings—Charlotte plumps for happy ever after, Emily for a tragic death, and Anne keeps her own counsel. How are we to read the ending of your novel?

MM: In the section where the sisters are discussing happy endings, Emily argues that a romantic death is the only possible conclusion—and she gets a romantic death. Anne, who offers no views on endings, departs into an open ending, full of possibilities. And Charlotte, who wants a happy ending, but can't quite bring herself to believe in the happy-ever-after of marriage, gets the kind of consummation she truly wants: recognition through publication.

JB: In order to become a novelist, Charlotte must leave Australia and go to London. Isn't that a rather pessimistic conclusion for a book that purports to be about the birth of an Australian literary culture?

MM: This is a book which celebrates some of our national myths: the gothic horror of our convict past, the pathos of the child lost in the bush. The artist who cannot be appreciated at home and must find artistic fulfillment overseas is another powerful myth—one which, for many years, was absolutely true, although I don't think it's true anymore. One of the unexpected upsides of globalization is that you can live in Australia and be at home in the world. In Australia we're accustomed to getting our culture from somewhere else, but now it seems to be possible for the traffic to go in both directions, which has to be a good thing.

Reading Group Questions and Topics for Discussion

1. The life of the real Charlotte "never quite matched up to her own capacity for experience," says Angela Carter in the epigraph. But the limitations of society aren't the only things that make real life different from imagined life. Many of us regret the gap between the way we are living and the way we could be living if things were a bit different. Do you think such discrepancies are necessarily unfortunate? Or is the fact that our imagination sometimes outpaces our reality perhaps something to be tolerated or even embraced?

2. Our introduction to Captain Wolf occurs just after he's been shot, at a moment when his heart is, in Charlotte's account, "exposed to the air, so vulnerable . . . ticking his life away." In fact Wolf's heart is unharmed; the bullet has struck elsewhere. Why do you suppose McConnochie selected this moment, and this particular image, as our first glimpse of the Captain? What does it tell us about him, and how does it influence our feelings about him as the novel goes on? Remember that Anne and Emily were witness to the scene as well. How do you imagine each of them might have described it?

3. In novels, as in life, people often hold views of themselves and of each other that conflict with what might commonly be considered the truth. What does Charlotte's description of her sisters—"Emily was pathologically shy" and "Anne was bad-tempered and lazy"—tell us about Charlotte herself? Discuss Emily's faith in the Irishman, whose trustworthiness remains one of the book's unanswered questions. How do other incidents of self-deception influence *Coldwater*'s plot?

4. Charlotte is the only one of the Wolf sisters who finally fulfills her vow to become a published writer. But early in the novel, it is she who asks, "What's the point of writing yourself a book? You already know how

it's going to end." Why do you think she ultimately chooses to be a writer, after all?

5. Like *Coldwater*, many novels these days incorporate a collage effect, including bits and pieces culled from journals, recipes, lists, and other sources. How does the inclusion of reports from Captain Wolf, letters, and parts of the Wolf sisters' novels change your experience of *Coldwater*?

6. "A secondary penal colony must . . . have an exemplary, symbolic function. It must be a warning and a threat; a living hell," writes Captain Wolf in *An Account of an Australian Penal Settlement*. Later, Wolf goes on to say that "prisons are designed to stamp out individuality, and induce a state of docile tranquility." How does what you know about prisons today in this country compare to *Coldwater*, and to Wolf's view of what a prison should be?

7. At the time when this story takes place, Australia was a giant penal colony in the hands of the British Empire; McConnochie has set her story in a prison within a prison. But in this novel, the concept of what imprisons us—and what might free us—is far more complicated than that. In a world in which one prison seems to lead to another, what do you suppose to be the ultimate release?

8. "I don't want a husband," Charlotte wails to Glade. "I want you. I don't care where we go, or what happens to us, I just want to be with you. We'll have our love. Love is enough."

"No it isn't," Glade answers.

With whom do you agree?

9. In a man, Charlotte looks for intellect, spirit, and passion; Emily likes a "look of defiance" and "a decision in all his gestures," while Anne seems attracted to the Diver's mystery. Is there any common ground in

their desires? How would you define what it is that women want? How do you suppose your mother might answer it? Your daughter?

10. Emily says that tragedy is less dishonest than other forms of literature. In the end, is *Coldwater* a tragedy? Do you prefer to read books that end in "wedded bliss" or those that end with their "characters surviving their misfortunes and learning to live with disappointment"?

11. Who started the fire?

12. Discuss Branwell's role in the story and his influence on the lives of his sisters.

13. "Even the most dangerous ideas can be handled safely, if they are considered in a thoughtful and intelligent manner." Which of the novel's characters says this? Do you agree or disagree?

14. Have you read any work by the Brontës? How does that color your reading of *Coldwater*? Does *Coldwater* change your reading of the Brontës own work?

© Gene Rose

About the Author

MARDI McCONNOCHIE is the author of several plays and currently works as a TV scriptwriter and editor. She lives in Sydney, Australia.

Praise for *Twelve Mighty Orphans*

"Great stuff, and there's no question *Twelve Mighty Orphans* has drama in droves."
—*Austin American-Statesman*

"[A] riveting tale about underdogs . . . [The Mighty Mites] were America's Team long before Tom Landry and his gray fedora. . . . Dent tells the story vividly, a wonderfully inspiring story."
—*Philadelphia Daily News*

"This may be one of the most compelling Texas sports books—or any Texas book—of the year."
—*Abilene Reporter-News*

"As he did in *The Junction Boys,* Dent brings the era to life with a myriad of historic details. . . . [A] compelling story for those interested in the history of Texas high school football or Texas during the Depression."
—*San Antonio Express-News*

"Dent is an oral historian of the first rank, capturing the voices and writing great pictures."
—*USA Today*

"Dent writes in what sounds like copy for a movie campaign but fits all of the facts. The Mighty Mites were the most popular team in Texas with a cult following that stretched from New York to California."
—*The Washington Post*

"Jim Dent, himself on intimate terms with adversity, has captured the underdog spirit . . . his affection for the subject lights up the page like a modern scoreboard."
—*Dallas Morning News*

"Jim Dent's *Twelve Mighty Orphans* is a bestseller waiting to become a blockbuster movie."
—Jim Reeves, *Fort Worth Star-Telegram*

"*Twelve Mighty Orphans* is a shout of joy and of gladness, and reaffirmation that character and determination do matter . . . a great book to read and give." 　　　　　　　　　　　　　　*—Scottish Right Journal*

Praise for *The Junction Boys*

"One-time *Star-Telegram* sportswriter Dent has made a valuable contribution to Texas lore. *The Junction Boys* is not just a sports book. It should, rather, be considered a volume of social history."
　　　　　　　　　　　　　　—Fort Worth Star-Telegram

"From high school to the pros, the history of football in Texas is steeped in tall tales and tall deeds. Amazing stuff. I loved this book."
　　　　　　　　　　—Randy Galloway, Fort Worth Star-Telegram

"[Dent] takes a cue from the best sports writing and aims for a human interest tale in which football plays an integral role. . . . It will be appealing not just to Aggie faithful but also to football fans throughout Texas." 　　　　　　　　　　　　　　　*—Houston Chronicle*

"It's the best sports book I've ever read."
　　　　　　　　　　　　　　—Pat Summerall, Fox Sports

"Engaging." 　　　　　　　　　　　　　　*—Sports Illustrated*

"I heard the story of the Junction Boys from Gene Stallings when he was on my staff with the Cowboys. Jim Dent has really brought the story to life in a book any football fan would like to read."
　　　　　　　　　—Tom Landry, former coach of the Dallas Cowboys